Reviews

"The author, Tony Smith, has produced an enjoyable, high quality historical fiction novel from an era not well covered, being the period of the Malayan Emergency in the early 1950s. Woven into this period piece is an entertaining mystery involving several well drawn, multi-dimensional characters. The key protagonist, the Colonel, is chief among these, but each of the Colonel's three wives feature importantly in the story and they are ably supported by other strong characters.

Modern readers might at first consider Tony Smith's style quirky or old fashioned, but my advice would be to read on. This style not only lends authenticity to the period, but cleverly draws the reader back in time and into the story. Much of the behavior and dialogue of the characters is anachronistic but it is on point for the story's characters, most of whom are portrayed within the context of their position within the British class system during the "end of Empire" period following World War 2. The book is realistic of this portrayal and this adds to its charm.

Tony Smith's use of letter-writing between various characters is masterful. From these various letters the reader learns much of which would usually be learned through dialogue, but in a tangential way. The role of letter-writing, and the content of those letters, supports the characters and time period entirely. The plot is well developed and plausible, deftly woven to give the reader just the right mixture of knowledge and anticipation. Of course, it is also a love story of sorts. The author may not characterise it that way but through the telling of the story, as the title suggests, we learn a great deal about the enigmatic Colonel and just how he came to have three wives — all eyebrow raising in their own way."

— Michael Pert, author of *The Kissing House*

"An enthralling saga entwined in a web of love, betrayal and intrigue. Riveting tale from a bygone era."

— Vivian Waring, author of *When Tears Ran Dry*

"Words from the mists of the early Twentieth Century and on through the years, settle sagaciously on the pages of A.C. Smith's latest novel, *The Colonel's Wives*. It is a satirical work of extraordinary proportions, filled with metaphors, alliteration and language that reflect ages past.....*ornamenting those black clouds like a string of pearls.* The words read as poetry.

The story is told through the dialogue of the main characters, and just when you think you have the measure of the story, you are thrown for a six. Colonel Newton, the lead character, expresses his thoughts on this when relating an incident to Nancying – *"Anything you come up with is best consigned to posterity, if only to appreciate how wrong you will be."*

— Judith Flitcroft, author of *Step Back in Time*

THE ENGLISH COLONEL'S WIVES

A.C. Smith

Published in Australia by Sid Harta Books & Print Pty Ltd,
ABN: 34632585293
23 Stirling Crescent, Glen Waverley, Victoria 3150 Australia
Telephone: +61 3 9560 9920, Facsimile: +61 3 9545 1742
E-mail: author@sidharta.com.au

First published in Australia 2021
This edition published 2021
Copyright © A.C. Smith 2021
Cover design, typesetting: WorkingType (www.workingtype.com.au)

A.C. Smith
The English Colonel's Wives
ISBN: 978-1-925707-48-9
pp526

About the Author

In his early-twenties, A.C. (Tony) Smith made voyages as a ship's engineer between South-East Asia and the west coast of the United States and Canada, Australia, and New Zealand.

A thirst to learn as much as he could about life and a fascination for politics saw him complete a law degree. Legal practice as a barrister extended over the next thirty years.

In between, he managed to fit in a stint as an MP, co-publish a fortnightly news/magazine and indulge a love of amateur theatre.

Since retiring from the Bar, he began writing in earnest. This is the sequel to his first novel, *Deeply With The Sun In Our Eyes*.

Dedication

Few people have made such an impression upon me as did Lieutenant-Colonel Sydney Kyle-Little when he introduced himself and presented a signed copy of his book *Whispering Winds*. Tall and erect, a mountain of a man even in his late-seventies, it wasn't merely his experiences as a patrol officer in the Northern Territory nor his epic trek on foot across the forbidding Arnhem Land, the first white man to do so, that had me in awe of him.

Syd also served in Malaya during the Emergency under High Commissioner, General Sir Gerald Templer, whom he admired greatly. He was no stranger to desperate hand-to-hand combat with vicious communist terrorists and always led from the front.

Humble and unsung, Syd was a great Australian, and this book is dedicated to him.

Table of Contents

Malaya — pre-and post-World War 2

Throughout the 1930s and until early 1942, Marxist communism in Malaya enjoyed an increasing influence. It was stimulated by the rapid influx of unskilled migrants boosting the Chinese population to being at near parity with Malays and the Indian communities. The Malayan Communist Party (MCP) had been both active and organisational with a membership base said to number nearly twenty thousand. Largely centred in Northern Johore and Penang, its most prominent adherents were trade unionists.

Following the landings by the Japanese in December 1941, the MCP offer of support to the British administration as their forces fell back to Singapore Island was accepted. Frantic efforts by way of some basic training to its fighters and allocating what scarce weaponry was available followed, though by then it was already too late. Before any skills of real substance were imparted to the eager young communists, they were forced into the jungle while the invaders were marshalling for their final assault on the colony.

With the fall of Singapore in February 1942, the guerrillas regrouped and established themselves into units. More recruits were gained, boosted by the vicious treatment the occupiers meted out to the Chinese. Styling themselves as the 'Malayan Peoples Anti-Japanese Army', they became a hardened, effective and merciless band. Adept and lethal in their hit-and-run raids, they vanished into the impenetrable jungles no sooner had they struck. Time and bitter experience saw pursuits as not only largely futile but also counterproductive since it involved ventures into some of the most inhospitable regions on the face of the earth.

In such an environment, with their secret trails, ambush sites, assistance from the indigenous inhabitants and ever retaining the element of surprise, the communists were a fearsome and dangerous foe. In the course of tying up military resources and exacting a significant human toll on the hated Japanese, they also earned the acquisition of precious arms and ammunition. Aiding these activities, a committed core of supporters supplied food, clothes, money and medicines. They also became a reliable source of intelligence.

For its part, using the attraction of large bribes, the occupiers sometimes managed to pinpoint trails and encampments. Bombing and strafing of guerrilla hideouts and the capture of individual communists would follow. Yet the infliction of devastating blows was invariably forestalled by the capacity of the fighters to melt into the jungle and regroup.

On the guerrilla side, identification of informers amongst the Chinese or Malay villagers led to swift and brutal reprisals. It was a strong deterrent to those who might be minded to turn traitor. Anyone indulging such activity faced just one fate. And no one was spared if a member of a family was even suspected of collaboration.

By late 1943, as the Pacific War began to turn in the Allies' favour, the communists were reinforced by Force 136 comprising a group of British Liaison Officers. They had been landed covertly in Malaya and brought with them arms and explosives. Once they had linked up with the guerrillas, airdrops of food, medicines, equipment and weaponry were also made. The Britishers lived with the communists, teaching them how to use the weapons parachuted in, identifying targets and maximising the deployment of Japanese manpower to counter their activities.

With the constant propagandising in the camps, some of the Englishmen were swift to appreciate that once the common enemy had been routed, the friendships there established may be of rather limited duration. The communists never abandoned their dream of political conquest of Malaya and hegemonic control. To that end, preparations of their own were made in anticipation of a Japanese defeat and secret weapons caches lodged in strategic places all over the country.

At the cessation of hostilities in 1945, the guerrillas boasted a formidable army of seven thousand who weren't going to lay down arms quietly in favour of colonial masters.

Attempts were made to impose overt rule through gestures such as raising the hammer and sickle and propagandising a great victory on their part. These were short-lived. The wider population were savvier as things returned to normal. The British military and then civilian administration gradually assumed control.

Upon the establishment of the Malayan federation in 1948, Chin Peng, the young, charismatic leader of the communists and his followers returned to their jungle existence, this time in opposition to the government. Dumps were opened up and arms distributed to the secret undercover units. Incidents increased and intelligence experts warned that armed insurrection was developing. Murders abounded and there were calls for strong action. Terrorism became the modus operandi of the communist terrorists (CTs). Still numbering a respectable five thousand insurgents, the CTs committed acts of unparalleled brutality to planters and their families. They were willing to strike at their own people if they got in the way.

Despite ten thousand police, three British battalions, six Gurkha battalions and several battalions of the Malay Regiment arrayed against the CTs, a State of Emergency was declared by the High Commissioner in districts where they had murdered two plantation managers and were running amok. Increased powers were gazetted to the police and army. A Special Constabulary of thirty thousand was also raised.

So marked the commencement of what became known as

'The Malayan Emergency'. It ushered in an ongoing guerrilla war that was at its most brutal between the late 1940s and the mid-1950s.

From its craggy facade, its stones, its angles, its apertures and its chiselled shapes, *Magnus Hall* was submissive to an appearance of having been fashioned and rough-hewn by ancient Cornish fishermen who viewed the position both as a lighthouse to guide their craft into port and a weathervane from which to determine if the sea might accommodate the search for a bountiful catch.

Why an old soldier more accustomed to the sweaty confines of Singapore and Malaya was desirous of possessing such a two-storey amalgam plonked atop a cliff abutting the bracing and exposed coastline to others might have required more than hasty impressions to yield a solution. Not so the third Mrs Newton, who no sooner began her survey than she understood. The nub of that conundrum lay in aligning the dwelling with the Colonel's nascent attachment to assuming a future with his new wife not just remote from all to which he and she were used but unlike any they had ever experienced.

Walking its parallel rock-walled boundaries that dovetailed into a rear hedgerow, an eclectic atmosphere clung to her as she zigzagged the area. The afternoon air, buoyant in sweet and salty vapours, was invigorating, the grounds grooming with potential and, when she scraped at the earth beneath her feet, she glimpsed rich black loam. Yet she also had to be watchful, being importuned into adopting tremulous, tiptoeing movements to minimise the bulbous-orbed attentions of a cantankerous heifer whose elaborate horns rose and fell like a pitchfork when the animal jerked its head disapprovingly.

Mrs Newton saw prudence in steering towards an enclosed yard. Therein, the only structures consisted of a cobwebbed milking bale, shed and adjoining henhouse. She scrambled over wire netting, through the detritus of a vegetable garden showcasing briars and thistles, and still the brooding beast stalked her. Agitation reaching fever level, a series of trumpeting bellows were followed by high leaps where she thrust her back legs in Mrs Newton's direction as if poised to deliver a final ultimatum. Gaining safety by sliding through the bars of a bolted cattle gate to a cobbled driveway, she found her nemesis positioned so as to announce that there should be no resumption of the trespass.

Their eyes met and, refusing to flinch, she called out in her sternest voice, 'Who the hell do you think you are, little minx?' a demand that only a mistress dare make. After a morbid stand-off, the quadruped blinked. 'Now, off with you and don't carry on like that with me ever again! Do you understand?' Bested, though not entirely divorced from second thoughts, there followed a gradual lowering of the Jersey's head. From that day on, she accepted her place and would form a lifelong bond with the only person who had ever put her in it.

Back at the scoured shores, the Atlantic south-westerly flow freshened, caressing her collar-length hair and pinching at her cheeks. The new lady of the Hall viewed several outward-bound fishing craft pitching their colours against a blue-green and white-capped canvas as they advanced to the banks renowned for prawns and fish. She leaned reflectively against the mossy, oaken table, comfort drawn from the durable creaking telling her that it had weathered the salty mists and thick, trembling rain of almost as many seasons as the dwelling itself. Illimitably beyond the boats, a Celtic curtain shimmered more days of the year than any other patch of water surrounding the British Isles.

He was now beside her, their arms interlocked, and they forged a silent contentment words couldn't adequately calibrate. It was an outward demonstration for each of being certain in the knowledge that no better place than this would occupy the rest of their days.

Then came the first twilight, wind and wave piping its tranquil music, inspiring forgiven memories of all that had gone before. Spring hadn't banished its predecessor, content to surround the more darkness fell. She lit his pipe first before insisting on firing the hearth in their cosy lounge, turning aside with a serene kiss an offer of assistance. Soon the air was perfumed by the wood-burning combination of pear and ash and, not to be kept idle meanwhile, adjusting the combustion stove was her next challenge to perfect its function towards a lengthy browning of roast beef and potatoes to be followed by steamed duff and custard.

Mrs Newton wanted nothing more than this hearth to be a place for him to read, think, study, perhaps even write, as he had always promised to do. Beyond making its interior a joy to enfold him, she was determined to nurture, expand, diversify and mould the gardens as she deemed fit and welcome visits from son, daughter, families and grandchildren.

So began their lives together. Over time, she took to the land, fashioning and shaping it. Behind the Hall's shed and bale they had fenced off a yard that now hosted a bevy of Sussex hens and one indomitable rooster. Nearby, white ducks, left in the wake of an enormous speckled black drake, seemed intent on navigating every cranny of the spring-fed pond searching for titbits.

Here lay an acre and a half of some of the most productive country on England's south-western coast. She had assayed that the grounds would sustain more than enough year-round emerald pasture for the cow, now with calf at heel. That pernickety fixture had taken new-found motherhood to extremes, becoming matron superior to the ducks, chooks and all forms of friendly animal life that happened to populate her territory, and woe betide any creature that she deemed unacceptable venturing therein. Foxes learned rather quickly at the points of her horns that there was but one upshot in any attempted poultry raid. The Jersey suffered none save the woman's hands to work its teats morning and afternoon. She cropped the grass assiduously and maintained it six inches above carpet level until the poddy was weaned and began to chime in so as to even it altogether.

There was always more than enough to provide the house with the milk and cream that lay the foundations for butter and cheese, soon to become culinary specialities of the adjacent village. And to complete their ecological functions, Pixie and Polly, the names given to cow and progeny respectively, deposited more than sufficient effluent for a market garden that supplied the couple and local families with vegetables.

Affording her husband a length-of-the-strait start in innate experience of English growing conditions, Mrs Newton shed the tag of novice so quickly that he became the journeyman. Those who witnessed the transformation to *Magnus Hall and Farm*, a change in title on which she insisted, observed of the proprietress that her seeding, growing, harvesting and preserving proficiencies must have owed themselves to considerable prior experience. All combined, the returns provided more than enough discretionary spending to escort her man to the pub for dinner once a fortnight while being able to save a little as well.

It was one of the many characteristics that filled the old gentleman with pride. Regulars at the local Presbyterian church, he never tired of reminding worshippers how blessed he was. She sometimes tut-tutted and squeezed his hand in restraint at his fondness for so indulging his wife, though, for Colonel Newton, now regarded as the stately country squire, such repeated accolades were tolerated in Christian good humour.

An addition to their family of animals arrived with a dull thud at the door late one wild and rainswept evening during their second year of occupancy. It was preceded by forlorn scratching. What they saw moved their hearts and filled their eyes. A sodden, muddied, half-starved, mangy fugitive with a mix of as many colours as breeds, the dog had been beaten with a whip or some sharp object, was bleeding, shivering and terrified. The cringing bitch attempted to stand, but couldn't, and Newton brought her inside. Immediately apparent was her gratitude for not being flogged again, although by this stage there remained precious little resistance in her.

He washed and bathed her wounds. This operation was carried out with painstaking tenderness, for there were times when the lightest touch on her ribs provoked a yelp or tremor. Soft bread in warm chicken broth was gratefully swallowed before he relocated her to a rug by the fire. Other than an occasional run of snoring, she slept for the next eight hours without a sound, much less a movement, having been swathed within a cushion of old garments on Newton's side of the bed. It was the beginning of love for her and she gained strength with each passing day.

A sign with a photograph was posted in the general store and enquiries made around the village. No claim of ownership came about. Newton was disappointed on that account, not because the poor thing was overstaying its welcome but rather that he wanted to confront the person who may have been complicit in such cruelty. Another month passed and it was apparent that the culprit's identity was unlikely to be uncovered. 'Bridie', as she came to be known, asserted that their residence was now also hers.

For Mr and Mrs Newton, Bridie was made theirs so much easier by love bestowed in return and she never let them venture far from her. She brought back memories of earlier canines in a foreign clime: the fearsome and never to be forgotten German Shepherd, who had given his life to save the child most dear to Newton. The second Rommel, only begotten survivor of the first, had been just as precious. On succumbing to cancer at seven years of age, Newton had pledged this to be the last occasion his soul would be torn apart by a dog. But all that disappeared into the Cornwall mists once he had fallen slave to Bridie's eyes.

The highlight in their early tenure at the Hall was a visit of his son and her daughter. Neither family had ever socialised before, they wondering but never asking whether this stemmed from the product of their parents' separate though interrelated lives in the years following repatriation from Malaya.

Now as a married couple, it was thought time to open the door, not just of *Magnus Hall and Farm* but to all that lay within and behind it. However, as the occasion approached, he began to equivocate, questioning its efficacy and arguing that, rather than seeing an integration of an extended if complicated family, it could be the progenitor of its dissolution. Newton considered that the proposal could create a schism between them when still in the bliss of so recent a union. Against the longevity of their relationship, spanning as it did nearly twenty years, he was resistant to any possibility of this one being placed in jeopardy.

But ever the optimist, in her uniquely even-tempered and alliterative style, calling him out as being a 'perennial, pedantic and predictable pessimist', she wouldn't contemplate it. Eventually he was persuaded to her view that the risks lurking in all aspects of human interaction were outweighed by the benefits, and she had reached that stage in life where taking the chance was worth it.

'You know, Reginald, as much as I do about taking chances. Look where that got us. Some were good and some – well, we won't mention those. This is one we *have* to do. It's for their sakes as much as ours. And what a thrill it will give our grandchildren, an opportunity for them to become acquainted as well. And as usual, my dear bureaucratic husband, underneath it all you'll continue to fulminate over the logistics and long-term consequences, personal and otherwise, both before they arrive and long after they leave.'

His son had become a solicitor. While at university he

met his future wife, who was undertaking an arts degree. They had married as young students and she soon bore him a boy and a girl. Mrs Newton's daughter enjoyed academic tenure before marrying. Her husband was a builder who ran his own business, and they produced a daughter and son matched in ages with their cousins.

No sooner had the children taken over than Newton's anxiety evaporated. The Hall became their castle in the daytime, a place where the primary activity centred around eating and cordial, while outside was play. At night, the stone cladding secreted sleeping monsters who extruded from its interstices, changed shape and crept into their bedrooms, barred and locked windows of no deterrence. When the wind blew from the sea, the rustling hedges became the harbingers of dragons that would bear anyone who went near them over the cliff to be swallowed up in the boiling cauldron below.

Such was the aura consistent with the children's fantasies that even the elder Newtons became caught up in it. He was requisitioned to play a ghostly ogre covered by a white sheet revealing only his eyes scouring the room for hiding children. Each day he pleaded with Mrs Newton to be relinquished of his appointment. On the one occasion where his wife acceded, she was unceremoniously unmasked and the cloth sceptre redeposited upon the original.

Inside and outside bore the characteristics of a home so chock-full of food, noise, fuss, fun, laughter and never-ending conversations that it developed a unified energy. The animals were feted, fondled and fed as never before, with Bridie in the thick of it, the children treating her as their own.

Each youngster wanted to milk Pixie. That could only be achieved with the involvement of their 'Nana', as they soon came to call Newton's wife. With Pixie's head firmly ensconced in a bucket of meal and molasses, each child had a go and the milk they drank that night before bed tasted so much the better from their exertions. As a special treat for the next day Nana presented them with another by-product, lunchtime helpings of delicious homemade ice-cream.

Ten days had raced by, though not before the pinnacle had been reached, chartering a fishing smack and returning that afternoon laden with haddock and bass. Mrs Newton salted, gutted and froze the catch to permit preserved transport back to their respective homes. The flounder was another story. She had laid on a feast of the massive fish poached in butter accompanied by chipped potatoes and green vegetables. There was so much cake and dessert to follow that four exhausted children were ushered off to bed early without a whimper of dissent.

The last night began with a pallor that threatened to condemn the occasion. Questions thus far left unasked emerged, generalities followed and, when the awkward evasions and pregnant silences brought Newton and his wife to the point of emotion, Newton's son made a timely intervention. He invited his wife to play the piano and encouraged a duet with Mrs Newton's daughter. For two musical strangers, their harmonies were perfect.

The song, *Different Drum*, became their choice. Ever the philosopher and after-dinner sage, so unlike his father, the young solicitor proposed a toast. He asked the room to consider whether any man and woman could have been brought to perfect unity by a drum that had resounded to such different beats in so many multifaceted places, times and circumstances and over such a passage of years without having been kindled by an abiding love. Not a voice was raised against that proposition.

'So now, Papa and Nana, because we all labour on blissfully ignorant of the entire ins and outs of your lives,' he continued, 'it's time for you to sit down and let us and the world know about how you two, though seemingly ready and apparently able, waited so long to really come together.'

A discerning acknowledgement was all they were prepared to give away before an, 'Oh, come on,' almost in unison from the assemblage led to a hesitant undertaking to do so in good time as ever. The rest of the night was consumed, along with the wine favoured by the younger quartet, in lusty song and laughter. Some was of the contemporary kind, which saw Newton intrigued by the variety of sounds they conjured up, he preferring to listen rather than obtrude with what he readily conceded were his own 'croaky discordant notes'.

Not being of a humour ordinarily given over to what had become known, courtesy of *The Beatles* phenomenon, as 'pop music', ever after that occasion he would turn up the volume when he happened to hear *Different Drum* on the radio. It prompted Mrs Newton to observe more than once, 'Reginald, it's beautiful, a voice sailing across the waves, as pure as the breeze itself in these parts. But that conclusion is not for us. It's sort of sad and depressing where it goes, *And we'll both live a lot longer if you live without me.* You and I know what it does say to us because we'll both live a lot longer if you live *within* me,' her own voice singing, and not so distant from replicating that of the original.

It was to be the first of many regular visits by the extended family until the children commenced school, when such occasions slimmed down to alternate Christmases and occasional summer holidays. Both families had now settled in London and, as the couples worked, timing was difficult.

Newton was not fond of staying anywhere but in his own home and the city lent him no comfort. His family accepted this as being a primary marker of who he was. He always feared running into someone from the service and, from the tension of exposing himself to such an occurrence, he had retired. Despite such a facility, he never stood in his wife's way when she decided to visit her daughter and the children alone. She wanted to do this as much as she could knowing that the time was fast approaching when leaving him was no longer an option.

Those formative years at *Magnus Hall and Farm* were halcyon ones. Newton had strived to maintain an erect, grey figure to her, looking every bit the retired warhorse, yet wishing he rather seemed less so. Pithy resort to a walking stick was a concession to his pronounced limp, a permanent reminder of service to his beloved country. A once full head of regulation-cropped black hair had receded to become a misty grey, much less organised but still venerable. By contrast, the moustache had thickened and retained a graphite colour. He was happy to leave trimming, cutting and shaping of these accoutrements to his wife, and this was extended to most other things within the running of the property that by now had needed the assistance of a part-time hand.

While he had otherwise fared better than some of his colleagues from the war and Malayan service days, a factor of which he managed to keep abreast through a serviceman's monthly, in recent times she noted with concern the signs of wear and excessive fatigue descending upon him more readily than ever before. She encouraged him to write, and he managed for a time, but all too frequently she would find him asleep in his favourite chair, notebook in his lap and sometimes on the floor with his pencil, Bridie forever at his feet.

As his health receded, so his speech began to falter. It was time to take in all that he could give her as often as she might request. With gentle persistence and the scrupulous precision of which she knew he would have practised had he been the correspondent, she wrote down all that he was able to tell her. His diaries and personal papers occupied a sizeable portmanteau still to be accessed and would later enrich the voids that remained.

Silence and incomprehension, when it finally descended, arrived in a circumstance least anticipated. She had been out on an errand for two hours and, on her return, he was nowhere to be seen. Since her husband was all but immobile, it prompted a desperate search. Her frantic cries yielded no response save for the faint sound of a whimpering dog. It was Bridie, now as old as her master, but still able to provide the alert down by the pond. She was protecting the prone figure by interposing herself between him and the waterline. A neighbour helped return him inside. She refused any suggestion that he be taken to the hospital knowing his wishes.

On the day after he had been found, just as the sun gave up, Reginald Newton managed to leave four words through eyes wavering between her and another epoch: 'Finish it, my love.'

PART ONE

Three long, throaty blasts from the snub-nosed foghorn welded to a funnel wreathed by a blue star in the middle of a white circle bordered with red paint, caused enough hesitation amongst the multifarious traffickers about wharfingers and access roads adjacent to the Keppel waterfront as to almost jolt their movements. It was as if recollections of the darker days of Singapore's occupation, not so remote of memory, had returned.

Quayside, the ship's departure stirrings were mixed with a commensurate number of enthusiastic cheers from well-wishers. Some seen waving little corporate paper flags appeared rather nonplussed by the spectacle, one explanation being their appearance to enhance numbers and atmospherics had been incentivised by a handy gratuity rather than the product of spontaneous attachment to the event. When bells, car horns, whistles and clapping accompanied the send-off, unease could be read in the faces of some of the voyagers encouraged to join in and throw streamers from the upper deck.

Refitted and in immaculate condition, this was a ship of conventional lines whose passenger quarters were of a standard surpassing its contemporaries. The maiden voyage in these colours would see it plough around the Cape of Good Hope to England. That the owner's suite had been reserved for the company's principal shareholder and his family, a status respected rather than disclosed, suggested that Blue Star wanted their girl noticed for his sake as well as its own since this also was the commencement of the Line's long-term Far Eastern expansion.

Akin to the awakening of an inert dragon stirred from an eternal slumber, the *New Zealand Star* belched sparks and black smoke as eleven thousand tons of steel juddered into life. In a rare display of patience, Singapore's early evening colours lingered while a window of light bathed a catacomb of parchment-white superstructure, as all eyes followed the slipping of her moorings. The captain ordered 'dead slow ahead', the tugs shepherded her seaward and the third mate rang the movement telegraph to the engine room with as much flair as the drum major on the quayside leading the brass band into *Rule Britannia*, a choice many privately thought both extravagant and undiplomatic.

Port Elizabeth was scheduled as her first landfall, a passage occupying two weeks, fair sea days prevailing. Since no significant cargo was to be shifted in that South-East African port, the stopover was billed as a timely concession to the complement of paying passengers who wanted to regain their land legs, having been enticed by the prospect of experiencing a few nights on safari, thence another day's steaming to Cape Town where half its refrigerated shipment comprising bananas and coconuts would be discharged. That venerable destination would serve to replenish the icy holds with lamb and beef and cram other available space with timber, supplementing the bulk of its rubber cargo. The succeeding charts were drawn for a course tracing the West African coast, across the unpredictable Bay of Biscay and then to the homeward stretch, docking at Tilbury, the entire voyage occupying the month of May.

Publicity for her first visit to Singapore made much of speed and reliability in convincing shippers, unaware of the vessel's pedigree, to entrust their cargo. She was twin-screw, propelled by two ten-cylinder Burmeister and Wain engines. In good seascape, they could drive the ship to greater than its cruising speed, a respectable seventeen knots. The ship had weathered the perils of Cape Horn and the Atlantic for a dozen years on numerous occasions. She had eluded the attentions of U-boats and developed a knack of sloughing a course calculated to avoid the cannon-fire from planes that had strafed her. During those fraught times, South American ports were infamous for being honeycombed with saboteurs and spies. An alert watch-keeping regime had thwarted several malign attempts to penetrate her security blanket. So charmed in seagoing lore, she was charming after the fashion that blends the lines of age with the spirit of youthful refurbishment.

Not all who knew of her innards eulogised 'the Star'. One retired engineer drawn to the assemblage of maritime devotees, businessmen and ships' officers who circulated the pre-voyage briefing on 'this thrilling new refrigeration and passenger-cargo adventure ship', was more sceptical. While in the presence of the chief engineer, he was overheard remarking to another sage acquaintance of like disposition as the attendees sampled afternoon tea, cake and cucumber sandwiches that, 'Every main engine is still only as good as its last voyage, some less so.' It drew a sharp rebuke from the line's agent, who reminded him that he was their guest on reputation and sufferance and naysaying prognostications kept private might be wise if further invitations to such events were expected.

Such mechanical portents were not immediately realised. On the other hand, the captain's announcement just after the pilot waved farewell to the bridge and motored off that the passengers should expect fair seas and weather for the voyage was overridden after barely one watch when access to open decks was barred until further notice.

The next twenty-four hours at sea saw atrocious conditions. The ship, teetering at the extreme of a starboard roll sending a watermelon into a vat of semolina in the galley and smashing a rack of crockery, had given ample notice that, had a second been unleashed, it might have been sufficient to take the list past the point of no return. Loaded almost to the gunnels, the event became the signal for the vessel to change course and hove-to in a concession to the tempest.

Debilitating as it was for him after his inaugural forecast, the master strove to maintain an optimistic decorum not just to his officers but also to the few passengers who managed to show their faces on that ugly first day.

In the midst of the havoc above decks, the chief engineer who, through bitter experience, had harboured some sympathies with the old shoreside salt's observation, became strident in his endorsement of it when the port engine was required to be shut down with a seizure imminent. It had been racing uncontrollably as the forty-five-foot waves buried the bow, pitching the propellers out of the water. Nothing could be done except hope that the other engine would prevail until the situation improved.

And that encompassed a further three days of unbridled fury, mixed with a diet of bread, water and hard-boiled eggs prepared in a fraught space where cooks could only attend to that simple task by utilising makeshift harnesses. Not a single passenger bothered to enquire when the regular menu might be reinstated. All except one remained bolted down, save to attend to nature's requirements or answer the steward's rapping that announced the arrival of the day's victualling. The solitary exception hadn't made a sound or lifted his head after a prolonged emptying of every last vestige of his stomach's contents into the red fire bucket.

For the first day, a handful of sand from that container was used to expunge the odour from his retching. When forced access was made, he had refused assistance, including from the second mate who offered to administer tablets and hydration. The items were deposited in a holding rack for him before being left alone. The water was managed but not the tablets. It was all he had until the early morning of the third day, by which time the weather had begun to relent. Contemporaneously, the ship's South African coordinates were reinstated and the engine room complement sighed with relief.

Coinciding with the course's resumption, the sea, in a last, tempestuous show of venting its superiority, gave up an enormous rogue wave that blanketed portholes in green. It seemed intent on shearing each rivet from bow to stern. There was a loud thump against the bulkhead, arousing the two occupants of the double cabin adjoining the single gentleman's abode.

The passenger manifest listed their names as Mrs Nancyng Jenkins, widow, and Miss Charlotte Jenkins, her daughter. With a second thump even more pronounced, Mrs Jenkins couldn't refrain from investigating. Banging on her neighbour's door, she called out, and repeated the process but to no avail. She entered the cabin to find a pyjamaed man on hands and knees attempting to mop up the strewn contents of his sick basin with a towel. Steering him to his bunk, she laid him down and finished the job.

'You needn't have done that. I was just trying to get to the toilet when that infernal wave hit,' he muttered weakly, swivelling onto his feet.

She took the receptacle outside. 'I'll help you. It's all hands to the pumps, you know, in times like these.' Finding her grip on his upper arm strong and insistent he surrendered to being led to the private cubicle across the way. 'When you're finished, sing out or tap on the door and I can take you back.'

'Thanks, but I shall see to it.'

'As you wish.'

She called to the steward who had been slipping envelopes under passenger doors. 'What's that about?'

'Mornin', Mrs Jenkins. Sure to be a good day, and the saloon'll be open for breakfast,' came the rosy optimism matched by an entertaining accent that lit her face. 'The galley gets the weather,' and, glancing sideways, cupped a hand around his mouth and whispered, 'better than 'em upstairs most times.'

'Aren't you a real trimmer? What's your name?' the response confirming a predisposition that she was one passenger he would enjoy serving.

'It's actually Ronnie, madam, or steward or just plain stewie, anythin' yer fancy takes. These ships, whatever they might say about this particular one, run a bit less on ceremony than the full passenger types.'

'Ronnie it is, then. The man in the cabin next to me—'

'Apologies, madam. I was about to grab the slops when I finished me deliverin'.'

'Oh, I knew you would attend to the unmentionables, and the last thing you need is being reminded. No, the man—'

'Colonel Newton?'

Her head tilted questioningly and she effected not to appear surprised. 'I don't know his name. He's fairly fagged.

The gentleman doesn't seem to want me fussing over him but when he's finished in the bathroom, which shouldn't be long now, he might appreciate some non-feminine assistance along with this box of barley sugar.'

'Super, uncommon kind and thoughtful. I'll remind *him* so, too.'

Mrs Jenkins left her own door ajar for long enough to see the steward guide her neighbour into his accommodation. Re-emerging some time afterwards with her daughter, she looked on as he stood outside Colonel Newton's cabin balancing a tray on one hand and meeting the door with the other.

'Would you care for a brew madam?'

'No thanks, Ronnie, we're taking it with our breakfast. How is he?'

'Oh, he's quite the ticket, Mrs. Old school if ever there was one.' The door opened and the tea was passed over. 'You'll be takin' a light breakfast in your room, eh, sir?'

'Most certainly not. Breakfast at 0800 sharp, is it?'

Ronnie nodded and saluted with a canny merriment. 'Yes, sir.'

By that hour, wind and sea lent some respite, the only motion being a corkscrew roll gentle enough to keep the curtains swaying in the saloon. With a single engine still in operation, the *New Zealand Star* could only manage eight knots. Mother and daughter, arriving ten minutes after the appointed time, found a solitary occupant, smartly dressed in civilian clothes, his head absorbed in a newspaper and looking nothing like the crumpled form she had rescued from the floor. Ronnie greeted them as other passengers filed in.

'Good morning again, madam, miss,' he bowed. 'Any table you like save the one in the middle, which is reserved for the captain.'

Newton didn't look up as they sat down. Four triangles of toast arrived in a silver rack. He plucked two of those from their resting place, smeared them with butter and marmalade, took a bite and drank a healthy draught of strong black tea.

The sound of unswallowed food issued from his mouth. 'I'll have the kippers after all, thank you, steward,' he said, anticipating another enquiry.

'Right you are, and well chosen, sir, if I may say so,' came the breezy reply.

'Hello,' said Mrs Jenkins, catching his eye after several failed attempts. 'If your colour had matched the giant wave's, I wouldn't have chosen unprotected proximity.'

Not without a degree of embarrassment, Newton stood up and motioned to her. 'You're reasonably safe now and may decide to move closer, albeit at your own risk.'

'Well, I'm game. Come on, Charlotte, we've had an invitation from Colonel Newton, and daren't refuse.' They sat opposite him at the table positioned nearest to the starboard corner. To his rear was a longitudinal pane of glass that viewed a creamy wake furling like a sail canvas. On their right were square windows from which the curtains were now bunched up with matching ties.

'So you know of me?' he said, viewing her expressive eyes with elaborate care and realising that they weren't shy of being studied.

'Names pasted on doors are a fairly sure guide.'

'But not a rank, the last time I checked.'

'I respect a stickler for the facts, sir,' she said, inclining her head sagaciously, 'but, while loose lips were once said to sink ships, such are also wont to spread the word.'

'Do they, then?' he replied, less stiffly. 'Well, nevertheless, formal introductions shouldn't be avoided. I'm Reginald Newton. And you are?' he asked, taking the slender hand with purpose while she regarded him carefully before replying.

'Nancyng Jenkins, and I'm proud to introduce my daughter, Charlotte.' The young girl, whose skin was lighter than her mother's, blushed momentarily before answering, 'Pleased to meet you, Colonel.'

'And how old might you be, Charlotte?' he enquired in a tone much less formal than he had used thus far.

'I'm ten, going on eleven, sir.'

'For a girl of that age, you're so remarkably petite compared with your mother, but I also see you've inherited some of her other features.'

'Did I, sir? Most people are surprised by my age. But Mum says my father was short. I have no memory of him. He died when I was quite tiny.'

'That's sad.' He was taken with their unusual blend of accents and his mind worked on the permutations. The mother was more Anglicised. Though other similarities lurked, the daughter evinced a mixed brogue without denying her mother's influence.

'Excuse me, sir, madam.' It was Ronnie brandishing a quarto white cardboard embossed with the blue star logo under which appeared a freshly typed breakfast menu. Mrs Jenkins gave it a cursory glance.

'I heard a request for kippers and, as Charlotte loves them, we'll all join in together. Some toast would be nice, fresh fruit and orange juice, with coffee and cream for me to follow. No boiled eggs today, if it pleases the chef.'

'I'm able to vouch that it'll please him no end. A wise choice, very, if I might say so, madam. Would you like more tea, sir, or perhaps some coconut milk, good for the stomach, if you'll allow me to be so forward, Colonel?'

Newton parried the offer by testing the weight of the pot and shaking his head. Two couples and three children were shown to a table by Ronnie's female counterpart while he busied himself with their order. Then the last of the passengers arrived, a couple accompanied by a young man of twenty and a girl slightly older.

'Are you retired, sir?' Charlotte suddenly asked.

'My dear, you shouldn't ask this gentleman such a thing,' chided Mrs Jenkins mildly, trusting to receive an answer.

'Oh, Mother, you're not usually so formal,' came her reply as she continued to press the point. 'It's just that being a colonel and not wearing a uniform, I was a little curious.' There was a delay which saw Nancyng Jenkins eye them both. 'Oh, then my apologies, sir.'

'No need for them. The secret's out. Uniforms are only required when on duty.' He was surprised not so much at the question but by the articulation of so young an interlocuter. On the point of speaking, her mother stalled when three officers and Captain Malcolm Meeker advanced to the central table. They sat down while a different steward took their order.

The master, wearing white trousers creased to a knife's edge, matched shirt with indicia of rank on his shoulders, then rose with the stateliness of a plenipotentiary, rounding the tables to greet each passenger in turn by name, bowing to the women and shaking hands with the men. Commandingly elevated to near six feet in height, suited with a close-trimmed beard, eyebrows like tar and as thick as thatch, his voice by comparison paled, insipid and ingratiating. Before resuming his place at the head of the table, he tapped the water carafe with a spoon, a practised method which mustered the breakfasters' combined concentration.

'Sorry to interrupt, ladies and gentlemen. Before you take your first meal of substance in days, let me apologise at the outset for strictures the weather imposed on catering. You'll allow me, I'm sure, to have the chief steward type up two breakfast menus for the duration of the voyage, one with eggs and the other without. Speaking for myself, ladies and gentlemen, the former won't be permitted access to the captain's table between the current bearing and England.' There followed a few agreeable murmurs from the passengers.

'Now to business. Much as I'd like to adopt a Christ-like supervision, I've had no say in how the sea has behaved so far or whether it might misbehave in the future, though credit will be claimed for fair weather.' On this occasion the table reactions were quizzical. 'You'll appreciate that my announcement at the start of the voyage was based on the available forecasts which proved a tad awry.'

'More than just a tad,' came an interjection from a bejewelled lady.

'Indeed, madam. We've lost three days and, unless we can conjure up a miracle, we won't get them back. There's a further rider to that. I would invite the chief engineer to elaborate if he were here but, at this moment, under his expert supervision, major repairs are being undertaken about eighty feet beneath where we now sit.'

'Here comes more ill tidings,' the lady's husband observed.

'Not altogether too bad, sir,' Meeker continued uncomfortably. 'Testing weather necessitated one of the engines being decommissioned after overheating. A piston's replacement was required and restoration should be complete either late today or early tomorrow. Shutdown of an engine takes off half the power and likewise speed. It means an extra day's sailing.'

There were more mutters in the saloon.

'Every effort will be made to make up time,' Meeker ending them by breaking in. 'But we can't do the impossible. Under the circumstances, drinks will be provided on a gratuitous basis until we reach Port Elizabeth. For those fretting about the safari, the operators have been alerted and it's still going ahead. Thank you for your patience. Daily updates on our estimated arrival will be given. Folks, please enjoy yourselves.' There was sporadic applause as he resumed his seat.

'Is this your first venture at sea?' Nancyng Jenkins directed her question to Newton, who had poured more tea and offered same to her. 'One coffee is enough so don't mind if I do, thank you.'

'It's a maiden deep-ocean voyage,' he replied economically.

'Then what a harsh introduction to finding your sea legs.' When he coughed and drew closer to the table, she smiled and pressed him further. 'I wasn't going to ask if you were on a secret mission and hoping to steal some time on safari,' she asked roguishly.

'Such an excursion hasn't been included in my itinerary,' came the dour reply. 'I'm going to England the long way around. It's been some time since I've been acquainted with Piccadilly or Big Ben.'

'Oh, we're seeing them, too. I can hardly wait,' chipped in Charlotte, surprising her mother. 'We will also visit the Tower of London, Westminster Abbey, the Houses of Parliament, Runnymede, and Oxford University. I love everything Mum's told me about England.'

'So, you're familiar with Britain, Mrs Jenkins?'

'I've read quite a deal about your beautiful country,' she announced, as lean forearms vacated the table to make way for her plate, tapping her daughter to do likewise. 'Are you staying with tea?' she asked, as the spout ceased its dawdling with the cup half full.

'I might do that.'

'Ronnie,' she called with confidence, elevating the pot, 'there's a good fellow, could we have another?'

'Certainly, madam, comin' up in a jiffy,' his enthusiasm not for waning.

Newton studied them carefully as they ate. Charlotte maintained an even pace with her mother, ever-present the suspicion that she might have preferred to finish sooner. Occasionally, Mrs Jenkins met his eyes, nodding each time she did so, then brimmed with approval at her daughter's handling of fork and knife.

'Not being one to reprise,' Newton began.

'Go ahead. That's what a breakfast table at sea is all about.'

'Is it? Well then, I wanted to get this out of the way earlier but thought you would, as the captain said, prefer to take full advantage of your first decent meal in a while.'

'Never mind the captain's soothing. I think we've almost finished, haven't we, Charlotte?' the observation timing with her last piece of toast being ladled with strawberry conserve. 'So, you were about to say, Colonel?'

'It wouldn't have been a particularly attractive sight that my quarters presented earlier, and you rather saved me from further discomfiture.' She refilled his cup after dextrously rocking Ronnie's delivery to maximise the draw. He nodded approvingly. 'And you didn't drown the Earl Grey with milk.'

'Nor am I into lighthouse tea. There's no artistry in fluking a decent cup.'

'Lighthouse tea? Something nautical?'

'A Welsh joke of which my husband was fond to describe a strength deficiency, "blinkin' near water",' she said, offering a persuasive intonation of the language of the bards.

His lips moved in appreciation and he steadied with the several clearings of his throat. 'But that was no fluke. You saw the way I liked it and delivered the right mix.'

'Let's just say then that I've been blessed with modest powers of discernment.'

'Some could assume picking up things like that is either natural or acquired by experience. You must have made the late Mr Jenkins a happy man.' She didn't flinch at the return to a subject that he might have left alone and he then attempted to dilute the remark. 'Impertinence derives from the service, you know. Sometimes it's impossible to switch off the "acquired by experience" hoo-ha.'

'No offence assumed. Now, if you'll permit us?' Charlotte's and her mother's chairs creaked in unison. 'It was a pleasure to be of assistance to you. There's nothing worse than being alone when you're not well. Good morning. Perhaps we'll see you on deck later.'

'Indeed.' Newton, who had risen with mother and daughter, bowed as they departed his table to move around the saloon, pausing to meet the other passengers. He resumed an unctuous survey of the opinion pages of *The Times*, desiring to postpone the full process until the evening meal. It was not to be. Social comingling commenced and he put the paper down.

Jim and Iris Cahill shook hands, as did Colin and Ernestine McConsker, the latter outstaying their welcome by being especially nosey. The children remained at their table.

'So, Colonel,' she ruminated self-importantly, 'I would love to understand what particular corps you were in when the Japs arrived?'

What a question, he mused, since December 1941 bore no relevance to the present, yet so framed as to prevent the avoidance of giving an answer.

'Well, ah, just some insignificant Intelligence area,' he stumbled out.

'How tremendous for you, chasing down all those fifth columnists,' Husband McConsker chimed in, adding to the inquisition by asking if he had heard the story of a British spy in the services who hadn't been seen since the surrender. 'You would know about that fellow, I'm sure. Can't think of the blighter's name. Begins with "H" I think.'

'Nor me. Not my area, but presumably you'll read about it one day,' Newton offered with reserve, re-arranging his paper ostentatiously so that the questioner's wife felt the need to offer a miffed apology. 'We'll have plenty of time to catch up for deck golf,' he added, understanding that remaining incognito would require some skill but changing the subject might send a message. 'I'm told all of us will learn before the voyage is out,' he added.

'Oh, yes, jolly good show. We must make the best of the outdoors after that shocking weather,' said Jim Cahill joining in. Their daughter, a retiring girl of similar age to Charlotte, hung back. 'That's our sweet child. Say "hello", Marion.' She raised a timid hand and Charlotte, who was behind her, took the initiative by taking it and introducing herself. They hit it off immediately.

The final grouping hovered. Sir Lionel and Lady Margaret Onions, the couple who had distinguished themselves not so *sotto voce* during the captain's homily, seemingly reluctant to demonstrate any positive inclination to regard themselves as part of the others, went through courteous formalities, content to go by his and her titles.

'Newton, this is our only child, Henrietta,' Sir Lionel announced, puffing up with elaborate conceit. The twenty-year-old's lustrous bronze hair, garnished by a tidy assortment of facial freckles, was single-plaited, its puffy end dangling at her waist.

Enquiring eyes ran over him in a fashion that was more than casual and her long fingers, boldly ensnaring Newton's hand, made captive his attention to such an awkward extent that he felt constrained to break in with, 'So, what do *you* plan to do on this voyage and afterwards, Miss Onions?' Expelling air, he freed himself, pondering the slot into which she fell.

'I'm not sure yet. I've had a rather lengthy time of, well, reflection I suppose.'

'Yes, you are, Henrietta,' said her mother. 'I'm certain Colonel Newton would like you to elaborate.'

'I doubt if such a military gentleman cares a toss, Mother. Oh, attend University or something in London,' she remarked disinterestedly, her deep brown eyes projecting from lashes the length of which were startling and cradled in lids so moist that Newton contemplated whether some recollection had arisen. She repositioned a few golden strands of hair from her face and seemed intent on gauging his reaction.

'Henrietta will be undertaking a degree in business at the London School of Economics,' emphasised Sir Lionel, who was keen to dispel any first impression of taciturnity for which his daughter was renowned in fresh company.

'Father has my life mapped out, it seems,' she remarked caustically. 'He has a way of keeping on top of everything.' They exchanged glances before Newton spoke.

'Congratulations, Miss Onions. You've my best wishes for what seems like a bright future,' he replied. She warmed to the response and was about to add something further when Sir Lionel turned to leave.

'Good morning, then. I suppose we shall see you later, Colonel,' he cut in with authority.

As the group reached the entrance, Henrietta shot a parting glance in his direction and received a nod for her trouble.

Newton decided it was time to examine the library. Well-stocked mahogany and glass cabinets decorated the walls in the smoking lounge. He pulled out several volumes and flicked through them. Half of the books on display appeared maritime related, suiting his mood. Speculatively, he selected a copy of Dana's *Two Years Before the Mast* and W.W. Jacobs's green-bound book of short stories, *Cruises and Cargoes,* departing with them under one arm. On his path back to the cabin, white tips on waves and a modest swell outside as he peered through a porthole were enough to deter an intention to have a stroll around the promenade deck. Assuming calm may not return or swells even worsen throughout the afternoon if the breeze freshened, Newton regretted his utterances about golf.

Opening the door to a lavender freshness was proof of his steward's efforts, as, too, became the presence of clean linen and a spotless interior. Newton was upright on a bunk that ran at right angles to the cabin's bulkhead affording him seaward views. From this vantage point he considered the quarters that would house him for the next month and weighed it as being roughly equivalent to service accommodation in size and fit-out.

A bunk-side table with four drawers became an adequate resting place for his reading. The brightly-polished brass porthole was to the left of that. His eyes scanned the wall in front of him on which was hung a painting of a paddle steamer and paused at a cane captain's chair, indicative that more than one visitor at a time would require being attuned to intimacy. Nearest to the far corner was a fixed wooden cabinet, beside which a washstand lay with a mirror above it. On the other wall sat a dressing table, positioned over a rug that ran along half of one side of the cabin covering the linoleum floor. Fortunately, it had been spared the early mishap.

He was reminded of the solicitations from Mrs Jenkins and his ineffectual attempts to offer thanks. Not one to see her efforts left unappreciated, he would pursue the matter at the earliest opportunity. That she seemed to regard any mention of the event as unnecessary made him even keener to make the point as going to her favour. And the thought of doing so stimulated the drawing of inferences about her.

She was attractive but in no measure flashy, exotic in a manner that activated his biographic interest. He envisaged that, being a stylish younger woman, she must have married a much older man, possibly an ex-patriot. She seemed entirely at ease with strangers in a new social setting, suggestive that her late husband may have entertained frequently. With an accent almost neutral and possessing a flawless command of English, it was no surprise to see her daughter similarly endowed through an attentive upbringing. Every element of her personality debunked the commonly held imagery of an Asian wife, seen but rarely heard much more than in simpering adulation, meeting the demands of an overbearing sexagenarian.

He dampened a towel from the residue of an ice bucket and freshened his face after realising that one and a half hours had engaged this reverie. Straightening his tie and rubbing some oil into his scalp, Newton steered himself to his immediate neighbour. Charlotte called out the visitor's name. 'Won't be a minute,' came the hidden respondent.

When emerging from the *en suite* in the larger cabin, loosened hair alerted him to a figure that neither competed for space in blouse and slacks nor was unwilling to shape these garments. She displayed pleasure at seeing him, delivering a gentle rebuke to her daughter in not announcing the colonel by name.

'I should have waited outside, Mrs Jenkins. Pardon me for intruding on your privacy but I'm loath to leaving things unsaid.'

'In what sense?' she asked portentously.

'Oh, nothing to be alarmed about. It's somewhat awkward,' he offered self-deprecatingly. 'My first attempt wasn't managed well, overlooking the restorative barley sugar unforgiveable, but I just wanted to say that what happened this morning, next door, well, grateful and all that for your efforts in rescuing this non-sailor and saving him from a mortify—'

She inclined her head in amusement. 'Nothing more needs be said, excepting that you may buy me a cocktail before dinner so that we can traverse more edifying topics.'

'You're letting me off the hook, since the bar tab has been waived. Still, we can have that drink later. Perhaps when we hit shore I'll attend to that commission with more substance and formality. Shall we aim for something in Cape Town, maybe even dinner?'

'You have a deal.' She held out her hand and he didn't hesitate in shaking it. 'Good morning, Colonel Newton.'

Chapter 2 – *Foredeck Assignations*

O n the afternoon following his ungainly apology to Mrs Jenkins and seas more accommodating, Reginald Newton resisted being suborned into the golf party, preferring a lazy canvas deck chair arranged to take advantage of medicinal sunshine. Every so often his head tilted from the page when a cheer went up and, as they became louder, he chose for some discreet observance.

A fulsome group were gathered amidst much clunking from mallets colliding with pucks and sending them in directions other than their intended placement. Doubling as referee, the shipwright's patience was tested when many were dispatched to the ocean bed but he squirmed when two sticks earned the same fate. Ruefully, he accepted the inroads overnight manufacture of replacements would make into his own leisure time.

Mishits began to account for dwindling interest, with

a remnant of the older passengers persevering while the rest sought other diversions. The abating atmosphere saw Newton return to his position, choosing a reverie with open book slumped across his chest. When Henrietta and her mother arrived to recline on nearby chairs, he sat up and nodded at both, receiving a greater appreciation from the younger Onions prior to stretching out and arranging a towel over his forehead.

After a short interval, her ladyship appeared indisposed and opted to go indoors. Henrietta, waiting upon her mother's departure, then took the chair nearest to him with pronounced movement and shuffling. The afternoon breezes blew from multiple directions, confusing and neutralising the sea. Incessant squawking and diving by marine birds indicated that life beneath the surface had resumed its diurnal pattern. He avoided any glance towards the young woman, deriving comfort in anonymity and salty ambience, blissfully unaware that he remained the primary subject of her observations.

Shadows from the superstructure were marking lines across the deck and its cooling effect stirred him. Contending he was the last remaining passenger on deck with Miss Onions having vacated her position and the players long gone, he felt at ease until he heard thumping above and decided to investigate. Two able seamen were unrolling netting similar to that found on tennis courts. This was tied to the rails on the port and starboard sides.

'What's that for?' he enquired, calling to one of the sailors, who replied that it was to guard against equipment loss in future games.

'We 'ad a few mishaps with the sportin' gear today, sir, so the bosun suggested that we rig this up.'

Newton returned to book scanning with a tired sigh, caught between a decision as to whether he should find his place or skip a few pages altogether and settle on another chapter. In this desultory mode, he was startled by the nearness of a voice calling his name. Straightaway, he shook himself into an upright position and coughed.

'I wondered if you might be piking out on that cocktail.' Mrs Jenkins' exposed back was drenched by the platinum sky in the west. She had bound her hair under a scarf. 'Are we still on?'

Fumbling with a pocket watch, he scrambled to his feet. 'Is that possibly the hour?' It was past five-thirty. 'How long have you been here?'

'Merely enough time to appreciate that the sounds you were making suggest your brain works feverishly during an afternoon nap.'

'Did I mouth anything incriminating?' he asked, more out of blandness than humour.

'I learnt mostly of the English countryside and geography and was given a taste of what to expect,' she returned in amusement, as if relishing his disquiet. 'Miss Onions was kind enough to indicate where you were hiding. You might well have won a fan in that fair, wily maid.'

'A little presumptuous, don't you think, Mrs Jenkins,' he

responded acerbically. 'Now, if you'll permit me to go and revive, we can still fit in that drink,' he said, stacking the last deck chair on the top of a bundle.

'Oh, come on, you're quite awake,' she shot back disarmingly. 'Here's the ideal nook, moreover in the cool of dusk and suitable for asking you something in private.' A steward was passing below and she called, 'Can you send up champagne? And you will have a—'

'Lemon, lime and bitters.'

'You do partake, Colonel?'

'Occasionally, Mrs Jenkins. To your enquiry then?'

'Oh, it's nothing really profound. I just wondered why an officer of your rank would be taking the long way home when the army could have flown you to London just like that.' She snapped her manicured fingers. 'None of my business of course, as it might be military manoeuvres, state secrets or something.'

He couldn't help contemplating his visitor with a mixture of the benign and the tendentious. Already the voyage had become anything but the uneventful and unnoticed one for which he had hoped; the atrocious weather at the start and now a feeling he was subject to a scrutiny that was far from imperceptive. Granted she was intelligent and lively, but for someone whose innate preference was to fish rather than be the subject of a fishing expedition, more particularly from a not unattractive passenger, for once he rested at a disadvantage.

An added factor was that her question resonated with

his senses more broadly than she could have imagined. At such an early stage, Newton found himself questioning his decision to separate from the army, and the process invariably became a candid assessment of those twilight years following the war. He likened himself to a tree whose gnarled trunk was the only sign of a cry for pruning, shaping and fertilising. Not otherwise demanding attention, it could be left to rot and ready itself for the axeman.

He was certain that damage had been done to his reputation in the aftermath of his time with Force 136. That excerpt always came back to his association with the communist leader of the guerrillas, Chin Peng, whom he had regarded as a friend in the field but who he also kept at arm's length. Others, through jealousy, chose not to see it that way.

After Japan surrendered, the interregnum proved a torpid period for the percipient Newton. An acting appointment to colonel gave him some hope, but formal promotion and a decent posting continued to elude him. With the effluxion of time, the likelihood of it being gazetted had receded even further. Leadership in Far Eastern Command's Intelligence, once thought to be his for the taking, had slipped into Whitehall's budget-trimming never to reappear. The entity's very survival was being called into serious question.

Newton was also convinced that certain echelons of the military establishment were engaged in a war of attrition. He was the target and they were intent on seeing the back of him. Without a command, he was relegated to lieutenant-colonel and assigned the role of civilian liaison attaché on High Commissioner Gurney's Singapore staff.

Re-posting to London may well have been the surest path out of the stalemate but he had vowed to stay on, even if it acted as a retardant to his career. If such were to come as an order, Newton had determined to resign. His was a personality that had never lent itself to advancing his own interests. He was the antithesis of a networker, stoic in an ethic that proof of his capacity lay through achievements in action rather than self-serving missives and obsequiousness. Accordingly, he avoided any suggestion of service courtship or eliciting favours, stuck to his assigned tasks and never went out of his way to make friends. Such was a singularly negative trait he recognised only too well.

By early 1950 and still desk-bound, he had viewed the appointment of Lieutenant-General Sir Harold Briggs to the position of Director of Operations in Malaya as a positive step. One of Newton's own recommendations in a report he compiled just after the war had been establishing a commander in overall control rather than persisting with the various divisions led by men trying to carve out their own 'fiefdoms', as he offered in another notorious memorandum, an observation which those who were keen to get him shipped out never forgave.

Generating confidence amongst the peasant farmers was also a stratagem he had ventured, along with squatter resettlement on freehold land. If the Chinese felt they owned something and that their interests were protected, being granted legal title to small farm holdings and the fruits of their labour protected by the security forces, they would be less likely to remain beholden to the communists.

He could only reflect on these things from afar now with a grim acceptance, knowing that his suggestions must have been seen at some stage and another would take credit for their implementation. And so things had dribbled on until his patience had simply evaporated. Having been driven to assembling matchsticks in order to pass the time, he up and decided that any future in the army in Singapore couldn't be within any reasonable or foreseeable contemplation.

Impulsively, though with one imperative to perform along the way, he had taken to a lengthy sea sojourn as part of his pre-retirement leave, ultimately hoping to travel incognito and slip back into Great Britain equally disregarded.

'My, as you colonel types say, have I stumped you or something?'

It brought a fleeting concession to his mien. 'I'm not a full colonel, Mrs Jenkins.'

'At last an admission, a comedown, and that explains it all. Might this be the start of a thawing in that veneer?'

'I'm beginning to realise that anyone on this ship except you might have thrown me into defensive mode.'

'If that wasn't defence, lord help yours truly in any attack.'

'As you wish.'

'Ah, ever the contained, gentlemanly officer. Sink me for being impudent, but here's what I think.' She was imprisoning his eyes, stopping an impulsive riposte as to what he might care about how she thought and emboldened her further with, 'No, you won't care to be told but I'll say it anyway. My first presumption is that you have ended a long relationship of some sort and decided you need a month of solace and sea air to embalm your soul.'

'Seems I'm not attaining a great deal of solitude to permit the medicine to take effect,' he replied laconically.

She paid no heed. 'If you ever married, I think it was, well, rather short-lived. But who knows, that's a speculation too far. So, this was someone who's aware of everything, and it's uncomplicated because she's a woman you see somewhat infrequently. I fancy you're a prodigious letter-writer. You told me this was your first trip back to England in ages. Letters and maybe those occasional visits from her kept it going. The longer I think about it, the more my intuition tells me you're married in name only and that ensures the perpetuation of the status quo as well as no strings. I'll have to reflect further before issuing any other declarations.'

'You needn't trouble yourself on my account since your fertile and inventive mind won't be stilled it seems,' he replied somewhat curtly. 'Then again, it's sure to afford me rare and unexpected amusement.'

She flung off the remark. 'You're a closeted man, but my inclination suggests that beneath that opaque surface there are many diverse tributaries marking out your red corpuscles. That facility fascinates women, you would know.'

Newton was not minded to let her didactic analysis bear fruit by making any concessions to the veracity of her pronouncements. 'Perhaps consecutive nights of bilious insomnia induced convoluted daydreams about a friend of mine. Did I babble on so incoherently in just a few minutes or are you some kind of fortune-teller, gifted with a power to interpret facial twitches?'

'Don't take me so seriously, Colonel. Look at that,' she said. The quenching process had begun as they leaned on the lacquered rail to witness the sun being drawn into the depths of the Indian Ocean as if by transparent tentacles of a giant octopus. With each slide and a final tug, the last vestiges of warmth vanished with it.

'Are you cold?' he asked. Her shoulders twitched and he had his answer.

'In this latitude it's a strange phenomenon to experience such a temperature drop so quickly,' she replied philosophically, and he enquired if she preferred to retreat inside.

'Not yet. I'm still waiting for a reply to my question.'

'I've forgotten what it was.'

'No you haven't, Colonel Newton. Stop foxing with me.'

'Why don't we do it this way; let's get ready for dinner and I'll think about what you've said.'

She continued as if not taking his proposal seriously. 'You took this cruise for a purpose and I bet my suppositions have earned some currency. Me? Well, *touché* is *my* elliptical answer. After all, you started it,' her candour temptingly provocative. 'Amongst my reasons were cost and convenience. Like my daughter, I also wanted to see Africa. My husband visited there well before we met and told me many fascinating anecdotes about the place, most of all describing its vastness, wildlife, beauty and grandeur, to say nothing of the culture. Those matters would hold no interest to a man of your persuasion,' she asserted to the point of incommoding him.

'If I should swear that most of your suppositions and premises were wildly inaccurate, would that still your curiosity?'

'More likely whet it. I want to know about the ones that weren't far out.'

'You're quite unruly, Mrs Jenkins,' he responded in resignation. 'As a concession and, mind, no more, shall we meet tomorrow afternoon at this spot to continue and maybe set the record straight?'

'Then I should be satisfied with that. Come on. It's even cooler than a moment ago and I would hate to see a relapse.' She squeezed his wrist as they parted.

Over dinner with mother and daughter, no direct reference was made to their recent discussion. After initial congratulations for the young girl's efforts in securing a convincing victory in the kids' table tennis tournament, barely a word passed. A few times Newton spied Mrs Jenkins eyeing him in a fashion that had him wondering whether she was signalling a return to the earlier topics. He likewise moved his eyebrows in Charlotte's direction, and that seemed to amuse her equally insightful daughter for she straight-out asked if he was playing mind games with them.

'Colonel Newton was dreaming whilst awake and begs

me not to mention it.' The remark brought the table to life as Newton searched for a retort.

'In case you're looking for something equally witty, my apologies, Miss Jenkins. It is, however, gratifying that you seem to have more of your father's sense of decorum.' Rising, he added, 'Many thanks for the pleasure of dining with both of you and, if you could excuse me, the cheeses and crackers are all yours. Goodnight.'

*   *   *

In territory not of his choosing, Newton considered again what he would say to the subject of his thoughts as each day drew him closer towards to what would be their first meeting in over twenty years. It was a continuation of the self-same exercise that had carried over from his torpor on the promenade deck where these subconscious contortions had been captured by Mrs Jenkins. Despite a preference to regard his enigmatic fast friend as a subject fitted primarily for amusement, he was shaken by the number of coincidences between what he had been agonising over and the impromptu summation.

Prior to departing Singapore, he had written to the hospice informing her of his stopover in Port Elizabeth being the fifteenth of the month. The date was superseded after the nauseous weather. With both engines now in service and confirmation from the chief officer that there was little possibility of making up any substantial measure of the time lost, he drafted a ship-to-shore telegram with an amended date and gave it to the radio officer.

The next few hours had him rolling over to glimpse the occasional star, then back again until, abandoning the notion of sleep through the conventional means, he switched on the light and opened his book. Habitually it was the action that would send him off. Into the mix of matters conspiring against such an expectation, the cabin had become warmer the further the night advanced. Recalling again the slumber of the previous afternoon, he laid the blame squarely on that occurrence for his restlessness.

Exasperated, he was minded to take an extended walk on the promenade deck as a final antidote for his insomnia. He had but one pair of shorts in his kit. These were donned, along with a woollen shirt and boaters. Newton wasn't expecting to encounter a soul at that time of night. The air was exhilarating after the stuffiness of his confined quarters and he lengthened his stride. Having completed two circuits and about to enter the third, he was waylaid by an evocative voice.

'Can't sleep, Colonel Newton?' it said, and he turned to face Miss Henrietta Onions. 'I might be able to help.' Barefoot, wearing a nightdress suggestive of long and slender legs, she drifted towards him with a pronounced sway of her hips.

'You should be in bed, young lady,' he replied brusquely.

Even under intermittent moonlight the intention was apparent. 'We can be far more comfortable in *your* cabin and I guarantee that you'll succumb, well, to sleep, afterwards.'

Newton rounded on her. 'For the love of hell, talk about the baited hook laid with a view to making the taker mad. You're young enough to be my daughter. Now please, Miss Onions, go back to your mother and father and leave me to work out my own methods of counting sheep.' He began to walk away but she, far from rebuffed, bounded ahead to impede his progress by gripping a porthole lug on one side and a tightly strung spar on the other. 'Right, if you want to play these foolish games, shall we go and discuss it with your parents? I'm sure they would be pleased to have a report on what you've been up to.'

Instantly, the switch flicked to anger. 'That might be your report, but father will believe mine,' she said, tearing at the shoulder strap and bodice, 'and it will be a recounting of how you tried to—'

'And mine will relate what I heard and witnessed and that you concocted a foul lie to besmirch Colonel Newton's character.' Mrs Jenkins, coolly and calmly, emerged from the shadows.

'Damn you for a cockeyed old Chinese crone,' she spat out, her eyes blazing, as fiery as her hair that was loose and streaming beyond her waist. She descended on the intruder, fists flailing to little avail, when the object of her fury seized both forearms.

'You had best return to your parents' cabin,' Newton said, restraining her from behind. Feet, not so tethered, she lashed backwards against his shins, then wriggled free and pushed past her, pausing at the passengers' companionway.

'You haven't heard the last of this, either of you.'

'Off you go, ridiculous juvenile,' responded Nancyng Jenkins contemptuously.

He looked at his saviour with a mixture of astonishment and gratitude, which was replaced by an ascendant beam of amusement as the moments passed. It was a feature she found compelling and, when he spoke, his voice was placid.

'Well, on my simple arithmetic, that makes two rescues in not much more than as many days at sea. What shall I call you, Joan of Arc?'

'I'm not in her league, though give me time. Past reason not hunted in your case.' In speaking, she moved closer to Newton. He drew back towards the deck railing, comfortable in its support.

'A student of Shakespeare? That was the only sonnet *I* remembered.'

'More a lucky guess.'

'I'm not convinced that luck played much of a hand.'

'So, given that you weren't up to no good, what were you doing out here at this ungodly hour?'

'Suffocating and sleepless in my bunk, needing air. Seems to have proved somewhat infelicitous in hindsight. What's your excuse for being about?' he responded.

She closed the distance again, this time nudging at his shoulder with her fingers, prompting Newton to face her directly. Nonplussed, he asked the question again with raised eyebrows.

'Does it matter what I was doing? Nancyng happened to be here and that's all I need say. For such an intelligent man, you're disarmingly ineffectual when it comes to women. I'll leave you to answer your own question as to whether I'm angling for your companionship.'

'Mrs Jenkins, you have a knack of flooring me, and that may be part of the reason why I'm beginning to become attentive to yours.'

She was thinking, *Oh, to hell with your propriety*, but given the concession, resisted the urge to state it. 'Well, prove it and tell me about yourself. I'm not minded to return to my cabin with a daughter incognisant of her mother's absence. You're even more out of favour in your bunk after that farrago of insolence and me, well, the later the hour, the more receptive I become. Make a start and, on the morrow, we can move to the next instalment.'

Mrs Jenkins latched on to him and they walked aft, taking in strands of light magnifying the ship's wake. Releasing his forearm upon a prolonged silence, she swivelled around and folded her arms.

'Having dragged me this far, it's evident that you're intent on persisting?'

Her response lay in detaching two wooden chairs from the six pack where they'd been moored and set them together. Before he could say another word, she was seated, leaving no space for further prevarication.

'So, is it as I might hope, that some vestiges of the moon and balmy air combining with my other entreaties are sufficient to advance the process of loosening your tongue?'

He sighed in capitulation and joined her. 'I'm going to regret doing this.'

'Don't spoil it with that brand of nonsense or you will,' she snapped back.

'You would surely know what it is to have a good friend, Mrs Jenkins, so that's where this tale pretty well begins and ends. Magnus Sansim was more than that to me, a lost and, at times, lonesome brother, perhaps the greater so than one whose blood is derived from like genes. He was born on the same day that I was, in fact Guy Fawkes Day, the fifth of November 1904. Are you aware of the historical figure, nay, legendary disrupter and anarchist, Guy Fawkes?'

'I'm little acquainted with his notoriety but, at the risk of letting out a fragment of the impatient, rather than setting off bungers and so recently imploring you to begin, I assume there's some relevance to your pointing it out.'

'Well, I hope you would like to hear a meaningful account rather than one devoid of colour or situation, so I mention the coincidence more for him than for me. At the inception of my friend's life by mere juxtaposition of dates, the imagery provoked by that *agent provocateur* is by no means irrelevant to events of which I'm about to embark.'

'Forgiven, I think. Go on if you will, Colonel.'

'So, he came into the world in a little village called Hambrook about twenty miles from Bath in south-west

England. Mr Sansim Senior was a solicitor who practised from a compact office situated on the ground floor of their home. His mother acted as clerk and secretary. An only sibling, Rachelle, six years younger than him, died of diphtheria before she could walk. He adored the child, since she afforded him that unconditional love for which he had longed up until the time of her birth.'

'What, didn't his mother and father love their boy?'

'His mother couldn't breastfeed him and employed a wet nurse. Mrs Sansim suffered a nervous breakdown after he was born, you see, and, upon recovering, she didn't seem to want or possess the necessary instincts to bond with the child. His father was always busy with his legal practice and frequently travelled to London on business.

'As I indicated, the child worshipped his little sister and went out of his way to make her happy. He played with her incessantly, even changed her nappy from time to time. They had domestic help, of course, but he perceived that both parents resented his closeness to the child or, more particularly, Rachelle's willingness to gravitate to her brother rather than the parents. Frequently he was scolded and sent to bed without his dinner for trespassing on their time, as they saw it.

'He was too young to understand then that his mother and father were having difficulty in their marriage, although he remembered them arguing a lot. When Rachelle became sick, a curtain of gloom descended over the entire assembly. Magnus was castigated for interfering in her care and told not to be in the same room with his sister out of, perhaps, fear he would catch the disease. In the room beside hers and being a light sleeper, Magnus was often woken when he heard coughing and would creep to her bedside and hold the tiny hand. She would know he was there and kiss him or give him a feeble hug when he leaned over her. He was only eight-and-a-half at the time.

'A night in the middle of winter saw it beastly cold and the wind was howling so much that he couldn't sleep at all. At times the house was shaken with such typhonic vehemence as to almost wrench the edifice from its foundations. He had a premonition that things weren't right. When he went to check on the child, he saw that the nurse was lying on the floor, apparently senseless, an empty liquor bottle beside her. Magnus rushed to his sister's side. Rachelle's fingers were icy and, as he put his cheek against hers, his own body chilled. He slipped under the covers and took her in his arms, determined to warm the tiny remnants. At that point the tempest calmed and he fell into a deep sleep.

'His next recollection was being woken by the domestic, who had recovered from her drunken stupor with morning filtering in. As he tumbled out of bed, she shrieked at the sight of the infant and ordered him back to his bedroom.

'When the servant related what had happened, embellishing the story to cast the boy in the worst possible light and portray herself in the best, his parents blamed him for suffocating the child. No amount of protestation relieved his father's wrath and he was confined to his room for days.

Even when suffocation was ruled out, Magnus was never forgiven for his disobedience and not permitted to attend her funeral.'

'From this distance, it can only be wondered how this terrible event shaped the boy's life. Hard to picture anything quite like it,' said his listener as her tears threatened to appear. 'Surely they came to regret their stance after the medical results and with time?'

'It seems not. There were no apologies or a scrap of empathy towards their now only child. In hindsight, there must have been so much going on between them that this catastrophic event sounded the death knell on the parents' relationship as well. And Rachelle's passing had a more profound effect upon his makeup than anything that had ever happened to him at their hands.

'Thereafter, father and mother retreated into his and her respective worlds; they seemed content to see Magnus get by in his.

'I should tell you also that "Little Mag", a loathsome name, had been attributed to him by domestic help because he suffered from stunted growth.

'After Rachelle's death, he was sent to Kingswood School in Bath at the age of nine. By Easter term of the following year, his mother had moved to London and he never saw her again. Kingswood was where I first met him as I was a boarder there as well.'

'So, this was where he told you about all of these things?'

'Yes, but that was much later, and I'll come to the

establishing of our friendship in due course. Let me go back a bit for I left out the other pivotal person in his life at the time of his sister's death.'

'Oh, who was that at such an early age?'

'Her name was Esrelle Langhe. Now, Magnus, which is what I always called him, hated his nickname. It followed the boy to Bath because several of his Hambrook classmates came across with him. He was a terribly uncomfortable lad in company, an object well-fitted to be picked on by teachers and masters alike. He struggled with his marks. Unlike so many who were academically deficient yet bore sporting aptitude, initially there was no sign Magnus possessed either attribute. Other boys were not shy of teasing him about everything. That made him so, well, ineffectual, spreading rumours that he was a doleful excuse for a child, a coward and an idiot with it. Then, somewhat imperceptively, he began to change.'

'Children can be so cruel. My daughter has never been like that, always helping the less fortunate and going out of her way for anyone. She's generous with all-comers.'

'One can see that in her. She's a credit to you.'

'Well, her father had something to do with it, too. You mentioned that Magnus began to alter somewhat subtly. Apart from physique, what was he like to look at? I mean, was he handsome, plain or average?'

'Interesting question. He had good colouring, sandy hair, blue eyes, noticeable brows that almost met above a nose that was, well, bumpy but reflective. The combination with his other attributes created a worrisome, somewhat needy sort of demeanour. He was a self-taught musical all-rounder, especially dextrous with wind instruments. Consistent with that facility, his mouth was stacked with teeth giving a permanent look of having it wrapped around something and this, together with generous lips, created a startling embouchure when he played the trumpet. He didn't laugh much as he was self-conscious about those teeth. I should have mentioned his hands. Tapering, attenuated fingers were tender in nature as they caressed piano keys. He drew much comment from all who watched him play. As he matured, Magnus was offered lessons by the music master. He declined, saying that reading music was beyond his faculties. That was silly, of course, and, when I pressed him about it once, he became rather short with me.

'But I digress. Getting back to Esrelle, it was she who called him "Mus", and he adored her not just on account of its originality, but it conveyed to him a sense of natural affection, something he craved. Esrelle was a classmate for each of the four years he attended Hambrook Elementary School and became his childhood sweetheart. It was all very secretive in the manner of innocent children. Both had vivid imaginations and they best explored them together. Apparently, such potential for any number of artistic endeavours was never tapped into by their teachers.'

'I bet they read a lot and dwelt in their own make-believe world. It's something of a product of inventive minds.'

'Sounds like you're speaking from experience, Mrs Jenkins.'

She avoided his gaze as the observation hung in the air. 'Simple common sense,' Nancyng replied dismissively.

'Yes, I suppose so. They both loved animals and explored the countryside. By all accounts they were similarly encrusted as far as their home environment was concerned.' He saw Mrs Jenkins rolling her eyes. She shook her head, assuaging his disappointment at her lack of appreciation by waving her hand back and forward, urging him to ignore her.

'On his last day at Hambrook Elementary, they pledged everlasting love to each other and stole a secret kiss or two. He found a piece of tinplate about three times the size of a penny and scratched on the inscription, "M.S. loves E.L.", then managed to tack it onto a yew tree at the back of the school.

'They never lost touch. Magnus would see her when he came home for term holidays. And both wrote letters in between. When he was depressed, he showed me some of hers and they read in the most imaginative way.'

'How so? Was she the poetic type, romantically disposed or simply a combination of all those things, given her age?'

'I thought some of it was quite mature, certainly more than Magnus seemed to be, which made me think that she assumed a dominant nature in their exchanges. Others had a disturbing fatalism to them, but that's easy to say in retrospect. Let me recall just one that left an imprint on my mind like an indelible stencil. It went something like this:

Hello my dear Mus,

I had a dream last night that you became an elf and I was your elfin bride. We ate buns that you stole from Mr Fulcher's bakery because your parents had cast you out and you had nothing else to live on. One early morning he caught you and would have handed you over to a constable but you wriggled out of his hold in the flour pantry and ran to my window beneath which you hid until late at night. I helped you up to my room with sheets knotted together. We then kissed and plotted what to do next. After a few hours, we decided to run away. I crept downstairs and raided our larder, relieving it of a yummy block of Stilton cheese, some pickled onions and a cob of bread, knowing how much you love cheese!

Well, we ran off to the station and decided we would get on the train that would take us to Edinburgh where we would find a place to live. You told me that you only had threepence and you know what? I had just a penny which wasn't enough to get us even halfway. I was always thinking that because your dad was a man of law you would have lots of money because my father was just a coalminer.

Suddenly I became really sad and woke up. I felt poor and beyond my station in thinking of you in this way. I dream such rubbish at times. But it's always one about us being together. We will be one day, or will we?

All my love,

Esrelle

'That's a revelation, as well as something of a recollection.'

'It's always stayed with me. Magnus let me read it a few times and often brought it up. He kept the letter ever after.'

'I'm not sure I warm to this girl. She seems somewhat manipulative, or am I reading too much into pre-pubescent jottings?'

Newton's tardiness in responding, prompting a query about whether his memory had been further jogged, was met with a dismissive shake of his head and an excuse that he was distracted after hearing the sounds of crew setting about their early duties.

'Yours is a discerning observation.' Mrs Jenkins beamed in admiration at his precision in returning to her query. 'I had never thought of it before in such a fashion, being pretty reluctant to jump to conclusions about any situation. It's different when you run a set of circumstances past another person, more so you being of the opposite sex. And we both know that they are but children.'

'Esrelle doesn't strike me as so child-like, that's all. I will take your making the distinction as to my sex as a compliment.'

'Always view anything said during a detour in this monologue in that way, Mrs Jenkins. We must necessarily turn over a clump of pages now but, as you can see, with a tale so involved and so chronologically distant, sometimes things are out of kilter as another recollection comes to mind.'

'That's the charm of listening to you. Of course, I mightn't be grateful if you apologised too much for it could be interpreted as patronising.' Their eyes suggested that this little spar was a draw.

'Just after his sixteenth birthday, her letters abruptly ceased. That was not the only shock he endured on his return home for the Christmas vacation. When he stepped off the train, no one was there to meet him. That didn't overly concern him since by now he and his father were seriously estranged. He regarded his return to the village as a chance to reconnect with Esrelle, be relieved from the monotony of existence in what he held to be a doleful excuse for an educational institution and see as little of his father as he could.

'Against this critique of his boarding school, let's go to his intellectual blossoming. By that, I mean he managed to pass his exams but began to read so much on his own behalf that he acquired a knowledge and articulation of language. It was seen as a threat by the masters. He developed into a quick-witted young chap, always a moment away from an original and intelligent answer. It annoyed his teachers beyond measure and, by incurring their wrath, trivial infractions were severely punished as a consequence.

'The other thing was that he filled out dramatically, almost overnight in fact, and with it came a confidence to deal with his tormentors. There was an odious bully by the name of Gristass who had picked on him mercilessly, meting out several beatings. When he was asked to shine his boots utilising his tongue and some Kiwi black polish one morning before breakfast he just exploded. Years of ill-usage had created a well packed with gelignite, I suppose, like some of Fawkes' fireworks, and he knocked him down with one punch.

'There was an awful fuss about this because Gristass' jaw was broken. He refused point blank to offer any exculpatory reasons for his actions, affirming to the headmaster that he had no concern whatsoever about his father being called in.

'That is when I became involved, providing a detailed statement of the lengthy mistreatment he had suffered at the hands of the bully. Initially, my deposition was viewed as of little weight given our friendship was well known. But my declaration inspired others who had also suffered at the hands of the miscreant, so they came forward. An overwhelming body of evidence providing dates and particulars of previous assaults saw the headmaster focus upon Gristass rather than Magnus.

'Well, the rest, as they say, is history. Gristass left after a mutual agreement with his parents and Magnus became a legend within the school. I think it also marked a cementing of our mateship to the point that it was lifelong. As a symbol of the coalescence of our minds, we did a childish thing. I had a penknife and we decided that our friendship was of such a binding quality that it should only ever be broken by death. A small blood loss to one and the other of us was the sacrifice we decided to endure. Typically, he made his cut first, we mingled our blood, you know like the American Indians, and we had become one.'

'It's almost a *Boys Own Annual* story.'

'Every word and each action happened. I recall it as if it were last week and, more than that, remember my ineffectual cut produced an unexpected volume of blood. I tried for a trickle and tapped into a stream. I had to get a bandage put on afterwards, but he refused to do so. I see the sky shows streaks of light.'

'Yes, and well-timed as I should slink back before Charlotte wakes. So, when do we resume this tragic and fascinating story?'

'Mm, tragic. Later today, it can be, unless you need some respite.'

'Colonel Newton, you're not going to escape me so easily,' she said, making herself clear by capturing his hand.

Releasing him when convinced that he understood the meaning, Mrs Jenkins entered the passengers' accommodation through a narrow door opposite the davits. Her words and actions supporting them likewise opened the restraints upon his memory as if a life had urged itself back upon him.

Chapter 3 – *Awkward Interviews*

Captain Meeker was perusing an assortment of papers in his suite when Newton announced his arrival with a knock at the door that was ajar. As if caught unawares, he hastily turned the file to which they belonged face down, rose from a turquoise upholstered swivel chair and invited entry. Extending his arm was the first action motioning towards an adjacent low table; the second, when Newton didn't immediately accede to the request, became something of an apologetic shaking of the other's hand after advancing towards him. 'Ah, the perils of command: paperwork, issues, dramas and personalities. You know what it's like, I'm sure, Colonel.'

When the only reaction he received was a look that not only failed in lending itself to become a participant in periphery discussion but suggested a discomposure as to why he had been so summoned, it came as no surprise when the offer of coffee was declined. The captain closed the door behind him with a ceremony born of familiarity regarding matters of state.

'Of course, you must be wondering, and with every right to, why I requested the pleasure of your good self in my anteroom at this hour of the morning.'

Newton had never been inclined to indulge sycophancy and regarded him with an unflattering tilt of his head before responding. 'I've learnt never to wonder about anything in advance of its purpose being explained, Captain.'

'Oh, indeed. I wouldn't have expected anything less than such a professional approach.' Leaning forward, he coughed uncertainly. Effusive movement of his head did nothing to alter Newton's preliminary opinion of the man sitting opposite him. A faint stain evident on the tip of his shirt cuff and fingernails retaining traces of jet suggested inattention to early grooming as well. In these confines Meeker's voice appeared squeakier.

'Well, then, you will no doubt be pleased to venerate the request to see me by coming to the point of my being asked here.'

'Quite. This is a somewhat delicate matter, Colonel. I hasten to add that in so saying I'm not a man given to pre-judgment and—'

The knock preceded the chief officer's bursting in without invitation, his demeanour struggling to contain rage. 'Sir, excuse me, but there has been a physical flare-up between the bosun and a seaman over him insisting on seeing you concerning some note he sent up.'

'Ah, McColl, the Scottish menace.'

'Well, he's pretty worked up, says it's an important private matter.'

'He can cool his heels. I'll not bow to the likes of him. Use your own discretion and lock him up if needs be.' The mate's eyes equivocated between the bemused visitor and the captain before he removed himself. 'The perils of leadership, I—'

'So, Captain, you were about to tell me something?'

'Apologies for that, Colonel. Yes, where was I?' his discomfort more than fitting the intrusion.

'It was to the effect of not being given to form an opinion in advance of hearing both sides of the story.'

'I'm, well, just overwhelmed, Colonel Newton. If I only had your quality of officer amongst my minions I would never need to worry about such things and my life would be much, ah, well—'

'Simpler?'

'In a nutshell, yes. Do you have any idea why I asked you to come?'

'Don't play with me, sir. Interviewing people has been a lifelong vocation. State your point, please.'

He cleared his throat as if by routine. 'Well, getting to the issue in question, I regret to inform you of a complaint I've had from the parents of one of the passengers who have, ah, mentioned an incident that occurred in today's early hours.'

'You mean, was said to have occurred?'

'Of course, Colonel, and I'm indebted to you again for that

proper characterisation. It's such an irritation having to deal with matters I rarely visit and sometimes I—'

'What's the nature of the complaint?' Newton cut in sharply. 'Do you have a signed statement that I can peruse and decide whether I will dignify it by making answer?'

'Oh, dear me, please, no, don't be offended, Colonel. No, nothing quite so formal as that. I'm not in the business of promoting grievance. Rather, I see my charter as one where I stand aloof from these little tumults, like a sort of mediator, perhaps even a conciliator. Do you appreciate what I'm attempting to say?'

'Almost to the point of fatuousness.' His visage retaining its fixed urbanity, Newton figured that the master hadn't understood and decided a different tack. 'Sir, I appreciate your predicament and the obvious difficulties in having to handle the personal vagaries of every passenger whom you are required to please, especially on a long voyage. You have a pivotal function managing not only the helm of a ship on the high seas but guiding its soul and all those who sail in her.'

'Thank you, Colonel,' Meeker replied, warming to the change of tone as much as the flattery. 'It's not my experience to find so eloquent a respondent and it allows me to move on. I've been informed that you and Mrs Jenkins were abroad on deck late last night, ah, the early hours?'

'And quite exhilarating it was. I trust you discern no wrong in that?'

'No, nothing at all, Colonel, other than it being, ah,' coughing, 'that both of you, ah, meted out some, what was described to me as, well, if I may say so, "rough treatment" to the young Onions girl and, of course, these things sit ill with me, knowing that you aren't the sort of man who would go in for such practices. I'm sure that Mrs Jenkins isn't similarly disposed. There are marks on this girl's person, which her parents, Sir Lionel and Lady Margaret, point to as corroborative of their concerns. And, of course, their daughter's version to them was detailed so I must – oh dear, I'm constrained as master of this vessel to maintain the peace, order and goodwill that any passage on a British ship requires by the law of the sea. Are you with me, Colonel Newton?'

'I've said so already. Now, what is asserted as the particulars of the rough treatment and why haven't you taken a statement from the girl herself? She's hardly a child.'

'Henrietta Onions was too upset to speak to me. Even displaying the blemishes required some effort, she sobbing the whole time, and if you'll just pardon me for a minute.' He reached behind him to retrieve the sheaf of papers. 'Sometimes I wish I was better organised. Such is the price of command, it seems, but—'

'Marks say nothing about her credibility one way or the other, do they?'

'I agree wholeheartedly, Colonel. Look, I'm on your side, I mean, with you, and it goes without saying that you have a right to know what has been said to me.'

'I'm not sure what you mean about sides. You seem to be looking at various sheets and notes. I assume they are the ones made by you in receiving such information?'

'You are quite correct. I haven't spoken to Mrs Jenkins, by the way. To preserve dignity and a modicum of peace, I wanted to minimise any suggestion that this was a major issue or necessitated a formal enquiry. That doesn't mean I can simply dismiss or fob off the allegations as unfounded, for my position, as you appreciate, means I'm bound to look into such things in a totally unbiased fashion.'

Newton noted the inconsistency without comment. There was both a clumsiness and discomfort emerging every time the other man opened his mouth. 'I don't question your open-mindedness, Captain Meeker, even having regard to Sir Lionel's status.'

'Thank you for appreciating my position, Colonel.'

'So what's the substance of the allegation, for I can see that you're a man not given to imprecision.'

Meeker, savouring the remark, stiffened in importance and become more earnest as he strove to approach the level of oversight that he recognised Newton occupied.

'Then it's asserted that Mrs Jenkins accosted young Henrietta and said she was spying or eavesdropping on the two of you.'

'And?'

'Well, that you intervened and also laid hands on her but, I hasten to add, not applying the sort of pressure that she did.'

'Is there more to this fantasy or is it a tangled portion of some drip-feeding strategy designed to gauge my reactions?'

He huffed shortly but quashed any desire to protest. 'Well,

Colonel, I'm not adopting a pose of policeman or judge, nor writing anything down as we speak.'

'You mentioned not having spoken to Mrs Jenkins. Is it your intention to do so?'

'Ah, yes, well, I would have been happy to have her come up with you but she wasn't in for breakfast and, given the late night's, ah, events, entirely understandable. I'm not so convinced that the necessity exists to do so now. Did you want to make any other statement on the allegations other than what you've already said about it being a "fantasy"?'

'Captain Meeker, it's rather an odd thing. She's apparently alleging rough handling, by inference because Mrs Jenkins was annoyed at being spied upon, whatever that implies. What does it all really tell you, Captain?'

'Your point raises context, opportunity and practicality.'

Newton contained an urge to let the captain alone. 'I was taking a stroll on the deck in the early ocean air, nothing more and nothing less. Miss Onions materialised, there was some conversation and I told her to go back to her cabin. She wasn't thankful for the suggestion and began to argue. Mrs Jenkins appeared and it led to a racial tirade. I held her back and she left in a temper. Is there anything else you require?'

The finality of the question was made clear by Newton's movements. 'Well, just before you leave, no. Ah, oh, one thing. Did you happen to notice the clothing she was wearing?'

'Not really; some sort of loose night dress, I seem to recall.'

'It's just that the shoulder strap was detached and some

tearing of fabric. Did you know whether that happened in the scuffle?'

'That's your terminology and analysis, not mine.'

'Well, you described some interaction and applying restraint.'

'No, I recounted holding her back. As to clothing, I didn't touch or tear any item of apparel.' Newton reached for the doorknob. 'I want to make it clear that nothing was done either by myself or Mrs Jenkins other than was entirely appropriate in the circumstances. The whole episode viewed from my perspective is now closed. You might consider Mrs Jenkins' feelings in all of this. She would prefer not to become embroiled in it, I feel certain, but your ambivalence on that score is noted. If you do wish to speak with her, could you afford the courtesy of advising me beforehand because I would like to be present. Now, if you'll excuse me, Captain.'

Newton gained the smoke room for morning tea, determined to dismiss from his mind what had transpired. That resolve quickly evaporated. The indisposition of knight and lady when his greeting passed unrecognised, while predictable and faintly comical, foretold of difficulty. Much more of a diversion was Henrietta's contrived spectacle on his appearance. She rose from her chair, exhibited an extravagant snort behind a sly demeanour, swished the grand mane of hair back and walked out, followed by her mother. In tarrying, Sir Lionel's anguish was evident, which, judging by the protuberance of the veins in his forehead, portended some dramatic utterance that involved retribution. He thought better of it and left.

The coolness seemed to have migrated to the remaining complement of passengers, who occupied themselves in chatter after perfunctory acknowledgement of his presence. Newton, a veteran of being sent to Coventry, recalled a reflection from a retired master mariner that the confines of a passenger ship were "productive hotbeds of salacious rumour". Facing away from the others, he had obtained coffee from a mobile station and was poised to add milk when he felt a tap from behind. He turned to greet the dark circles framing his neighbour's eyes.

'I'd concluded that you had taken to your bed for an extended stay given your absence at breakfast this morning.' Newton hailed her with a residue of equable humour. 'You weren't the only no-show by the way.'

She returned his greeting with a friendly request for the same order that he had just fulfilled for himself. He passed her his untouched cup and repeated the process before sitting on a comfortable settee beside her. 'You've either had a pretty rough night or been so affronted by my introductory chapter that you're about to tell me to desist from further epistles on account of it having an adverse effect on your wellbeing.'

'Very amusing, but none of the above, actually. It's Charlotte. Unfortunately, she's been ill, and I've only now settled her down.'

'Is she going to be alright?' his tone evincing genuine concern.

'I think so. She was up with a splitting headache and sore throat when I returned after we separated. I procured some grated apple and her stomach promptly refused to accommodate anything. The dear thing has only now found sleep after having some peppermint-elderflower compound.'

'You have taken to serious herbal remedies?'

'Why are you so startled? I'm Asiatic. We've a cure for almost all ailments and we don't resort to instant artificial, short-term amelioration. Did you know that in our culture we regard illness positively? It's a natural effort on the part of the body to both rid itself of nasty incursions and, at the same time, immune our systems against serious predators.'

Newton regarded her with a mixture of perplexity and admiration while she remained impassive. 'Well,' he finally replied, 'whatever you say. Terribly sorry to hear of her distress. You must be hungry. Shall I ask the steward to make up something?'

'I chewed on some nuts, and lunch isn't that far away, thank you. You've been up and about, looking fresh as with the day, I see.'

He lowered his voice and leaned closer to her. 'Even more than that, I've not long come from a meeting with our illustrious master.'

'Sounds somewhat fateful, since I doubt he's your type for social calls. Let me guess. That little tart of an Onion sting has something to do with it.'

'A pretty informed conjecture, Mrs Jenkins.'

'Nothing too informed about it. I envisaged trouble

from the moment our paths crossed. Her disdain for me as a complete stranger was something experience learns to accommodate. A curious pull towards you was the other aspect.'

'You don't miss much, it seems,' he said with the makings of a querying frown.

'Never mind that. Tell us what his lordship upstairs had to say.'

As Newton outlined the substance of the conversation, she would incline her head from time to time and roll her eyes. 'I finished up by telling him that he shouldn't speak to you without informing me. A presumptuous thing, I suppose.'

'Maybe, but thanks anyway. No bodyguard required, Colonel. I'm quite capable of handling these matters myself.'

'As you wish.'

'More your good self is what troubles me. In thinking you have his measure and that he's not going to cavil with a colonel from Military Intelligence, you might be the presumptuous one.'

The raised eyebrows evened when she tapped the palm of his hand. 'Come on. You must remember what Dickens wrote about lawyers being shy of meddling with the law on their own account.'

He chuckled knowingly. 'I'm not qualified, not even halfway there.'

'Ah, I've just learnt something else about you, have I? Let's pass on. I shall simply assert that my analogy is apt.

You should never treat these sorts of things as beneath your contempt. They can sometimes come back to bite in uncomfortable regions. I've nothing to lose speaking with a ship's captain who might fancy himself beyond his station. However, on a ship, he's king, makes log entries to suit his ends, if so minded, and offers opinions to others. You need to avoid being cavalier is what I'm saying.'

Newton finished his cup, and she had poured and milked another before their eyes met again. She experienced an unusual phenomenon, a moment of inner satisfaction at being around someone to whom she had taken a real liking and who could be trusted without the slightest demur.

'Dear me, Mrs Jenkins, I would almost be prepared to swear that you speak from experience. When yours is the confessional and mine to receive, you can be certain of my utmost attention to that memoir.'

'Then you're bound to be disappointed, I fear. But you have some distance to go before I have to marshal my thoughts. Can we get back to Miss Onions?'

'Certainly. No doubt you'd like to know precisely what I told Meeker?'

'I don't care for any such thing. Rather, if I've assessed you correctly, it's certain that you didn't tell him of the threat she made.' Her brows tightened as she watched Newton before answering her own question. 'My assumption was correct. That may well have been your biggest mistake. It's not one that I will repeat if Meeker quizzes me.'

With the coffee pot now almost exhausted, the

smokeroom had also emptied. He assented to her suggestion that they utilise the next hour leading to lunch by continuing with his story. She excused herself, indicating that the check on Charlotte shouldn't see much time being occupied, but he urged her to do whatever was necessary.

Newton noticed some Blue Star writing paper, a pen and ink at a nearby desk. He made some detailed notes of the recent conversation with Meeker and had just dated and signed a sheet when Sir Lionel and his wife surprised him by their approach. Both wore confrontational expressions and it was she who spoke first.

'Colonel Newton, what needs to be said is something I never thought that we, as a certain class of English gentlefolk, would ever utter to a senior officer of His Majesty's service, so attend to me and list—'

'Before you do,' he interposed, taking the initiative, 'may I ask if you've recently conversed with Captain Meeker?'

'Yes, we have, and what of it?' returned Sir Lionel with venom.

'And you're not satisfied with the account?'

'Satisfied!' shrieked Mrs Onions. 'Horrified would be what I'd call it,' she expostulated, shaking as she spoke. Her husband, mightily put out, steered Lady Margaret roughly to an upholstered chair.

'Control yourself and be quiet, woman! I will handle this. You need to retain the calm that befits someone occupying your position.'

Turning to the object of his displeasure, he looked down

from a height approximating Newton's, only standing close enough as to prevent him from ascending to it. He began in the magisterial manner he customarily used when about to dress down and dismiss an employee.

'This won't take long, sir. Your behaviour with our daughter on deck in the early hours of this morning was not that of an accomplished officer, let alone someone who aspires to be a gentleman. Rather it was more like that of a brash private.'

Newton's attempts to speak were futile as Sir Lionel's voice reached a higher pitch in ordering him to listen. Taking in a breath that reeked of something stronger than English Breakfast tea, he complied with a calculated movement of his jaw, further infuriating the man addressing him.

'You think it's amusing? You want fun? I ought to punch you on the nose right now for your impertinence except that *I*, at least, *am* a gentleman. However, you may be laughing on the other side of your face after we reach England.'

'I wasn't smiling at you, Sir Lionel. Rather, it's my inability to fathom what you are on about. Spell it out and be off, or else stand aside and give me some liberty of movement.'

'I won't tolerate my daughter being touched in any fashion by you or your Asian friend. Retain your distance for the duration of this leg of the voyage and don't even look sideways at her, if you know what's good for you.'

No one in that room had perceived Mrs Jenkins' watchful attendance at the door, hands on hips. She could remain invisible no longer.

'Enough! Just the *Asian friend* here taking in this tommy rot. I'll tell you something now that you won't want to hear and that Colonel Newton has forborne from embarrassing you with. I witnessed Henrietta Onions' outrages last night. I heard all that she said. She made a clumsy attempt to seduce Colonel Newton, brazenly telling him that they might go back to his cabin where she would entertain him and—'

'I refuse to listen to this monstrous slander calculated to sully our precious child.' Lady Margaret was stayed from further utterances by the none-too-gentle application of Sir Lionel's right hand on her mouth.

'Keep quiet, woman, and let her heap ridicule on herself.'

'I also heard her say that she was prepared to make a highly improper accusation against Colonel Newton, tearing her slip in the process. And I wasn't the only witness, by the way.'

'Witness, rubbish, and all interesting, but completely at odds with what Colonel Newton has told the captain of this ship,' Sir Lionel retorted.

His wife spluttered something unintelligible and he overrode her. 'I wondered what you two have been talking about, pouring each other's refreshments and all sorts of intimate mutterings. Now it seems that you've both been concocting a plot designed to get him off the hook,' said an increasingly erratic Sir Lionel, wagging a forefinger at each of them alternately and raising his voice to a crescendo.

'Gentlemen and ladies, please.' The captain had entered, accompanied by his chief officer. 'This is no place for argument. I won't have it on my ship. Please settle down, shake hands and leave any adjudication of right and wrong to me.'

Rather than placating her, the statement reignited Lady Margaret's wrath. 'I won't listen to this pair of foul—'

Sir Lionel again intervened. 'These two are now saying our daughter's a liar and accused her of immorality, suggesting she harboured a prurient interest in a man nearly as ancient as me and, when rebuffed, says she cried rape or something. It's the oldest double take in the book. They've got their heads together, just as I told you they would, and think we'll simply cower in some corner. They don't know the Onions pedigree.'

'Or—'

'Stay your tongue, will you, Margaret. And it needs to be asked why nothing like this had been alleged before by the colonel to you, Captain,' he said, confronting the ship's master and then turning to Newton, who was lounging back in his chair at the turn of events. 'What have you got to say for yourself, Colonel?'

The subject of the question was unmoved.

'I would rather that we all calm down and—'

Meeker's attempt at governing the situation was blunted by Sir Lionel pushing past him and standing over Newton again, repeating his previous call to him in even more forthright terms. 'Explain yourself, sir, or be damned when the authorities hear of it.'

He stood up imperiously, such that Sir Lionel was forced to give way. Mrs Jenkins darted in beside him and they faced their accusers with a unity of composure. Meeker was rudderless and his mate equally flummoxed. The atmosphere was diffused when a sudden strong wind gust buffeted the ship.

Meeker seized the advantage that nature had provided. 'Please, Sir Lionel, you and Lady Margaret, if you will, depart in the company of my chief officer. He shall see you back to your cabin.' This time there was no dissent. 'Shut the door, Mister.'

'Captain, as you said earlier, this is neither the time nor the place for any discussion about last night's regrettable incident.'

'Are you speaking for yourself, Colonel Newton?'

'The colonel speaks for himself and I'm quite capable of speaking for myself,' replied Mrs Jenkins emphatically. She related the events of the evening in thorough detail using first person conversations that Newton found incredibly accurate. 'There's more if you like.'

'And you don't wish to add to Mrs Jenkins' comments, Colonel?' Meeker added discomposedly.

'Nothing, save to agree with every word.'

Mrs Jenkins wasn't finished. 'A man of your experience can see the awkward position that we both faced. Henrietta Onions' self-evidently vindictive behaviour has led me to speak more frankly than I would otherwise have chosen. That's all I intend saying about the matter other than to commend Colonel Newton's restraint in not wishing to bring disgrace upon that girl or her family.'

Meeker adopted a reverential tone when he replied. 'I'm satisfied with that and understand perfectly the reason why you chose not to bring it up, Colonel. We perceive that these are delicate issues yet, of course, one also must appreciate the position of the parents. They will always support their daughter. Oh, and, Colonel, you can report to your superiors that, against the odds, we have made up some time with the other engine on line,' he said, desperate to move from the subject, taking it that Newton would praise his efforts elsewhere and additionally hoping to regain some lost dignity.

'Good for you, Captain,' came Newton's disappointingly flippant reply.

'Well then, on present indications we expect to dock at Port Elizabeth in about a week. I anticipate that some strain has been created by recent events. Might I suggest that, at least until we arrive, dining arrangements might proceed on a basis where we ensure either an earlier or later sitting for you and Charlotte, Mrs Jenkins.'

'My daughter is unwell and I don't anticipate that she will be taking solid food for a day or so. I've already spoken to the steward.'

'Dear me, I'm sorry to hear that, madam. Is there something we can do?'

'No. You have your own responsibilities, Captain, and I mine.'

'I'll be dining with Mrs Jenkins, Captain.'

Meeker coughed awkwardly, 'Of course, Colonel. It goes without saying—'

'I'm glad that it's clear with you and settled.' The master tipped his cap and withdrew, much as an apprentice being sent back to work.

Newton was at the liquor cabinet as the door closed and caught her glance. She acquiesced and a gin and tonic was mixed. 'I'd be ready for several of those but for Charlotte's indisposition.'

'Well, though tested by all this, I'd best stick to ginger soda.' He remarked. Sitting opposite her across a card table, they clicked glasses. An unduly studied analysis of her drink prompted his next observation.

'I couldn't avoid hearing mention of the "witness", Mrs Jenkins, and wondered if I wasn't the only one?'

'That thought crossed my mind, Colonel. Reminiscent of that well-known Biblical adjuration, "Be sure your sin will find you out".'

'How much longer are you going to keep me in suspense?' he asked.

'I've always admired the Scots, rough and tumble types of the likes of Seaman McColl. Saw everything. Even jotted it down and dispatched an envelope under the captain's door. He was frank enough to concede that his own brushes with the law taught him much. Hasn't been able to follow it up with Meeker but was good enough to seek me out.'

Newton's head movement was considered. 'That's priceless, and pretty much game over for this little fakement. Now to the rest of the day. The morning has been thrown out. Can we meet this afternoon, taking it as given that she remains stable?'

'It's safe to predict that Charlotte's main problems are past her, as with ours. You know, Colonel,' she said, rolling the glass in her hand, 'I'm not one for disappointing the other guests who might otherwise languish through not having anything to talk about if they don't see us together.'

'You seem to have a witticism for a multiplicity of situations.'

She toyed at the remnants before replying, standing as she did so. 'I'll tap on your door or, better still, a note for when next we meet, if not at lunch. Notes are the in thing, aren't they?'

Chapter 4 – *Henrietta's withdrawal*

As with the mood, sunlight remained a capricious commodity since the contretemps. The weather continued to be indecisive throughout the morning, the sea choppy and swell rising. Fears of a return to the bothersome conditions of recent memory were being voiced among the passengers but, by the noon watch, relative calm prevailed.

The unsettling event involving Henrietta Onions, along with its aftermath, exercised Newton's decision to avoid public dining and he ordered a plain luncheon repast of sandwiches in his cabin. Such isolation went against his instincts. On two occasions, mindful of Meeker's request, he had loitered outside, long enough to see the Onions trio being entertained at the captain's table despite an interval of forty minutes between viewings.

He had attempted discretion when making a first intrepid pass across the entry door's porthole but suspected the young woman had spotted him during a second such episode of surveillance, fleeting as it was. That served as sufficient impetus to retire indoors, although true it was that Mrs Jenkins' continued absence lent additional force to the move. His tray arrived accompanied by a cream-coloured envelope addressed to him. Inside was an invitation, inked in expressive flair, appointing three o'clock as the time and the viewing deck as the place for 'continued recitation of your poignant account'.

Bearing his *Two Years before the Mast* that wore the appearance of being through scores of hands before it had found his, Newton occupied a sheltered corner of the boat deck nearest to the stern on the starboard side. There was a briny authenticity driven by its proximity to the ocean's surface as the ship rolled gently and occasional sprays flicked past, with sailors paying out and greasing a chain of interminable length while singing a lusty shanty.

Occasional scudding showers had thwarted the open-air position and also snuffed out the patience of the deck golfers. Newton remained unable to pass the sixth page of the novel, but, before he could dampen his finger in order to move to the next, he tipped the book over and rested his chin on upturned thumbs. Struggle as he might, an impetus to read absented itself. His mind was yet again drifting ahead disconsolately in contemplation of the rendezvous that loomed after the docking at Port Elizabeth.

The promise he had made would be kept. Nature, breeding and long association had inculcated him to army life. Newton was accustomed to undertaking tasks that might cause lesser men to refuse, buckle against or waiver. In this particular case, he expected that the encounter after so many years would be exacting and the application of a significant degree of self-discipline necessary.

What could he say to her? Might the composure that time and her parlous situation had brought him evaporate when he heard her voice or would those features he recalled sometimes too clearly in moronic visions that never quite abandoned him lead to concessions? Recoiling at the last thought, he experienced an involuntary spasm.

'My, dreaming again. Let me guess: at its wickedest, a bevy of dusky African maidens plying your receptive mouth with grapes or a rather mundane form of automatism causing that waggle of your head matched by the jittering of your feet?'

Unable to hide, an ineffectual clearing of his throat made matters worse. Mrs Jenkins' pleasing form peeped from a knee-length, bright red towelling cape loosely draped around her shoulders. She was wearing a white halter-neck top and high waist shorts. Soft ivory tennis shoes contained elegant feet and pleasing ankles. Upon removing her wrap, she appeared kitted to match him on the walking track that circumnavigated the ship and was paced at one-tenth of a mile per circuit. Suggesting such a turn, his indecision produced mock irritation.

'Well, are you going to acquiesce, say anything complimentary or remain open-mouthed? If the latter, I might need to do some doctoring on you again.'

His response began with an easy laughter she found almost unbecoming in one so staid. He reined it in. 'As usual, Mrs Jenkins, you defy every prediction. There was a time, not all that long ago either, when I would have adroitly avoided someone of your uninhibited disposition.'

'I wouldn't have permitted you to do that,' she hit back without a blink. 'No more avoidance, for now you see me as a patriot decked out in red, white and here's some blue,' pointing to the band on her hat, 'and don't pretend to be miffed. I can read you like a novel. Speaking of which,' she lifted up the object in question and noted the page, '*you* haven't been doing much of that.'

'I was collecting my thoughts in preparation for your attendance.'

'So this is the erotic section of the account, judging by your body language.'

He tensed his jaw before remarking. 'And how's Charlotte?'

'Oh, much better, thanks. She's a Jenkins.' Her expressive eyes narrowed when enquiring, 'Has anything further happened on the Onions front since I've been in lockdown?'

'Well, nothing that would warrant reporting, except to relate the obvious glares as redolent of not being confident that I would win bachelor of the forthcoming ship's ball. They dined interminably with Meeker and I deemed it prudent to take refreshments in my quarters.'

'I expected nothing less of such a lot. That unholy English caste system can sometimes be worse than the Indian one.'

'You've had some experience of it?' he pursued, exhibiting deep curiosity.

'For heaven's sake, Colonel, do you see me as so well-travelled?'

'Sometimes, Mrs Jenkins, I'm not sure how I see things when it comes to you. You're a puzzle.'

'I'm certain you're not particularly interested in my lineage, but you tend to ruminate far beyond any practical necessity to do so.'

It was a response that left him flummoxed before the inflection in her jibe wrought another concession from him.

'For a sage so right on many things, it's surprising how wrong you can be on some.'

'My dear Colonel, let's declare a "matching-of-wits" truce. Rather than any saunter, can we journey to your tale or have you misplaced another bookmark?'

He signalled towards the sea and indicated that it had found a watery grave. 'I think I was about to touch upon a fateful homecoming for term holidays after that business with the bully stuff obtruded itself.'

'I believe you were, as I recall.'

'Thank you for confirming it. Sometimes continuity is not my strongest suit and recollections can be fallible.

'Not being met when he stepped off the train necessitated a twenty-minute walk before Magnus arrived at the front door. They were waiting for him as he shuffled past the manservant. His father, along with a young woman employee he knew as Miss Mason, regarded him severely, as if he were an overlooked legatee suddenly turning up to claim a rightful inheritance in the lands and estate of a recently-departed uncle.

'Magnus soon realised that her appearance in the parlour beside his father was unconnected to the scope of her employment. She had originally been engaged as a junior typist, recently out of school, whilst his mother was at home. After her removal from the house, Stephanie Mason was promoted to personal secretary.

'Without ceremony or even as much as an explanation, his father presented Miss Mason as the second Mrs Sansim. She wouldn't have been even his third choice of stepmother had he been asked. Magnus had never got on with her from the occasions she would surreptitiously poke her tongue at him when he was quite young to, as time advanced, her talking down to him or telling tales calculated to inflame his father's wrath. Magnus had sensed something odd about her influence within the household that seemed to increase with each passing year. She never disguised her resentment at the boy's appearance on vacation and welcomed the approach of the new term heralding his departure.

'On one occasion after his mother had gone, he overheard a conversation in which she told Mr Sansim that he had been obnoxious to her, was disdainful of his father and was so sick of being around "this ugly house" that he wanted to return early from his holiday. That same evening, when confronted by Sansim Senior, he denied any such thing even being in contemplation. Seeing such a denial as false, this insubordination so affronted the head of the house that he threatened to put him on the train the following day unless he apologised. He duly complied.'

Mrs Jenkins frowned and disposed her head to demonstrate a picture of genuine sympathy. 'The poor, sad fellow. I had nothing but love from my father, kind and wise, an exceptional man. It's unthinkable.'

'Magnus had always wondered why Miss Mason boarded at his father's home when he was younger, given she only lived a few miles away. Now just that little bit older, he drew his own inferences. As I mentioned previously, no longer physically stunted, he had also matured considerably. Being well into adolescence, Magnus recalled the unusual degree of intimacy between his father and Mason that seemed to proceed from the moment she arrived as a fifteen-year-old. With his maturing, this took on another meaning.'

The listener asked, 'Do you think that Magnus suspected something might have been going on right from the beginning?'

'I don't know about that, but my own memory begins from about four or so and he was five when she turned up. Children have a unique perspective. They don't understand what *it* is, but they may perceive a wrong, I think, more quickly than an adult,' he said pensively.

'That sounds rather clever. And you obviously believe it?'

'My belief is irrelevant to the tale, Mrs Jenkins,' he replied, returning to inscrutability in demeanour, a characteristic that tested her patience.

'Oh, go on then,' she urged.

'Mistress of the manor at twenty-three, his father gave her that and a few more years' start, but in every other respect she assumed an unrestrained supremacy in the household.'

'It gets worse. I can just imagine its abject effect.' He swore that her eyes were moist when she spoke again. 'What a terrible position for a young boy, with no balance from a caring mother's tenderness either. But, sorry, I forgot to ask this earlier, when did you meet him?'

'Oh, good heavens, my memory fails me again. I should've mentioned this sooner for it was not too long after he'd met Esrelle. So, I'd say he might have been eight or nine. Magnus had a phenomenal memory, probably one of the most photographic I've ever encountered.'

She found the answer odd as to timing but chose to overlook it. 'Obviously more so than your intelligence officer's recall for detail. Come on, don't take umbrage, I'm not trying to take a rise out of you.'

'Well, others might have judged us as nearly on a par but—'

'Never mind. It was a silly question. Now, this is so compelling. As much as I want to hold back the diminishing light, I see that sun is ornamenting those black clouds like a string of pearls. I'll need to attend upon Charlotte soon, but I really don't want to hinder your interesting account.'

'May I just finish this section and you'll have time to get back to her before much longer?'

'Go on, please.'

'Having never forgiven his mother for leaving so suddenly and refraining from either saying goodbye or making any effort to contact him, he began to rethink the entire situation. He became cognisant, shall I say, of a possible version of the event other than in the context of his father's abridged account of being deserted by "that woman who doesn't deserve the title of mother". He did not dare ask the unforgiving gentleman where in London she might be lodging. With his own resources so limited, local enquiries proved pointless.'

'I have a question, and perhaps it's a touch premature, but did he tell you this when you were at school together?'

'Yes, it *is* a little premature,' said Newton with a hint of reproof. 'Shall I go on or would you prefer we adjourn until tomorrow afternoon?'

'Goodness me, don't get precious, Colonel. Finish what you were saying.'

'Well, there were bits and pieces all along the way from the moment I met Magnus. I mean, we were just eleven years old when the home dysfunction unravelled, and one can't be precise about sequences but I believe we talked a lot about our respective lives from the first moment of our meeting, and we became closer as time passed. It was more of an aggregation of information from both sides.'

'Do you mean to sound so affected? I'll answer my own question. I doubt that you really do, but, rather, it's an unfortunate habit acquired through ineffable connection to your sphere of intrigues and plots.'

'Somewhere in there I heard grudging praise. If I may continue just a little further. Magnus probably came to believe that his mother must have died. She wouldn't have found life easy after the divorce – well, that's assuming there was one. Given that there were some legal entanglements, one would expect that she might have been given a sum of money as a settlement. Looking back on it, my friend remarked that he didn't see any alteration in his father's financial situation immediately after Mrs Sansim the first decamped.

'However, a change came not long after wedded bliss had been pronounced. Magnus noticed that Mrs Sansim plus one was, as the Americans say, "high maintenance". And he also observed that his father became morose, depressed and withdrawn as time passed. Sadly, for Magnus – for father and son, I suppose – the relationship between them remained fractured and had led to Esrelle and he drawing support from each other.'

'Yes, back to her. What about *this* girl's background? Was the absence of parental love something that they had in common?'

'I think that may have been so initially. What I mean is that Esrelle might have perceived that to be the case or, being less charitable perhaps, traded upon it to develop that commonality between her and Magnus.'

'Calculating, you're suggesting?'

'Be patient, Mrs Jenkins. But I don't think her home life was so bad in actual fact. He said that she and her parents often quarrelled as she got older. Esrelle stayed with her grandmother on a few occasions, then left home abruptly when she was in her mid-teens. I'm jumping ahead here but he was later to establish that her leaving was unconnected to any discord making it impossible for her to stay there.

'So she has suddenly gone. After hearing gossip, Magnus was prompted to make some enquiries. He was informed by several students that she had been seen in the company of a tutor from Esrelle's school, a married man in his thirties. One of his friends, actually we both knew him as Roper, who was at the same school, told him that the tutor – I forget that fellow's name now, but it doesn't matter – resigned his post and severed his ties with the area around the same time as Esrelle left home. It wasn't a long bow to draw.'

He exhaled loudly and raised his eyebrows. She took his cue.

'That's not a bad spot for a break in your – or, rather, the story of Magnus. I'm sure you've been told this before, but you've such a penchant for detail and precision, retaining all that information for, what, at least three decades. I'm not sure that when my turn arises I'll be able to replicate your efforts.' She offered her hand and the smile on her face was accentuated by a squeeze from her fingers.

'You'll manage, Mrs Jenkins. The further I've gone, the memories, details, ins and outs, call them what you like, they just keep on drifting back. Mind you,' he said with the makings of a twinkle, 'I'm accepting nothing short of being furnished with a full and unabridged narrative from your lips.'

'My dear Colonel, how could you possibly entertain doubt about our reciprocal bargain?' Her hand was on her heart as she leaned towards him. 'These lips are my bond. See you at two on the morrow, or maybe even dinner?' She bowed, kissed her own hand ostentatiously and left him.

Newton remained where he was. The ship's lights were gaining prominence. He stretched and ascended the stairs to the promenade deck where he loosened up. He soon found a lively pace, bidding 'good evening' to the Cahills, who were strolling along hand-in-hand in the opposite direction. They returned his greeting with nods that seemed no more and no less than being polite to someone to whom they hadn't conversed since their first meeting. By the time he completed another circuit, they were about to quit when Mrs Cahill swung around and spoke. 'Are we going to have the pleasure of your company at dinner, Colonel? We also skipped drinks.'

Newton was momentarily caught off guard by the question and paused in his stride to look back at them. 'Ah, yes, I'm going to take a seat around eight. I may see you there.'

'Indeed, it will be our pleasure. Have a lovely walk. It's cool and fresh now after the rain. Decent atmosphere out here.'

'Yes, very.' She had remained in the same position and he walked back towards her. 'Was there anything else?'

'Not now, dear. I'm sure the colonel would prefer

to maintain his momentum.' It was her husband who anticipated what was on her mind.

'That's alright, Mr Cahill. I'm anxious to hear what your wife might have to say.'

'I just wanted you to know, Colonel, that my husband and, well, I think I can safely speak for the other passengers, never believed the rumours that wilful girl circulated for one minute. Given she's owned up and exonerated you from any wrongdoing, we would hope that's the last we'll hear of it.'

'You can't blame her parents, old fellow,' her husband added. 'You'd support your child in that event wouldn't you?'

Newton opened his mouth as if to speak but waited. 'I suppose so, although, never having been in a similar position, reactions might differ from person to person. I'm relieved to have learned of my having been "exonerated", as you put it; pleased also that the ship's company never doubted my veracity and, overall, humbled by the experience. Just one thing, may I? When did you learn that the complaint had been withdrawn?'

'We'd tried to avoid the gossip about the business with your, ah, Mrs Jenkins and Henrietta originally, not wishing to get involved, of course, and then couldn't help over-hearing snippets,' said Mrs Cahill plaintively, effecting to appear indifferent, 'when the captain was, you know, having lunch with them.'

'And I just came out with it,' offered her husband, 'and asked him, that's Sir Lionel, what was going on. He said the whole thing had been a mistake, a misunderstanding, and their daughter had suffered a lot of trauma when she was young; something about seeing a school friend hanging from a rafter after suiciding and this terrible experience made her an attention-seeker and prone to exaggerate as she got older. He was frank with me. Anyway, no doubt you have been, or will be, acquainted with the details in more thorough terms.'

Newton remained imperturbable. 'Well, nice to see you both again. I'll keep going and clock up a couple of miles to secure my appetite.'

Having covered the estimated distance by hard slogging it over the last two furlongs, he had worked up something of a sweat, if not hunger. What he had heard from the Cahills, given what he regarded as the deplorable ineptitude in which the whole episode had been handled, came as no surprise. The delay in communicating its apparent resolution to him on the part of the ship's master was an entirely different matter. And he was certain that if Mrs Jenkins had become aware of anything she would have told him.

There was adequate time to get ready and even a cocktail, if he so wished. The steward had laid out a dinner jacket and he casually glanced at the menu. A favourite fish, mackerel, caught his eye. The entrée consisted of prawns with tartare sauce wrapped in lettuce leaves and Swiss cheese. Freshly baked rolls were a familiar side to every meal. He ignored the dessert, finding syrupy sweets anathema. Replacing the menu, he noticed a small envelope containing an invitation to dine at the captain's table. It was the reading of that note that clinched his decision.

Captain Meeker's expectation of contrite, if not fawning, approbation on greeting Newton outside his door was quelled by the colonel's unbending question.

'What's the meaning of this?' he demanded, brandishing the paper. Meeker offered Newton a seat inside in a bid to pacify the questioner. 'I'll remain here, sir, as I have a dinner engagement with Mrs Jenkins and must change soon,' he replied pointedly.

'As you wish, but I'd hoped we might put to rest that disagreeable business.'

'If you've something worth listening to, say it now or not at all.'

'Your assertiveness wounds me, Colonel. I've supported your version of events throughout and not once have I detected gratitude for my pains and hard—'

'Let me be clear. I don't appreciate receiving information concerning the outcome of a false allegation of impropriety not merely second-hand but significantly out of date.'

'To whom have you been speaking, Colonel, for I can assure—'

Newton cut across the hand gestures, not least because of the aversion he felt at seeing any man holding command whose wrist bore a gold bracelet and who decorated three of his fingers with flashy, consecutive rings. 'Have the allegations been withdrawn?'

'They have.'

'What time did that happen?'

'Well, at luncheon I had a pleasant—'

'Just facts rather than inanities, thank you.'

'I was saying before you interrupted me that there was an apology delivered today by both Miss Onions and her parents.'

'Time?'

'I won't be badgered on my ship, Colonel. Formalities take time and mean that I can now provide a statement to that effect.' Meeker retrieved a typed sheet of paper signed by Henrietta and Sir Lionel Onions and passed it to him.

After studying it, Newton felt somewhat deflated by his impulsivity, yet was far from wholly mollified. 'Thank you. By the way, I see no reference has been made to Mrs Jenkins. She stands accused as well.'

'I considered that. But, given the delicacy of the matter, I felt she would be satisfied with the lengths to which the Onions family had gone to put everything to rest as far as you were concerned.'

'So you haven't spoken to her?'

'No. I'm leaving that to you, sir, appreciating the shared interests you have in the outcome and what you've said previously to me. Of course, she can speak to me any time, if she so desires. My first priority is to see the ship resume its happy equanimity. We have a break coming up in Port Elizabeth that will be good for everyone and with many sea days to go after. I'm sure you follow me, well-rounded man that you are, Colonel, much more in touch with worldly matters than a mere ship's captain of a modest passenger/cargo steamer.'

He began to take his leave of Meeker, who insisted on a handshake. For all that he wanted to ignore the gesture, Newton relented for as brief a time as it took to engage the hand, avoid looking at its excessive ornaments and deprecate its limp oiliness.

Before changing, he tapped on her door to be greeted by a healthier Charlotte followed by her mother, who was wearing slippers and a dressing gown. Her makeup had been applied, and she asked if there was anything the matter.

He produced the letter and her lips parted to reveal a winning freshness.

'So, we're off the hook, Colonel?'

'I was thinking consideration might be given to the absence of any mention of *you*.'

'Why? I'm used to such slights, goes with the territory. Let's be grateful that the matter is closed and you rise totally vindicated.'

'But what about Nancyng Jenkins? There's been a deal of gossip, and the whole thing is more unsatisfactory from your perspective than mine as it happens.'

'Colonel Newton,' she said, advancing so as to have him inch backwards into the companionway, 'move on. I'm not long out of my bath, a pleasant place to be and one you might next consider, sweaty man. What have you been doing, chin-ups or Meeker firing *you* up? Be there at eight.'

'Unruly in my direction and elsewise the diplomat, Mrs Jenkins; what can I say?'

'I will listen to you over our seafood cordon bleu, but what you can do to assist the process is permit me to get dressed and yourself to follow suit. See you anon,' the last words coming as she withdrew to make the cabin's confines her domain.

It became the most congenial night of the voyage. Nancyng even managed to extract a shambolic dance from Newton before she went on to take turns with several officers and Captain Meeker resplendent in full blue uniform. She was the essence of sociability as the evening advanced, the spark at every table, including the one occupied by the Onions family, drawing admiring glances from each person present who couldn't help noting her svelte, effortless class and goodwill. Newton was awestruck at the *joie de vivre* emanating from this remarkable woman.

A veritable chorus of those same admirers urged Newton to accede and join in the spirit as she held out arms of entreaty towards him after her last partner, the captain, resumed his seat in such a state of exhaustion that he had to be fanned by one of the stewards. It would be a bold refusal in the face of universal insistence. More pertinently, what he perceived as Meeker's emerging recovery was decisive in his accepting her challenge.

Once they began serious movement, it became evident that the retiring colonel was far from taking baby perambulations at her leading and behest. Soon his princely steps told not only on Nancyng's repertoire but also her indefatigability. As the end of the rhumba heralded an interval for the band, she fell into his arms and, pursing her lips, planted an artistic kiss on his. They sat down to enthusiastic and appreciative applause from the onlookers. An unsolicited bottle of champagne arrived, was uncorked and poured before Newton could emit a word of protest.

It didn't cease there. The passengers and officers, with the captain taking the lead, gathered around them and sang, *For they are jolly good fellows and so say all of us!* It was repeated three times before the ensemble picked up their instruments and resumed with a gentle waltz. They followed the dancers in silence for a time, their next move foretold when Nancyng rested her hand on his. Newton acquiesced to her plea of one more turn provided it be accomplished without ostentation. She was led to the centre of the floor and promptly forgot what her feet were doing when nestling against his shoulder.

Chapter 5 – *Magnus in Uniform*

'Before it escapes me, just wanted to say that the more the conflict between Magnus and his stepmother continued, the less his father was inclined to have him remain at home so that, when son announced that he wanted to return to school early, his request was acted upon with unseemly haste.'

Newton's opening to their discussion the following day preceded only by a cursory nod was soon regretted.

'So last night didn't happen,' Nancyng responded frostily. He rushed an apology when she sat beside him at their preferred location above the promenade deck. 'You can be such a wooden character, Colonel. How many times need I remind you?'

'A few more, perhaps. Last night some of us may have had a little too much champagne for their own good and—'

'Us, my posterior. I'm reaping the sower's harvest while you consented to the one you couldn't refuse amidst being doped up on lime squashes. Oh, why do I make dissent? It would be hard even being an ordinary female around you, damnably so for one with spunk.'

The colourful riposte left Newton speechless. Frowning, he extended the silence before making a grudging concession to tactlessness, a few observations about feckless attitudes to life, his disdain for partying and frivolity almost as a soliloquy to the sea, which was equally unimpressed.

A delicate finger directed a curl of hair over compact ears, persisting as the consistent flow of air, motion and breeze defied repeated attempts to keep it there. When his eyes sought a comment from her, she offered a pithy aside, obfuscating a perception that all she thought unlikeable about the man was in truth an attribute. He was not quite old enough to be her father, yet, in so many respects, behaved as if he occupied that position already.

Nancyng was drawn to older men and, as she continued her assessment, discovered an inability to take in what Newton was saying. Her mind migrated to a time and place of early womanhood, and in another blink, she had been widowed. What her late spouse, the Welshman Xavier Jenkins might have given Newton in years, he could never match in latent composure. It was a dewy-eyed recollection that failed to escape the subject of her distractions when she spoke again, and that shook her even more.

'Um, you were saying, Colonel? Oh, my godfather, I'm done with these antiquarian English formalities. What can

I call you? And don't dare reply "Reginald", for that, with deepest apologies to your parents, reads more like a sentence.'

'Then,' his laugh disarming her, 'you might be happy to learn that that less than insular club has inducted a new member of which, incidentally, I was the first. How about, "Grayg"?' He spelled it out. 'It's the nickname Magnus invented.'

'He seems interesting, telling me more about yourself than you seem disposed to, for I warrant that you were old-fashioned from birth. I'd say, perhaps, even forty in a bonnet. Gray without the "g" for me.'

Newton's facial expression remained gentle. 'And what shall I call you, "Nancyng" or something shorter?'

'That'll do. And as you've either developed a case of buyer remorse or are merely keen to avoid any difficult issues, I'll thank you to return to our worthily named, Magnus.'

He managed a repentant nod before recovering with, 'While I might refrain from specific comment, you should not take it to mean one thing or another about last night.'

'You've already mentioned him going back to boarding school rather earlier than was due,' she said, not without a sigh of exasperation.

'He offered a plausible reason for doing so even though it was something he could have undertaken at home. Magnus announced that he wanted to swot up for an examination after he had, off his own back, applied for a scholarship to enter Sandhurst Military College. When he told me that this was his ambition in life, I laughed at him, suggesting that it was an excuse to avoid spending time at home. Somewhat put out at first, eventually he agreed that it was the primary reason.

'Once his stepmother seized proprietorial control over receipts and expenditure, I think Magnus resented being accountable to a stranger's purse strings. When the headmaster, who had become quite fond of him after that bullying business, saw the potential in the chap, he floated a service career citing Sandhurst as a possibility, dangling the offer of scholarships to pupils who might be suitable candidates. Magnus jumped at the suggestion. The intake was for 1922. When he told his father, more than a flicker of interest was ignited.

'"A military career could finally be the making of you with the qualification that you are your mother's child,"' he grumbled, '"but at least a bursary might relieve your father of the crippling fees at that infernal school."'

'That was all the ever-conniving Mrs Sansim needed to prompt some fervent questioning as to whether he had enough time for study and if he would be prepared for the entrance examination, "Might it be likely to occur soon?" After he replied, "Within a month of Monday week is the exam and I'll find out after that if I'm to be accepted," it was as if some ready-reckoner instantly clicked into action wiping away her perpetual scowl.

'"Then does it mean you'll go straight over there and learn how to be an officer without any cost to *us*?" she asked.

'"It's a full bursary, but I won't know the whole thing just yet. There's the initial induction and basic training and to the officers' school some months later."

"'Well," she gushed in an unaccustomed display, "if you desire so honourable a career far be it for us to prevent it. We want you to follow your dream, don't we, Mr Sansim?"

'It's not difficult to picture the ageing solicitor acquiescing meekly. Magnus recounted that since he'd last seen him, his father had wilted, much like a seedling too old to transplant. And, as he ably mimicked, there she stood, waxing, whining and waning, wagging her finger at him and declaring that his father's practice had experienced a downturn, that Mr Sansim was careworn with its upkeep and other strains on his finances, that she was the self-sacrificing and long-suffering wife. I remember commenting sarcastically that the alteration in his domestic affairs played no part in her analysis.'

'You obviously allude to him marrying the young secretary. There may have been many reasons for his decline. Some marriages are unaffected by disparate ages between the spouses,' Nancyng declared touchily.

'Quite so and point taken. Magnus was not one, irrespective of my goading, ready to lay the deterioration at her feet, as he looked for the best in everyone despite what I believed was detestation from his stepmother and any clear indications of feeling from his father.

'However, Mr Sansim wasn't so devoid of instinct as to be incapable of meeting his conjugal obligations, for, almost as an afterthought it seemed, Magnus was told before a trap delivered him to the railway station that he would have a new brother or sister within five months. As it happened, he got both, twins, a boy and girl.

'The knowledge that a new family was in the offing became foremost in his mind on the train to Bath. During the journey Magnus decided that he would never go back to the house again, even if he failed the Sandhurst entrance exam.'

'He must have been almost desperate to get away from them, Gray,' remarked Nancyng Jenkins, gauging his reaction on this, her first, use of the nickname. She was unsurprised at the absence of any outward show.

'Yes and no, it has to be said. There had always been times when he looked forlorn in the discussion of intimate issues pertaining to family life. Clearly, he dreamed of something better. I had learned early on that it was best to avoid mentioning my own circumstances and—'

'So you did embark upon them with him?'

'Well,' Newton answered awkwardly, 'I suppose I did, but decided, as his woeful recitation of filial estrangement unravelled often seeing him retreat into a corner to mope for hours, that it was best to refrain from saying anything much at all about myself, more so if it was positive. I think he was inclined not to ask for the very reason that he couldn't conjure up an existence where children might be loved and cherished.

'He had, during those early years, told me enough to let me believe that at one stage the plan for his future involved the lad taking Articles of Clerkship with Mr Sansim as master. All of this must have been before his parents' separation, for, after the divorce or whatever and his father's remarriage, the topic never resurfaced.'

'Hang on, I'm confused about this. You mentioned a tad vaguely, "divorce or whatever". Did he ever get told the truth regarding his mother? I mean, his father, being a man of the law, would never have committed bigamy.'

'No, he wouldn't have. It wasn't spelt out by Magnus. I recall him remarking on one occasion that he regarded his mother as dead, meaning dead to him, and that follows in a youngster's mind, I suppose. His father may have encouraged such a belief for obvious motives.'

'It's all rather dastardly, Gray, isn't it?'

'Unthinkable,' Newton replied with distaste. 'But I'll pass on. Given those internecine developments that he surely regarded as calamities, Magnus knew a career in law was off the agenda. Whether he would ever have followed his father into the profession, even if the marriage had survived, is speculation. A new family rammed home to him the consequences of another child in the house, let alone children, as it turned out; nothing much there for Magnus.

'He was happy and surprised to see me in school as, somewhat fortuitously, I had returned early as well.'

'Why had you?'

'Oh, I can't recall all that detail now,' he replied, passing over her question with a speed that forestalled a follow-up remark. 'I'll never forget the commitment he put in, studying day and night. Although by no means the top student in his class, Magnus had developed an omnivorous passion for military history, was otherwise tidily well-read and no slouch at written expression. I helped a bit, hunting down some references taking in the Napoleonic imbroglios and later Crimean War, for which he was appreciative. I brought him buns and cocoa and he got me to ask random questions from the books in the brief moments between his cramming. He seemed to know his stuff but getting anything wrong rattled him so much that he would note the mistake and have me follow up the next day. I could see that there was no shaking his resolve to reach his goal.'

'Did he go to ordinary classes as well?'

'No. They were reduced to revisory lessons because of the recess and he was excused by the headmaster. Most of the time Magnus closeted himself in the school library during the day and afterwards burned a candle well beyond lights out. After he sat the test, he blithely declared that it was as easy as a flat-country hike.

'Initially, I regarded his statement as rare descent into hyperbole and thought he was putting a happy face on it all to mask a despairing conviction of failure. He proved me wrong, and I lauded his incredible feat of absorption and endurance when he waved a piece of paper in front of my eyes and jumped about all over the shop with an exuberance foreign to his personality. He had won a scholarship, in fact earning a grade of ninety-four per cent, the highest ever recorded in such an examination.

'Within a week, Magnus was gone. One of the requirements of entry to Sandhurst was that he would enlist in the British army for the preliminaries, as he told his stepmother. With that behind him almost a year later and scholarship in hand, he could skip on to Sandhurst. Thus, a career of the finest officer pedigree should have proved a formality.

'It didn't quite work out that way. Magnus was identified fairly early on as a recruit with considerable potential and offered an overseas stint. I'm assuming, because the scholarship indicated an outstanding theoretical ability, he was asked if he would like to go out to the Far East for a year based in Singapore. The offer to serve so soon in an exotic location was beyond refusal but he was canny enough to ask the right questions beforehand. When he raised the issue of Sandhurst, Magnus was told that enquiries had already been made and the situation could be deferred to suit him.'

'Such minute detail. You're the one with a photographic memory. Did you write a lot or something, and are you embellishing it with literary flourishes?'

'Nothing embroidered about it,' he affirmed. She rolled her eyes mockingly. 'We corresponded regularly and saw each other occasionally as the years went by and he filled in the gaps. As you know, I ended up in His Majesty's service and also went to Sandhurst, but that's another story—'

'A topic tantalising my interest, Gray, and about which I'd like to hear from your lips sometime.'

'About which you won't be hearing since your story is

scheduled to follow my explanation as to why I happen to be sailing on this passenger tramp, and I won't countenance any rearrangement of the order of things.'

'Gray, one day you'll tell me if my name isn't Nancyng Jenkins.'

'I'm certain you don't wish to pique me by pressing on with such silliness,' he said firmly.

'Well, excuse me, your highness. Go on, if you please.'

'So a year stretched into two and he became an acting lieutenant. He seemed at home in the role. They wanted him to stay on and offered another promotion. He politely refused.

'This time he asserted himself, showing them a cable from the commanding officer at Sandhurst stating that the scholarship wouldn't be deferred again and if he didn't return it would be withdrawn. So, in 1924, Magnus, a subaltern, walked into the venerable confines of Sandhurst in Camberley as much an undergraduate as any other inductee, although destined, upon graduation because of overseas experience, for much bigger things.'

'All very interesting. But Esrelle seems to have vanished without trace. I hope she, like his mother, hasn't disappeared forever.'

'How timely. While in Singapore, completely out of the blue, he received a letter that had been forwarded on. Despite everything, his memory of Esrelle retained a sweetness that effervesced like a Malayan breeze wafting through his tiny quarters at dawn.'

'Not just the historian but a poet also.'

'They were his words to me,' Newton replied drily. 'In the letter she'd begged forgiveness and explained what had occurred to see her leave Hambrook and cease communication with him. Magnus was won over by the candour of her disclosures and the warmth transmitted from the only human being he believed had ever loved him.'

'She sounds more the crafty Machiavelli preying upon his inherent decency rather than anything else.'

'Probably justified, and a rather kind comment on Magnus' decency,' came a delayed response. 'I've seen the construct between the two of them in that light. At the risk of sounding repetitive, he didn't cease to love her.'

'More fool him, but that's men, I suppose.'

'Subjectivity, Nancyng, can sometimes be an unreliable informant.'

She deflected the observation with, 'No more exercised than any woman my age. Men can be such dears, and pretty awful when they choose.'

'Universal *human* traits, perhaps. Anyway, worshipful love was obvious because he often used the term "scoundrel" in referring to that older, married tutor. He never uttered a bad word about Esrelle and would suffer no one to do likewise. The only time he erupted with me was when I voiced a throwaway line about him being better off without her and he told me never to say such a thing again if I wanted to retain his friendship.'

'That must have shocked you.'

'Well, it did, because he looked into my eyes so fiercely that I just froze up and quietly apologised. But that was the end of it, for Magnus held no grudges.

'Anyhow, getting back to the correspondence, he actually sent me a long letter explaining the whole episode. Esrelle had become involved with a man who she avowed as "no good". He assumed that referred to the same fellow with whom she ran off, as she didn't elaborate on his identity for fear, I suppose, of opening the door a little too wide.

'Pregnant and abandoned in London after the father discovered her condition, she was left to fend for herself. A miscarriage followed. She couldn't face her family and managed to obtain work as a library assistant. There, she flatted with another girl and had wanted to contact Magnus sooner but was ashamed to.

'Enthusiastic and, in retrospect, naïve, he replied to her letter, expressing his profound sympathy for what she had gone through and offering support, and not just verbal either, as he actually sent her a sum of money he admitted as "not being much". She hadn't asked for anything but happened to mention she was struggling on a pittance of a salary.'

'Not many men would have gone so far or, perhaps, been so foolish. Your Magnus is quite honourable and noble even if predictably incautious.'

'Yes, I suppose, in the fashion to which a few men of that era aspired. This marked the start of a protracted period of confidential correspondence. He was far from home and, while not entirely friendless, kept to himself. I was always wary when writing to him, knowing his moods if any hint of reproof could be discerned in my language.'

'Mm, understandable. What about local women? One would think any young man might be open to the wide variety of attractions the oriental East had to offer.'

'Before he heard from Esrelle, I probed him in a roundabout fashion concerning what his colleagues did for "entertainment". He was quite derisory of their behaviour and declared that he had not thought about a casual affair. Once Esrelle reconnected with him, the only outlet he looked forward to was receiving her letters, to which he was never dilatory in responding.'

'Irrelevant question at this point, I realise; did he ever write to his father?'

'Not to my knowledge but, ah, in a chronological sense, you've managed to jog a recollection and remiss of me for not having acquainted you with it. Approaching the end of his tenure in Singapore, he received a letter from solicitors advising him of Mr Sansim's sudden death and—'

'You forgot to mention *that?*' she asked, somewhat perplexed.

'Ah, yes,' he baulked, 'I overlooked the occurrence on account of it having been appended as something of a PS,' adding firmly, 'Magnus was cut from rare cloth you need to appreciate.'

'So it seems, and even more tragic, I suppose.'

'If one pauses to reflect on the loss of an only parent, you're right. The estate lawyers enclosed a copy of the last will. He was not mentioned as a beneficiary and the whole of the estate, real and personal, was devised and bequeathed to his widow.

'The solicitors informed him that he had the right to make an application for provision, reminding him that such applications rarely succeed where adult, able-bodied males are concerned, given the competing interests, as in here a widow and two young children.

'The letter requested an indication as to whether he was intending to make a claim. The house apart – of which he was the remainderman and, given the widow's age, of no real practical use to him, she being a tenant for life – there was, to his surprise, another valuable property, together with the goodwill in his legal firm listed as the assets of the estate.

'Magnus recounted, not without some flourish, that they had provided a *pro forma* document for him to sign giving notice of whether he wished to bring proceedings against the estate. He crossed out the "do" and the "don't" and inserted the words "Do Not Ever!"

'But back to Esrelle. His letters tended to minimise the pace of emotional attachment, perhaps fearing I might warn him off and wanting to preserve our bond, a stand-off on both our parts, to be sure. Once he started talking about their renewed association, it was transparent that his feelings for her were as strong as ever they had been and their "friendship", as he designated it, was heading in an inexorable direction.

'At least twice weekly they would write. Three letters arrived together, all expressing concern for his safety and suggestively curious as to how he spent his time away from duty. Impetuously, in my private opinion, he sent her a not inexpensive sapphire and gold ring as a gift rather than a proposal. I guessed he didn't want her to think that he had any social life and probably also made the gesture as a pledge of constancy. The subject of marriage had never been broached by him.

'For her own purposes, she chose to interpret this action somewhat differently and wrote back saying that she loved his shyness, understood his careful way of doing things and was honoured to be asked to be his wife but would need to think about it further. "We will discuss it all when you return, my darling," she concluded.'

'Did you see what was written?'

'Yes. He showed that and others to me years later. Even with what had happened, as he did so I held my peace. At times, Nancyng, I struggle putting this all together from the mix of our letters and conversations where he opened up to me.'

'It's an understandably tough recall when it's a childhood friend. Might you have wanted to upbraid her behaviour or denounce his foolishness?'

'It crossed my mind, and hindsight is said to be a universal trait. I regard it as discretionary in the voice of all men.' She shook her head incredulously and suggested that Newton might be a perfect subject for Freudian analysis.

'After I'm dead, go for your life. My body has been willed to science and who knows what they'll find.'

'Perhaps the mind of a genius, Gray?'

'You mock me, Mrs Jenkins,' he sniffed.

'I'm sure one day the cutters and dicers will discover a tiny ounce of humour, perhaps even fun somewhere in that Reginal Newton brain.'

'Ask the Freudian devotees for an inquest,' he responded, benevolently this time, and she further warmed to him.

'On with your tale, Colonel,' she laughed, 'or you might find me too readily getting nosey concerning you.'

'Magnus was surprised by the response yet relieved at her circumspection. Although I now think he harboured an ingenuous fantasy about them never being apart, I was far from certain that he wanted to marry her at that time either. They were still quite young as well and not in a sound financial position to plan a future.

'True, he had a little money saved but that was to tide him over when he returned to England, for there were no prospects of earning any meaningful income to support a home and family until he graduated from Sandhurst and obtained a formal posting. But the long period alone, his father's death, uncertainty and/or indifference about his mother made him singularly vulnerable.

'He desperately wanted to belong to someone. Magnus became certain that Esrelle was the one for him even though, in the imagery of Hardy's heroine, this Tess was no more the girl he had imaged throughout his childhood.'

'Angel Clare, get thee behind me, Magnus,' issued her reply that Newton soon appreciated wasn't meant to be jocular.

'As the overseas assignment drew to a close, his sense of longing increased and I believe he came to think of nothing else but spending the rest of his life with her.

'Their reunion on the docks at Southampton was one he wouldn't forget. Esrelle wore the ring matched simply by a field-green frock trimmed at the collar with white lace. A womanly shape had displaced the sylph-like teenager he last recalled. Though matched in age, he appreciated their separation in maturity and doted on her self-confidence, exemplified by the imperious putdown of a porter who had mishandled his bags.

'At her instigation and shortly after his return, he formally proposed and she gleefully accepted. Esrelle, having brokered a rapprochement with her family, Magnus made a chivalrous application to her father for his consent to the marriage. It goes without saying that she hadn't told the parents about her pregnancy. The couple's obvious lengthy association, his long-term prospects as an officer, his respectful presentation and, perhaps, sanguinity that Esrelle would settle with a steady, conservative man, won him over without hesitation.

'During the engagement, she remained working in London whilst he was finding his feet at Sandhurst. I meant to remind you that I was there also, having entered courtesy of scraping through the entrance examination rather than by winning a scholarship. My father had secured a placement and it was a costly thing. I had also done my basic training.'

'Was it sheer coincidence that your paths linked up again?'

'We'd hoped to be there together and canvassed the

possibility even before he left school, but luck played the biggest part.'

'And you would also have expected to be the prime candidate as best man after the banns were posted. Had you met Esrelle at this stage?'

'I hadn't actually. It perplexed me a little. Magnus seemed in no hurry to introduce his fiancée. Perhaps he feared my reaction to her might have been reproving, as he knew I was sometimes fond of airing my opinions at our personal level.'

'An understandable caution on his part,' said Nancyng Jenkins, standing up and retrieving field glasses when she heard a commotion from the golfing deck. There was a pod of whales moving parallel to them thirty yards distant, diving and surfacing. One, whose entire body arched above the waves, created a mammoth displacement of water and the spray went close to bathing the ship. Newton joined her at the railing, accepting her binoculars in time to observe a repeat performance.

'Extraordinary. It surely must be the leader of the pack, a sperm bull whale, if I'm not mistaken,' he said, transfixed by the spectacle. 'Over fifty feet long if it's a foot.' When she remarked on his knowledge concerning the animal, he stammered something about having read quite a good deal on the subject.

The pod had slipped away to the stern before they resumed their canvas recliners. 'We can quit now if it's beginning to sound wearisome,' he told her.

'Look, if you're happy to continue a bit longer, it's at an interesting stage.'

'Yes, you're correct, but it appears we are about to receive some company that might decide the matter.'

The Onions family, Sir Lionel taking the lead with a downcast Henrietta at the rear, approached. He wore a cap, blue jacket, white pants and boaters, much as a commodore preparing to ascend the dais and fire the starting gun in a Cowes regatta. His wife, holding a broad red hat, had chosen a smart pink pantsuit and heeled sandals while Henrietta, in mustard shorts, a loose sailor's blue and white striped t-shirt with an anchor insignia across the front, appeared somewhat fuller of figure than her lean legs would have expected to suggest. Sandals tendered her feet.

'I trust you'll excuse us, Colonel Newton. Having seen your ogling of those superb creatures and the bull, we thought it might be timely to impose briefly upon you and Mrs Jenkins. There's something I wanted to say that the written word alone never can.'

'Not at all, sir,' he replied, relaxed and confident, the thought of any confrontational predilections removed by his demeanour. 'You have *our* ears,' Newton added after sensing Nancyng's interest in what might be forthcoming.

'I'm a man who can't abide even residues of festering discontent. Given recent events and that we have a long voyage ahead of us, speaking for my family, I wish to extend an earnest offer of goodwill towards you both. There was a misinterpretation. Lady Onions and I jumped to conclusions.

Henrietta is on this voyage with us after a period apart. There are times when her health doesn't serve our daughter as well as it might. Do you follow, Colonel?'

'There's a saying, Sir Lionel, to which I've long been attracted. *Least said, soonest mended,* and, as far as I'm concerned, the matter is closed.'

'And no hard feelings, Mrs Jenkins. Last night you were magnificent.'

'Absolutely none at all,' she replied, stepping forward to take each hand in turn. Newton followed, noting that Henrietta's was the least reassuring of the Onions trio.

Chapter 6 – Love and Marriage

ancyng Jenkins was on the verge of calling for another drink when Newton arrived at their designated place of meeting unusually later than the appointed time. One ice cube, barely visible in the idle fruit cocktail, remained. He was apologetic, saying that Sir Lionel had been the cause of his tardiness.

'When he asked if I could spare five minutes, I almost expected a recantation of yesterday's penitence until he glorified his robust corporate structure for fifteen, before managing to mention whether I had ever considered a career in business after army days expired.'

'Really? Did an offer emerge at the end?' Nancyng pressed.

'No,' he laughed, 'but he went on and on, principally about his extensive interests in the Far East, hinting that someone of my "vast experience" in that part of the world would be an invaluable acquisition. I was dumbfounded yet vague about the future and, save for saying that I was presently content with my life though would be happy to discuss it further when I had time, was late for another appointment.'

'And his reaction was?' Her eyes forecasted the answer.

'He discerned yours as being the preferable project. Sir Lionel isn't accustomed to a fobbing off, if quite content to let others experience such a dispatch when it suits him.'

Nancyng Jenkins handed the glass to Newton, who swallowed a goodly portion.

'Project, mm? I accept your characterisation rather more warmly than you may have intended. Well, my interest is piqued. How the worm turns, as they say. Please do keep me abreast of further developments.'

'Of course. So, are we ready to go on with Magnus?'

'It's your story.'

'Yesterday, did I mention that Esrelle was residing in London?' She nodded. 'Having secured a promotion, it emerged that she was now earning a good deal more than her fiancé. He felt somewhat insecure on this account.

'Esrelle constantly maintained that she needed to scrimp and save as much as possible to ensure their future. They saw each other on average about once a fortnight when she caught the train. Magnus found the arrangement disconcerting for her time off didn't always coincide with his. Regulations forbade him from absenting himself from Sandhurst for longer than a few hours without written permission. He was also anxious at the imposition on her travelling every other week, returning late on a Sunday. He urged her to wait for when they could arrange a full day together, even if it meant their assignations would be limited to once a month rather than snatched fissures of time.

'She insisted on the situation continuing. On one occasion, I recall specifically his recounting of Esrelle being quite seriously agitated over this and asking her whether there was anything wrong. Magnus related what they discussed quite vividly. It was the day I first encountered her, and more on that soon.

'"Oh, don't be silly, dear," she replied dismissively to his reticence about her seeing him so sporadically. "You really need to comprehend women, don't you?"

'It was an answer for which he might have sought clarification, but she was adept at reading his mind and assiduously steered the topic away from her to one of where they might live once they became man and wife. Married undergraduates were permitted to reside away from the confines of Sandhurst.

'"I've already had a look around and we can get a half-decent flat nearby for reasonable rent. It will be tight but, with my allowances and the money in the bank, we'll have sufficient to get some furniture together and overall will be enough to carry us through. After I graduate, because of my decent overseas stretch, it's possible the army might be inclined to send me—" His hesitation drew a frown from her and he qualified the answer with, "But you know the army tries to look after its officers who have a wife to support."

'He had often told me she was capable of being quite taciturn and, at this point of their discussion, he was no doubt decidedly uncomfortable. "I hope so, dear, especially when children come along. They need a good education in our English system. Married people have been known to have babies, you know."'

'I sensed that one could have heard a bobby pin fall on the carpet at this juncture. You sketch the atmospherics so comprehensively,' observed Nancyng Jenkins.

'Ah, that really was Magnus for you. He used to mesmerise me with his uncanny ability to draw you into the environment as if you were where he was.'

'Just as you're doing now. It's obviously a facility you both shared.'

'Generous of you to say so,' he said, scrutinising her for any reaction beyond that which he initially assumed she'd intended. Receiving none, he continued.

'Magnus slid her hand into his and petted her arm in an attempt to propitiate the darkening air. It would've sent an ague through his body. The last thing he could bear was any signal that might jeopardise their future, such was his desire to please.

'I recall thinking – and remember I was older now – as he was relating this awkward conversation with Esrelle that I'd never met anybody so palpably self-doubting. He kept assuring her things would all work out no matter what the posting. Yet, when he took in the alteration in her tone of voice, he sorely appreciated his submissions had been futile.

'"I realise the army has become your life and, yes, it will be our lives." He held her to him and apologised for being insensitive. "Your future is settled, for you've already been out in the field, unlike other classmates, Magnus, and I'm not complaining. I, I just don't like talk – no, I'm scared of talk about going away. Your little blossom here is frightened and insecure, that's all, with what I've been through," she concluded simperingly.'

'So she used that ploy to play on his diffidence. Pretty low stuff. This relationship is unravelling before its consummation.'

'Well, let's not jump too far ahead. Esrelle was a complex and mysterious female. There were two prominent sides to her. One, kind, outgoing, vivacious, spirited, the other—'

'Self-centred, scheming and underhanded,' Nancyng cut in with undisguised relish.

'I wouldn't put it with quite such blunt force. The many substrata to her makeup, be they for good or ill, enthralled him. Sometimes I wondered whether Magnus chose to flirt with the dark side pretending it was from a secure distance, but don't we all have foibles of one sort or another?'

'I will need three long voyages like this one to work out what, if any, *dark* categories enshroud your makeup.'

'Nancyng, you have a persistent habit of foisting me from the periphery of being a narrator into the centre of the topic under consideration.'

'As I said, you're telling the story and I'm sure you're about to relate some poor me display by this little lady.'

Newton's tongue remained planted within his cheeks. 'Esrelle made a tight ball of her handkerchief and wiped away tears that she seemed to will at materialising. He knew it wasn't the time to inform his betrothed that the army would decide on his posting rather than him selecting one that suited their circumstances or convenience but went on to placate her, suggesting for the umpteenth time that the service always attempts to understand the situation of married couples. She had remained aloof, standing, shuffling her feet, before thrusting the tear wad sideways and distancing herself further from him. When he moved to follow, she made her preference clear and he remained where he was.

'"We have so little money," she responded as if he hadn't spoken, never leaving off the fidgeting with her eyes. "My life is a week-to-week mausoleum existence, paying rent, eating plain fare, having so few decent clothes and almost no jewellery to show on the rare occasion I go abroad in the evening."'

'Sounds like a real Drury Lane performance, Gray, that is, unless you're being overly melodramatic?'

'Not a bit of it. The shame is that injecting even a hint of a comment along those lines was beyond the lad. Dress and latest fashion was the one thing she never stinted upon. Esrelle liked baubles, the Far Eastern sapphire ring now residing on her right-hand wedding finger, evidence of its displacement by the one-carat diamond solitaire on her matching left that had salted off not a little of his reserves.'

'Judging by their conversation, her gratitude was short-lived?'

'Magnus was incapable of viewing what seems obvious to us from this perspective. Anyway, then came the bombshell in a lengthy dissertation when Esrelle informed her fiancé that she wanted to keep their forthcoming nuptials a secret.

'"If I were to tell the manager that I was getting married it would be the end of my situation. Not all about you, Magnus dear. I have employment, remember? I can continue to stay with my flatmates at least until you receive your posting and come to you when the army deigns some weekends off. Don't be disappointed because, in the long run, it will be best for us. You can conserve our money by living in at the barracks and finding a casual situation when I visit. My rent is not so bad, and I can train down Friday and return on Sunday. It's the perfect arrangement. And we wouldn't want to be in each other's hair day and night."

'Of course, Magnus couldn't bring himself to canvass an opinion that he was inclined to think marriage was about being together. At the time of being told this, I perceived that he was stunned at the sudden emergence of a decision she had conjured up well in advance of its announcement. He was also worried should the ruse be discovered as it might put them both in a poor light.'

'You said before that you met, or rather "encountered", I think, this woman on the day they had the conversation you're presently relating. Are you going to mention how that came about exactly?'

'I was in due course, but, since you've raised it, I shall, the thing being quite accidental and a trifle unusual. It was an inclement Sunday and my first attendance at Sandhurst. I hadn't yet been accepted but was called down unexpectedly for an interview. At this stage, I was living at Islington after my parents had moved there and had been completing an arts degree at London University.

'I recall the train journey from where I lived to Camberley station, being the nearest to Sandhurst. There had been some commotion at the other end of the carriage, it, apart from myself and the couple concerned, being empty. When I heard the shouting, I witnessed a lively verbal exchange between a young woman and a middle-aged man. The language was, to say the least, somewhat—'

'Blue?'

'You could say that.'

'Don't be bashful. I'm sure you recall it word-for-word.'

'The female was giving quite as much as she got, more even, and you might understand the feeling of loitering in the background, torn between putting a stop to it because no woman should have been spoken to in such disgraceful terms yet thinking she might be the type to reconcile with her protagonist and remonstrate against the intervener.'

'Understand, yes, but, come on, like what was said, Colonel. Spill it.'

'The man said, "You are nothing but a plummy-mouthed tart, always were and always will be." In turn, she was less than complimentary about his private person—'

'Oh, lord, help me. Told him he was unable to get it up or something?'

Newton cleared his throat and emitted a faint smile. 'She slapped his face in the process, he seized her by the shoulders and I became a rescuer of sorts.

'I deflected his punch with my elbow. He was a stocky man, though inclined to corpulence, and not overly grateful for my intervention. I noticed that the train had come to a stop virtually at a railway station after she pulled the cord. As we glared at each other, he cursing vociferously, the guard came on the scene. In a flash, he sized up the situation and the man was marched off the train along with the woman. Two policemen happened to be nearby on the platform and, eventually, they took him away.'

'What happened to the female?'

'Spot on. That was the strangest thing, or perhaps not, as I suggested earlier. I could see her arguing with the police. It was as if she was attempting to confound them when one would have thought she might be doing her level best to offer thanks for their support.

'At one stage a policeman began to walk to the carriage, I assumed coming to speak to me, but she rushed up and called him back. The sergeant, who had stayed with the man, motioned to her to reboard, and that was it. In some distress, the woman was taken to the guard's van and the journey resumed.'

'Are you going to keep me guessing much longer or simply point me in the direction of its relevance?' she asked snappily.

'Nancyng, I'm certain you've guessed the identity of the changeable young woman.'

'It's hardly something that requires consultation with a fortune teller, but fair comment.'

'As mentioned before about my having travelled down to Sandhurst, I tried to track Magnus down but couldn't find him for obvious reasons. At five or so in the afternoon, heading to catch my train home, the weather, by now appallingly ugly, cold, damp, and me settled in my seat, I spied them in a clinch on the platform. She had her back to me, and I was about to yell out to Magnus when she turned to board again. It was, as you guessed, the woman from the earlier entanglement. She didn't see me, and I determined that she wasn't going to.'

'But you told me earlier that it was the day you met her.'

'Well, it was, speaking retrospectively. I didn't say it was the day we were introduced. That occurred on a subsequent occasion.'

'You can't resist reverting to form, Colonel, and I use the term advisedly. So, the actual introduction came later. And, knowing you, not a word passed your lips at any stage to the hapless Magnus about the altercation on the way there?'

'Correct. But I shall return to that original conversation—'

'My, this is becoming more complicated by the minute, as with you. And don't even think about getting huffy,' her tone indicative that he should demur.

'If you so please, Mrs Jenkins. Before we get to the introductions, Magnus was worried about her suggestion that she withhold information from her employer because it could leave a "terrible and unearned black mark", as he described it, and pressed her further.

"'Do you think it's wise to hide being married from your manager? I mean if he were to feel that he'd been practised upon, he mightn't take—"

"'Nonsense," she cut in assertively. "He'll never find out about our marriage. You know, I sometimes wonder whether you are trying me out, as in virtue-testing, because you don't trust me and it's really hurtful that you're doing it, Magnus. I've a right to a private life. And it's not the army *I* must salute, you know. They're the council running the library. No document has ever been put in front of me to sign nor am I under a duty to inform them of anything. I labour and toil and do it bloody dashed well, I'll thank you to know."

"'Of course, dear, but your engagement ring, surely he can work out—"

"'Magnus, you are so naïve it's embarrassing. And you aspire to be some Intelligence Supremo. Do you think I wear that thing to work?"

'I apprehend that my dear friend was as equally crushed by the disclosure as by the description applied to the showpiece of his love. But Magnus stayed cool, contained and submissive under her withering comebacks and kept his own counsel. I said before that he hated arguments. Rather casually, she mentioned something that caused him real unease.

"'And he would blame me outright for the missing money if he saw such a thing as that on my finger."

'"Missing money? Dear Esrelle, what are you talking about?"

'"Will you please settle down and try to develop the habit of trusting your future wife. That had nothing to do with me," she said with vehemence. "It's getting late and now's not the time for idle gossip."'

'The train approached Camberley station and he held her tighter than he ever had done, frightened he might lose her if he said anything on the subject that had so torn him.

'"I must dash, or the train will be off while this gabbing goes on. Goodbye and *adieu*, darling."

'He threw his Mackintosh over her and they ran to the carriage. Magnus opened the door and stood bareheaded on the platform, waving until the train was out of sight. Despite the weather, he decided to walk back to the college. I could almost see the disconsolate figure trudging along. None of it made sense to him. There had departed the love of his life living one that seemed so artificial with other girls around her. *She must be making out she's single to them, too,* he surely ruminated. Yet did he, I wonder.

'Along the way he stopped at a pub. He wasn't a drinker but downed three pints in quick succession as it was near closing time. It gave little comfort to the feeling of unease about Esrelle's dismissive attitude.

'What he regarded as ordinary candour and propriety in dealings between an employer and an employee was not seen in quite that way by his future bride. The old doubts he had about her following the unforeseen severing of their relationship as youngsters returned. It was five to six. This time he had a double brandy and felt immeasurably better as he walked the rest of the way back. The rain clouds had broken up and his spirits lifted.

'He was hopelessly in love with her. There's no other way to describe it. That old saying, "Love sees only what it wants to see", or some such thing, comes to mind. I can't help concluding again that she was the first adult person in his life who, for whatever strange quirk, made him feel wanted, and he was terrified of doing anything that might alienate her affections.'

'Was he intimate with her?'

'I don't know, and was hardly in a position to enquire on that account and—'

'But weren't you his best, or even his only friend?'

'Well, I wouldn't have asked anyway. If my opinion at the time was worth anything, later events suggested I might have been accurate.'

'Dear me. Need I be forced to extract teeth with tweezers, again? *What* later events served to form *what* opinion?' her frustration dispersing at his meek frown.

'I'm reluctant to speculate, other than express a doubt that Magnus' relationship with Esrelle had reached such a level.' An exasperated sigh constituted her only reaction.

'The day following, she rang to assure him that if he was against what she was doing she would abide by his decision.

'He was ecstatic after the call, so thankful for the apologetic tone of voice. It made him love her all the more, helped him to rationalise the situation and gave him peace of mind. Her strongest point in allowing him to make the decision for them was the fact that she wasn't working for a private firm.

'I grappled with the distinction, asking him what difference he felt it made. He explained that, having thought it over, a local authority running a library sometimes made exceptions in the case of married employees, particularly those in poor circumstances. He was persuaded by her that they were in a difficult financial position and, while she could have asked for a dispensation, it was too risky. Furthermore, the situation wouldn't go on once she became pregnant, of course, and he knew that she was keen to become a mother. Thus, he went along with her, saying it would be best to remain "mum".

'He was the kind of chap who, when he thought more on a topic, always ended up making concessions for Esrelle, she being a girl of many contradictions and strong opinions. She forever expressed a desire to have children and, as a means of boosting her stance, was fond of posing the question that since young married people always want a family why should they be any different?

'It became a position tinged with irony that seemed to have escaped her, yet it quite naturally might have evoked a painful memory for him. Family aspirations in one breath and, in the next, she was keen to keep their forthcoming wedding a secret for reasons that defied his standards of good faith.

'If that was another sigh, I quite understand and apologise for the prolixity. I'm in the home strait, about to detail my formal introduction to Esrelle, the nuptials and the aftermath.'

'Mine was more an acknowledgement of having to join the ship's company again for cocktails, dinner and the much-heralded card night. Have you paired up yet?'

'I avoided putting my name on the list drawn up by the purser.'

'You'll be allocated, trust me. Given the interest in our ongoing sessions, it probably won't do that we take on all-comers. Perhaps we should contrive a row concerning cheating to provide more fodder for gossip.'

'Go on, then,' he smiled wryly, 'may as well be hung for a sheep rather than being troubled by inconsequential whispers. Concerning your daughter for a moment, I'm not for inserting myself between mother and child.'

'She's quite happy to have a break from me during the day. Marion Cahill and Charlotte are becoming inseparable.'

'That's good to know. At the start of this chronicle, I had no idea it would take so long. With the memory being enlivened, the more I'm bringing to mind other events as if they'd happened only yesterday. The incident on the train refers.'

'As you relayed the event, I thought it such a striking recollection; sometimes so poignant, as if something like this had actually happened to you even. And that's the mark of an exceptional correspondent.'

She studied Newton keenly and wondered if a fleeting

episode of blinking was really referable to his complaint about soot from the funnel in his eye. His refusal of her offer to look at it, followed by some extravagant rubbing, did nothing to disabuse her curiosity.

'What was that you were saying?'

'Never mind. Are you coming, I mean, inside?' Nancyng's mock frown pressed with some mischief, intuiting that on this occasion he either preferred to avoid an engagement with them or had shifted his focus entirely.

'Gray, did you hear me?'

'Sorry. Ah, if you wouldn't mind, I'll pass for now.'

'Have you had another of those many flashbacks?'

'Not a flashback so much as a missing piece of the jigsaw deciding to drop in. It's a history demanding as much concentration to maintain continuity and interest as I'm sure it does to take in.'

'I find it rather easy and interesting actually, without trying. Still, I understand how difficult it must be to pull it together. You're doing well, and swaying into the esoteric whets my appetite even more,' intrigue at what was coursing through his mind apparent.

He perceived the path she was on and chose abstraction. 'In such a quest, being a slave to exercise doubles as a spring-cleaning of the mind. I'm going for a turn. You well remark that I need to collect my thoughts for the denouement. Thereafter, my obligation will turn to that of listener, one who might refrain from comment along the way.'

She bit at her cheek, stilling the urge for a caustic

comeback. 'You should ready yourself for disconsolation when that stage arrives. Nothing I might relate could outdo this by half.'

'Do you think so, Nancyng?' he asked, fixing her with eyes that this time arrived willingly.

'Now I know so, Gray,' encouraged, then disappointed when he stepped back to fold his towel and walk away as if she had already gone.

Chapter 7 – *Poor Rich Girl*

As an only child, Henrietta Onions had experienced the privileges of a background few her age could have realised. Her father, with whom she was primarily attached in infancy, had been a successful merchant in England. At the apex of commerce and industry, Sir Lionel made his fortune in textiles. His companies were extending their reach and diversifying both at home and abroad. They included interests in mining and shipping. The Onions Group held a substantial stake in two shipping conferences, including shares in the company that owned the vessel transporting them to England. He had married his secretary at thirty-eight, she being of similar age. After it became clear that his wife was unable to bear children, they adopted a baby daughter. When she arrived, Sir Lionel doted on her.

Henrietta learned early on the techniques of entwining her father around whatever finger she elected to utilise.

Even in those early years, her mother couldn't be so easily ensnared. Prone to defer to her husband in most things, when it came to this child she was more assertive. Up to the age of ten, Lady Margaret was wont to warn Sir Lionel that her upbringing was not profiting by his excessive tolerance, overindulgence and what she termed 'demeaning protectiveness'. Sir Lionel paid mere notional heed to those views. Such had the bond become that his wife's efforts to break its habitual neediness seemed to have the reverse effect.

As Henrietta grew, Lady Margaret began to consider the totality of the household in an altered light. It coincided with the cessation of marital relations and led to extremes of jealousy, regarding her husband's affections as being alienated towards the girl both at her instigation and perpetuation. She started to question whether some abnormality in the relationship was manifesting itself.

Having reached an early puberty, confoundingly, Henrietta gravitated towards her mother. This Sir Lionel welcomed, regarding the development as a natural progression. His benevolence didn't persist as mother and daughter grew closer. He became suspicious when they once talked late into the night in Henrietta's bedroom, even imagining that his wife might become incautious respecting marital intimacies when, the following day, he was treated like an overstaying guest.

No sooner was he devising means such as sponsoring journeys abroad with her friends than, just as suddenly, with blooms of young womanhood taking hold, Henrietta re-engaged with Sir Lionel of her own volition. Lady Margaret was relegated to an insignificant position and even greater estrangement from her husband ensued. Tensions would sometimes arise when she wanted something and her mother was resistant. Discerning their fraught relations, she was adept at playing one off against the other, knowing her father would always win out.

One issue that proved most troublesome was her insistence on going to a Swiss finishing school in 1946. Her mother had been worried about Europe after war's end and felt things were unsettled, what with mass movements of people and the Soviets occupying substantial influence in Germany and the Eastern Bloc. For Sir Lionel and Lady Margaret, it provoked ongoing rows leading to one of volcanic proportions.

Following her parents' attendance at a function and arrival home in the early hours of the morning, Henrietta was roused by a noisy conflict. Her mother's suggestion that Sir Lionel harboured prurient motives of his own in wishing for her to be fashioned into young womanhood overseas reached a feverish pitch.

'Since you don't want me in your bed anymore, you'll have a free hand with her.' A dull thud and screaming ensued.

Entering the living area, she saw her mother lying on the floor holding her face with Sir Lionel bent over her. The ferocious eyes with which he met his daughter's entry were instantly checked and, in modulated tones, he told her that Lady Margaret had tripped over.

Henrietta wasn't convinced and knelt to comfort the fragile woman.

'My dear girl, your mother is merely upset. Discussions about the proper placement for your education are always difficult when I support your preference and Lady Margaret has a different goal for you.' His daughter's attention transferred in an instant when vehemence punctuated the atmosphere.

'How could you so demean *me*?' she gasped at him. 'And in front of *her*, too.' His wife's narrow lips pinched white, she having scrambled to her feet.

'Lady Margaret is beside herself, Henrietta darling. It's rather late to expect rationality. Families must always strive for unity even if things are complicated and difficult. Mostly, sanity wins out,' his hand taking hers. 'We're sorry you've been inadvertently drawn into it what is between your parents and all will soon be worked through for *your* betterment.'

Henrietta realised from the fixed stare alternating between herself and him that her continued presence wouldn't be helpful in bringing about any resolution. Having appreciated the role she played in their lives more than for which they gave her credit, she disengaged from him and returned to her bedroom.

Remorse for the physicality towards his wife saw the topic quarantined from further discussion whenever Henrietta asked them separately what was going to happen. His unease and prevarication led to an inference that her mother's wishes had triumphed and Switzerland was now out of the question.

When it came to attaining her own way, Henrietta shared Sir Lionel's guile and resolve. A plan evolved courtesy of the insistent attentions of a young admirer, the son of one of her father's closest business associates. He had become lovestruck with her. After listening to Henrietta's impassioned plea, 'Surely there must be some influence you can bring to bear on your Daddy for my sake? Why, we could meet up over there without them around,' he undertook to champion her cause.

Sir Lionel revisited the issue with Lady Margaret when his colleague detailed how a Swiss interregnum had delivered an efficacious result for one of his daughters. His view strengthened as he urged that such a placement could establish a broader social repertoire, 'give her time away from us and equip her for a prominent and expanding position' within his corporate structure.

Even though at first blush the proposal amounted to a capitulation, his wife was able to appreciate its merit. Lady Margaret, having retreated into an emotional enclave, had lost the will to engage in any meaningful way and bowed to her husband's wishes. Despite a residue of ill feeling, she rationalised the surrender by informing acquaintances that Henrietta was more mature than girls of equivalent age.

The young beau had fulfilled a purpose. Henrietta humoured and teased him before setting out for the Continent, but any illusions about prosaic bliss in future were left unrealised, his stream of correspondence, described to one of her friends there as 'romantic mush', falling away when not a jot of a reply was earned.

She was to remain at a school in the Swiss town of Lugano for a year. Cached next to the Italian border and within a twenty-minute train journey of the tantalising luxury of Como with its lake and villas, it became the perfect habitat for a capricious and flirtatious young woman destined to be noticed.

In addition to a bookish persona binding the finishing skills effortlessly assimilated at the school, Henrietta learned a good deal more about what it took to satisfy the urgings of men. Nearly eighteen, she combined a persuasive naiveté with an ability to hold a mature and intelligent conversation.

Convincing most who met her that she was as meek as a spray of olive flowers on its host in mid-spring, at the makings of interest from the opposite sex, Henrietta could perform effortless conversion so as to exhibit a variety of irresistible feminine wiles. Older males were unfailingly attentive and, when necessity drove her, she pitched to this fraternity. It required but casual exertion to keep admirers hooked. A middle-aged Italian count saw the bestowal of rich adornments and expensive jewellery as small change to win her company.

But the day she met her counterpart in intrigue, if not chicanery, ended a charmed existence that had seen her the centre of admiration promenading along footways, riding in motorised conveyances, a topic of discussion in suave restaurants and a particularly favoured frequenter of the Villa d'Este, resting majestically on the shores of Lake Como. There, she encountered the young French duke endowed with demonstrative attributes: charm, smashing masculinity and as handsome a man as had ever set foot in Italian society. It was all of those personal characteristics rather than his title that saw Henrietta, for the first time in her life, trembling and anticipatory at his every action. That he was a good-for-nothing waster in comparison with her other paramours escaped her.

She had discovered what it was like to be wearing the shoes of the pursuer, debrided of reason and blind to the debilitations of the object of her pursuit. Henrietta was fixated on the duke as the man she would marry. She loved him obsessively, extravagantly and tirelessly.

A libidinous pattern emerged with him ready to thrust other women into her face as if it was a test she must pass. On one occasion when she pleaded restraint at his associations, he became furious. He held her down and, when she tried to escape his grasp, tightened his fingers on Henrietta's throat, telling her that she must learn 'the ways of French noblemen' if she intended to retain his heart.

Resistance to his demands wavered with the repetition of threats to end the relationship. She drew the line when he suggested that it would earn his respect were she to engage in intimacy with one of his friends while he remained the voyeur. When his sobriety returned, the duke accepted that it was one step too far. By delivering a tearful apology, he earned her undying plaudits.

The enslavement evolved still more when he made decadent excursions into bookmaker dens. Rather than emerging the beneficiary of his expeditions, as losses mounted the duke became parasitical. Money she didn't have at hand to satisfy his gambling creditors, so the many expensive prettifications past amours had provided were the obvious target. She pawned rings, brooches and bracelets in unseemly haste, as if they were street stall trinkets. When the supply was exhausted, at his insistence she wired for more funds from her father on the pretext of several break-ins by robbers.

Once, inflamed with wine, he told her she would make any man a wonderful wife. Taking it as a proposal, she accepted and promised undying duty, whereupon he erupted into uncontrollable laughter, before coughing so hard that he vomited over the bedclothes and himself. He told her she was an 'idiot', seasoning the affront by declaring her responsible and trying to force her to lick the particulate from his feet, before throwing Henrietta out into the icy rain. She had to be hospitalised for pneumonia.

Having barely recovered following her discharge and arriving at the duke's lodgings, she was confronted by a sign indicating that there was a room to let. Thumping on the door to no effect, and still weak, she collapsed on the stairs outside, beating her fists on the pavement, shrieking and sobbing. The landlady helped Henrietta into her parlour.

'Young woman, please contain yourself. I warned of the terrible mistake you'd made getting involved with that devil. You're another in a long line who's been here looking for the charlatan.' She administered some brandy, taking a liberal dose for herself, before telling the tormented girl that it was believed he had skipped away in the company of a middle-aged dowager and wouldn't be returning.

'Do you know where he's gone?' Henrietta implored.

'To the lake of fire, I hope, for all the trouble he's caused me in unpaid rent and the disarray in his rooms. It's worse than a pigsty.'

With Sir Lionel's encouragement and assistance, she was able to extend the term to catch up on missed schooling, becoming a different personality for those remaining months from the one who had arrived radiating confidence and vitality. On attaining her certificate, Henrietta Onions forsook the traditional graduation ball and left Switzerland for the solace of England.

At home, her health remained problematic, experiencing a period of depression, introspection and social isolation. Henrietta alternated between seething about how she'd been used and vowing that life would henceforth involve taking, not giving or appeasing on the one hand, to, on the other, one of complete indifference to any situation, most of all how she presented herself.

Weight loss so denuded her frame that she became gaunt and colourless. Her garments hung off her as if they were oddments draped over hangers. Henrietta was moody, listless and introverted. Mentally, she had suffered much more inside than the physical symptoms manifested. She was seen by medical specialists for a mysterious nervous condition that plagued her, unable to help formulate a treatment plan because she could never reveal the true reason for her difficulties.

An incident of shoplifting led to more medical consultations. When it appeared that charges were going to be laid despite Sir Lionel's plea with the local inspector of police, he was driven to take the matter to the Home Secretary, a close acquaintance. A medical report was furnished in mitigation and the reprieve secured when the shopkeeper dropped the complaint.

Sir Lionel's and Lady Margaret's relationship that had cooled appreciably during their daughter's Swiss stay deteriorated even further throughout this period. Each blamed the other for their daughter's declining mental integrity. They were advised by her psychiatrist that it was in her best interests for differences to be kept minimal. An uneasy amity was reached.

Perceiving his daughter's condition to waiver between improvement and backsliding, matched by pendulous alterations in mood, Sir Lionel and Lady Margaret received a further medical recommendation that summering in the southern hemisphere might just be the antidote for her. The family embarked on the maiden Christmas voyage of the *RMS Orcades*. Amidst the odorous acclamation from weary locals eager for a break from post-war rationing and despondency, the glitzy passenger liner departed Southampton on 14 December 1948 at the start of its Indian Ocean–Australian odyssey. She would arrive some four weeks later, finding moorings in the port of Fremantle before continuing on to Melbourne and Sydney.

Halfway into the voyage, to the parents' great relief, improvement began to show. The levelling in appetite arrived with the temperate weather, combining to produce a dramatic palliative effect. She reclaimed the colour that had so long deserted her cheeks. The trademark shock of hair, like the southern sun, now bore a blazing, lustrous sheen. Henrietta soon regained much of the shape she once had. No one was rendered more ebullient than Sir Lionel, whose open-cheque patronage of the endless array of dressmakers' shops saw his daughter emerge resplendent, self-assured and accomplished.

Nonetheless, there were odd periods of gloom and brooding, but her father was always there to provide support. Lady Margaret, true to obeisance respecting doctors' orders, maintained strict decorum in her dealings with Sir Lionel and was ever ready to lend advice on the emerging woman's wardrobe whenever it was sought.

Henrietta resumed her place in society and embraced shipboard frivolity as if it was second nature. A new-found readiness to flirt sometimes occasioned dissension between her parents, he all for it, his wife not so. Lady Margaret knew it was pointless, yet couldn't resist voicing an indwelling and ever-present disturbance concerning their adopted daughter. Intuition that this was the underlying cause of her breakdown after Switzerland was cavalierly dismissed by an increasingly impatient husband as the fractured spouses sauntered the deck.

'She repeatedly denied getting involved with anybody other than being triflingly immature, and the doctors rejected your theories out of hand,' he told her firmly. 'Permit the poor thing good times and let us be thankful that she's back in the world again.'

'Of course, Sir Lionel,' as she now perpetually referred to him. 'One only has to look at the flush in her cheeks burning even bolder on the frequent occasions you manage to pay a compliment. Those of her own flighty persuasion even seem to have found a new star,' she tittered, missing her step after the long dinner and bottomless claret.

The family disembarked in Melbourne. They travelled by train to Sydney, spending six weeks there before taking the return passage through Suez. By the time the ship docked at her home port, Henrietta had gained a stone-and-a-half.

It wasn't long after their homecoming that a crisis in one of his holdings necessitated a rushed trip by air to Singapore and the Malayan Peninsula, almost sure to involve a prolonged stay. His daughter accompanied him. Her mother, whom by then she'd come to despise, had given up any hope of influencing her against such a course and remained in England. Eventually she would sail out and link up with them.

Sir Lionel had warned that a return journey home by sea could only be taken on a passenger/cargo vessel, a much less grandiloquent manner of travel than the *Orcades*. Henrietta showed the spirit Sir Lionel loved in his daughter when she declared, 'It will make a nice change after all those pretentious first-class passenger boys playing at being men on a grand vessel. Anyway, didn't you say there might be a surprise in store for me when we reach Port Elizabeth?'

*   *   *

Henrietta Onions was plainly unwell. Attaining her majority a few days' steaming from the East African coast, she cared nought for its acquisition as she gained the open deck on that auspicious afternoon. Fighting a condition akin to seasickness was one thing but, since the vessel's motion was almost indiscernible, she associated the malady with another bout of depression.

Henrietta had requested her parents not make a public celebration of her birthday. She explained it in terms of avoiding any further focus upon herself after the earlier humiliation concerning Newton. However, her father had hatched a plan, calculating that a diversion was needed to restore her credibility as well as erasing the 'misunderstanding' from memory. Sir Lionel accepted postponing the announcement he most wanted to make, Henrietta assuming a one-quarter holding in his worldwide interests, until they arrived home. Instead, he had arranged for an elaborate cake and a presentation.

While these preparations were afoot, she, being

encouraged to take in the sun and sea to 'return some colour to her cheeks', as her mother put it, had no set plan to hear anything passing between the colonel and Mrs Jenkins. Nor was Henrietta Eunice Onions engaged in an entirely abstract meander. The gist of these habitual discussions had become a vehicle for corroborating a suspicion of familiarity not contemplated with absolute indifference.

Having caught the flavour, the heiress paused and positioned herself behind a lifeboat. Nancyng Jenkins, who at that moment happened to be boxing Newton playfully on the shoulders, had risen. The action was interpreted as an attempt to cajole him into following her suit, but he wasn't buying it. Eventually she desisted and moved off to a ladder, a shortcut that took her down to the passengers' accommodation.

Henrietta fed her hayrick tresses into a band, secured them tightly to her head and nervously adjusted her clothing, as the conditions cooled and light began its inexorable retreat with Newton almost at the end of his first lap. She waited in the mask of the portside funnel casing, emerging as he doubled down the stairs and commenced a casual ramble towards him. He nodded courteously, not slowing, as she had done, and reached the barrier at the end of the funnel. Swivelling about, he steered towards the for'ard extremity and crossed to the starboard side, quickening his pace. It was an incommodious route that defied interception given its narrow circumlocution, but she was determined to stick with him. Wearing sandals and coming close to matching him in height, where the deck opened its way towards the bow, she adapted her stride with ease to level with and remain abreast of him.

'If you'll excuse the interruption, Colonel Newton,' her tone conciliatory, 'but I couldn't help noticing your regimen at this time of evening and waited for you.'

'The decks aren't off limits to anyone, Miss Onions, except for young girls who prowl and loiter late at night,' he offered coolly, savouring the sweet dusk air as he stretched out as fast as he could go, trusting to his meaning and actions. The slight lead he gained, increasing as he departed from his usual route and swept down to the golfing deck, was soon whittled away as she caught up to him again.

'Is it so difficult even to tolerate me, sir?'

'Not even given to consider it, Miss Onions. You announced yourself once and I've yet to see any practical recantation from being the put-upon, haughty princess.'

'Colonel Newton, I beg you,' she said, trying to arrest his momentum and, with the slightest narrowing of the trajectory of their combined movements, came into contact with his person. 'Would you be so understanding as to hear me out?'

'You touched me. Pray tell, another malodorous technique inviting a walk to the captain's cabin to file a report of the interaction to cover myself against a second round of contrived allegations?'

Her eyes semaphored a stand-and-deliver code which left no room for equivocation. 'Don't be absurd. That business has passed us.' Having gained his attention, she resumed in a less forthright manner. 'I came with favour in my heart to apologise in person.'

Newton could be a pedant for protocol, though within him welled a milk of forgiveness that in others subjected to similar denunciation might forever lurk the vial of ill will. He paused this time as her hand detained his forearm, eyes wide and unblinking, 'I'm sorry for the trouble I brought you.'

'And to Mrs Jenkins? You will go likewise?'

'Of course, and to her I feel the same way, but, rather than giving any expectation of further offence, I pushed a note under her door in which I said much the same as I've done to you, as well as offering to meet in private.'

'To *Mrs Jenkins?*' he insisted.

'Yes, to Mrs Nancyng Jenkins.'

'Was it so hard for you to say her name? You may not appreciate her ethnicity, but surely you've been raised to exhibit the minimal duty of common humanity.' She lowered her head, apologised again before sobbing took over. Unsteadiness became a stumble as she told of feeling faint.

Fearing she would topple over, Newton motioned her towards a davit stanchion. Henrietta leaned against it, then faded towards him, unable to remove the dizziness. She didn't respond to the question of wellbeing, her head seeking his shoulder and resting momentarily before she straightened and stood at arm's length.

'Thank you.'

He remained in the same place, observing a complexion almost matching the colour of the superstructure.

'Are you sure?'

'I apologise again. Like my black moods, it's something that's been happening lately without me having much say in the matter, and who knows what, ah, it is, its cause.'

He waited as she took in several breaths before conciliatingly, 'I was a little harsh. It's just that it would be helpful to know what possessed you to make those allegations in the first place? We can leave explanations for another time.'

'No, it won't do,' she said, her colour improving. 'You deserve more than paltry excuses and I shall try to provide some context.' She began slowly, before an unexpurgated release detailed her experiences in Switzerland, ascribing them to the appearance of a mysterious illness she had acquired, coupled with personal setbacks that she left unattributed to any particular event. Severe depression was consequent upon the condition and she was suicidal. It had baffled the best specialists Harley Street could offer. A wrenching instance of foolish shoplifting, she said, led to a psychiatrist's recommendation that a cruise to Australia might help take her mind back to a place where she could exist without fear and feel needed for who she was. She concluded by saying that the absence of genuine filial affection felt throughout her life was at the forefront of the problem. That the doctors weren't taken with this rationale had left her despairing.

'To be frank, Miss Onions, I've seen little open signs of it on this ship,' Newton responded, unconvinced that her account was a recitation of the whole truth. 'I'm sorry but you've loving parents, surely, and that's a sight more than some other much less-privileged young people of your age.'

'Have you ever been in a house having all that money could buy, surrounded by two people who outwardly make a show but, in actuality, abhor each other? One is jealous for who knows what, while the other attaches to me in a manner that I don't fully comprehend. Perhaps it was his way of showing love or even needing it himself, but I never felt it to be the right sort of love a child might be expected to receive. It became quite strange.'

He directed his gaze towards the west, eyeing the crimson light that gilded through the clouds before turning to her. There was a softening, unlike anything she'd perceived before in this usually detached man. She waited for a few moments to see whether it was an illusion before speaking. 'You do understand, I trust, what I'm saying.'

As formally as he could, Newton replied, 'No person with a heart would be other than distressed to hear such a cry from any human being, Miss Onions, and in someone so young.'

'Not that young, actually. Still, it's been hard trying to cope with, well, everything,' she replied, taking in the horizon for the first time.

'It's not my intention to treat you unfeelingly. I have to say, though, that many children have no parents and a terrible start and yet they seem to get on and live their lives as they mature, like those poor mites in times gone by who came through the Foundling Hospital in London. Have you heard of it?"

'I don't, I haven't, what does it do?'

'For nearly two hundred years it has taken in children left and placed there as babies. "Bastards", they were called. I read of one young girl who was deposited there by her mother as a suckling. She experienced an upbringing no child should ever have to suffer, no one to kiss her good night or tuck her in or read a story. No one to give love and none upon whom she could bestow hers. In was abject loneliness, not for a season, but one that endured for many. She rose and broke the chains to become a famous soprano.'

'Hers must have been a terrible cross to bear. What happened, how did she survive and achieve so much?'

The question went unanswered. 'Absence of family and having nothing except a roof over her head, miserable food, sometimes harsh keepers and poverty is a bad start. That's not said to downplay your regrettable illness, but you have a family and, whether you think they love you or not, they demonstrate their concern by caring for you and taking you on luxury sea journeys, something of which foundlings could only dream.'

'Are *your* parents still alive, Colonel Newton?' she asked, her directness unsettling.

'My advice, Miss Onions,' he straightway responded, 'is

you should thank God for what you have or count yourself lucky.'

'You're right to say so. I've led a selfish existence. Hearing about the girl you mentioned does suggest so, no matter what I feel inside. A wonder that *she* climbed above it.'

Newton saw the words as coming from within her but, fearing the perilous waters into which the conversation was being piloted, put an end to it. 'I still haven't covered my three miles, so if you'll permit me—'

'Can I just have one more turn around the ship with you?'

'Yes, as long as you refrain from asking personal questions.'

'I promise. You are wise and that's why you're a bachelor, as everyone speculates.'

Newton couldn't shield a trace of amusement. 'Well, no one will ever know what I am, nor should they, Miss Onions.'

It was another statement intended to foreclose discussion, but she was undaunted. 'As I said, you should realise I'm not as young and silly as you think,' the last few words rushing by, her breathing faster through his quickened pace. 'Would you like to hazard a guess?'

Her request to ease down was given only slight notice. 'I didn't hear you.'

Louder, she declared, 'Today I turned twenty-one.' He marched on as if trying to lose her. 'Not even a "happy birthday"?'

Finally, his sigh signalled an easing off. 'If it pleases you, best wishes, Miss Onions.'

'There's one thing I didn't mention.'

'Far be it for me to stop you mentioning anything, young lady,' this time coughing.

'Not wanting you to think I was trying to elicit your sympathy as a means of excusing my bad behaviour to you and Mrs Jenkins.'

'Oh, really, Miss Onions?' he replied, as her voice fell behind him again. In resignation, he came about and advanced towards her.

'I'm also one of those bastards, as you so finely reminded me, rescued in fact from the Foundling Hospital, but my parents don't know that I know.'

'You're what?' he asked in astonishment.

'Yes, another lie. One big lie, I am. The ignominy of my real status was the motivation to seek you out. I saw something in you, now even stronger because you're acquainted with the institution.' She wrung her hands as if their entwining might muster confidence. 'And how can it be, really, that you know of it?'

Her shrewdness alarmed him and she took in his reaction before continuing.

'Underneath that granite exterior you're a decent man, Colonel. I'm desperate to get away from my,' she paused, her emotions precarious, 'lecherous – yes, that's what I think he is – father, and my mother is verging on I don't know what because of it.' She paused again to gauge his reaction. 'Are you able to assist me?'

Henrietta sat down on a splicer's bench. They were in the teeth of a wind that habitually met the ship's bow under full power. 'Can you, please, as a decent human being?'

'I need to think about what you're saying, and you surely must apprehend that I would harbour some scepticism. You seek my help on something almost unimaginable, you ask me about foundlings, then claim to be one. Putting it kindly, I don't understand you, Miss Onions. And why did you occasion me so much trouble?'

She sprang up again taking his wrists. 'A cry for help, stupid attention-seeking, I don't know. He has always sort of preyed upon me as no adult man should, let alone one's father, even if not a blood one. It messed with my mind. You're the first person I've ever told the truth to even after all those doctors, and how could I ever tell them anyway?'

Newton looked on the piteous figure, hands at her side and shoulders drooped, tear-laden eyes imploring for kindness and belief in her. 'Come here, young woman.' She didn't move until he stepped close enough and then sank into his arms. He held her for some minutes as she cried.

'I'm such a silly fool,' she finally said, and thereupon he told her that he understood, would do what he could to help and try to come to terms with all she must be feeling.

'Thank you, sir. I'm afraid there's one other thing, and I'm sorry for throwing it all at you simultaneously, but if I don't say it now you will really believe I'm making all this up.'

'What is it, my dear?' he asked, gently stilling a tear on her cheek.

There was a moment's hesitation. 'I, I have been trying to locate my birth mother for several years. That's the real reason

I'm on this odd cruise, though it suited my father anyway. After endless enquiries, it's certain that she's living in South Africa. And that's where I intend to disembark both from this ship and forever from the life I have lived to this point. I want to know my mother, be with her and nowhere else.'

*   *   *

The evening witnessed a small celebration in the dining saloon. The decorative cake was wheeled out with the requisite number of candles. In an act of composure that renewed questions within Newton, Henrietta, wearing a sleeveless mauve gown stood beside, though apart, from Sir Lionel, who made a short speech. He presented her with a string of pink pearls and a multi-encrusted diamond signet ring which he made great moment of placing on the small finger of her right hand. Newton followed every action intently and, when she glanced in his direction for a fraction of a second, he understood.

To the strains of *Why was she born so beautiful* she, with her head arched forward over her bodice, expended three breaths in extinguishing the candles. The birthday chorus rang out with Sir Lionel's off-key voice prominent in its rendition. All joined in the spirit of the occasion and a loud round of applause followed. The bandsman announced a waltz and her father claimed precedence. Henrietta maintained a discreet distance from him, resisting any attempt to bridge it.

Newton divided himself between conversing softly with Charlotte about what she could expect of the prevailing English weather in the 'old country' and evincing a conspicuous indifference to the celebrations. His demeanour prompted an intervention from her mother.

'Still unable to forgive her?' she asked, arching her eyebrows.

He felt a little like a man holding a guilty secret. His reply had to be crafted to cover the possibility that their interaction on deck had not gone entirely unnoticed, yet any declaration that might be inconsistent with his demeanour could be his undoing in this discerning woman's eyes.

'I, ah, haven't actually given Miss Onions much further thought after some earlier attempts by her at appeasement when I was on my pre-dinner turn.'

'She *spoke* to you?'

'Yes.'

'What, without—'

'Rather, with apologies. Was that what you meant?'

'No. Go on, this *is* a turn up.'

'Yes, apologies to both of us. You'd be interested also to hear that she left a note under your door and would follow it up in person, if that was acceptable to you.' Mrs Jenkins appeared puzzled. 'Am I being told by your reaction that you've not received such a communication?'

'I haven't seen any such thing as yet. Charlotte, would you mind going back to our cabin and check if an envelope has arrived?' She returned in a few minutes.

'Well, I was wrong. Right, as foretold, though I'm certain it wasn't there when we left for dinner. Anyway,' she said cheerily, 'Not worried about the timing, although I guess you probably are.'

He embraced a short glance before saying casually, 'Perhaps I shouldn't be, but I think you have called it yet again, Mrs Jenkins.'

She paid him an interrogative smile. 'How long did she walk with you?' Before he could answer, Charlotte excused herself to accept an offer to join a tap-dancing session from one of the other girls.

'How long?' He cleared his throat several times. 'About fifteen minutes or so with a break in between.'

'Between what?'

'The walking. She, well, was pretty apologetic, really. I wasn't surprised by anything she said,' he went on elliptically. 'A fairly mixed-up sort of girl, that one.'

'Not a girl anymore after tonight, Colonel, but I give her credit for that. It's an action that misperceives the adverse opinion I formed about our Miss Onions.'

'She definitely hasn't approached you though, has she?'

'I would have told you,' her voice evincing some irritation. 'Hello, I think you've spoken a little early.' The subject under discussion had arrived and stood beside their table.

'Mrs Jenkins, without him overseeing me, I'm sincerely sorry for my behaviour towards you.' She offered her hand and it was taken.

'Congratulations on attaining your majority. Sit down,

Henrietta,' said Nancyng. 'Good grief, never has a person been so apologised to. Colonel Newton has conveyed the earlier regret you extended through him. I've read the note and—'

'I suppose,' she hesitated, 'he's also given you some background, but I'm not offering any excuses. The apology is unreserved,' she said with convincing impact.

'No background at all. Accepted, and that's where we shall leave it, Henrietta, and again, my best wishes on your birthday.'

Sir Lionel strode to their table, his face fixed in cheery pride, crimsoned by the effects of liquor. He emptied the glass of champagne in his hand and returned it to a lingering steward. 'I was going to be bold enough to suggest that we might all join in on the dance floor to form a sort of passenger and crew conga line. Mrs Jenkins?' He took her hand and, with the other, motioned towards his daughter. 'Colonel, I'm certain that Henrietta would regard this occasion as an opportunity to make amends in the spirit of shipboard collegiality.'

'Henrietta has reached adulthood, Sir Lionel, and will mark her own chart in the future, as I'm sure you'd want this young woman to do. As far as I'm concerned, she has nothing for which to make amends.'

Chapter 8 – *No Such Bliss*

The unexpected visitor gave Newton more to think about than the penultimate stages of the Magnus phenomena. During the time spent waiting for her mother, the colonel had been kept entertained with Charlotte's mix of merriment and awareness. Glimpses of an Australian accent stirred happy recollections, extended by her thirst of events in the lead-up to Singapore's capitulation.

'I always love war history and have been taught some of it. We were told that it was a heroic defence against overwhelming odds. Was it that straightforward?'

'A perceptive observation for one so young, Charlotte.'

A yearning to know more about his assignments over that period was proving to be unquenchable. 'Did you have to fight the Japanese in hand-to-hand combat?'

'Good heavens, none of that, too much of a coward.'

'But didn't you say some snuck back into Malaya and lived in the jungle, so you must know more—'

Nancyng's arrival occasioned opportune relief and prompted an acerbic observation.

'After last night's party, I was wondering if Onions might have collared you for a gin and tonic but, meantime, your daughter has ever been the penetrating inquisitor.'

'Good for her. Oh, and there's the clock. Well, for you, anyway, that's lateness. Give a woman some latitude, Colonel. Charlotte, are you going to join the others in a game of Monopoly?'

'Aw, alright, I suppose, and thank you, sir, for telling me of the thrilling escape just before the Japanese came, the Australian man left behind, a happy ending, so nice. And I would like to be told more, *Mother.*'

'Miss Jenkins!' She sprang to her feet, pretending to be miffed. 'So what was that about; a foretaste of daring I'm soon to hear, or are you going to add a postscript?' she asked, eyes gleaming provocatively, her twang not nearly as evident as Charlotte's.

'Had you been able to tear yourself away from the great mercantile baron and his other passenger favourites you might have been first to hear that little story. It's completely irrelevant to the balance of Magnus' doings and I shan't be repeating it.'

'I'll contrive to cajole it out for the second half of this voyage after you've listened to me.'

'You're welcome to renew the application but by that time I doubt you'll bother.'

'Alright, Mr Colonel Never-Depart-From-Precedent

Newton. No mean feat enduring Sir Lionel and his disordered wife, not that she contributed anything, spending most of the time, when not ogling me, staring into space.'

'Was there rudeness?'

'I didn't take it as such. There's something much deeper inside that triumvirate.'

'What do you mean?'

The pungency of his query was left to hover as, eyebrows active, she said, 'I'm perfectly aware that you've noticed the family unit, as have I, but it's of no especial interest to me trailing off in that direction right now.'

'Certainly,' Newton's tone corrective, 'I wasn't seeking to do that. We're nearly at the conclusion of the Magnus and Esrelle story, having already wrestled with the notion of whether you might trouble yourself to drop by for the denouement.'

'How you can change and deflect, just like that,' she returned, snapping her fingers. 'You're possessed of one of the driest senses of humour ever attributed to mankind. And if I didn't know you better, I might think your interest in my movements could have another explanation.'

Newton remained po-faced. 'Since you raised it, what sort of fellow is Sir Lionel, um, from your – a woman's perspective?'

'He can be charming. Not without bombast, as one might have expected, even given the climb-down following her retraction. There's a certain, ah—'

'Familiarity?'

'You were watching last night. I felt your eyes you may be sure. I'd go a little further than that and say he wasn't too restrained in the clinches.'

'He touched you?' Newton asked with feeling.

'Well, no,' she replied questioningly, 'at least not in the manner of overt impropriety, rather a blustery, negligent sort of fashion, consistent with a man accustomed to brooking no opposition. An ineffectual wife hovering within yards of him failed to exert any restraint. She's used to that existence, I'll vouch. And it was rather odd that his daughter refrained from displaying the jewellery so soon after its ostentatious presentation.'

'You weren't the only one to notice.'

'She seemed to withdraw to parts unknown. I didn't see the young woman for the rest of the evening. Did you happen upon her at all?'

'No. I became the near-mute supplicant for Mr McConsker's prophecies about the imminent political collapse of Malaya and the spread of communism throughout South-East Asia. I did hear someone suggest that Henrietta could have retired early because she was indisposed or something. She never looked comfortable, and it followed on from being somewhat giddy on the open deck.'

'Mm, may have been the same bug that hit Charlotte. If it is, she'll be grounded for a day. Now, are we going to return to the tumultuous Magnus realm near to the part for which I've been waiting?'

'Just so. If my recollection serves me, I was on the point

of revealing that formal encounter with Esrelle, in fact the day before they were due to get married. By this stage I was at Sandhurst with him. A few of us decided we would send the boy off in the customary manner for his final night of freedom. We had managed to persuade the tentative bridegroom in waiting to repair to the wet canteen and—'

'Were the buxom wenches behind the bar in on the action?' she winked.

Newton chuckled. 'Such pedigree is unknown at Sandhurst, though wenching is coming up, as you'll soon hear. Some of the chaps had put quite a few pints under their belts before Magnus literally broke out into a cold sweat and started to shake after realising that he'd forgotten where he had put the ring. As best man—'

'Oh, you failed to mention the appointment.'

'Another memory lapse on my part even though I recall your anticipating it.'

A warm grin and shake of her head followed. 'Yes, Gray?'

'As future custodian of the priceless band up to the point of its production for the Vicar's blessing, it was my concern, too. Magnus wasn't used to drink, and two were more than enough. He rummaged through his pockets as if some ill spirit had taken hold. I asked him to trace back through the sequence of events. Esrelle had found the style of ring she wanted. That was the previous day. He remembered her saying that he had to "guard it with his life", believed she placed the box in his hand but was unable to recall what he did with it. Well, bucks' night suspended, he and I raced back to his quarters and turned the place inside out to no avail.

'On the eve of his marriage, obviously he couldn't face her with an admission that he had misplaced it. He begged me to try the only option left for, if that failed, a new ring had to be procured in record time and would be impossible to replicate, as it was in no sense plain. He told me she was meeting some girlfriends from London who were treating her to a private soirée at the *Whistler's Arms* pub. Back at the canteen, having tipped them of my intentions, the lads assured me that he'd soon forget about it and be well looked after in my absence.

'I hailed a taxi to that location, a ten-minute journey away, and was a little puzzled to learn from the innkeeper that no such "ladies' night" function was taking place. He confirmed Esrelle was a guest and that she had left with a few girls about an hour earlier to a party but didn't know where. Incredibly, as the taxi was taking me back to give Magnus the bad news, the chatty driver started gabbing on about having run some "mighty tipsy" girls from the *Whistler's* to a dance venue a few miles away. Naturally, I enquired of him whether they gave any indication of their plans and he said it was pretty obvious that it was some sort of a "hens' event", as he put it with a twinkle. I took the punt and he dropped me off there.'

'And did you ask him anything else?' the inflection in tone unmistakeable.

'Mrs – ah, I mean, Nancyng, your insatiable curiosity is only outdone by a sagacious capacity for prophesying.'

'Blather on Gray, knowing your form as I do.'

'No comment, but a concessional "yes" to meet your intuition. This fellow was from the East End, a real character. I asked him whether the bride announced herself. He told me that she did most of the talking, being tighter than the rest of the bunch put together.

'The red hair started it, and his memory was jogged as she pattered away. He could've sworn she had been a customer on a prior occasion some years ago when he was driving in London. My antennae were poised to elevate but I merely observed that he would pick up so many fares and all would seem alike in this type of occurrence. He countered by saying the lady in question became one who was unforgettable.

'When he arrived at her flat, she afforded the cabman a kind "thank you" and began walking away, oblivious to his call for the five bob. As he caught up to her, she opened her blouse and offered herself on the spot. Well, not quite all of herself but, to attempt his accent and quote him, "Mate, the coppas calls it 'gobblin', and with a missus at 'ome, guvnor, I wasn't one bit ruddy interested."

'She was somewhat blunt at the rebuff. "S'Cockney arse'ole. Here's your effin' money!"

'She threw the coins down on the pavement, stormed inside and slammed the door. As you might envisage, the picture of the woman on the train and the harridan from the cab grew as close to one and the same as turf planted in squares amid a green field after two weeks' growth. I resisted the temptation to ask for a fuller description in case he began to suspect me of being a pervert or something, so I made up a story about looking for a group of like-minded girls who might be interested to meet up with some soldiers at a party.

'"You won't go wrong with that lot, mate", he chortled. Asked if he could recall what they were wearing, he replied that he only noticed the one who he believed was in his cab that other time. Quoting him as near as I can, "Dressed in a black numba that left nothin' to the imaginin's."

'He offered to wait but I told him not to bother as it might take a while. I gained the impression he had become more interested in assisting my quest to locate those females than touting for fresh business.

'The place was crowded, it being a Friday night. A reckless band blurted out offensive noise and the mission of finding her appeared futile. After five minutes or so, I needed to get away from the din before my head blew apart.'

'You seemed more tolerant of the ship's ensemble the last couple of nights. Perhaps older age brings liberality rather than the reverse,' offered his listener sarcastically.

'I rather think it's the quality of the musicians and the tunes being played, or rather murdered. They were a ragged outfit.'

'If you'd been swinging with a sensual female, you wouldn't have been troubled with the music. Stop looking indignant and resume, Colonel Blimp!'

'I was on the point of leaving when the music suddenly broke off, with the ensuing racket sounding like a lorry losing a load of paint tins on a sharp corner. There followed a good deal of shouting and screaming. A couple of men were fighting and a female in a lacy black top was in the thick of it. At first I thought she was inciting the protagonists, but she seemed to bring them both to their senses before the muscle arrived, quelling the disturbance.

'I was pretty certain it was the woman on the train and one of the scrappers was the individual who was with her. The band was ordered to resume and I found a discreet vantage point.

'By now, the woman's friends were milling around. She said something to the older fellow and, indignantly, he strode to the exit. Gesticulating towards her companions as if asking them to wait, she ran after him. At the doors, the couple embraced and went outside for more. I know because I followed, spying them in a lively clinch, petting and kissing. There was no let-up in their ardency on a zigzag path to his car, and in it, before driving off.'

'She just left her friends cold?'

'Apart from the hand signals, something was said, but I've no idea what, on account of all the din. The ubiquitous cabbie was outside. At my instigation he seemed only too ready to whip me back to the hotel, and at speed, after I acquainted him with what had happened. He was enjoying himself rather more than I was, let me say.'

'That dash seemed a wasted effort and his disappointment was as palpable as mine when there was no sign of them. I waited a bit before giving up. After paying him off, a quarter of an hour passed and still nothing at the *Whistler's Arms*. I was at a loss as to what to do next. I couldn't hang around indefinitely but would appear awfully silly returning to the bucks' bash empty-handed, to say nothing of any awkward questions that might follow. Something told me that I should register as a guest and one way or the other get to the bottom of the missing piece of jewellery—'

'The more so to satisfy your curiosity about Magnus' future wife.'

Newton squirmed a little. 'That done, I settled into a little reading arbour adjacent to the staircase where comings and goings might be observed. I'd just finished an article in *Punch* when, arm-in-arm, she and the man with the big ears, bald-pated little head and beady eyes, came down the stairs. I followed them to his car, secreted around the back. My detective work was fairly amateurish in those days and as luck—'

'Not now though.'

'You might well say that, Mrs Jenkins, but I could never voice such self-praise.'

'My lord, you're so snooty.'

Newton's features tightened as if rebuked. 'And you can't resist delivering reminders, Nancyng. So, then she waved him off and I flew back inside. On her return, boldness, given the time of night, as opposed to caution, was my guide. I asked if her name was Esrelle. She became defensive, answering with a careless, I suppose, inebriated, "And who wants to know?" The voice defiant, it was a pose belying her looks while viewing me with a mixture of suspicion and inquisitiveness. She assumed more the appearance of a collared bag-snatcher contriving an explanation on the run.'

'Sorry to interrupt, but she didn't recognise you, from the train?'

He rubbed his chin before replying. 'It seemed not, well no sign or suggestion.'

'Probably the situation, drink and all that, and you wearing a uniform.'

'Yes, all makes sense. After announcing who I was, a remarkable turnaround ensued. She grew attentive and sober. Something suggested that playing the innocent might disarm her, so I said I'd come from Magnus' "last night of freedom drinks" as best man envoy after he'd mislaid the wedding ring, that he was wracked with anguish and despair and became desperate to do what he could to recover the precious item. I apologised for inconveniencing her the night before the nuptials.

'She descended into a fit of raucous laughter, took my face between her hands, kissed both cheeks, started gushing how good it was to meet me after so long and fulminating about all she'd heard concerning Magnus' "blood brother". Literally moments after making out with an occasional lover of some longevity, Esrelle was now spouting about her future husband and how he was such an adorable, absent-minded duffer, as steady as Lady Macbeth importuning her husband to do away with Duncan. It was a marvel to behold. And there was something else that I found amazing.'

'She made eyes at *you*,' Nancyng Jenkins offered with her head inclined.

'I wouldn't quite put it so, but it was evident how electrifying she could be to men without needing a prompt. I was asked to wait a minute, she adding coquettishly that it wouldn't be proper to have me going to an "anticipatory bride's boudoir", before returning with a tiny receptacle that she had intended her bridesmaid to deliver over to me. She opened the box and put the ring in my hand, closing my fingers around it. I thanked her, and she promptly directed her lips onto mine not so dispassionately before telling me to pass on to Magnus a taste of what he was likely to expect.

'"It's your solemn task to ensure he's in tiptop shape on the morrow so as to do his duty by his virgin bride."

'They were her actual words. My, I marvelled at how she almost persuaded me to regard them as authentic. And that's how I came to meet Esrelle, simply extraordinary.'

'No one forgets a shyster, more so the skittish variety,' Nancyng offered in derision.

'I began the long walk back to the canteen, for there was no way I could have risked staying there after such a ruse. Magnus was making a grave mistake and my gut wanted to prevent it. But the moment in which his life was so fully invested loomed just hours away and telling him about what had transpired became unthinkable. Though not a religious man, I must admit to uttering a bland plea into space that by some miracle it would all work out for him.'

'You've never believed in God?' Newton considered the question at some length. 'That's not asking much is it?'

'No. At that time I rarely went to church but we all sort of—'

'Agnostic perhaps?'

'Well, not being one to be pigeonholed, though I came to a surer belief after a man I had known for a short time effectively gave up his life for a relative stranger in rather exceptional circumstances. He had a grounded belief rather than a vapid one.'

'Yes, and?' Her hopes that he would expand were left unrealised.

'I digressed. They were married at eleven o'clock on that first day of spring, 1926. Esrelle didn't bat an eyelid at me when I duly produced the ring. I should have mentioned that this was the day after his graduation from Sandhurst. While a fellow-inductee and myself held umbrellas aloft, the newlyweds exited the little chapel within the grounds, Magnus beaming with pride as if he'd just won first prize in a grand lottery. They breached a guard of honour made up of other officer-graduates braving inclement weather and we stood back cheering them away, me rather more contained, as they set off in a chauffeur-driven car.

'They honeymooned for a week at a seaside shack in Kent. Magnus told me that it was the happiest he'd ever felt in his life. After the first couple of days, it became unusually warm and the fields where they walked, talked and ran were sprinkled with the season's first appearance of bluebells.

They picked little sprays of them and he wove some into her hair. Magnus was captivated, never once considering that she was other than *his* virgin bride. It was a splendid illusion and nothing from her past ever obtruded into their daily communion.'

'I can't feel anything but sorrow for this boy, the only description for one so naïve and vulnerable. I'm almost tempted to recreate the ending.'

'Anything you come up with now, whatever it might be, I'll vouch is best consigned to posterity, if only to appreciate how wrong you will be.'

'Well, I won't even try,' she responded with a toss of her head.

'Following return to the mundanity of duty and, for him, a terrible longing at being separated from his new wife, he was additionally demoralised at the army's inertia. Still no posting and, after three months of weekend visitation, the strains had begun to emerge. Their surfacing was aided by the inordinate dithering and incompetence on the administrative side. Andover was originally to be his placement, but that was countermanded. Esrelle's exhilaration after being notified of its confirmation by telegram was replaced by fury after receiving another the next day to say it was off.

'Almost immediately after this disappointment, Magnus was informed that he had been assigned to undertake a training course in Military Intelligence. It would take him to Scotland for a month. She was annoyed by this commission and railed against the establishment for its indifference to their marital life.

'"How can we ever have a family if the brigadier's lording it over you and keeping us in separate beds?" she whined, rolling away from him to sit on the edge of the only marital one they owned, smoking and indulging a bout of cursing. It left Magnus wide-eyed, not the least because she seemed unable to appreciate the irony of her own position in remaining at London.

'"I thought we weren't going to concern ourselves with this until we got on our feet," he replied shortly. Magnus became frayed at the timing of her remark. She was exasperated after an unsatisfactory coupling where he had been unable to effect coitus.

'Mortified, he stroked her hair. She twitched her shoulders and wriggled away from him, signalling a preference that he desist before descending into something he found hurtful; insinuating that her doctor had suggested his fertility was the one needing to be checked. Magnus' tearful recounting of her words had me almost as upset.

'"We have made love at times when I've been ovulating, as I am now, and damn well told you so, and it's not happening, as you weren't interested. Don't you find me to your liking anymore?"

'He was both humiliated and perturbed at the thought of occasioning offence, but she rebuffed placatory overtures and attempts at a resumption of intimate touch were firmly refused.

'Magnus pleaded forgiveness with expressions of wanting her, admitting he had no idea that making babies was something that they were even trying to do at that time. In turn he was met with a statement that she meant so little to him that he didn't know her fertility cycle and wasn't connecting with her needs. She fled from the room, showered and dressed.

'Venturing to suggest that it might be a little early returning to London as he watched her gathering a few things together, he was visited with another stern rebuke. She announced to being "heartily sick and tired" of all army rigmarole, not her most coherent point, "bored and frustrated" with the impasse in their marital affections and complaining of the train travel, it taking over two hours to get to her front door. She was prone to exaggerate as a ploy to win sympathy, but Magnus held his peace.

'"Some *home*, as we haven't yet set up the hint of a *home sweet home*. From now on, how about we say 'digs'?"

'He insisted on walking her down to the station and did everything he could to soothe his volatile wife. "I'll try and postpone the course and do the next intake in four months' time. Esrelle, please, we need to be together. And, yes, I'll get the army doctor to check things out."

'"Oh, don't cancel your bloody manoeuvres on my account. Get them over and done with."

'The tension during that awkward and unusually brisk pace she made to Camberley railway left him feeling sick. Once on the platform, he held her in a tight embrace and she remained limp, telling him they weren't child lovers anymore and he needed to grow up. That jibe cut him deeply, but there was more.

'"A real man understands his wife's needs, not merely the physical, but the maternal, when it comes to the natural instinct of a woman wanting to bear and raise children. The past is the past, but I hurt so much sometimes, if you must know."

'He begged forgiveness and was even pushed to remind her of the wedding priest's retelling of "wonderful times and then times of trial". The goodbye shredded his nerves. Supplanting her lips, she inclined a cheek, not simply made cold by the dampness of her tears but devoid of giving, bent, as she was, on boarding the train and even steering clear of his wave. The guard's shrill whistle drowned out any bedraggled hope for a "goodbye", his name or even a last glimpse of her. Esrelle's preference for keeping her seat was unequivocal confirmation of her withdrawal from him and, after this, Magnus sunk into desolation.

'He was confiding in me more often now. After hearing my thoughts about what he should do next, Magnus chose not to risk adding information about his fertility to an army file, even if outside consultation took longer than the in-house pathway. It came much sooner than expected. While in Scotland, he received the shattering advice by the post from a private specialist.

'Magnus rang me immediately. I knew he couldn't possibly admit to infertility. He resolved to fudge the issue by nominating delay if she happened to raise it after his return from Edinburgh. Beset by fears she might forever be lost to him, he trusted to the vows so recently pleaded to her in understanding, recalling the girl he once knew still remained somewhere inside the increasingly fickle Esrelle.

'But this wasn't to be his only dilemma. Perhaps driven by such a major personal setback, the young officer's star sputtered further during the practical interrogation phase of his post-graduate course in the Highlands. Magnus was given the news that he would need to re-sit the examination when interviewed by his commanding officer, Colonel Tweddle-Wright, on his return. It being the first time he'd failed a test, he was beside himself.

'"Shame you've not quite got the ticker, Sansim," bombast his favoured manner of address. "From all the reports about how clever you are, I thought you'd have topped that class. What's ailing you, man? Troubles on the home front I'm bound to wonder, given all that travel the little woman endures so graciously?"

'Magnus, who had never taken to Tweddle-Wright from their first salute, intuited the commiseration as utterly insincere and not without ulterior motive. Though preferring to leave socialising to others, more so now that Esrelle was in his life forever, Magnus was a considerate fellow who related to almost all of his peers. But not this character, whom he regarded with scorn, and about whom I'd heard one or two other things as well.'

'Had *you* encountered him much?' Nancyng asked thoughtfully.

The question seemed to take Newton by surprise. 'Ah, not really, but there was barracks talk that he was something of a sneak who enjoyed the discomfort he meted out to recent inductees by unannounced visits to, and inspections of, their quarters late at night. Even more significantly from the viewpoint of Magnus, Tweddle-Wright showed an unusual degree of inquisitiveness, bordering on an abstruse interest, in his and Esrelle's interpersonal situation. He seemed to enjoy peering into the nuances of relationships those under him had with their wives and girlfriends, masking this odd propensity by pretending to be concerned about their wellbeing and arguing that it affected general morale.

'For Magnus, insolent questions, as they were, and infuriating him to the point of tempting a response that he would have later regretted, he exercised his notorious and admirable restraint, recognising the constriction of rank. And his course failure also served to stymie any reaction that might have other ramifications.

'And profound apologies, I overlooked some highly pertinent background. The CO had already met Magnus' wife—'

'Yes, I wondered,' interposed Nancyng.

'Quite so. They'd run into the Tweddle-Wrights at the railway café within Camberley. A latching sort of rapport was on garish display between the couple and

Esrelle as if it was a meeting of old acquaintances after a lengthy separation. She was a masterful tactician, as you've seen already, when it came to imbuing favourable first impressions. Magnus, who told me that he felt like a ghost the whole time, winced at her chummy and cosying incaution, though he would never admonish her.

'To Tweddle-Wright's prying about the young couple's marital situation, his subordinate told him that they were managing well enough.

'It was a typically pared reaction. Knowing Magnus, I could hear the firmness in his voice with a clear intention of stymying any trespass into intimate territory, but it was brushed off with high-handed indifference.

'"Glad to hear it, Sansim, even if I'm far from being convinced that's the uncut version. Your business, doubtless. Now let me see, hell of a fine young woman, that *Estelle*, who my wife found enchanting. You and she will dine with Maeve and I next Saturday evening when, no doubt, she will be on visitation indulgences."

'He corrected Tweddle-Wright on the name and pleaded that she was often exhausted on arrival from London. A dressing down followed his protestations.

'"I won't accommodate any answer in the negative, Sansim. One thing you must understand about army ways is that your commanding officer is not only always right, he's the person at which you click heels when a summons is directed your way. An invitation from me is a privilege afforded to the few. Harken to it and consider yourself fortunate. You know where I live, and we shall expect you for cocktails at 1830. Good morning."

'For the next few days pending her visit, Magnus was not himself. He even got testy with me once or twice but quickly apologised, explaining why. The morning she was due to arrive dawned cold and miserable, a throwback to an ice-blowing late-January day. As if to enliven his soul, if not his body, he plunged into a bath filled with cold water that had eked its way from semi-frozen pipes. Dressing in his best uniform, Magnus was determined to show off the man in whom he thought she would want to believe.

'He was encouraged by her acquiescence in arriving at lunchtime Friday, rather than the evening, when he told her he had been given the day off after extended duty, but a meagre embrace as he greeted her suggested his expectations had been misplaced. Dark lines under her eyes and lethargy at seeing him for the first time in weeks made Magnus reticent about disclosing the social engagement at that time, or even later, given Esrelle slept until dinner. She ate well and drank several glasses of burgundy from a bottle he had purchased to celebrate their reunification. Lassitude returned as he caressed her and, when she was unresponsive to further blandishments, he desisted.

'Esrelle protested ongoing distress the next morning when he enquired how she was feeling and what she might like to do for the day.

'"Can't you understand me? Why is it you ignore the signs when I'm fertile and haven't the slightest degree of empathy when that other time of the month sets me low?"

'Later, delivering coffee and toast to her bedside, he made cursory mention of the invitation, hastening to add that it was neither mandatory, nor demanding compliance in the event of indisposition, and that he would deliver an apology. She sprang up, pushing to one side the half-eaten breakfast as though a gong had been struck bidding her to an audience with royalty.

'"You'll do no such thing." She glided to the dressing table, brushed her hair and made a series of movements at the mirror, tilting her head to the left, the right, up, then down, revolving her lips and studying her nails. "Why didn't you tell me sooner? Colonel Harry and his lady wife, lor' save me, looking such a fright and nothing to wear. Mus, you'd better amuse yourself somehow today because I need to find a beauty parlour and buy an outfit."

'He was astonished at the alteration overtaking her. Once in their company, she pulled it off with exceptional aplomb for someone who had woken so out of sorts. Esrelle presented like a debutante at a county ball and enjoyed herself more than at any time since they're wedding. There was such an aura surrounding her, something Magnus had never quite appreciated. She was another person entirely, relished being noticed, admired and complimented upon.'

'He had fantasised that they would always remain loner children under their fairy mushrooms and in lolly houses,' remarked Nancyng Jenkins with a wink.

'That might be the pessimist's view of it. I think Magnus felt gladdened to be getting to know her more, hearing of life in London through what she relayed to their hosts rather than anything ever disclosed to him. She was no homebody and liked the theatre.

'Champagne was liberally dispensed and unveiled another facility, her more than passing familiarity with it, having little difficulty in emptying a glass before he had taken more than a quarter of his. She surprised him at how well she could hold her drink. When the moment called for it, Esrelle exhibited an admirable forbearance in being a model listener and compelling flatterer rather than some fatuous lush. Magnus really felt the novice, dithering husband just beginning to appreciate his vibrant, outgoing wife and yet frightened of what it portended.

'By the time they returned home, a tinge of light in the east had squeezed through their bedroom curtains. Rather than it serving as notice of the lateness of the hour and overcoming her, she exploded with sexuality. That, given the earlier remark about her cycle, was lost on him when I pointed it out. He said they made love as never before.

'When he finally awoke, Esrelle wasn't about. A scratched note was left for him saying that she had taken a walk and would return well before three, an astonishing hour to nominate. After the chimes rang thrice, Magnus had become anxious to see her before it was time to leave. Carrying her case like a lost waif, he surprised her in the High Street and the response was not what he expected. She seemed in another world, gaily humming a tune. Their conversation really stuck in my head:

"I said I'd be back. What the hell are you doing with my suitcase? That's private property and I'll thank you never to touch my things again."

"Sorry. I, I saw the time and packed it. You're sure to miss your train. Where have you been? I was worried."

"I told you I was going for a walk. You silly, foolish man, I can get the next train."

"But you told me that you hate catching that one because it stops at all stations and gets back to London so late."

"What's this now, are you conducting an interrogation? Well, go for it. From what I understand, you need the practice."

'That Esrelle knew stung the more because he couldn't remember specifically telling her what had brought about his "fail" mark for the course nor had he heard it mentioned by Tweddle-Wright. A belief that he must have told her collapsed when she hinted suggestively at "hearing something". Magnus knew that the host had been the culprit, but when and why? It bothered him.'

Nancyng Jenkins sat up suddenly. 'Seems the rather long walk took in the Tweddle-Wright's abode. Anyway, after that appalling revelation, I think it's time we all had a soothing round of deck golf.' On her feet, she offered her hand. 'Colonel Newton?'

He hadn't connected with her and became apologetic

after she repeated his name and said, 'Aren't you listening? Coming or not?'

He shook his head without meeting her eyes. 'Thanks for asking, but you go ahead. A stroll will better serve me.'

Chapter 9 – *The Consequence*

'You are, *were*, so aligned with Magnus,' remarked Mrs Jenkins. Newton hadn't shown for dinner and she had found him alone on the sundeck the following morning after missing him at breakfast. The remark drew a crafted response.

'But not so much as to see the pit into which he was sleepwalking, for I didn't intervene.'

'Could you have?' she added in a barely audible voice. 'Anyway, introspection may have sent you off for some respite from me, perhaps?'

He was thankful for the chance not to dwell on her proposition. 'It seems I can never get away for long, Nancyng Jenkins.'

'Mindful of my perseverance, you might like to end the suspense and favour me with the outcome. I have requested tea and scones, for two, by the way.'

'Good show. Well, yesterday, I told of one of those

ineffaceable recollections ending with Esrelle cutting Magnus to the quick.'

'Didn't I remark on the opportunity to learn something about his failings?'

'You have a telling recall and insight.'

'Not such as to match yours.'

'One day we shall debate the topic.' Opportunely, their morning tea arrived. She filled each cup and he buttered and jammed the scones.

'Thus,' he continued after his first bite was blended with the tea, 'that initial intermingling marked the start of a succession of such occasions hosted by the Tweddle-Wrights. Within a short period, these events became routine. Sometimes acquaintances of the hosts would join them, but that was more exception than rule and, even then, the others invariably called time before they did.

'Consequential sexual explosions ended after the second dinner party. He was becoming more frank with me now, Nancyng. Esrelle was spirited and not altogether unguarded when enjoying her drink. As they rarely had wine together, Magnus pondered whether his abstemious habits might need to be revisited, not least to the extent of his frowning on her imbibition.'

'He desperately wanted to please her. Have you ever had those feelings, Gray?'

'This isn't about *me*,' his reply cancelling the line of enquiry. 'Yet those thoughts of pleasing Esrelle were modified when he detected a waning of desire towards him as the weeks went by. None of this was consistent with her earlier decrees about wanting a child. The test results never came up for discussion. She was habitually tired on Fridays, but soon after Saturday lunchtime, busied herself in all manner of preparations for the evening ahead, taking especial care with choice of apparel and hairstyles.'

'Mrs Sansim had developed a penchant for the good things, as with her husband's stepmother.'

'Incisive recall for detail again, telling even, Mrs Jenkins. At these occasions, Tweddle-Wright was fond of voicing opinions on innumerable topics. His wife was no less expansive when an opportunity arose and far from anchored to her spouse's elbow.

'Magnus described her as a stoutish woman of average height, who appeared to fill, to the exclusion of all else, any garment she happened to wear. She exploited her best features and delighted in choosing shoes that exemplified incongruously tiny feet. Ashen-haired, she appeared older than her fifty years through a predilection for wearing gowns of gaudy décolletage. Within closer confines, her face was agreeable, if somewhat harsh. Arching greyish eyes worked ambivalence; welcoming, yet inclining to portray mistrust in roughly equal measure.'

'A dame with an agenda?'

'Patience, Nancyng. Her mouth was large, with top teeth so set as to make her lips appear fuller than they were. She had borne three children. Twin married daughters settled in Lincolnshire. A younger son was in his final year at a

London college.

'Initially, I probably need not say, Magnus was a casual and near-mute observer. Tripartite discussions tended to dominate. He didn't mind this, feeling uncomfortable in his commander's company. Expressing a keen interest in the colonel's magnificent library, he was encouraged to browse after dinner when the others talked on at length.

'Subtly, Maeve Tweddle-Wright began a drift in his direction. She would praise him over trifling matters, such as the ties and cufflinks he wore. Trending towards a spicy intimacy of voice when they were alone, the lady of the manor posited that anyone could pick him as of academic persuasion; that he was "the strong, contained type, philosophical and understated", the first dinner guest in living memory who, on entering their library, gravitated towards Shakespeare, Chaucer, Herodotus and Livy rather than military reading.

'He attempted to downplay the characterisations, suggesting that it was doubtful whether anyone saw him quite the same as she did, being something of an antiquarian when it came to reading and needing to pull himself away from an odd fascination with ancient history. From these lavish praises, Magnus felt compelled to avert his gaze, an action that seemed to encourage her to advance closer to him on the settee.

'A perpetual expression of inquisitiveness, accentuated by a tendency to widen her eyes and lift heavy brows became a feature she put to good use, seeming to revel in making him feel self-conscious, with constant urging that he go on before feigning, that's how he saw it, amusement when he did. He would try to turn the conversation her way with, "You read a little Mrs Tweddle-Wright?"

'"And will it make any difference if I say I don't, Lieutenant?" as she held her glass towards him. Magnus obliged by topping it to a level with which she demonstrated agreeability by tasting no small portion, the liquor taking some liberties in her dialogue.

'At this juncture she announced that it was high time they became less formal.

'"'Maeve' will ring nicely coming from you, young man. I've heard your wife sometimes adopting the contraction. I prefer 'Magnus' myself, and I'll be wrecked if I know why people want to strangle so distinguished a Christian name. My husband tells me that you have a guaranteed future; born officer, he says, will go places and all that."

'And "go places and all that" founded a suspicion that this was confected adulation. He continued a vain search for collateral subjects on which they might converse as her not-so-stealthy survey persisted. She told him not to worry about his "flop in Scotland", saying that there would be other courses and that he had proved himself to someone who matters. Rather than trying to work out whether she was expressing a personal opinion or echoing another's, he simply nodded. It was no further resolved when next she spoke.

'"Actually, I'm being rather a tease. Harold didn't say any

of that to me as we never talk shop, but it's an opinion I've formed after these months of dinners and chat."

'She slid ever closer to him and placed a manicured left hand on his arm. He was struck by the abundance of jewels squeezed onto her fingers illustrating how chunky they were and became more than a little unnerved when her red nails decided to forge impressions in his skin.

'So ostentatiously portrayed, Magnus felt a directed compliment might see her discontinue, pointing to a large ruby bordered by a crescent of diamonds on her wedding finger. He shuddered and she desisted, asking why he was so anxious and assuring him that she had never been known to bite, unless provoked. He was spared from making an answer by the appearance of Tweddle-Wright leading Esrelle into the room as might a martinet.

'"Now, what have you two bookworms been up to?" he asked, and Magnus later swore to me that husband and wife hosts seemed to exchange telephonic smirks.

'Replying as if he'd been caught red-handed unbuttoning a dowager's gown, Magnus muttered that he was at the point of requesting a loan of the books deposited on a sumptuous reading chair.'

'Or at the point of being propositioned with another kind of loan,' smirked Nancyng Jenkins, riveted by the library escapade.

Newton refused to be side-tracked. 'The telepathy continued with the colonel posing to Maeve whether it was best to part with their guests now for a few weeks or work out some other arrangement over port and cheeses. Tiring of the whole charade, Magnus remarked that he had some special duty in the morning, to which Esrelle was minded to offer, only just audibly, "Poor boy". Maeve spared additional embarrassment by suggesting that the book selection be sorted out on another occasion, perhaps even if he would find time to pop over for afternoon tea during the week, a sentiment endorsed by her husband.

'Still Esrelle wasn't finished; her speech slurred. "Mus so loves his bed, just when we're having such fun as well. Can't you excuse him from chores this once, Harry?" she implored in a manner indicative of more than one after-dinner sherry. Magnus told the Tweddle-Wrights that it was Esrelle's way of saying she was done in and that the literary offers were kindly appreciated. His assertiveness surprised all in that company and impressed Maeve.

'Not just the late-evening air was cool on the drive back to, and arrival at, their little flat, Esrelle being less than easy-going in manner as she undressed, with a pithy comment about him curtailing the entertainment. Inside, he was fuming at the familiarity adopted in addressing Tweddle-Wright, with only the time of night conspiring against an impulse to raise it. She, having rolled over, though as good as the widest points of the North Sea distant from him, made it definitive when the silence persisted to his turning off the light as her sounds of sleep became tinny.

'The following day, Esrelle kept to her bed and he was not going to question her claim of feeling out of sorts, regarding it as a matter peculiar to his wife's changeable moods. He found some afternoon relief when she got the earlier train, having insisted that he need not trouble himself to see her off.'

'This is building up for one great calamity. I can feel it, and yet I'm almost pleading to have you say that my thought processes are misconceived, surely?' Nancyng's breaking in allowed him to drink some iced water the steward had left after their tray had been removed. It refreshed her, too.

'Are you right to go on?' the touching query leaving him to further ponder the issue.

His head shook as if ridding itself of an extraneous recollection. 'Not much more to relate. Somewhat exceptionally, a number of evenings after, Esrelle telephoned him. Her greeting was as flat and mechanical as any Magnus had heard and he reacted like a white knight to an intuition that here was his wife for once eliciting his support on some troubling topic. Anticipation was no less acute on account of it being so late to be calling.

'He was given over to sentimentality, thanking her for phoning, saying he hated it when she left early and spoke of breaking inside every minute they were apart. The answer to a question as to whether there was a problem preceded a fit of coughing down the line. He told her that she needed to see the doctor about it. The conversation Magnus relayed thereafter was again one that never faded from my mind, her voice calm yet hesitant:

"I'm not bothered about things such as a minor cold. I've

something really important to tell you, Mus, and beg that you won't find this uncomfortable. I know the timing isn't right. Are you sitting down?"

"What's the matter, my darling, please say it?"

"Oh, you absent-minded, naughty chap, haven't you guessed? You're going to be a father. Isn't it the most wonderful hour and second of our lives?"

'He told me she shrieked with joy, heedless to his stony silence.'

Newton and Nancyng exchanged glances. 'Oh, my godfather, this must have been, to him, the equivalent of losing an only child before its heartbeat had been heard. I can't begin to visualise his distress,' she said. 'How was he at this point in telling you?'

'Outwardly, and perhaps inexplicably, he showed not the slightest emotion, this despite his guts, pardon the crudity, having been rearranged. There was a moment when he wanted to believe it was true, that somehow or other the doctor's assessment had been wrong, but it couldn't have been since, and I should have informed of this in proper order, so perturbed was Magnus by the first diagnosis that he had consulted a specialist who expressed one hundred per cent certainty.

'The phone fell from his grasp and he could no longer suffer the sound of the voice asking for him, so Magnus ripped the cord out of its socket. The following day he requested an urgent transfer to any overseas placement. He wrote a long letter to Tweddle-Wright setting out a multitude of reasons, physical and emotional, why he possessed no aptitude for Intelligence work and sought an unassigned position.

'More than ever, Magnus was dreading the inevitable interview with a commanding officer he had come to abhor.'

'And perhaps even suspected?'

'Perhaps, though he never voiced any suspicion. Much to his surprise, by four that same afternoon a letter arrived signed by a brigadier who, unknown to him, was acting down in Wright's position after he had been called to London on some urgent matter. His request, coinciding as it did with an immediate vacancy, had been granted with regret. He would go to Malaya Command and be assigned to one of the Straits' settlements. On Friday of that same week a ship was sailing for Singapore and he was given three days leave to organise his affairs, having regard to his marital status, before embarking.

'He had his kit packed and settled with the kindly landlady by leaving the furniture and a week's rent in consideration for terminating the arrangement early. Typical handy Magnus, he re-connected the phone just before leaving. I hadn't gone into the flat, really only marginally superior to a bedsitter that he secured on good terms after acquainting her with his marital situation and the irregular occupancy.

'With a few days to kill, Magnus opted to blot himself out on the first and couldn't remember how he managed to make his way home. He repeated the process at a different pub the next, although scaled down the quantum. On returning, this time in reasonable shape, he extended the intake from the security of his abode.

'The searing Thursday morning headache told him that alcohol disagreed with his constitution, but, by the afternoon, constraints had fallen away and Magnus resumed, if with marginally more circumspection.'

'Where were you, Gray, during this ghastly interlude?'

'He didn't tell me about the posting and avoided any contact during what would have been a harrowing situation,' came a worn reply. 'It was a wretched period, as you rightly point out, and why would he want to confess his folly?'

After a pause, Newton continued in a similar tone. 'Having gone past six o'clock when he settled at his flat, this time able to stand without props and showered, there was a knock at the door.

'It was his CO's wife, thrusting books into his arms with the familiarity of someone with whom he had only five minutes before been chatting. Taken aback at the sudden appearance, Magnus made plain his disgruntlement at the unsolicited attention by being offhand. For her part, there was blithe, insinuating dismissal.

'"Since you've been unable or unwilling to take up my offer, I brought over the ones which excited your interest. Might it be an imposition to request a cup of tea or even something a little stronger?" she persisted, advancing beyond the landing and forcing his retreat inside, where Maeve promptly made herself at home.

'He told her that she needn't have bothered, explaining

that returning them after a respectable time, if ever even, was an influential reason for not troubling herself. She ignored his pleas and a neat half dozen volumes eventually found their place on the sideboard as he scrambled about, lost at what next to do.

'Over-coiffured for an occasion purported only as a dropping off, Maeve eyed him covetously before remarking that she'd heard of his posting, suggesting teasingly that it was rather sudden. How she knew about it at first riled him, but her coincidental appearance gave all the proof he needed. She circled the tiny living room, paying scant attention to his excuse that an offer too good to knock back had presented itself from nowhere, Intelligence work proving a little beyond his interests, if not capabilities.

'The dour, moving to careless manner in which he was speaking rather alarmed her and she took him by the upper arm as if to stem his rocking about. Seeing the clutter of empty bottles in the far corner of the kitchen, she implied that he was more than a little drunk.

'He laughed off the suggestion, slewed away from her, grabbing one of the books and flipping through the pages. She steadied him again, saying that they didn't matter one iota. He picked the bundle up as if to deposit them outside and she, more gently this time, reassured him they wouldn't be left in his custody, adding that a man who wore his own mind on his sleeve was someone to admire.

'It struck a chord with Magnus and he asked her whether she would prefer tea or a glass of wine. When the only response was an extended parting of her lips and the smile he remembered from the library, he apprehended that her felicitations about his reading and movements weren't entirely altruistic and demanded to know what precisely she was seeking from him. The question was snubbed by an expression of interest in champagne.

'"Dregs of cheap claret is all I have," was his capricious response, and he swung into action, managing to keep the tiny splash in the receptacle that he passed to her. Admitting finally to a session at the local, Magnus insisted he was now much less confrontational and began more like himself, even apologising for his rudeness.

'"To say I'm surprised to see you at this hour is an understatement. What then really does bring you here?"

'"I was merely passing and saw the light on."

'"Bearing an armful of literature?" He called out from the kitchen, uncorking a bottle and returning with two more ample glasses.

'"I've hardly tasted this one, thank you," but then polished the balance off, a schoolmarmish intonation spicing her voice.

'"No, I didn't just happen along. I've been visiting friends and had that lot in the car just in case you happened to be home. Is it so bad, my handsome-when-angry, Magnus?"

'The opening gambit passing him by, he apologised for the absence of accompaniments and sat opposite her. She removed soft pink gloves, slipped out a cigarette and waited, her tongue not reticent in moistening painted lips. Finally, he reached over with a struck match and she clasped his hand before drawing back. A fashioned smoke ring emitted seductively. She regarded him much as might a therapist visiting a patient, which, I needn't add, he was.

"'Ah, that's good. You never became a smoker, did you, even though your Esrelle acquired the habit in earnest under Harold's attentive guidance?"

'Mention of her name, the association and the intimation stung, reminding him how puerile his influence had been. Magnus' eyelids twitched as if he was going to speak but only managed a jerk of his head. Eventually he remarked that the habit settled her down after a hard day at work just as, fortuitously, the kettle started to sing, and he admitted being out of sorts having lit up the gas for the tea they weren't having.

'He scrambled to the stove and extinguished the flame. Returning to the sitting room unsteadily, he tripped on the edge of the rug. She was a strong woman and, but for her quick reaction in grasping his forearm, he would have fallen. She tapped the place next to her on the two-seater and they drank more wine.

"'That's anything but cheap, Magnus. Quite good. Mm, 1921, a satisfactory year in Bordeaux. My, you look a little shaken and tense. Just allow yourself to float away all those immense cares. You've been told on a number of previous occasions to relax when with me, as this woman isn't prone to bite."

'Having removed her shoes, she positioned herself behind

the chair and began to massage his shoulders. Receiving no resistance was all the encouragement she needed to apply herself more assiduously to the task. They drank in between. She wasn't ready to abandon the ministrations and he allowed his body to lean into hers when she sat down.

'This phased into a kind of pregnant pause, if you will, until he abruptly freed himself to face her, announcing that he wasn't comfortable with the situation. A cupped hand prevented further speech. Gently she nibbled on his neck and her tongue traced a line to his ears before he stood up.

'"This isn't right. We're both married. I still love my wife."

'The words were out before he knew what he'd said. The use of "still" didn't elude keen ears and her lips rotated.

'"Your lady is fortunate. No doubt you'll miss her. Well, here's to the tour of duty all alone, though she needn't worry about *your* constancy."

'The inflection hit home, but they clinked glasses and he seemed to view Maeve Tweddle-Wright in a benevolent fashion as they toasted the future. Shoes returned to their rightful abode and Magnus followed her to the door, where she held out a relaxed hand. He took it and she clasped his formally.

'She expressed regret at making him feel uncomfortable, admiration at his being an "honourable and decent young man" and a ready hope that, should he feel inclined to correspond, his letters would be received in the strictest of confidence. The visitor remained at the foot of the stairs as if deliberating before ascending them again.

'"Magnus, I had wanted to tell you for some time if ever you felt lonely, if your, ah, needs weren't being met, one word and I would have been happy to supplement them. You are leaving, so it's irrelevant, but making my position clear gladdens me. I shall miss you."

'Her cheek touched his before darkness prevailed. With him, insobriety never excused wrong over right, yet her last offering, coming on top of the earlier ones, confused him. He was careless with the door. In the lounge he stripped to his singlet, casting his garments about in frustration.

'Magnus began drifting into an erotic contemplation of the lady Tweddle-Wright's propositioning. He might have taken it up had he been staying on and to blazes with the risk. Sex with anyone but his wife, and perish it being with another man's, instead of looming as abhorrent a practice as could be imagined now energised desires long repressed by abstinence, gradual rejection and final humiliation.

'While so possessed, elusive were the sounds in the making or the footsteps that had crept up behind him until he was conscious of uncovered breasts fondling his back. In no time her lips had found his and he couldn't hold back. They made love on the floor rug and, when she was gone, he tried to blot out its recollection by finishing the claret and diving into a bath where he scrubbed himself red raw. The next day he was on the real sea, sailing to Singapore, and never saw her again.

'Obviously, we stayed in touch. He detailed it all to me when I arrived in the Far East. Magnus was pensioned off with a spider's web of illnesses, including malaria, and hung around the peninsula after that. We met up from time to time. He lived a pretty shambolic and dissolute existence, though never went near European women. Eventually, he settled down with a Malayan widow of modest and secure means, ludicrously asserting her status as one of housekeeper. Seemingly old enough to be his mother, technically it sounded right. Naturally, I had my doubts. Was there more? He never said anything to me and, of course, I didn't ask, but she was good to him. A civilian at this stage, some way or other, not the least being the persistent widow's ingenuity, he managed to survive the Japanese occupation.'

'Perhaps Magnus had found the mother figure that he craved all his life,' Nancyng mused as she recovered a handkerchief.

'You could well be correct. Are you alright?' She nodded after addressing her eyes.

'Well, leaping on a bit, we lost touch until about a year ago, when the enduring housekeeper, Mrs Iris Shananger by name, sent word that he was seriously ill and had asked if I could come and see him. Of course, I agreed without a second thought.

'The sight was pitiful. It had been years since we'd seen each other and that made me feel guilty. Magnus was as thin as a matchstick and desolate. I knew immediately that the malaria had returned, and his mind's fragility was painfully evident. He had a request of me as his one ex-pat friend. I was ready to do anything I could for him but was startled by the nature of the plea. Magnus told me that Esrelle was living in Port Elizabeth. Yes, of *all* places.

'Somehow she had managed to track him down, no doubt calling on a wide circle of contacts, yet another mercurial element to the woman. Esrelle disclosed that her own health was precarious, in hospital enduring a battle with cancer. She begged him to come and see her as soon as he could arrange passage and even sent some money for the fare, unaware, of course, as to his own parlous predicament.

'Had he been marginally better, such is the mark of the man that he would have gone without hesitation. Indeed, that was his intention, for he wrote and told her that he would get there. But as the malaria and other maladies tightened their final hold, he sent for me, asking if I could see my way clear to act as his emissary.

'It was impossible to refuse and, though reluctant to part from him at this perilous stage, he urged upon me that duty to the service was my first priority.

'I assured him I would visit again the following week as a matter in Kuala Lumpur had called me off and wouldn't take long. I returned in under seven days but, as I approached the bungalow, a pathetic wailing signalled that fate had intervened.

'Mrs Shananger was inconsolable, surrounded by her relatives. The room was a mass of flowers and orchids. Magnus loved them. Someone mentioned that she had kept an unyielding vigil beside his body over the entire twenty-four hours or so since he passed.

'The funeral was the next day and I remained for it. She was grateful for my presence and told me of his wish to be buried privately. Just before I departed, she handed me a scrap of paper on which was the name of a hospice where Esrelle was in Port Elizabeth.

'"He was most insistent that I give you this," she said through a veil of weeping, her head shrouded in a heavy black covering. "He also adjured me to remind you that doing such a thing would go a long way to comfort and help me."

'At this point I had to hold her in my arms as she could barely articulate the words.'

'You seeing Esrelle would help and comfort Mrs Shananger? How extraordinary.'

'Not if you knew Magnus, Mrs Jenkins.'

'I think I've come to know him, yet still wonder.'

'Finally, the grief-stricken woman managed, "Magnus said he would regard you visiting Esrelle on his behalf as the act of a saint."

'I knew it would have been close to his very phrase. My friend was more concerned about this Port Elizabeth woman's health, his widow now in truth, than his own.

'And that, Nancyng Jenkins, ends the Magnus narrative and is behind the reason for this elongated excursion back to London.'

'Could I ask something, and it may sound somewhat odd: what was Esrelle *really* like, her looks, the thing that makes a woman, that *is* the woman?'

'The short answer, you may be surprised to hear, is this: now that you have seen and had some experience of Henrietta Onions, you will go somewhat close to having seen and known Esrelle Sansim.'

212

It became an inobtrusive moment of analysing him, creative fingers interlocked across his chest, seeming to use as a point of focus the blue and white deck footwear deriving purchase from the intermediate bar of the ship's railing. Finding him thus was a rare pleasure, since she had arrived nearly an half-hour shy of their appointed time with a view to marshalling her own recollections in private and transported an earnest longing into the mind of Nancyng Jenkins. *Would that it was Magnus paring away at the ceiling of _Newton's_ life allowing me to be lowered into more than the fleeting spaces to which he had permitted entry, rather than me indulging rampant speculations about him.*

Time might also have been expended in preparation for the inevitable probing questions. Thoughts of pursuing this strategy evaporated when one of the two persons about whom Nancyng postulated he was contemplating took on bodily form, approaching as the putative younger version only to immediately revise such intentions upon perceiving her near presence. The interplay between the two might have opened up tantalising theories in him had it been witnessed.

'You're here already, Gray.'

'So I am.'

She could only smile. 'I want to warn you up front, and trusting the colonel won't be put out by my happening at this spot early, but what you're about to hear is going to be a letdown measured against the detail of the enthralling history you so recently concluded.'

Mrs Jenkins' amusing pretences and perpetual light-heartedness had the ameliorative effect of dismissing his ruminations as they settled in under the mid-afternoon shade of a canvas awning and opened a welcoming response.

'Allow me to be the judge of that. Throughout my monologue, you have been kind, humorous and instrumental in keeping me to the mark with astute and timely comments, sometimes quite testing. Never a dull minute having you as a scrutineer.'

'What a generous remark to make. If I may say so without giving offence, in lensing Magnus' life through most intimate details and marking its sad, pathetic ending, you evolved into a very different personality to the one I encountered and struggled to comprehend at the beginning. I'm not referencing the part you played – small, of course, albeit essential – to everything that unfolded. Yet, having satiated my appetite along this journey, there exists a holler for the postscript, if only reading something like, "to be continued".

'Anyway, perhaps you might care to dovetail it after your impending visit. One thing occurred to me as we separated yesterday. Some of the events were confided obviously when you were both boys. But later, as young men, all the involved and intimate detail must have emerged following his second posting to the Far East. How did that all come out? I know you touched on it in a broad way.'

'We went back to writing to each other. It was a shock that he'd just abandoned England without a word. No one knew what had happened until I received a cryptic wire from him after his ship sailed to the effect that he was seconded to Malaya at short notice and would contact me again by mail. Over the next twelve months the mess gradually unfolded.

'He stuck to his guns in never criticising Esrelle or painting himself as the victim. Though tempted, I didn't reveal the wedding eve shenanigans or the earlier fracas on the train. The knife had been plunged deep enough and I wasn't minded to prise it around. The one thing I deduced, though, was that the individual on the train, at the hotel and who knows where else, and the tutor who was first involved with her were one and the same man.'

'How did you come to that view?'

'Why,' he hesitated, 'I recognised him.'

'Really?' She pressed her shoulders back and cocked her head, seeking to recall mention of his ever having set eyes on the elusive tutor.

Newton's mind was earnest in its travel until he picked up on the point. 'I know why you're surprised now. Actually, he *was* pointed out to me once way back in early school days as being somewhat of a favourite amongst the girls. He was glib of tongue and always made himself available to help them beyond what he did for the boys.'

'Yes, interesting.' She nodded. It was one of a few occasions where Nancyng found herself at something of a loss and seemed about to follow up when he settled back on his elbows, saying in a jocular fashion that it was her turn to be ready for 'the rack'.

Curiosity was subsumed by the time Newton searched to see why she hadn't begun. 'Alright, it's here goes, I guess.

'My early childhood was unremarkable save that my mother died when I was three. I never knew her. Father didn't remarry. I had a wonderful upbringing under his loving care and the teaching of a spinster Englishwoman. She was employed as a kind of governess. Father spoke English fairly well and, of course, was fluent in Mandarin and Cantonese.'

'You didn't say where you were born?'

'Sorry. Canton. My father knew the value of a good education and was an astute businessman. Starting out as a humble fisherman, he eventually acquired a fleet of junks that plied the waters off the southern coast of China. He moved into cargo trading on larger boats before selling out and buying a number of commercial warehouses. I had an older brother by eleven years, and he worked with Father the whole time.

'As well as English, my governess taught me Latin and French. I was fluent in my native language and became proficient in five altogether. I loved English most of all and read any book put before me. It was my father's intention to send me to University to further my studies, until disaster struck.

'When I was almost sixteen, a terrible thing happened. Fire broke out in one of Father's warehouses and spread to adjoining buildings and properties. In the conflagration that followed, he and my brother perished. The fire had consumed many other factories. As there was no insurance, the claims exhausted every last penny. I was orphaned, of course, and there were no other relatives save for distant ones who weren't going to take on the responsibility of a young girl seen as marriageable or quite capable of supporting herself.'

'You won't mind me commenting on what a appalling thing to have faced,' Newton broke in. 'Yet you relate such events in the fashion of someone divorced from them having happened. That requires a discipline few possess, since you aren't old enough now for these things to have occurred much more than half your life ago.'

'That's a diplomatic way of saying that I can't be all that ancient. It's a sentiment I'm pleased to accept and not elaborate further upon,' she replied with a hint of sauciness.

'The Chinese are notorious for being, as something or other goes, "as inscrutable as the proverbial Sphinx".'

'And some Englishmen are equally unfathomable,' giving

rise to a rare separation of his lips that gave her a glimpse of even teeth.

'Sorry if I've drawn you away from your train of thought.'

'What makes you think you have, Gray? My governess, Shirley, was not about to relinquish her tutelage of me. She obtained a position with an English family living in Canton. They were kind and allowed me to live with her. Because of my proficiencies in languages, I assisted her as understudy. The youngest child, a girl of thirteen, soon became a particular favourite of mine.

'They gave me my board and keep and, once they saw what I was capable of, also treated me with a small wage. A number of other British families got to hear of our teaching and a mini-school sort of sprang up.

'A year or two after this time, the militarists in Japan were embarking on adventures in the northern regions of mainland China and an opportunity arose for a particular family whose children I had tutored to move to Sydney. There was a close relative living there, an important businessman with interests in wool processing and exports.

'I had been employed with his younger brother's children. They didn't want to lose me, or, I should say, the connection with the children to whom I was close. The dilemma I faced was explained and they gave him glowing references about me. With the businessman's links to government, it was fixed that I would accompany them, but not my old governess.

'I didn't want to part from Shirley, nor she from me, but it had to be, and not long afterwards she accepted a position in England. We had to separate and lost touch. I don't know what became of her.

'Sydney was where Mr Jenkins and I met. He was the managing director of the company, a widower in his late fifties. I was not quite eighteen. I became his personal secretary and, less than a year later, his wife. It happened just like that, Gray, so why do you frown? People do fall in love sometimes. Look at Magnus and Esrelle.'

'I'm not disagreeing with you, simply the rapidity of it.'

'Magnus was a poor citation, and you're kind not to have called it out as such.'

'Charlotte was born before I was twenty. Despite the age difference, perhaps even because of it – and don't sneer – we were happy.

'I think our marriage outraged some of the hoi polloi with whom Mr Jenkins was aligned in commerce and I daresay it caused him some trouble, the whispering and so on. But an even greater obstacle was his grown-up children, who were older than I was and who never acknowledged me as a legitimate stepmother. How could they, I suppose? I understood their reticence and accepted my place at dinners, functions and family get-togethers. Despite every endeavour, in retrospect, stooping as close may be to grovelling, I was unsuccessful in gaining their approval. It put a strain on things, not just between us as man and wife but literally across the board, the more so when Charlotte was born, for she was the delight of his life, as fathering a child at his age would be.'

'Was there some respect for you on account of your—'

'Proficiency in language?'

'Well, being the mother of a baby girl related by blood to them, his wife and your commendable standard of education generally.'

'My education, such as it was – and I wouldn't rate it as highly as you so suggest – probably made things even more difficult, for I had no formal qualifications.

'Alfred, that was my husband's name, urged me to apply for a university degree. He thought that if I could point to a piece of paper awarded by the prestigious University of New South Wales it might silence the carping voices that were all too ready to write me off as some over-egged, distorted-eyed, lucky-charmed governess.

'I jumped at his suggestion but there were hurdles. I hadn't matriculated and wanted to undertake a Bachelor of Literature. They required me to demonstrate that I would be a fit candidate, so I did a six-month course and sat an examination.'

'The results of which stunned the examiners?'

Nancyng Jenkins twirled a lock of hair and gave Newton the canniest of smiles. 'Are you telling the story, or am I?'

'Well? Was I right?'

'They went as far as admitting your humble historian to the master's degree, which I elected to undertake by writing a thesis.'

'I won't speculate again,' he interjected self-deprecatingly, eager to hear the outcome. 'How did you manage and what happened?'

'Well, I had to go that way, given my responsibilities for Charlotte, and couldn't have achieved it through coursework. I wrote my thesis on the romantic poets.'

'Something you obviously liked and knew a good deal about.'

Her answer flattened him again. 'I selected the topic for the very reason that I knew nothing, or only a passing, girlish smattering of that era and wanted to enhance my knowledge. As well, it was not a subject on which there was a horde of animated discussion. Surprising to me was how my interest flowered. Dear me, such a glow of reproach, Colonel. That's the last attempt I will make at poetic flourish.'

'You mistake my demeanour, Nancyng. It was admiration you were witnessing. I'll feel rather deprived if you remain true to your word.'

'I'd like to think there's a romanticist lurking in some cranny underneath those cobwebs, Reginald Newton. Anyway, as the months went by, Alfred was extremely kind to me. I needed rare books and lots of them. I had only to say the word and they were procured.

'It took me the greater part of a year to complete the task and I was advised that notification of the result would be made in twenty-one days. After two nervous months without a word, any optimism about a good, or even acceptable, result had evaporated.

'When I finally received a request to attend the Faculty of English for afternoon tea with my supervisor I was fully prepared for the bad news. Reckon at my surprise when the head of the English Department and his deputy were also on hand. *Oh well,* I thought, *I expect this is how they let a little foreign failure down lightly.* They welcomed me at the door. Effusive handshakes and many pats on the back followed. I was completely nonplussed. The quality was of a standard that pleased them and I would be awarded the degree.'

'And?'

'What do you mean?'

'"Standard that pleased them" says a little, but students who compile theses don't usually get summoned to the faculty to meet the head and deputy unless the work was exceptional and they have something else on their mind.'

'There was another matter,' she continued with unassuming clarity. 'A position as tutor was offered. It was turned down, of course, but they pressed me, saying this was the first time a woman of my culture had been so honoured. I tried not to blush. Charlotte came before any aspirations of mine and she needed me, as did my husband, whose health was disquieting. I didn't mention this before, but he had been under a good deal of stress from both his business and the family.'

'Did things not improve after the degree was awarded?'

'To the contrary, they deteriorated further between me and them. The conferment was framed as a perverted symbol of avarice pitched to him as conniving cover for my scheming and plotting. Subtly, it began to creep in between us. Alfred would snap at me over the slightest thing and, if I went out anywhere, a full inventory of my doings was required.

'Thereupon he'd apologise and sigh under the strain of their poisonous insinuations that I, being so young, couldn't possibly love a man so old and had to be leading a double life; I was, and always would be, an interloper determined to make off with their inheritance and regarded as too smart for my own station as well. Such a perception was hard to shake off.

'It all came to a head one Saturday afternoon prior to Alfred's children arriving for a discussion. I suspected it had to be something to do with financial matters judging by the pile of papers my husband was poring over when I brought him some lunch.

'The dear one was anxious, sweating profusely and separated himself in spirit, at least from what I perceived. I asked him straight out what was wrong. Unconvincingly, he denied any problem worth mentioning apart from his distrust of every lawyer and said all they wanted to show him was a simple deed the solicitors had drawn up. Soon afterwards, the morose group arrived.

'I couldn't hang around in those circumstances. To compound my isolation, they refused to even acknowledge Charlotte, just as she was reaching out and starting to talk. It was cruel. Since he seemed to waver between stress and confusion, I whispered to Alfred that, after the meeting was over, he might like to spend a few nights away. We both loved Katoomba, and he thought it was a great idea. Charlotte and I would go there and book in at the Victorian-era Carrington Hotel where we'd stayed a few times. I wrote the hotel's phone number down and gave it to him. Oh, and, never meaning to namedrop, let me add that Edward, The Prince of Wales, had lodged there back in 1911.'

'Did you request the suite in which he stayed?'

'If I didn't know you better, that remark could be filed away as demonstrative either of a disdain for royalty or a rare attempt at levity.'

'More like at a loss as to how I come away with an enhanced reputation by trying to characterise it for you.'

'Now, that *is* vintage Colonel Newton. So off we were to Katoomba, which, by the way, is a small town, west of Sydney perched on the summit of the Blue Mountains, an idyllic location. I'm reminiscing, perhaps even dreaming. Bad things seem less so as I digress a little. Do you mind?'

'Of course not. I'm not familiar with Sydney or its surrounds but have spent some time in Brisbane.'

'You might want to tell me about that and much else when *your* memoir is dusted off for release. I saw your lips mouth the words, "Not likely", so never mind.

'The Blue Mountains are home to the famous Three Sisters, rugged outcrops standing side by side that act as sentinels on Sydney's western flank. You can view them at close quarters at various vantage points around Katoomba, which is, have I mentioned, two hours by train from Central Station.'

'That about coincides with the travel time from Brisbane to Toowoomba by car. It's also westerly, situated on a range not so imposing, given your description, as the Blue

Mountains, but with views to the plains below that are spectacular.'

'When were you there?' she asked with a keen eye.

'Ah, just after the war ended.' She waited for more as he shrugged his shoulders indifferently. 'We had a meeting of the services in Brisbane. A few of the chaps went for a drive after someone suggested an outing. Anyway, you were saying before I interrupted your train of thought?'

She saluted the pun. 'Interrupt as much as you like, for there are no set rules as to who talks and who doesn't.'

'Yes, but this is your story, and I held the floor much longer than was ever intended.'

'And I came away with all so little concerning you, but there are many sea days ahead, eh, Gray?'

'Indeed, there are, Nancyng.'

'Charlotte and I settled in at the Carrington. There was an ominous stillness about the evening air. I remember seeing the sky and thinking that it seemed unhappy. It can snow up there and we were in late autumn. I was expecting Alfred's arrival in time for dinner.

'When it had struck eight o'clock and I'd put Charlotte down for the night, I called home with the intention, first, of seeing whether he had left and, if not, telling Alfred to postpone coming until the morning. There was no answer and I assumed that he must be on his way. He still hadn't arrived by eleven o'clock and I became a little concerned. I concluded that he may have gone out somewhere with his children and ended up staying with them. It puzzled me why he hadn't telephoned but, given that he was a man who hated conflict and knowing their antipathy towards me, I regarded it as not wanting to do anything that would bring me into the frame of delicate inter-familial negotiations.

'Well, I was right about the elements, for they were unleashed. It became a truly horrid night, an unrelenting blast of freezing south-westerly air that whistled and moaned through the window apertures. It was actually the first time we had been apart since our marriage. Being chilled in body didn't freeze my mind. It remained incessantly active. Charlotte, on the other hand, slept as if nothing would wake her.

'When a tame mid-morning sun had been unable to melt the overnight sleet on the terrace and grey clouds were signalling a snow dump, I rang again and still nothing. By now my imagination was in full flight. I felt there was something wrong. On the instant, I decided to return home. While we were waiting at the station for the train, I was approached by two police officers. Being called by name released fears that are difficult to relate even today so I won't even try.' The compassion in Newton's face encouraged continuance.

'"We have a forlorn duty to perform, Mrs Jenkins," the senior officer explained, and immediately I knew. "Your husband collapsed after a heart attack late yesterday afternoon. He was rushed to Saint Vincent's Hospital in Darlinghurst but couldn't be revived."

'His notebook was pulled out before he spoke again, as if

something needed to be verified. "He died at seven minutes past six last evening. We extend our deepest condolences. I have been instructed to offer conveyance back to your home."

'From then on I was in a stupor. The younger one, I think, held Charlotte while I had a sort of convulsion. I couldn't speak as many questions pressed upon me, for whenever I tried, nothing came out of my mouth. I remember drinking something strong at the police station and being taken to a private hospital, where I was comforted by a nurse. I began screaming for my daughter as I suddenly felt I'd abandoned her. A doctor came in and assured me that they were looking after Charlotte, who was surrounded by toys in a little playpen. I had to come out of it for her sake, but I wasn't going to be satisfied until they took me to her. She looked angelic in innocence and seeing the little darling, and her father in her, had a palliative effect upon me.

'I wanted to know where Alfred was and the sister, a kind soul, told me that he would be at the morgue. In a situation of sudden death like this there had to be an autopsy undertaken before funeral arrangements could be made. I asked about his family and whether they knew about what had happened.

'She seemed amazed by my question. "The police told me that his children were with him when he collapsed and throughout the time he was at the hospital. Did they not contact you?"

'"No."

'"That's so strange. Perhaps I shouldn't say this, but, when they brought you to the hospital, I overheard the sergeant saying that the family members had been ringing and ringing the Carrington but you couldn't be reached."

'I replied that I was expecting my husband to join us last night; that at no stage did I ever leave the hotel and the only time I ventured out of our room was when I used the lobby phone to try to get through to him. And I also remembered alerting the manager that, should Alfred try to call me, I was to be notified of it no matter the hour, he being the sort of man who might show up quite late. The manager said the road conditions had turned nasty with ice and sleet and possibly some snow, adding that it wasn't a good time to be driving. At the end of hearing all this, I burst out crying from sheer despair and incredulity that these people could behave in such a despicable manner towards me.' She removed her handkerchief and bit on it. 'Hang on just a minute. They couldn't have known I was even staying in Katoomba never mind the Carrington, since my husband wouldn't have told them.'

Newton watched on as she swallowed hard and chewed some more. This time his hand steadied her wrist. 'Such pain as yours lingers forever.'

She forced a smile and he excused himself. A few minutes later when he returned with a glass of lemon barley water, Nancyng nodded in gratitude and drank slowly. 'Would you prefer to leave off for now?'

Face averted, he waited for an appreciable time to hear her say, 'Fancy only realising after all these years another lie had to be added to their farrago of deceit. It's as if a flashbulb went off. Sorry for that digression, Gray.'

'I understand where you're coming from.'

'Do you? Let's pass on. I was gratified for the ride home in the police car. Charlotte was not of an age where saying anything in absolute terms about her father would mean much. She did ask in baby talk where "Daddy" was and I merely replied that we would be home soon.

'It was a strange thing going into what was my home knowing that neither I nor Charlotte would ever hear his fatherly voice ringing out again. I needn't go into much about what happened over the next few weeks. However, there is one important detail which I haven't touched upon and might do so now as it's integral to the story.

'Less than a week after Alfred's death, I received a legal letter postmarked Hong Kong. I was told that the firm acted for the estate of a woman by the name of Mrs Ten Yun Mee, who had passed away leaving a will in which I was named as a beneficiary. A copy of her will was enclosed. I was gifted the sum of three thousand pounds. The residue of the estate was left to a person bearing her name and described as her son. The astonishing thing was that my late father had been named as his father. So here was this unknown brother a good deal older than me. Apart from Charlotte, he was my nearest living relative.'

'You mentioned having a brother before. Was he the one we're now talking about and how did the Hong Kong people find you?'

'Had I already referred to him?'

'I thought you had.'

'Oh, sorry, yes, the one who was killed in the fire, so obviously not him. Anyway, as to tracing me, even with a mind as inventive as yours, the answer is almost beyond conjuring. It took the solicitors a long time, more than a year in fact, to establish my whereabouts. They advertised in England as well as locally and found me through my old governess who happened to see it and somehow knew I had married Mr Jenkins. Apart from all the formalities, the letter added that my half-brother was residing in Penang and wanted to meet me. They supplied particulars of his address. He owned a business there and my imagination ran riot. If a nothing like me received so much money from someone – what shall I call her, "stepmother" – that I never knew existed, the estate must have been substantial.

'All sorts of things went through my head. How had Father kept this woman secret for all those years?'

'There are invariably many more layers of curtain behind the first,' he said reflectively.

'I suppose there are. Well, he managed to lead this other life and the will thus spoke. These were many shocks, and everything merged into a fragment of time.

'One minute I was the settled and loved wife of a successful man, having his world at my feet, along with his unstinting encouragement to go into academe.

'The next moment I was a widow with a fatherless little girl, disgruntled and conspiratorial relatives by marriage who not only despised me but were devoid of human feeling for Charlotte. They handled the funeral arrangements, as if I was a maid who their late father sometimes bedded in the wine cellar.

'I will say nothing of the ostracism at that event. Charlotte and I didn't exist. But, before three subsequent sunsets had passed, there was more correspondence, this time by registered mail, from another set of solicitors. I was getting quite used to their jargon. They demanded I vacate the property where we'd lived since we got married within twenty-eight days. A will was attached in which neither me nor Charlotte were mentioned as principal beneficiaries; in fact, I didn't rate a mention at all. And while I wasn't expecting anything much by way of a benefit since we'd only been married a relatively short time, I was unprepared to be reading a document purportedly executed on the day he died in which he had left Charlotte the residuary estate. To this day that I wasn't included is something beyond my comprehension.'

'As one with Magnus' father's estate, though a bit different in his case. But you, as the widow with a young child, surely that would have placed you in a strong position to contest the will, given all of the circumstances?' Newton prompted.

'I most certainly could have. I vacated the house quickly and stayed with a friend from university while obtaining some legal advice. Oh, I failed to say – this is ironic now that I look back on it – the problem was I'd been gifted a substantial legacy myself, or at least been advised that it was forthcoming. The lawyer informed me that such an amount would be relevant to any claim for me being left without proper maintenance and support.

'But there was a much more weighty matter making any possible award to me or Charlotte academic. On that same day, and before he signed his last will, he put his name to a deed effectively divesting his assets to a trustee, the family's accountant. All he had was some cash at the bank and furniture. The value of the actual estate was less than three hundred pounds before funeral and testamentary expenses. Even if it had been ten thousand, that wouldn't have mattered to me. I wanted to get away from such a combine for good, and now I had a place to go.

'My newly-discovered brother had asked me to come and set up home in Malaya. I could stay in one of his vacant flats in the meantime. There was nothing to keep me in Australia and I accepted his offer of shelter. I had the legacy from my "stepmother", and, within four weeks, we'd arrived.

'The relief I felt must have been written all over my face when my brother met me in Singapore after the ship docked. I couldn't get over the likeness he bore to my father and he was also able to see similar characteristics in me. He pointed out a few things such as the shape of our noses, being a little less flared than Chinese ordinarily possess, our prominent cheekbones, that we were both tallish, me slightly more than him, chuckling in the recollection of Father being shorter than his mother. And he gravitated to Charlotte as any uncle would have.'

'Your brother must have had a little to do with your father when he was alive?'

'He did, although I'd no idea how, since Father managed to keep that other life he had totally secret from us. As you said, curtains and more curtains and, for me, smoke and mirrors.'

'Nancyng, even on this very ship, I daresay that we'd all be surprised at what we saw if souls yielded up bodily mysteries.'

'Are you thinking of Sir Lionel and his lady?' she asked suddenly.

'As it happens, they came to mind.'

'And Henrietta?'

'Now there's some material for a psychological seminar. Such a cryptic question. Why does she enter your mind?'

'I'm not without eyes. Intrigued, perhaps; the likenesses, the memories. At the risk of being blunt, would I be correct in suggesting you view her somewhat differently to the girl that struck out in the early part of the voyage?'

'You were going to add?'

She sighed in frustration. 'To me, it's as if you've discovered something that might either lead to a Damascene conversion or to purgatory.'

'That's esoteric, for I'm neither fitted to be saint nor persecutor deserving of hell.'

'I'm not factoring in the horrible accusation she made. She's rather become central to the mystery that you'll move heaven and earth to solve, as if a line of enquiry suddenly opened and has ignited your mind. My overblown imagination at work, pray tell?'

The trap snapped shut the moment she met his inscrutable eyes. 'No wonder the faculty was enthralled by your thesis. I would love to read it one day.'

'Is that meant to be a compliment or a riddle, a putdown, or shouldn't I ask in case the answer disappoints, or maybe the surprise would offend?'

His features lightened and she stood and stretched, arms extended seaward by way of concealing eyes that gazed resignedly at the ocean.

'Your powers of observation to date have been exemplary but this time they're a little wide of the mark. Are you inclined to resume your account?'

When she addressed him again, a pink flush had impregnated her cheeks. 'Sometimes I'm caught between a dilemma as to whether I should slap your face or wait for you to kiss me as if you wanted to.'

'I can't begin to interpret what that poppycock is intended to convey, and I won't even try to.'

'I know you will at some stage in the near future,' she hit back hard, intended as demonstrative of possessing a facility of which fun should not to be made.

That she had a ready answer to everything intrigued Newton. 'How about you stop concerning yourself with my face or yours and concentrate on Penang, for instance, on the timing of your arrival there? The Japanese can't have been far off making a decision to seal the fate of the entire

Malayan peninsula.'

'Right on the sums historically, as always. Alright then, maestro,' she chortled, resuming the security of her canvas support. 'My brother was a well-established merchant. He was married with a couple of children under five. His wife was predominantly of Malay extraction. We stayed in a two-bedroomed place rather than one of his flats.

'He offered me a position in his business but, being me, I wanted to make my own way. Lim, though a little taken aback at my preference to be independent, understood and, to be honest, I wasn't comfortable landing on someone's doorstep like that. I desired to know him better.

'I didn't want to deplete the money from my late stepmother and wondered about what to do. The old faculty came to my aid after I wrote to them explaining the predicament. They went so far as to send a recommendation about me to the Anglo-Chinese school. It was a fairly fragmented operation as funds were tight. The primary school was run at Chulia Street, the middle school in a lovely old building called *Suffolk House* and the high school was conducted separately again in Maxwell Road. Do you know Georgetown at all?'

'A little of the place, and I've heard of the street names you mentioned. I've not had anything to do with the school, of course,' he replied in considered tones. 'Come to think of it, I've no recall of either of those schools.'

'Oh, go on and admit that you always know more than you say.' When not receiving the dawn of a smile on Newton's face, she accepted it, but this time with less than customary equanimity.

'I'll pass over the geographical aspect. Without canvassing the ins and outs, I received an offer of a position to teach at the high school. It suited me to work for them, but I hesitated at the prospect of being away from Charlotte. They came to my rescue again.'

'I'm not surprised. There would be few of your age with a master's degree in literature.'

'That didn't hardly matter a fig,' she said unassumingly. 'There was an unoccupied caretaker's residence and they offered it to me. Fortune favoured us and, modest as it was, it served the purpose and became our home. I was able to employ a nanny for a little time until my brother's wife offered to help out. This became the perfect arrangement. From the outset, she idolised Charlotte and the children all interacted well together.

'I worked there until the war came. In the lead-up to the occupation, a number of English people were repatriated to Singapore. These included some of the teachers. I had to make a decision about our future as I was concerned for Charlotte, as were my brother and his wife.

'There was no leaving my daughter alone with air raids and the like, and so I resigned my position and went to live with my brother and sister-in-law. I did so at his invitation, mind you, but, as I didn't want to be seen as sponging on them, I offered to help him in any capacity, and he gave me clerical work to do from an office he had at home.

'Charlotte was now approaching school age, however, given the circumstances, I took it upon myself to begin lessons for her. In those early years, Charlotte looked more Chinese than she does now. I always dressed her Malay fashion whenever we went out anywhere during the occupation. We were fortunate never to be bothered by them.

'However, as Lim wanted to be as inconspicuous as possible, his enterprise was shrunk, and he leased what was remaining of it on a handshake basis to a Malayan business associate who had some reliable Japanese connections. My half-sibling became a sort of silent manager so that he could keep an eye on things from a distance neither too close nor remote and never appear to be more than an innocuous functionary.'

'So, as for yourself, Nancyng, you pretty well sailed through the war incognito and untouched,' he said, straightening his back and fingering his moustache. 'Extraordinarily fortunate for someone in your position.'

She answered with a nonchalant, 'You might say that,' without facing him.

Sounds extended for longer and became more significant than at any previous stage during their discourses. In expectation of an enlargement on her initial response, Newton twisted to an upright position. Out of the corner of his eye he detected the gestation of a problem made more awkward as the seconds passed.

Being unresponsive beyond his elegiac enquiry as to whether she was alright suggested that Nancyng Jenkins' mood wasn't becoming any more appeased or that a resolution was near. A thrust of wind drumming on canvas, an occasional whiff of smoke from the thudding funnel and the squawk of seabirds diving into a cauldron of wake as a shoal of fish came under marauding attack, combined to permit a number of distractions capable of forestalling the gloom that had imparted itself so suddenly upon their gathering.

He turned his head, hoping a second time to break the impasse with a friendly smile, but that soon erased itself with Newton's conviction that she was desirous of being anywhere other than beside him.

Chair cords, straining and creaking under his weight as he wriggled his torso, served as a reminder of his presence and she flinched. In the context of their habitual good-natured banter, loud sighing punctuated the intermission and Newton dared not flinch or signal a breath. When it was finally found, Nancyng's voice, cloaked in suspicion, coincided with her striking a folded-arms pose well apart from him.

'You know a lot, Colonel, but, for a man so knowledgeable, you might have been expected to realise that there is indeed a good deal more to the story. And you might have done me the courtesy of listening in the manner to which I reciprocated when you held sway.

'It has become obvious that you don't regard my experiences during the war years as deserving of your concentration, respect or time. Well, that suits me just right.

We survived the war, otherwise we wouldn't be here. Life has moved on and we're on our way to England, as are you. Enjoy your voyage and, henceforth, don't trouble yourself to interfere in mine or Charlotte's.'

Throughout her declaration, Newton had been regarding her with an incurious expression. She raised a hand as if to wipe that look away with a final denunciation, before easing it by her side and using the other to retrieve the towel on which she had sat. Nancyng balled it up with some vehemence, pitched it at his feet and walked away. Still, she hadn't finished, calling back, 'I'm not as easily patronised as you think, and *Uberimma fides* is a two-way street. If you care not to brush up on your Latin, Colonel Newton, it equates to a moral duty, mutual in operation if not in nature, to act in the spirit of the utmost good faith and not trifle with the feelings of other people.'

Chapter II – *Storm at the Stern*

Newton's incomprehension at what might have prompted Mrs Jenkins' rebarbative outburst saw him anchored to his perch pondering her actions far beyond the space in time that it took to watch her receding form hurry down the brass-ridged stairs and onto the deck below.

For a goodly period, he persisted with an expectation that she might soon materialise as if nothing had happened and the autobiography resume. In this frame of mind, he occasionally turned to peruse the direction she had taken, sanguinely hoping that, having attended to Charlotte in some fashion in concert with a cooling off, she might think better of her actions and resurface even a smidgin contrite. But as the minutes advanced, in inverse proportion so also did his optimism recede.

After rehashing as much of the latter stages of the conversation as he could in the light of what he supposed as his minimal contribution to it, rather than blaming himself for any possible indelicacy, he tried to put the riddle surrounding her behaviour aside as one best served by being discarded as insurmountable. For a man of his temperament, such a course proved to be difficult.

Even examining his mannerisms, voice inflections and omissions to comment, he couldn't discern any infraction on his part. He hadn't intended to offer offence nor, he reasoned, could an objective bystander in possession of all the facts have anything but sympathy for his plight. Nevertheless, it rankled him and had soured an assessment of being disposed to treat her account as touching to entertaining a doubt that it might not have been wholly unimpeachable.

Given their adjoining cabins, there could be no escaping her altogether. He had the choice of either devising the most tactful measure open to mollify her feelings or let time work the objective for him. Such was his outlook that there could be no overt conceding of fault occasioning her distress unless she made a direct allegation, in which case, for the sake of harmony, he would apologise.

However, no amount of trying could shake off his contemplations of the event and, the longer he dwelt on it, the less disposed he became. As he compared the vehemence of her reaction with the innocence in the dialogue, the more so when astringent analysis supervened, his mistrustful nature questioned whether she had constructed the outrage on account of reaching a position in the story that was either too embarrassing or, perhaps, even too compromising to recount. Nancyng was, Newton reasoned, in a tiny minority; a relatively unprotected Chinese woman who had survived the occupation of Malaya unscathed, it seemed. Either way, her urbanity had taken punishment and she had become a diminished figure to him.

It came with some relief when Henrietta Onions, who had returned with a view to broaching the topic she had earlier postponed and had taken in his internal dialogue, stepped into view, thus putting an end to his dilemma.

'I'm sorry, but may I have a few moments, knowing it's yours and Mrs Jenkins' practice to spend time out here? I'd wanted to speak sooner but am reluctant to interrupt or bother you. I came upon her travelling with spirit along the companionway and for some reason she seemed not to notice me. Might she be coming back?'

'Ask her yourself, if you wish,' a somewhat abrasive tone seasoning his voice, of which he quickly repented. She didn't move to do so and it was evident Henrietta was in no better strength than the last time he had seen her. 'Look, why don't you sit for a moment?' He motioned to the recently-vacated chair and witnessed a face whose colour required the precaution of a steadying hand on her upper arm from a standing position. She seemed unable to decide and declined water.

Henrietta's features were drooping and, when he renewed the offer by sliding the chair towards her, drew back from him. 'I'm not myself. I don't feel well.' She was breathing rapidly and only accepted his help when he steered her into a sitting situation and shifted closer.

'Are you faint? What is troubling you, young lady?' When she failed to answer, he added with empathy, 'Wait for a while and it must surely pass.'

'I'm obligated to your kindness, but you wouldn't want to know. It's gone.' She scrambled up, her colour far from replenished. 'Maybe some other time. My apologies for being a right, regular nuisance. I don't know what came over me. You must now really believe I *am* crazy.'

He followed the unsure movement that eventually led to the stern. Her back to him, she seemed transfixed by the two streams of boiling white water displaced by the dual propellers. Newton concluded that this was shaping to be another of those days on the *New Zealand Star* best forgotten. After a few minutes, he checked aft again and Henrietta was no longer where last she had stood.

With the lethargy of a fading afternoon, along with a disordered and weakening sunlight, the deck amblers had dispersed, leaving Newton to ponder what might best uplift his own spirits. A stiff breeze had emerged and force of habit suggested that only a brisk walk could bring relief. He had completed a third round of the track when resonances of a punitive ruckus inclined him to reverse his clockwise trend and seek out the source. From his position on the mezzanine deck, he saw Henrietta sitting on her haunches, the back of her hand pressed against her face. Lady Margaret was standing over her, foaming venom. He moved close enough to hear what was being said.

'I belong elsewhere now that I know who I really am and where I stand. Nothing you can say will hurt me further,' the young woman sobbed as she edged onto her knees.

'From this day, we disown you. Your name is not Henrietta Onions. It may as well be Lily Langtry. It so happens that your real mother lives in Port Elizabeth. Sir Lionel wanted to surprise you. We even know where she is and had thought you might like to meet her. I've a better idea now; she can actually have you back with our blessing.'

Stooped over in form, she slowly raised her head in the attitude of one pleading to be spared some terrible fate. 'Please, could I have my mother's address, I beg of you?'

'Beg, go on, beg. Do you think I would give you anything you wanted after all that's happened? Find her yourself.'

'But you just said you don't want me, so why not?'

Lady Margaret continued to view her contemptuously. 'Almost from the moment you arrived at my home I sensed you had been fashioned by bad seed, a potent example of a foundling, if ever there was one. We gave you the distinguished name of "Onions". I had hoped that under our influence your wilfulness might be corrected and purged. It wasn't for lack of trying. But by the age of eleven, when my husband's weakness succumbed to your budding allurements, I realised it was too late. He wanted you in every way but that which a daughter should be. You played him off against me and—'

'At eleven, are you saying? Did you hear yourself utter

those words? How could you even think I had a mind and will of my own? Can such perversity ever issue from a mature woman, let alone one—'

'Shut your filthy little mouth, harlot,' she ejaculated, arching over so as to deposit spittle on the girl that scattered around her cheek like speckles of spray from the sea. Henrietta caved back on haunches, wiped her face and dry retched before attempting to scramble free. She was pinned against the flagpole. Newton's innate reserve to keep away from family matters not of his own exerted restraint upon him, save for pronounced throat-clearing that went unheeded.

'Have you quite finished, *Mother?*' she said derisively. 'Or perhaps I should emulate the religious hypocrisy you rammed down my throat and offer you my other cheek? Yes, I will. Here it is.' Henrietta angled her head and leaned forward.

The remark and the action served to aggravate the tormentor, elevating her tone. 'You never had the slightest feeling for me as the mother you so ill-used and now easily deride, one who gave her life for you. By the time you were thirteen, I was banished entirely from your feelings as you alienated my husband from me. Go on, say something, trollop, if you dare. Now's your chance.'

'I was a messed-up girl, a child, really. He was my father. How could I do anything? I trusted him and I needed love.'

'Ah, a concession at last from the little strumpet. *You* were messed up. And has the hide to call it "love". How do you think *I* felt as *I* watched my marriage unravelling, a husband's affections stolen courtesy of a strumpet with limbs like sticks, more preying than mantis and breasts larger than mine?'

'I was a *child*! I didn't do anything that was my fault.'

'Anything? Fault? Don't make me laugh. You exemplified guile, you exploited every last inch of your flesh to take control and ensure that, by satiating my husband's lust, you would spite me. I couldn't meet his needs, so you stepped in. You might have been thirteen or whatever, but you implemented the schemes of a creature of twenty-five, and one singularly accomplished.'

Henrietta assumed a foetal position on the deck when Switzerland and her illness were thrown in scornfully.

'Yes, and what happened there, Miss evangelical purity?'

Her head twisted in terror. 'I couldn't—'

'Stop yourself,' she sniggered, and then with menace, 'I know much more than you think. But Sir Lionel wouldn't have it when I finally told him today. He said I was mad. I'm not mad, or am I, Henrietta? You will find out from here on and pay for all you've done.'

She took the words as if they were jabs from the tips of poisoned spears, there being no doubt of the hatred confronting her. Henrietta cast about as if looking for something with which to defend herself, before she fixed upon it, retrieving a stout length of rope from the foot of the flagpole. It was knotted at either end. Forcing herself to a standing position, she brandished it in her hands.

'Am I hearing this? Don't you come an inch closer to me. You knew what was going on and stayed silent. *You* turned your eyes away because *you* had to save your position in society rather than your daughter. Now, skew your wretched vision back to this.'

Dropping the rope, she lifted the blouse covering her slacks to expose her midriff. A blaze of purple, much like fragmented lightning within rain-laden clouds impregnated the face of Lady Margaret as she walked away and then turned around. A bullocking shape of woman, she rushed forward, leading with her shoulder towards Henrietta's stomach. But, instead of crushing her against the stern gate, Henrietta managed to stand her ground and absorb most of the impact before uttering a painful cry and falling forward under her mother. The intent to deal with the winded body was obvious, as she thrust Henrietta upwards with a strength her rage had mustered.

Newton sprang down the ladder and seized the furious older woman. He broke her grip and pushed her away, where she almost lost her footing and took Henrietta in his arms. Lady Margaret continued to rain wild invective at both before transferring her wrath to him, suggesting he was just another in a long line of middle-aged deviates. Newton turned his back on the source of these accusations, shielding the young woman and trying to calm her.

He didn't see the same piece of knotted rope that Lady Margaret had managed to lay her hands on but felt the first cut across the back of his head. Newton shunted Henrietta to the side as Lady Margaret stepped back a few paces before coming at him again. This time he caught and wrenched it from her grasp. The rail was insufficient to arrest her raging momentum and it was followed by a bloodcurdling scream as she toppled over the side.

The urgency in Newton's voice was unmistakeable, 'Man overboard!' He repeated the cry several anguished times as he flung out a lifebuoy. The bobbing figure in the water was already two chains adrift of the ship and rapidly slipping further away to the starboard quarter. By the time the alarm had registered, the orders communicated and the telegraph rung to stop engines, only the ship's diminishing trail could be seen.

The chief officer had arrived with a powerful set of binoculars. Walking from one side of the stern to the other, he scanned the confused sea and swell before hailing the master, who had been doing some scouring of his own. 'No sign out there, sir.'

'And none from this position, Mister,' Captain Meeker replied. 'Launch two lifeboats. You lead a search in one, the bosun in another.'

Meanwhile, the passengers, alerted by the commotion, had been requested to remain on the games deck. When questions were asked as to the whereabouts of Sir Lionel, it was whispered that he was paralytic drunk in his cabin and couldn't be roused.

The captain ordered that a radio call be put out to any nearby shipping. The speed of the lifeboat launch was as efficient as if a drill was in progress. Having seen the rescue craft under power, he returned aloft to his command post, seeming to luxuriate in his directorship of the rescue operation.

Newton, with Henrietta hysterical and unable to let him go, asked that first aid be rendered after he had traced the blood on his trouser leg to a laceration on her ankle. He had ripped part of his shirt to act as a temporary tourniquet. She consented to be carried to the sick bay by several crew members after assuring her he would come once the wound was bandaged.

Having been acquainted with the disaster, a shocked Nancyng Jenkins moved to Newton's side and, in the disintegrating light, strained her eyes with his in a vain effort to pick up any sign of a person in the water. When Charlotte brought field glasses, Newton ascended to the bridge, circling the sea through a three-hundred-and-sixty-degree arc.

The captain had hoped that the *New Zealand Star* could be anchored but the ocean floor was several miles beneath the hull. As darkness came over, Newton was unable to pick out even the lifeboats, only succeeding when the searchlights made their random sweep of the waters around them. The ship's engines had been restarted to maintain its proximity to the rescue craft, now reduced to one boat.

As the hours went by, so passed any hope for the woman in the water. Save for Newton, all of the passengers had retired inside to an atmosphere where hope had given way to melancholic resignation. The boats were being hoisted. Newton, at the captain's bidding, visited the sick bay, finding Henrietta conscious though under sedation.

In response to her question, he told her that Lady Margaret Onions had vanished in the deep and, this far from land, would never likely be found.

Coroner's Court

Port Elizabeth

Before the Honourable Judge Kieter Smidzen

9.30 am, 19 May 1949

Court Official: 'All rise!'

Coroner: 'You may be seated, ladies and gentlemen. Because the *New Zealand Star* has a sailing schedule requiring her to depart late this afternoon, I have convened these inquests as an interim measure in relation to the disappearance and possible death at sea of Lady Margaret Onions and the death of Sir Lionel Onions, both said to have occurred on the same day.

'There are several onboard witnesses, and I acknowledge the efforts of the ship's master, Captain Meeker, who has obtained statements from all relevant witnesses. I have read and considered them. A statement has not been required from Miss Henrietta Onions, the daughter of

Sir Lionel and Lady Margaret. In the circumstances, it is quite understandable that Miss Onions has been seriously affected by these terrible events and can't be meaningfully interviewed at this early stage. I have been provided with a short psychiatric report attesting to the fact that she is presently confined in a hospital and undergoing treatment. If, having regard to the material I have read, there becomes a need to request a statement from her, I will revisit with the doctor when this can be done and, with that limitation, any findings will necessarily be qualified.

'If, on the other hand, as seems possible from the deposed material thus far, I am satisfied that there is evidence before me from the witnesses who have provided statements and are present to give oral evidence in order for me to be sufficiently satisfied as to the cause of death and presumed death of the subjects of this enquiry respectively, I intend to make my provisional findings based on that evidence.

'The depositions I have are from the captain, the chief officer, the second mate and the bosun from the crew side. On the passenger side, I have Mrs Nancyng Jenkins, Mr James Cahill and Mrs Ernestine McConsker.

'Captain Meeker has explained that they were chosen out of the passenger manifest on account of their interaction with Sir Lionel and Lady Onions at the birthday celebrations of Miss Henrietta Onions and the following day. I have also been provided with a statement from Lieutenant-Colonel Reginald Newton, on retirement leave, formerly attached to Sir Henry Gurney's staff, High Commissioner,

Federation of Malaya. Apart from Miss Onions, he is the only eyewitness to the events at the stern.

'I am assisted in this task by Mr Akerman, who is counsel instructed by the government solicitor. No deponent has requested legal representation nor have the ship's owners, though their local agent is present as an observer.

'Given the close proximity in time, place and circumstance between the death of Sir Lionel and the presumed death of Lady Margaret and considering the relationship between these two persons, being one of husband and wife, and given the tragic incident involving the disappearance of Lady Margaret at sea that seems to have followed, chronologically speaking, Sir Lionel's demise, I intend to conduct the inquests together.

'For legal reasons, a finding needs to be made in respect to each such person separately for the purposes of the Coroner's and Inquest's Act. I must determine how Sir Lionel died and whether sufficient evidence exists for me to conclude that Lady Margaret is also deceased. Yes, Mr Akerman.

Mr Akerman: 'Thank you, Coroner. I formally tender the statements of each witness listed on the schedule. If it pleases your Honour, I call Captain Meeker.'

Captain Meeker, sworn and examined:

Mr Akerman: 'Just a couple of questions, Captain. Your statement is thorough and clear. Throughout the voyage you were able to observe Sir Lionel from fairly close quarters.'

Meeker: 'Indeed so, yes, I was.'

Mr Akerman: 'Did you at any stage identify any signs that

might suggest Sir Lionel was severely affected by anxiety or was exhibiting signs of depression?'

Meeker: 'No, not for a moment. None whatsoever. There was only one short period of a day or so where a misunderstanding arose between himself and Colonel Newton where he might have been anxious.'

Mr Akerman: 'What was that about?'

Meeker: 'It concerned an incident that occurred between his daughter and Colonel Newton that I have recounted in my statement. The situation was quickly examined and rectified by me adopting best practice ship protocols and there were no signs of any problems from there on. Quite the contrary in point of fact.'

Mr Akerman: 'Thank you for the observation. Your deposition states you saw him the night before he died over an extended period. I take it that in your presence there was no indication of further trouble or discord between Sir Lionel and anyone else?'

Meeker: 'Further trouble? If you mean dating back to the earlier misunderstanding, no, there wasn't.'

Mr Akerman: 'Yes.'

Meeker: 'The night before was Sir Lionel's daughter's twenty-first birthday. Colonel Newton and he were on good terms. Apart from his formal speech of congratulations to Henrietta, I must say he seemed slightly more restrained during the party though he beamed a great deal. Sir Lionel was so proud of Henrietta and tender towards her when she retired earlier than expected on account of feeling indisposed. He and Mrs Jenkins got on exceptionally well, so, no, there were never any smouldering issues. All had been long passed.

'He drank a good deal of champagne, but he was the sort of man who had a sound tolerance of his liquor. By the time I left, the party had pretty much wound up, with Lady Margaret also having departed, leaving just Sir Lionel, Mrs Jenkins and one other couple remaining, that being Mr Pistorac and Miss Prudence Mackay.'

Mr Akerman: 'Were you aware that Sir Lionel had sleeping tablets?'

Meeker: 'No, only that he told me his wife took them from time to time due to insomnia and that he had taken a couple earlier in the voyage when we were experiencing atrocious weather and sleep was almost impossible.'

Mr Akerman: 'That's all I have, sir.'

Coroner: 'Does any other relevant person have questions they would like to put to Captain Meeker? I can see all heads signifying in the negative. Thank you. Captain Meeker, you may stand down.'

Coroner: 'Call Dr Vorster.'

Dr Vorster, sworn and examined:

Mr Akerman: 'Doctor, you are a pathologist having thirty years' experience. In your opinion, what was the cause of death of Sir Lionel?'

Dr Vorster: 'At a basic and fundamental level, it was heart failure. I have stated that the analysis of his alcohol to blood ratio demonstrated the presence of a high percentage of alcohol. It was of an alarmingly high order as my statement attests. Such a level was potentially lethal in combination with his ingestion of barbiturates or sleeping tablets for a healthy individual, let alone one with severe coronary heart disease.'

Mr Akerman: 'You mentioned "alarmingly high" for any particular reason?'

Dr Vorster: 'The blood and stomach analysis was conclusive on the mix within his body. I was surprised by the reading of alcohol in his blood. It would suggest that, when he retired on the Saturday night, he had consumed a great deal and, given that he had three large whiskies prior to lunchtime and more wine during a limited meal, I'd expect that the carryover from the previous night and the additional alcohol would, at least in part, account for the analysis, but we don't know how much he drank after returning to his cabin. The contents of his stomach suggested that he had had little to eat that day.'

Mr Akerman: 'How many sleeping tablets could he have taken to see him lapse into a coma from which he might not emerge?'

Dr Vorster: 'With that amount of alcohol in his blood, I suspect three or four would have been all it needed for a fatal outcome. I'm told the bottle was under half-full and it contained some twenty-five tablets originally. My view is he could have had more, but I would put it down to carelessness perhaps brought about by his level of intoxication rather than a deliberate plan to end his life. It's completely out of character having regard to the background he has and apparently his business was exceptionally sound. From the statements I have read, including material wired from his board in London, no other personality factors were present either on the information with which I was furnished or in the checks that have been undertaken. By all accounts, he was a happy, larger-than-life, successful man.'

Mr Akerman: 'Thank you, Dr Vorster. Pardon me, one other thing, and, if the Coroner permits, this concerns Lady Margaret.'

Coroner: 'Proceed, Mr Ackerman.'

Mr Akerman: 'If someone fell overboard at the stern of a ship at sea from a drop of about fifty or so feet and assuming the person couldn't swim, how long would it be likely for that individual to survive? This is also taking into account moderate swells and choppy wave conditions.'

Dr Vorster: 'I am being asked to speculate to some degree, though I have dealt with such situations on prior occasions. With such a caveat, this occurrence is reasonably clear-cut. I would think a person in Lady Margaret's perilous predicament would have been unlikely to have survived beyond ten minutes in conditions like that and with no innate ability to maintain flotation. Indeed, the chances of survival even in a lesser time would be remote. And that's assuming the fall into the water was a clean one. The height above the surface with the vessel in motion, how she hit the water and what part of her body did so all throw up serious hurdles even for an excellent swimmer. In my opinion, an uncontrolled fall from that height could alone and of itself be fatal, or at least occasion serious injuries.'

Mr Akerman: 'I have nothing more to ask at this stage, your Honour.'

Coroner: 'Dr Vorster, with regard to Sir Lionel, from the blood tests you undertook, are you able to estimate how much drink Sir Lionel might have consumed on that fateful day after allowing for the whiskies and wine at lunch?'

Dr Vorster: 'Again, some of this is quite speculative. But the blood to alcohol equation demonstrated much more than his intake before and during the luncheon. I would think that there might be something of the order of another half-bottle or so of spirits taken. That is confirmed to some extent by the remaining liquor found in his cabin. His wife, we are told, drank only wine. As I said, his alcohol level was extraordinarily elevated; for some men high enough to have knocked them out altogether. But, in his case, it apparently didn't, given his resort to sleeping tablets. I say that having not seen or heard any evidence of malevolent administration.'

Coroner: 'Is it possible that the sleeping tablets could have been administered by someone other than himself? I'm not suggesting that was the case, rather just asking you to consider the possibility.'

Dr Vorster: 'What, forced down his neck or administered by stealth?'

Coroner: 'Perhaps either. Could that have been done if he had been out to it or significantly affected as a result of the alcohol? Regrettably, we have to, difficult as it is when regarding the demise of a highly respected individual, consider every potential cause.'

Dr Vorster: 'Almost impossible to do by force. There was no indication of fluid in his lungs, which one would have expected to see in such a situation. That's assuming they were dissolved in water. I understand he was in his cabin with his wife for a good deal of that afternoon. I believe from the toxicology results that the sleeping tablets were self-ingested.

'I suppose it is remotely possible, if highly speculative, that Lady Margaret may have given them to him by some surreptitious means such as mixing the tablets with his whiskies and soda. Apart from any supposition that a wife such as her would set out to implement a murder scheme, and so far as I'm aware there's no such suggestion, I regard the situation as one of an unfortunate accident. Excessive alcohol in combination with a number of sleeping tablets and a suspect heart proved fatal. His heart was, I say with respect and in no measure wishing to be cavalier, not many beats away in relative terms from a catastrophic seizure. One can never say with precision, however, when that might have happened.'

Coroner: 'You told Mr Akerman you thought he may have had three or four tablets. That seems not a high number as far as occasioning death is concerned?'

Dr Vorster: 'It may have been more, but the point is that, in combination with his blood to alcohol percentage, he had no chance of surviving such a cocktail, given also the presence of chronic coronary artery disease I've already canvassed. Sir, the number I selected has an element of variation and guesswork about it. Nobody will ever know the precise quantity consumed.'

Coroner: 'With respect to Lady Margaret, you have opined that it is entirely conceivable that she could have suffered injury as a result of that fall thus making it more likely for her to succumb by way of drowning much quicker than, for example, merely toppling over the side of a dinghy?'

Dr Vorster: 'Before I deal with that question, if I may, I would like to add to my last answer about Sir Lionel. There was no evidence of any marks or bruising on his body that might have been consistent with him being held down in some fashion as to facilitate a person with ill motives trying to force tablets down his throat.

'Now, if I may return to Lady Margaret. She could well have so fallen as to immediately have swallowed sea water in significant quantities or she could have been rendered unconscious by the fall. I am told that she was seen, whether alive or not is unknown, or at least a figure appearing to be her was observed in the water for a short period before she slipped out of sight. If this is correct, it would suggest to me that she suffered a significant shock on entering the water, as would be expected, and there was no prospect of surviving thereafter. Her body was not found and, short of a miracle of heroic proportions, I'm in no doubt that she's deceased.'

Coroner: 'I take it there's nothing arising out of that, Mr Akerman?'

Mr Akerman: 'No, your Honour.'

Coroner: 'Thank you, Dr Vorster. I understand the last witness to be called is Lieutenant-Colonel Newton. Is that so Mr Akerman?'

Mr Akerman: 'Yes, sir.'

Coroner: 'Colonel Newton, will you please take the stand?'

Colonel Newton, sworn and examined:

Mr Akerman: 'You have provided a lengthy and comprehensive statement under your own hand about the tragic events that occurred on the stern of the ship. Are you able to tell this court whether you detected alcohol on the breath of Lady Margaret?'

Newton: 'I can't be certain of that. However, may I expand on your question?'

Mr Akerman: 'In respect of whether she may have appeared to be affected in any way? Yes.'

Newton: 'Thank you. She was behaving in such a manner that, on my somewhat limited interactions with her, exhibited a degree of heightened emotions beyond which she had ever previously manifested in my presence. I had seen her somewhat upset once before concerning the incident detailed in my statement where an issue arose respecting Miss Onions. On the occasion with which we are dealing, something seemed to be troubling her. She was berating her daughter in a manner I couldn't quite follow.'

Mr Akerman: 'You mean it didn't make much sense?'

Newton: 'I would agree with that, save to the extent that I wasn't presuming to understand their relationship.

'Not long after I arrived on the scene, the disagreement they were having reached a point where I felt I had to intervene. I can't comprehend Lady Margaret's motivations but, at one level, her behaviour might have been regarded as consistent with someone who had had a shock or whose inhibitions had been released through some means. I won't speculate on any issues pertaining to drink because, not being certain, it would be unfair to the lady. Miss Onions was in no way provoking her. If anything, I think this young woman adopted a retiring, defensive approach, trusting that her mother's energies might exhaust themselves and she would leave off altogether.'

Mr Akerman: 'And it never quite levelled to that point?'

Newton: 'I think it almost did but, for some reason, Lady Margaret was unable to let go of this fateful eruption, if I may put it so with the utmost respect, and it preceded that ill-advised movement detailed in my statement that saw her overbalance and fall into the sea.'

Mr Akerman: 'Now, what were your actions thereafter? Perhaps you could just expand a little more on your statement.'

Newton: 'After assisting the somewhat distraught Henrietta, who was bleeding profusely from the injury mentioned, I stayed on deck for a little while before migrating to the bridge until the lifeboats returned. Unfortunately, the news was far from good. Lady Onions had not been located. From some knowledge picked up in the service, I knew there was little prospect that she would be alive, even had she been a strong swimmer. Miss Onions subsequently advised me that her mother couldn't swim at all, as my statement deposes.

'At this stage, I was unaware of any other developments on board. Through an intermediary, I think it was the third officer from memory, Captain Meeker asked me to attend in his cabin. I did so, and both he and his chief officer were present. Given the circumstances of what had transpired at the stern, I thought it preferable that I speak with them in the presence of another person. At my instigation, Mrs Jenkins, who had not witnessed the incident, was happy to sit with me during the entire interview.'

Mr Akerman: 'You mean that you wanted an "independent witness" if you like?'

Newton: 'I wanted a person who wasn't part of the crew present.'

Coroner: 'Why was that, Colonel?'

Newton: 'I had had some prior experience of Captain Meeker not quite getting the entire picture in relation to that other issue involving Henrietta which my statement has covered. Experience suggests that, to avoid later potential conflict, it is always better to have an individual unconnected with the matter under investigation present.

'In saying so, I'm not casting aspersions on Captain Meeker. I noticed at the outset that the chief officer was making notes of the discussions in what appeared to be a log. The concern I had about that, though in no way intending to suggest anything improper against either gentleman, was that such a process needed to be vetted by someone other than crew. It's a practice that has served me well in the King's dominions.

'What I requested was an opportunity to read the notes at the end of the interview. If I didn't agree with them, I could point to the relevant areas and we could discuss any issues there arising. The captain was kind enough to assent to that proposal. As it happened, at the cessation of our discussion, save for one trivial matter about the clothing Lady Margaret was wearing when she fell, the notes encapsulated a faithful account. The summation, if I may so call it, was not, nor did it purport to be, word for word what we covered. Afterwards, I signed each page.

'At the end of this process, Captain Meeker informed me of the death of Sir Lionel. As I mentioned in my statement, I had only been aware second-hand that he had been in his cabin. I knew nothing of the reason for his inability to attend the decks as most, if not all, of the other passengers had done. My assumption, if it's correct to go that far since I was preoccupied in trying to assist with the rescue effort, was that, given his obvious devotion to his family, there must have been good cause as to why he couldn't be there.

'It would be fair to say that the last thing of which I expected to be advised at that time was *his* death. Captain Meeker further informed me, without comment, that a half empty bottle of sleeping pills was found on the bedside table.

'I saw Sir Lionel the previous evening during Henrietta's birthday celebrations. At that time, he appeared in high fettle without being rowdy. He was certainly free with his alcohol as, I suppose, many a father might choose to do on such an occasion. I've no idea how much he drank. I left the venue at about ten in the evening and didn't see him again.'

Coroner: 'Are you able to shed any light on why it would be that such an extraordinarily tragic chain of events could come about whereby, not just two people who happened to be passengers on the ship, but no less both parents of a daughter travelling with them, could have lost their lives in such proximate circumstances? I appreciate that the question does involve an element of conjecture, but this is a Coroner's Court and I'm able to source evidence from wherever quarter, however given, and afford it whatever weight necessary in the exercise of my inquisitorial function. If there was some connection between the two, I must pursue it. Naturally, your extensive military Intelligence background, Colonel, is not entirely irrelevant to my seeking any view you might hold.'

Newton: 'Thank you for explaining the process, sir. I understand the question and the basis for asking it. May I say, with respect to your Honour, that it's doubtful whether any opinion of mine would assist the inquest, with all due deference to the court. I have no expertise, psychic abilities and, despite my background, don't possess qualifications that would add especial credence to any observations I could make. The skipper of the tugboat who shepherded us to our berth in Port Elizabeth might not be any less informative if provided an outline of the tragedy.

'That said, at its highest, I regard the whole of the

circumstances as a sad and tragic combination of events for which no single reason can be ascribed. But let me say this isn't an opinion, rather, it's a statement, and the inquest will decide what occurred. Why Lady Margaret acted so apparently out-of-character as she did on that calamitous evening is something that anyone would find difficult to comprehend.

'I remained convinced that any bad blood, even residual issues, that might have remained on account of the earlier misunderstanding had no effective influence upon what happened. The complete written material from Captain Meeker which I have read about the event, the public apologies ensuing thereafter and the actions of all involved attest to a righting of the disagreement.

'It's true I'm not privy to the dynamic of the Onions family, nor would I presume to know or perhaps even want to venture upon. I can only say from an observable distance that, up until this terrible evening, they appeared to be going about their normal business.

'As I understand recent history, this voyage was not the only one they have taken together. Given Sir Lionel's business interests, they were well accustomed to journeys on passenger ships. That this one should have ended in catastrophe is both extraordinary, as your Honour has intimated, and perhaps completely by mischance. I hasten to add again that, in passing such an observation, it is not my intention to usurp the function of an inquest in its determination of what appears to be the coincidental deaths of this unfortunate couple.

'The last thing I wish to speak about is the most difficult situation in which Miss Henrietta Onions finds herself. I am not a cleric, nor do I pose as some arbiter of moral probity. That she is with child had no outward bearing upon the argument leading up to her mother's loss of balance.

'I heard no denunciation of her on that account by Lady Margaret at the ship's stern. It is shocking that we have seen this young woman lose both father and mother almost in one fell swoop. She deserves the utmost consideration and support.

'Thus, it's completely understandable to me as to why she's been unable to muster the necessary emotional reserves to provide a statement of what occurred, other than a manifestation of profound distress of her mother having perished after falling into the sea in circumstances she neither foresaw, nor could have prevented or in any fashion explained.

'I know this because I heard what Miss Onions said to the chief officer not long after the accident occurred and she, no doubt in combination with her condition, has been confined to specialist medical care. In the meantime, it is incumbent on all of us – I'm not speaking of your Honour of course, and I feel a certain duty myself – to ensure that she is cared for and protected from harm. That means that I've decided against going on with the voyage to London and will remain in Port Elizabeth until Miss Onions is well and provide whatever assistance to her that I can.'

Mr Akerman: 'Thank you, Lieutenant-Colonel Newton. I have no further questions of this witness at the present time. Your Honour, in the circumstances of the ship's imminent sailing and the health of Miss Onions, along with the intimations of Colonel Newton, would the court be inclined to make some preliminary findings?

'Given the state of the evidence, I do not propose to call Mrs Jenkins unless your Honour requires her.' The coroner shook his head.

'Since the court accedes to that proposal, for the record, my intention wouldn't be to seek the testimony of any further witnesses unless your Honour so requires.

'My current submission, having regard to the statements, the oral evidence and the exhibits, is that, in both cases, death has been established beyond any reasonable doubt, that both were accidental and unrelated and that no negligence attaches to the ship's owners, the captain or his crew. Thereby, no person could be committed for trial.'

Coroner: 'Thank you, Mr Akerman. I will adjourn to consider your submission and all the evidence. As pointed out, the vessel is sailing this evening and, given that both Colonel Newton and Miss Onions will be remaining in Port Elizabeth, at least in the short term, I intend to deliver some interim findings at two-thirty.

'I would, as presently advised, subject to Miss Onions' medical condition, at a later stage prefer to hear from her as a witness directly concerned in the mishap at the stern. She may be able to shed more light on her father's earlier actions and movements on that day as well.

'In the court's view, it is preferable that preliminary findings are made so as to give some closure as to matters concerning the estates and business affairs of Sir Lionel and Lady Margaret, as well as to the ship's owners on account of these events having transpired in international waters on one of their working vessels. Colonel Newton has indicated that he wishes to be excused from further attendance on account of his concern for Miss Onions and, since his evidence has concluded, I see no reason not to grant his request. The court is adjourned.'

Newton, remaining unmoved, bowed to the coroner as he vacated the Bench and delivered a sideways acknowledgement of Nancyng Jenkins. She made towards him as he retired from the court.

'After you,' suggested any further exchange between them might occupy a narrow compass.

At the foot of the forbidding grey steps, she waited and watched his deliberate ascent while being met with the blandest of expressions.

'You aren't fooling me,' she winked. 'I trust it's not merely goodbye, good luck and all that kind of stuff, although, if you are to be believed in there, I guess you might prefer we had no further opportunities to reveal some of *our* life stories.'

'I believe I said something like this before when our

discourse was even, mutually beneficial and cordial. You may well think so, Mrs Jenkins, but far be it for me to ever say it. I sincerely wish you and your daughter well,' and passed by as if her first few words hadn't been said.

'*Auf wiedersehen* then it is to be.'

*　　*　　*

On the stroke of two-thirty, the coroner, whose aspect was distinctly more funereal than at the commencement of proceedings, entered to the bailiff's cry, 'All rise!' Apart from public officials, counsel assisting and his instructing solicitor, a single newspaper reporter and the ship's agent, there were three curious bystanders who had not managed the morning session and one other person who answered the call. That was Mrs Nancyng Jenkins.

Coroner: 'Ladies and gentlemen, here are my interim findings. A full decision will be provided after the inquest receives evidence from the final witness, Miss Henrietta Onions, who, because of ill-health and the loss of both her parents, was unable to come to court today.

'At or about 6.30 p.m. on 16 May 1949, The *New Zealand Star* was just over one day's steaming from Port Elizabeth in moderate seas and swell. Clouds on the western horizon meant that, to all intents and purposes, it was sunset.

'At the stern of the ship, Lady Margaret Onions and her young daughter were engaged in what is perhaps less than adequately described as a "lively discussion". The subject matter is not pertinent to my findings in this case, suffice it to say that emotions were running high on Lady Margaret's part. An inference can be drawn as to why that was but, until I hear from Miss Onions, I'm not prepared to go further save to observe that the young, single woman was in the early stages of pregnancy.

'Colonel Newton, who had come upon part of the quarrel held off until he deemed it prudent to intervene with a view to easing the tensions. For reasons not fully known, as he was assisting Miss Onions, Lady Margaret attacked him from behind with a length of mooring rope that was knotted at either end, and which is an exhibit in these proceedings. He was hit in the back of his head. Lady Margaret made a rush towards him attempting to wield the rope again, but Colonel Newton dispossessed her of it. The momentum and her loss of balance saw her fall overboard. She was a woman said to be significantly overweight and I have viewed photographs of her Ladyship taken during the voyage.

'No effort was spared to locate her in fading light and persisted for several hours into the evening without success. She was not a swimmer. In my opinion, having regard to the evidence of the pathologist and the absence of any vessels in the area that might have picked her up, I conclude that she is deceased. I make no adverse findings against the captain, the shipowners, Henrietta Onions or Colonel Newton.

'A stout guard rail of a height mandated by International Shipping Regulations was in place but, notwithstanding this deterrent, she fell overboard. There is no evidence of any involvement by Miss Onions or Colonel Newton that intentionally or negligently caused Lady Margaret to fall. His removing the rope from her grasp was entirely reasonable. I find that the cause of death was an accident due solely to the ill-advised actions of Lady Margaret.

'As to Sir Lionel Onions, the matter is clear. He was pronounced deceased at approximately seven-thirty that evening. It appears he had been dead for less than an hour as there was still faint warmth to his body. The pathologist who undertook the post-mortem found that he had a high level of alcohol in his blood, had taken an unknown quantity of barbiturates and suffered from serious heart disease. Dr Vorster's conclusion that all of these things combined to bring about heart failure is accepted, and I so rule.

'There is no evidence of any involvement by a third party in respect of the death of this man. I find that he did not take his own life. There is nothing in the family history to support such a conclusion or in the events leading up to his death, he having recently celebrated his only daughter's coming of age with her, his wife and the ship's passengers and crew. He was a successful and enterprising businessman with the world to live for. In the circumstances I find that he died of natural causes. His death was a tragic coincidence to that of Lady Margaret's demise.

'These inquests are adjourned to a date to be fixed. Thank you, Mr Akerman, for your assistance. Thank you, Mr Bailiff, close the court.'

Bailiff: 'The Coroner's Court is now adjourned.'

Chapter 13 – *Goodbyes*

For Nancyng Jenkins, the twelve empty seats arranged in two lines of six on the right-hand side of the courtroom stood out as never before after the rotund, black-robed figure of Judge Smidzen had retired to his chambers. It founded a realisation that the Port Elizabeth Court served the criminal jurisdiction as well as the civil and sometimes, as today, functioned in the capacity of a Court of Inquiry concerning death, accidental and otherwise.

With the bench vacant, counsel, his solicitor and the entourage of belongings, law books and papers having swept off with them, the bar table was devoid of everything except an empty water jug and four glasses. The public gallery was also deserted, and Mrs Jenkins felt more conspicuous than at any other time. Within that void and on its wooden floor, hesitant steps in heels sent an echo that resonated throughout the building.

A genial conversationalist, the bailiff was used to the

odd person hanging back wanting to chat or thirsting for some unspoken gossip about a case. Never one to shy away from the public or any member thereof, more so when the subject was attractive and tastefully attired, he was eager to be engaged. Having satisfied himself of the courtroom's fitness for the next day's proceedings and knowing that the woman seeking him out was a witness not called to testify, he was expecting some expression of disappointment.

It was not to be. Her right hand fingered two envelopes. The addressee was the same in each case. The thicker of the two was handwritten, the other typed.

'Excuse me, sir, I'm the Mrs Nancyng Jenkins who was mentioned in court. May I request an enormous favour?' she enquired sweetly. 'Would you be so kind as to see that these are delivered to Colonel Reginald Newton. I had hoped to do so myself, but time is short. You see, the *New Zealand Star* is casting off soon and, if I don't get aboard promptly, my daughter will be on her own for the rest of the voyage. Could you be a darling or tell me that I'm too much of a nuisance?'

It was a proposition so charming and so resistant to refusal that he was tempted to ask if she might repeat the request, advancing so close as to be able to take in her perfume. 'For you, dear madam, nothing could be any trouble. I'll be driving past the hotel where he's staying on my way home later and can leave them with the concierge, who is known to me personally.'

Nancyng thanked him and advanced her hand, which, having passed the items, was warmly shaken. Without a backward glance, she found the street and a taxi, arriving dockside with minutes to spare. Only two passengers positioned well apart were leaning against the rail, one of these being her anxious daughter. They exchanged waves as she boarded. Soon after, the gangway was lifted and the *New Zealand Star* slipped her moorings. That it wasn't feted for her to see Newton for the last time, as she searched shoreside forlornly in case he had relented, gave the entry onto the ship's upper deck an entirely hollow feeling. And it wasn't confined to the inner harbour.

Captain Meeker doffed his cap at the pilot transferring to the little boat that had shadowed the large vessel until she cleared narrow waters and it tooted back. Meanwhile, the sole remaining passenger's forlorn action almost went unnoticed. Other than her dutiful cabin steward peering at her from seclusion and whistling to himself at the confirmation of a suspicion, no one ashore could possibly have witnessed Nancyng Jenkins' kissing the crimson petals of a long-stemmed rose and flinging it over the starboard side. She made herself believe that the four ten-second blasts from the ship's horn following upon her gesture, knowing the sounds would be heard by all in the town, including the irascible English colonel, was no coincidence.

As the port faded from view and the pilot boat receded to a mere speck astern, she tried to expunge a foreboding of loss, things not only left unsaid and in limbo, but unaccomplished, a prospect gone forever. Nancyng pledged to retain something inside her that wouldn't be consigned to a pleasurable interlude or, worse still, an historical footnote, not at that point, nor for the immediate future.

Spilling a tear or two, she trusted that the phantom upon whom her emotional energies had been spent might, after reading her written thoughts, at this moment or on some subsequent occasion, be entertaining, if not similar considerations, perhaps wondering what might have been.

*   *   *

In Port Elizabeth, with dinner the guiding issue on his mind, Newton had advanced twenty-five yards from the entrance to the hotel when the bellboy came running after him waving two envelopes.

'Colonel Newton, sir, these were left at the concierge's desk by the court bailiff.'

Once in his hand he dismissed the notion of a few minutes reading in the open and followed his pursuer back to the lobby in order to peruse the contents.

Lieutenant-Colonel Newton

At sea en route Port Elizabeth

Dear Colonel,

After we separated yesterday, Henrietta, in solemn frankness, spoke to me. I feel bound to record for you the various things that she related and what happened as a result, knowing your penchant for possessing every detail.

Before our discussion on deck had come to so telling an end, there had been a confrontation between Sir Lionel and his Lady after she had surprised them in a compromising position in Henrietta's suite. Sir Lionel had tried to explain to his wife that he was drunk and didn't know what he was doing. He conceded that things had got out of hand and maintained that Henrietta was the initiator. All hell broke loose when she admitted carrying her father's child, accused her mother of 'making a belated show with her protests', left them to it and took herself away.

What happened in that cabin afterwards between them will never be known, but it is almost certain that two people have perished. Much later, with normality of sorts resuming and Charlotte asleep, Henrietta came to my cabin and we had a long conversation.

Initially, she was composed and told me of learning that she had been adopted and her birth mother may actually live in Port Elizabeth. There had been some sort of arrangement proposed for all to meet up with her while the ship was in port. It was to be a surprise. Henrietta pressed Lady Margaret for details during the bitter argument at the stern and she refused point blank to reveal where her mother lived.

As we further talked, her distress became intense. Understandably, the captain had locked her parents' cabin, and this also denied access to her suite. Henrietta had been given other quarters. She still retained a key and asked what I thought if she were to go in there to search for her father's diary. This, she believed, would contain the address. She didn't have a name but would take down whatever addresses there would be for Port Elizabeth.

Naturally, I didn't think it would be a good idea for her to go in there and prowl about. Not without some hesitation, I volunteered to be the bunny but wouldn't be rushed into doing so without thought or preparation and persuaded her to take my bed. By the time she went to sleep it was nearly three o'clock, a pretty sure hour for some on board 'larceny', knowing that the watches didn't change until four and it was unlikely anyone else would be up.

Wearing thick socks and dark attire, I stole in like a burglar albeit with a good deal of quivering at the slightest sound. She had been precise with her instructions as to where things were located but, small torch in hand, I didn't bank on the dresser being locked. The only objects that might be fashioned into 'house-breaking tools' I took from my hair.

The lock was one of those old-fashioned ones and easily resisted my amateurish manipulation with the first bobby pin. In the second and last effort, this time having two such implements plaited together, I managed to pick it, and the diary was the first thing I saw. I flicked through to the letter 'P', and, sure enough, the page contained just one Port Elizabeth address.

Henrietta woke early, seedy and ill. After she emerged from a long spell in the bathroom, I handed over the diary. She wanted to return to her allocated cabin, and I have to say that this suited me as well. I didn't want Charlotte to know what had been going on. I suppose I could have just written down the address and replaced it. Also on my mind was the fact that this girl was now alone and there might be things in the diary that could help her later on, important contacts, etc. Who was I to think about all the illegalities, enquiries, investigations and that sort of thing? She seemed content to retain the item anyway. So, that seems to be it for I haven't laid eyes on her since.

In Port Elizabeth

Well, we are now here and you've left the ship for accommodation ashore. You're going to stay over in Port Elizabeth to see how Henrietta gets on as a sort of interim guardian to her, so says the gossip on board, and there's been plenty of it going on. How noble of you, though probably also a fortuitous thing given your other duty in that place.

I couldn't help but think how life can be full of unlikely coincidences. Here's you, on a gallant undertaking at the request of your late friend, Magnus, going to visit his ailing widow in the same city where Henrietta's biological mother is said to be living. Perhaps you will all link up somehow. I'm not trivialising the circumstances bringing this about and suppose it's meant to be.

In passing, may I say, though, that it was with a tinge of sadness and disappointment that you didn't fill me in with all your plans. I understand why my behaviour on the day we should all forget contributed to your decision. No doubt you had ample reasons.

Sooner or later, perchance, an explanation of everything on both our parts may bring about an end to the many suppositions.

Yours,

Nancyng Jenkins

Newton reflected over the contents and read the letter a second time before extracting the slimmer communication.

Dear Colonel,

I compiled this note after we parted at lunchtime court recess today.

I perceive that by the time you are reading it, we will be well and truly steaming down the coast to Cape Town. It's regrettable that the events of recent times have turned out this way. It will take time to realise that I must settle on the absence of your company for the remaining weeks of the voyage on the *New Zealand Star.*

Despite the little contretemps between us (before the ensuing calamity), I can't tell you how much I enjoyed listening to the fascinating tale about Magnus, at times sounding like something out of a novel with lots of spicy and crafty characters thrown in. I know there's much more to it and, of course, the postscript, given the assignation in Port Elizabeth with Esrelle, and was hoping to tease that and all the other bits from you in the weeks ahead, but it isn't to be.

I haven't considered that we shall probably never meet again and, judging by your attitude today after the court adjourned, it may well be a more agreeable situation to you than to me. I trust I'm mistaken. You are a contrarian by nature. Perhaps I should also say a contradiction. Anyway, these and other things happen to be one of the reasons why I find you such an interesting man.

If you should ever toy yourself enough with the notion of wanting to contact me, while my daughter's education proceeds over the next few years I will be living at a relative's house. The address is 26 Vivesta Lane, Sonning Common RG4 Reading, England.

I wish you the best of luck with whatever you choose to do and hope that your life will be a happy one.

Fondly,

N. J.

*   *   *

When he entered the street, Newton was met by a recumbent afternoon suggestive of moderate satisfaction with prenoon business. Even the merchants lacked perseverance as his attention was drawn to an individual of gargantuan proportions dozing behind the wheel of a taxi. He crossed the road and kept on walking for half a block then reversed direction to retrace his steps, noting a scrawled 'for sale' sign in the rear window of the same cab.

'Swartzkop Sanatorium, please,' he said, stirring the mildew-bearded driver, whose halcyon days of once fronting a Springboks' scrum may well have been far behind him but who retained his Afrikaans belligerence. At the controls of a Jaguar sedan whose appointment with the panel beater was long overdue, he grunted assent in the fashion of one who had long ceded manners to size rather than polite satisfaction at gaining a fare.

'Znot much outadere mizda,' he speculated after five blank minutes where Newton was left to ponder whether the engine's need for a thorough overhaul might just be postponed long enough for him to reach his destination without requiring a tow. Like so many of his breed the world over, the Afrikaner read minds.

'Ah, getcha easy. Shiz guid for zanotha zousan' yet, mizda.'

'Been out to the Sanatorium before, I take it?'

'Mm, moisda zem move, place zis buggered. Zemolished any zay.' Newton suspected he was angling for an open fare from the labile tilt offered through the rear-view mirror. 'Bez wait 'ere if za person not dere.'

'Alright, since you seem minded to do just that.'

Brakes, as if in suspect harmony with things mechanical, finally managed a creaking halt. They were beside a grimy, two-storey brick building possessing every appearance of being readied for a demolition gang. Newton flinched at the dilapidated entrance, hoping it to be an incorrect address. The driver's prophesying was gaining currency. A lanky and concentrated African with a large broom was sweeping cracked and uneven stairs. On being asked, without raising his head, he simply lifted a finger that pointed to a small side entry to the left of barn doors hinged precariously, bolted and padlocked. He could see a starch-pressed woman in the office as he rang a bell. The enquiry made, she leaned over a filing cabinet and viewed him suspiciously.

'I take it you're family?' she opened in heavily-accented English.

'To the extent that I'm here, well, as her husband.'

'We have no such patient with us.'

'You might recognise her somewhat unusual Christian name, Esrelle?'

'Oh, we did have a—'

'She may have been calling herself Langhe.'

'There was someone staying here, *"Estelle* Langhe". Discharged home I'm afraid,' she offered choosing her words carefully.

'I see; that could be her. She had written advising me that she hadn't been well. We haven't lived together for many years. I would like to see her if I could. I sent a ship-to-shore telegram here. Can you give me an address?'

'I'm sorry we don't have it, the telegram that is, but, as to forwarding address, I can't – ah, she didn't disclose her marital status and we're unable to release that information.'

'Not even to the man to whom she's married?'

'I'm sorry, sir, you are?

'Mr Reginald Newton.'

'Oh, another problem I perceive, for we are yet to establish this is the same woman to whom you say you're married.'

'You see, madam, it's like this: I've come a long way on the chance of seeing her for what I realise may well be the last time. She requested me to come and I promised her that I would do so. If you doubt my *bona fides*, telephone her and it will be confirmed.'

'I can take your details, sir. Could you please provide me with proof of your identity? A passport, and I would also need to see a certificate of marriage.'

Newton stifled his elevated impatience. 'My passport is back at the hotel and I'm afraid I'm not in the habit of carrying a marriage certificate on my person.'

'Alright, then here's a suggestion. I will make an appointment for you to meet with our superintendent. He has the authority in matters like these.' Newton had not observed the driver who was hovering behind his shoulder.

'I haven't that sort of time to spare, I'm sorry. Would it be inconvenient if you could let me speak to her on the telephone? The lady would confirm me as her husband.'

'Oh, I couldn't do that, Mr Newton, without proper permission and—' An alarm rang out and the woman rushed off. Newton raked fingers through his hair and proceeded towards the foot of a stairway upon which she was now doubling up. Meanwhile, his driver was foraging around behind the desk.

'Excuse me, what the devil are you doing?' Newton's tolerance in full retreat as he returned.

'Oy couldn't zelp 'earing all zat. Juzda 'unch.' He was not looking at Newton but rather a notepad in which he was writing while peering into a file. 'Ereze de address, are ya ready to go?' The passenger followed him out to the vehicle. 'Sheez dere. Anoder ten minutes and we're atze place.'

'You've got her name and address, just like that?'

'Vell, never ask juz like, juz think cosda bit more. Esrelle Langhe, ze gettin' varm?'

When he stopped outside the whitewashed brick structure, nodding in its direction, Newton augmented his tip when the driver's reaction to the initial denomination failed to deliver complete approval.

'Seems I've misjudged you, at least in some respects,' he offered in supplication. Newton wasn't thinking of the residential details purloined as if such tasks were part of his trade.

'Za bloody inzulen, limey bastarz,' the stubble audibly muttered, grunted, expectorated and tipped his cap almost in the same motion before the rattletrap gained traction and faded away.

Newton stood outside the wrought iron gate, painted black and hung between two stout wooden poles in the middle of a cream-coloured paling fence. The front garden bore the mark of impeccable English tendering and roses, its most decorative feature, were in full pink, orange and red bloom. One side of the large block had a row of apple trees extending on an imperceptible slope to the rear. The other held a series of segmented and stepped beds of potatoes, tomatoes, cucumbers and lettuce bordered off with ears of corn, prominent and ripe.

The brick building had been rendered and coated in an ivory hue recently, it seemed, judging by paint spots at the footings. Its roof was made of iron and slate-coloured. Such a fine, if unpretentious dwelling in a neat, tree-lined and concrete-sealed street was nothing like he had expected. Newton began to question whether failing to secure verification of the occupant before paying off the taxi may have been incautious. Salutary barking from within silenced the thought and also sent him on a determined quest to acquire more courage. Shaking his head as the nerves reached a pitch he needed to dispel, Newton kept to the footpath and followed a continuous line of dwellings similar in construction but never so neatly gardened and manicured as the property under surveillance.

While the deviation purchased more time to compose himself, it did nothing to allay the gathering droplets of cold sweat. Mopping his brow at regular intervals served as a reminder that his preparation for this meeting had been woefully deficient. Striving to conjure an excuse to postpone it for another day, he hit on the one idea that appealed to his penchant for procrastination. *What could make more perfect sense than to secure the services of an enquiry agent to be absolutely certain that this was indeed the address and the right person?*

Hardly sooner than the thought entered his mind that he scotched it and meandered on, taking in perfumed jacaranda trees, the purple carpet of their flowers beneath his shoes emitting little popping sounds and becoming another fortuitous, if evanescent, diversion. Newton imagined that he was sitting opposite himself at one of those interviews where the subject of his interrogation was floundering. Any pathway became a reprieve to be grabbed, except for the one that would take him to the inevitable appointment with truth.

The black and white photograph in his possession of the day when she accepted the proposal of marriage was the only one he had of her, and he guarded the item as if his life depended on it. Twenty years sealed, he opened the envelope marked 'Strictly Private' in which it rested.

The first thing he saw was a tiny, demure face peeping around the folds of her hair, thick and flowing, and overpowering confirmation returned. That day she wore a short-sleeved suit of British racing green, formed around a fragile figure of middle height making her appear much taller than she was. Legs and arms she regarded as an affront, bony and wretched, he saw as slender and comely. Her brows were intense, lashes long and mischievous, eyes guarded, a feature he preferred to overlook. He turned again to her hair, sunlight shimmering within its smouldering redness, his mind having imaged a technicolour dream.

When it came to the comity of marriage, Newton had lived with a proverb first drummed into teenage boys by the school chaplain, the adaptation of which required them to remember that it was appointed unto man once to fall in love and thence to marry and thereafter never to fall out of it or divorce. Despite all that went on around him, he had followed the instruction to the letter, if not its theological underpinning remembering that somewhere Christ had decreed an exception for divorce in the case of adultery.

If reconciliation was beyond reach and removed from mortal hope, Newton also believed that staying married, no matter what might cross one's path to do otherwise, would become a sole spiritual absolution, more especially as he accepted responsibility for what occurred and nothing had, or would, alter that view. All these years later, the same air she breathed, being so proximate to that which nourished him, induced an overpowering recollection of the woman he never ceased to love.

He halted again. This time his fingers weren't trembling as he brought the portrait so close that his lips almost touched it. As if some indwelling motor started and large hands piloted him like a blindfolded prisoner, Newton gave way. Prevaricating was pointless, postponement worse, and, tapping his back pocket ruefully, wished only that he'd thought of a hip flask.

Hesitant with the knocker, the seconds turned into an agonising, noiseless minute so he closed his hand to apply it with greater purpose. Thankfully, there was no barking this time, just movement, occasioning a bizarre presentiment that he was expected, as if objects were being repositioned and things hastily arranged in something of a fluster.

Light steps were coming closer and his breathing ceased altogether. The door opened and there she was, the afternoon sun catching her shimmering hair, coiled and entwined to rest at her shoulders but, instead of being nondescript, the suit was of that same green fabric, exactly as he imagined it a lifetime ago, and at one with the sapphire ring.

PART TWO

Chapter 14 – *Coming out*

Port Elizabeth

8 September 1952

Dear Mrs Jenkins,

I sincerely apologise for permitting over two years to pass before replying to your thoughtful and generous letters. You would have been entitled to give up ever hearing from me and it's apprehended that receiving this might shock you to the core.

That the delay was nothing short of unconscionable requires no reminder. Rather than wish you well and slink off into deserved oblivion, can I begin by pleading that a great deal has happened and, on hearing about it, you may feel more disposed to forgive this tardy answer.

First, I'm indebted to you for all of the now dated background provided, especially that with which Henrietta Onions acquainted you after the events at sea, best allowed to pass unrevived. This should put into perspective many things that I trust will shortly be revealed.

Rounding everything off, despite some anxiety about the inquest coming back on, the Coroner's Court wasn't reconvened for the purposes of Henrietta giving evidence or at all. It was an outcome with which you may conclude she was comfortable, as was yours truly. Need I elaborate further?

Under the Eastern Cape laws, interim findings are made final if the coroner doesn't reopen the proceedings within a year. I felt this was the inevitable outcome when Miss Onions renounced all of her right, title and interest in the estate of her parents. You might accept that our English courts may have been more diligent before being asked to certify as to the deaths of Sir Lionel and Lady Margaret, as well as the cause of their demise had Henrietta sought a grant of probate of either or both wills.

It won't be a surprise to read that the Chancellor of the Exchequer and several children's charities (Henrietta has since learned) were rather pleased by her selfless renunciation. You will also understand the young woman's motives for adopting this course.

With all that out of the way, let's return to our various exchanges, now seeming so distant though still remarkably fresh in my memory. I begin by recalling the prescient observation you made about coincidences.

With a modicum of good fortune, I was quick to locate the place where Esrelle resided in Port Elizabeth albeit not without qualms as to what to expect. You would appreciate my rank astonishment when the person who opened the door to Esrelle's home was none other than Henrietta Onions. Upon seeing her, it was as if the scales were shunted from my eyes, for I knew almost straight away that she had to be Esrelle's biological daughter adopted out all those years ago. As unbelievable as it now must read, the whole thing was incomprehensible, too. That makes little sense, but I can't think of any other way to put it. Yet there had been a resemblance, as I mentioned to you at the time.

Now, of course, Henrietta didn't know why I was there other than she thought I had somehow found *her*. We had a discussion first in which she said that her mother had been living here for some time before having treatment for cancer and being sent home. She was bursting with excitement to introduce me. When I saw Esrelle, she was shrunken into a rocking chair, reading, while facing a bay window with the curtains drawn to admit natural light. Henrietta motioned for me to steal quietly in and wait while she approached and turned her around to face me.

'You have a visitor, Mother.'

Apart from long, plaited hair which retained patches of the colour she had passed on to her daughter, I wouldn't have recognised her. Gaunt, wafered layers of pallid skin seemed to be willing themselves to waste away. Her face dreadfully mummified, she appeared in a kind of half-house, as if death had already invited itself in, and as near to welcoming it as any person still living could be capable.

For all that, recognition was swifter than I expected, and the makings of a tiny rally ensued. She shed a tear that led to a spring coursing down her cheeks. The effect was, well, awful. It took some restraint not to feel for her, a suspicion that she could become more distraught through regarding my moistening eyes as mere drips of pity, powerful.

So I began to relate a little of the history you already know, while betraying some awkwardness with Henrietta still looking on in wonderment. All these connections, I suppose, really threw her.

As we conversed – and this probably sounds somewhat ghoulish with recollections being raked like motley leaves in autumn – she increasingly assumed a renewed lease on life. (Henrietta's materialisation had, rather than anything else, begun that process.)

'Henrietta and I haven't held back with each other, Reginald,' she said, warming to the topic, as her daughter's adoration saw her draw near and place a longing arm around and a kiss upon 'my dear mum's' neck, as she put it.

'I know she's with child, who the wretched father is and, more particularly, am content to envisage where that monster might be, since he could occupy no better place than the eternal torment so richly earned.'

'It's going to be tough for Henrietta, given her condition. She will need courage and resilience in the months ahead,' I offered, adding, 'and now that she's found you, what greater solace could there be than in looking after you?'

It was evident that Henrietta had taken to her mother

as if she had known her from womb to womanhood rather than for not much more than a few days. Truly astonishing was the reciprocity of adoration. They touched and caressed each other without ceasing. A domestic's frequent comings and goings were closely monitored by Henrietta as if she was determined to learn what was required and become her substitute.

'My daughter will stay here with me. She has nowhere else to go. We will both get through this our journey together,' she said with considerable emphasis.

I couldn't answer because it seemed to have become a fantasy into which Esrelle had succumbed and, at such a precipitous stage of her life, anything I added would have been counterproductive.

'This home is my largest asset, Reginald. I've been thrifty. All that I possess will become hers and she'll manage somehow.'

Two people were within the house. The coloured servant, of whom I've already spoken, was tidying the lounge room when I entered, and a nurse was in the kitchen with a syringe extracting clear liquid from a small bottle marked 'Morphine'. It was all brought home to me as being extremely ominous. But back to what was happening with Esrelle.

'If your continuing reticence to speak is a revelation of scepticism about my survival chances, let me set you straight, Reginald. Oh drat, my awful hair,' she said, struggling to arrange it.

'Let me, Mother.' Henrietta released the plaits and

retrieved a brush. With the utmost tenderness she began, snail-like at first, becoming, with great patience, more expansive, to smooth out the lengthy, tangled strands, thence to shape and define her mother's locks as if they were extensions of her own.

'Reginald, I appreciate that you've known my daughter as the beautiful young woman she is much longer than I have. God has been kind to let me see and touch her. Such a surprise that it has almost jerked me back from the brink. Henrietta, I adopted out and never expected to meet again. Now I'll die a happy woman.'

She flinched in pain. Henrietta left the room saying that she would fetch the nurse.

'From my heart, thank you for coming, Reginald. This is the happiest day of my life. My Henrietta, I thought I would never top that, but now you *and* her. Are you going to make anything of that to this decrepit old skeleton who once long ago you saw as the blushing bride?'

'Please don't say that. I'm almost speechless, Esrelle. The link – I had no idea, of course – well not until the door opened, and there became a sort of metamorphosis.'

She began to weep again and I hung back awkwardly. 'I'd always wanted to tell my husband to his face how sorry I was for the past, all that had gone before,' she managed to say before breaking down again. I pleaded for her to stop, but she persisted. 'I was genuinely repentant, if remiss, in ever writing to express it.'

'Your husband never stopped loving you. He never held

anything against you,' I chimed in, trying to be breezy and inventive. 'You could do no wrong. In the mess, there was one occasion when he overheard a couple of the fellows talking about you in sly terms. He burned up on the spot and dealt with them, one for each was all it took.'

'Some man I threw over,' I think she whispered through damp, visionary eyes taking on a remorseful sheen.

'Esrelle, the past is what it is and the future is your beautiful daughter,' I replied, apologising as she seemed to become dreamy. She proved me wrong again.

'I don't know what to say to that. Sometimes I feel I deserve to languish in hell along with that creature who stole my daughter's childhood. But, yes, it's Henrietta's future, as is the precious life inside her, which we must consider now. Reginald, you could have just seen me quickly and left for England. Why?' She was far away and I began to think she would soon be asleep before her eyes took on a renewed intensity when they returned to mine.

Other than a brief shrug of my shoulders, I didn't add anything, and I placed my hand on hers trying to soothe her.

'My daughter wants to look after me,' she suddenly said. 'I was moved back here to die, on finite time, they never say it to you of course, and look longingly for the next shot of narcotic, which,' she groaned, and I crouched down holding her hand, 'shouldn't be – ah, here comes the elixir right on cue.'

The nurse struggled to find a vein in her right arm and affixed a stout rubber band to the left with success. Esrelle waved her away dreamily when she was about to check the pulse.

'I'm a real livewire now,' she said, and her face brightened as Henrietta knelt on the other side of the chair. 'Oh, that you were the child my husband and I had produced, but you're my daughter and that's all I need.'

She began to ramble as if her mind had reached back all those years and the events flooded in upon her reasoning.

'Mummy, are you alright?' Henrietta asked, and offered her a glass of water which she sipped slowly.

'Damn lucky, my dear. I'm sorry to you, to him, too. But now that you're both here, there's a request I have.'

'Would you prefer me to leave the room, Mum?'

'I most certainly would not.'

'Then, dearest,' Henrietta replaced the glass and held her hand, 'don't you dare even blink a hint at getting rid of me.'

'She's just one with me, isn't she, I think, Reginald?'

I wasn't qualified to answer and left it with a short nod before she continued. 'I did a terrible thing, and he repaid my wrongdoing by never really seeking some happiness of his own. He knew that, try as I might, *I* never would, and he was right there, until now of course. It sounds churlish, but I thank him for his sacrifice. If I did anything right in the last twenty years it was to continue to regard him my husband and, after you were born, I was never unfaithful to him again.'

'He wouldn't want you or anyone else to regard him as perfect,' I chipped in, somewhat incautiously it appeared, since I received a frown.

'Mummy, don't you want to rest a little? You're looking weary.'

'Oh, it's that wretched opiate, a hit followed by a downer. I should have waited but, before heeding your words, Henrietta, there's some more to do, to say. I have no right to ask this of you now, Reginald, but I do so knowing of your character.'

'That's most undeserving,' I managed to say awkwardly.

She seemed not to hear and stared in a strange manner from Henrietta to me with her eyes almost glazing over. It was as if she was in between two realms or even three: the past, the present and what little future remained.

'Can you bring yourself to taking care of Henrietta during her pregnancy?' she finally asked, focused again. 'You can live here. She has no one but me, more a hindrance than anything, and halfway towards her first child, deserving every assistance, into the second trimester.'

She switched to matters financial. 'I am leaving my daughter all the money I have, and she'll get this house. The solicitor came, a new will done, and she is protected.'

I was astonished at the rapidity of it all. We were venturing into perilous territory. As you know, Mrs Jenkins, I had originally planned to keep on for a time with the inquest and all that remained hovering to see if there was something I could do for Henrietta in her unenviable predicament. Now this. I was unsure about staying in the same house, pleading for time to think about it. I had a reasonable income in my retirement year but, after that, the pension was modest, as were my reserves.

'I will allow you a day to do so,' said Esrelle. We all laughed at this. She was a woman who always knew her own mind and, from what I've told you about her history, not unused to getting her own way either. She placed Henrietta's hand in mine and, keeping hers there, repeated, 'Can you, Reginald?'

I left them without making any firm commitment. More than mere emotion was required to get through the next stage of any plans I might make. Had I returned to England, with further army service pretty much out of the question for reasons upon which needn't be elaborated, I had thought there might be enough for me to set up a little business or acquire one, perhaps even a corner shop or some other thing where I could be my own boss. My temperament wasn't of the type that lent itself to working for someone else and I had seen enough of the civil service, where so many finish up after military duty. And how could I just up and leave those two women, each needing a male to help get them through.

Upon returning to the hotel, I remembered the 'For sale' sign attached to the rear window of the old taxi that had carried me out to where Esrelle was living. I began to think about it, and he wasn't hard to find again. The taciturn seller was the sole employee and driver, a character called Gerhardus Szaught. He informed me that the goodwill of the business was on offer and the wreck of the conveyance that constituted its entire stock in trade came with it for free.

Well, I threw caution to the wind; unlike me, I suppose.

We haggled about it on the spot and came to an in-principle agreement whereby I would drive it with him for a week and capitalise its worth based on the takings during that period. I insisted on a set-off against the refit for which the car screamed out.

Expending next to nothing, apart from the repairs which weren't so cheap, I had bought myself an income, albeit with scant knowledge of the byways of Port Elizabeth. Gerhardus agreed to work for a percentage of the takings during the first month and would train me as well. After that, I paid the outlays and gave him a monthly stipend for the privilege of using his name as 'owner'. That was the catch because he still had to hold the majority interest in name at least, as I was not a citizen of this country.

It was a big call to trust someone in that way but I was comforted by Esrelle vouchsafing him as a person who would honour the arrangement we struck. After that, we developed a good relationship. Getting much out of him was like prising teeth from a lion. Then, once he happened to drop that he had served in the French Foreign Legion of all things, the sluice gates sort of opened up. He spoke of his active service in Morocco and other parts of North Africa. Thereafter, we exchanged quite a bit militarily, so to speak, and he became more than a little interested in Malaya and the Far East, a place that he informed me he might be inclined to visit one day.

Anyway, back to the domestic intricacies. As you no doubt have deduced, I accepted Esrelle's further offer that

I might live with them after ascertaining that there was a disused storeroom attached to the rear of the house which, with a slap of paint, a little bit of patching and a tidy-up, has suited me. I've become quite the handyman.

From there on something of a miracle happened. Over those next months, Esrelle rallied. The doctors found it quite inexplicable and opined that the cancer had gone into remission. They are still scratching their heads.

I never thought I'd seen such devotion and attachment between mother and daughter, yet it was nothing compared to what I witnessed when Henrietta was delivered of a rather bonnie nine-pound-four-ounce baby boy. I was made to feel part of something special and, for me, it became rather unprecedented.

And there you have it. I'm running a tidy little earner of a taxi service in Port Elizabeth and a de facto father, I suppose, to a little fellow who is already looking at me with his saucer eyes and saying 'Dadda' and more (and getting some encouragement!). What better life might one ask for? To be more frank than I would prefer, my answer is, 'There can't possibly be one.'

If you have managed to get to the end of this rather lengthy missive, you'll be pleased to know that I won't try your patience further. Trust this finds you and Charlotte well and look forward to hearing some of your news. And please don't be sparing with it.

Yours Sincerely,

Reginald Newton

P.S. I meant to mention the one occupant of the house who I most feared. His name, 'Rommel', said a great deal and, from the moment I stepped over that threshold, he sized me up, trying to decide whether I was a legitimate invitee or one to whom entrance was *verboten*. While he may not have been the largest German Shepherd ever to become tamed, he was most certainly the fiercest and strongest. It was his jaws and teeth that separated him from most other canines I've ever encountered.

He took an instant fancy to Henrietta, unlike to me. I sorely needed her assistance over those first few weeks before he tolerated the only male of the house, even so, if I as much made a movement he interpreted as untoward, those same jaws stayed it until he received the command from his mistress to release me. It eventually became a game with Esrelle as her health and spirits lifted. Henrietta joined in, and you can easily guess that there was one person who didn't laugh or get the joke.

When the child was brought home from the hospital, I swear after that moment the dog regarded the boy as one of his own. I was kept at bay until the little chap started to crawl and play. Only then was grudging permission granted for me to join in. Young Magnus (yes, that name again) took great delight in throwing his toys around for Rommel to fetch.

Incidentally, Rommel's mother had been run over. The driver of the vehicle was Gerhardus, the event occurring outside Esrelle's house. He was said to be terribly upset over the incident, something that I would have found totally out of character before I got to know him better. Esrelle offered to care for the pup and he became a permanent fixture in her household ever since.

RN

Chapter 15 – *The Promise*

'Could you please spare a few minutes prior to going out in the taxi today? There's something I need to say, Reginald.'

That she had called to Newton hesitantly as he was about to depart ignited a premonition. 'Don't worry about the work. We've ample time to speak, Esrelle,' he replied, shutting the door behind him. A few minutes passed before he approached her bedside. 'I telephoned Gerhardus. As you have always said, he's something of a lamb when you cut through the armour, insisting on taking over for as long as may be necessary.'

Esrelle's reactive smile waned just as quickly as she lay at the disease's bidding. Its not so short remission had defied the best medical prognoses. All had ascribed her renaissance to Henrietta's appearance, the birth of Magnus Reginald and the happiness of the little family blossoming throughout this period.

Her strength had waxed by the time of his first shaky steps and more besides was superimposed with him as a toddler. It was something at which to marvel, and Henrietta's fervent prayers for her mother began to ask questions of Newton's agnosticism. Esrelle had become ebullient with Magnus' chattering, his bustling, giggling and running up and down the hallway, peeping playfully around corners. When either discovered the other, squeals and shrieks culminated in a limitless conferral of kisses and hugs on his revered 'Granna'. On such occasions, Rommel was an ever-willing participant before Henrietta, sensing her mother's near exhaustion, would intervene to put the little fellow down and assist her into the favourite window rocker.

It came to an ear-splitting end when, after one of these frolics, Esrelle collapsed, screaming in agony. Her femur had broken like a twig and the X-rays told the story. Radiotherapy was no longer a realistic ameliorative and no other medical inhibitor could withstand its relentless march, the specialist declaring that the carcinoma had entered her vital organs. The visual signs couldn't be denied. Her intermittent coughing sapped what little stoic resistance remained.

'Henrietta, can you leave us for a few moments, please, if you don't mind?'

'Of course, Mother. I shall take Magnus out for a walk.' She pressed her lips to the fading woman's cheek and momentarily squeezed Newton's wrist before shepherding her son to the door.

'First let me be clear, and no post-mortems just yet. I can't bear long faces, Reginald.' She took his hand in hers, failing to impart the same asset as the resilience of her eyes.

'At the start of my delicious reprieve – what is it now, two years ago – Henrietta told me all that had happened in her unenviable life. When she mentioned you, I couldn't comprehend what I was hearing. I knew you would come to me, but to have heard from her lips the way she treated you early on in the voyage and the trouble it caused, her really needing help, that Margaret woman—' he eased her head onto his chest.

'Please, my dear, those things are passed and best forgotten. You've proved yourself as her mother, Esrelle, and a fine one.'

'From you, Reginald, that's something to take in. I've never been predictable, and I expect you'll forgive me for requesting this on the instant but I must do so for time is short. Is there a chance that you might take one step beyond that solemn promise I had wrung from you to be there for Henrietta and my little darling grandchild?'

Expecting she might ask whether he could entertain the possibility of formally becoming the boy's male guardian, he responded by accepting adoption was a huge responsibility but that he wouldn't rule it out, if Henrietta was also agreeable.

'Were it that simple, Reginald. I've looked into it already, at least unofficially with the solicitor. I have mentioned in the past the other legal matters concerning her and this house, and they have been fully settled.' She paused for breath and drank some green-coloured liquid. 'No, I'm afraid it's not merely that. This is a commitment much more profound, not only to him but to his mother as well.'

In a man who expressed his feelings with as much frequency as a lunar eclipse, the question had the effect of releasing an adulthood of pent-up years. Shaking, he knelt at Esrelle's feet. After a considerable interlude of basking in memories as she stroked his hair and came to settle on his bowed shoulders, Newton regained himself, taking Esrelle's hands, now just a shadow of those he once held in praiseworthy devotion so long ago.

She resumed after drawing his head against her breast. 'The little mite has your name unofficially, but the scar of his conception could reappear to crush him. He has to be given more than a casual presence for a season or two. While you will look after her and him, you can't do so in the same house on a pretext and, as he gets older, attempt to rationalise it. He has to always believe that you are his father.

'And look at yourself, Reginald. You're a different person, the same – well perhaps not quite the same old stodgy fellow who knocked at this door, but now your actions, what you say and do. I never tire of seeing you with young Magnus. He adores you, and you're the only real father the boy will ever have.'

It seemed like an interminable period of touching, stroking and recollection before she prompted him to speak. 'Are you going to say something, anything?'

'Esrelle, please, my darling, it's not just up to me. Have you canvassed her about it?'

'As a matter of fact, I have, in a roundabout sort of fashion.'

'I think I can guess the sort of roundabouts you tend to employ.'

'And that's why you fell in love with me. Well, dammit, she believes you care about her and I told Esrelle that a love would grow, and you will come to love this young woman more as time passes. I'm not going to compromise you, Reginald, and enter into a scam, declaring you've become a hopeless head-over-heels pussycat for her, but I've watched you two in the same spaces, and she's not entirely unaware of the tenderness towards her that you held even on the ship when she came to you for help.'

'What you have said makes eminent sense,' he reassured in abstract devotion.

'Oh, Reginald, please don't go down that old track. What's your answer? If you need to have it straight from me to tip you over, here it is. Please can you? I want you to ask my daughter for her hand in marriage.'

It was a proposal unlike any other and the ironies were too abundant for words to express. He nodded his head several times as if contemplating how to make answer.

'Yes, I suppose I could take that step, if she saw fit to have me.'

Her face managed to find a thread of colour and she kissed his forehead. 'But never mind jumping to any conclusions, for I don't intend granting you a quickie divorce. So you're going to have to postpone any wedding plans for the moment.'

'You're never going to change,' and he found her lips, tenderly.

'I felt that, decrepit state and all. Why ever so, yet at this hour how could I be otherwise with you? But I promise one thing, the wait won't try your patience.'

'I want it to be a long wait, Esrelle.' This time he stroked her cheek. 'It's as well that we come clean, I mean, myself, really. There's something I must confess.'

A knowing twinkle spread to her wasted face. 'Who was she, the general's wife?'

He trusted his disquiet hadn't shown for it was one memory too many. 'Ah, not quite.'

'Come on, Reginald, please, not a good time to hold back. I didn't expect a score plus years of celibacy on my behalf. Say it.'

'It took around about that space of time to occur. Just nothing much; wealthy society widow, older. Lady Clementine Blunting was her name, happened to witness my street reproach of a drunk and disorderly junior officer just as she was about to be ushered into a nearby car. Afterwards, she advanced on me, introduced herself; overflowing, or rather over the top, she was, at the manner in which I had dealt with the unfortunate chap. I was somewhat taken aback but respectful, receiving a hand that didn't wish to give way.'

'Displaying that dispassionate charm with which she was instantly fascinated. Go on.'

'Her guide, an art director with whom I had but

a nodding acquaintance, joined us. An invitation to cocktails at the Old Museum that evening, I could hardly refuse when she seconded the suggestion. With a host of dignitaries present, she drew me into her circle like a prodigal nephew.

'Being well connected, she was determined to exert the leverage it gave her with the Singaporean expatriate community, my superiors and the boffins in Government House itself. She was a renowned patron of the arts and had pledged a large sum up front, along with ongoing stipends, towards the reconstruction, restoration of and acquisitions for the Museum after damage, neglect and plunder had denuded it during the occupation.

'She needed to be humoured, amused and entertained in consideration of the subscription since it had not yet found its way into treasury coffers. I was alerted to these imperatives and informed that it would be considered as part of my duties to ensure that she remain committed to the project while being on hand as her companion as and when desired. A rider was that the request had emanated from the top of the local administration.'

'I'm feeling better already, Reginald. Don't short-change me now, please,' Esrelle offered, clasping his hand with a grip that had regained some fibre.

'Had I been operational, such a request would have been rejected as not being within my remit. But I regret to say I succumbed to what was to become a vacuous and dissolute diversion with my promotion in limbo, perhaps trusting thereby that my patience might not be in vain. I became her choice of partner to each event on the local social calendar.'

'Dissolute. *And?*' she asked, her eyebrows communicative.

'Well, beyond the third such escorting, all I shall admit is that Lady Blunting's demeanour betrayed more than the mere lending of an arm in, and connected with, her being squired to and from subsequent luncheons, balls and other functions.'

'At last, it's like some D.H. Lawrence intertwining. *And?*'

He was slow to answer. 'Well, again, after some weeks, these activities, outings—'

'Were wearing thin, Reginald?' He sighed and she smiled, then grimaced, attempting to straighten up.

'When her homeward bound vessel finally tied up in Singapore, the lady equivocated over whether she would embark or remain until the next cruising season. My forbearance had reached such a precarious state whereby, having exhausted diplomatic methods of extrication, drastic avenues of absolution began to course through my mind until an unexpected respite arrived.'

'Surely not *another* woman, ahem no, not you. Perhaps a substitution?'

A contrite grin ensued. 'I became aware of a lieutenant's return to England on the same ship. This officer, blessed with attributes at which Adonis himself may have paused to blush, was the perfect replacement. Engineering to be indisposed with a fever on that last night before the liner was due to leave and her own travel plans, even at the eleventh hour still undecided, I swooped on the youngster, sweetening him through the bestowal of generous out-of-pocket expenses. He accepted the commission, and I knew he wasn't the type to waste time. The plot succeeded and she sailed on the morning tide, leaving me a perfunctory memorandum trusting that my health would soon improve.'

'Reginald, with some apprehension, I sense that's not the end of the story, and I do want to hear it from your lips.'

'Indeed. My assumption that Lady Blunting would never trouble me again proved inaccurate. The ensuing cruise turned sour when the self-same lieutenant found more enticing pleasure in the allures of a young woman passenger after not even a week's steaming. In the frightful conflagration that followed, the cad – and that describes him perfectly – verballed me with some pejoratives to the effect that I had considered the esteemed woman as little more than a "clothes horse" and was willing to unload her for the mere exaction of "thirty pieces of silver".

'The payback was swift and scornful. Any suggestion of me being ever confirmed as a full colonel, something with which I had rather incautiously acquainted her when she enquired as to my future prospects, was shelved, although it's fair to observe other factors were in play. Also postponed indefinitely was the fulfilling of the Museum commitment. Into the bargain, I was upbraided for speaking about promotion to a civilian and left to stew upon my incaution after the dressing down.

'Subsequently, I was informed in writing that I must

resume the uniform of a lieutenant-colonel and consider my position. Given the stated preference for remaining in Singapore, the end for my career was only a matter of time.'

'And no doubt you took the demotion without uttering a murmur of protest, changing your insignia as if you were swapping a pair of socks and admonishing yourself for the lapse in judgment. Again, am I right?'

He was spared from further embarrassment when the front door opened. 'Hello, I think she's back from their outing and no doubt the little fellow will be out like a light. Nice timing. Makes no difference to me or the proposition. Go see and bring her in, Reginald.'

Henrietta entered first, right hand trailing behind her as if searching for Newton's.

'He's fast asleep,' she offered with a curious smile.

'With Rommel close by, my dear daughter?'

'You nailed it, Mother. So, how goes things, darling? Oh, here comes old Dadda. I say, that was a lot more than just a confirming glance,' she quipped.

'I just wanted to make sure his teddy bear was beside him,' Newton offered benignly. 'He loves that crumpled little thing. And Rommel ensured it was all I was intending to give.' Both women returned his affectionate smile.

Esrelle spoke with renewed purpose. 'Sit down on the sofa and just pretend I'm not here. I'll endeavour to hold my tongue for as long as may be.' The frail woman's eyes sparkled more than they had since the doctors had made their pronouncements.

Henrietta combed them both before her face lightened, 'What have you pair of conspirators cooked up now?'

'I want to marry you, Henrietta. Your mother has given me permission to ask, but she won't do more than that, for it's my request to make. Will you have me?'

There was no stilling Henrietta now. 'Reginald, there is nothing more in this world I want than two things. I have prayed and prayed that Mummy would get better. She came back from the brink. Those prayers were answered and for a reason. The time allowed me to come to love you as I have never loved before. But please understand also that I was, in an offbeat sort of way, drawn to you before this moment, and you must have known that.

'And Mummy *has* spoken to me about the future, this topic much to the forefront in recent times. I accept and understand completely that you do not love me in the same way because of your vows all those years ago.

'Much as your patience has been rewarded in finding, not merely the mother I always needed but the family you wanted, my patience in knowing you will come to love me the same will see us through. I realised at the outset what you were, what you remain – a careful, kind, considerate and honourable man – and I like what I see and love what I see. Your loyalty is real, as you've proved to my mother.'

'Not entirely loyal, I'm afraid.'

'You still love her and have given up your own plans to remain here with us, an example of the loyalty of which I speak, if ever there was one.'

Esrelle managed to stand, refusing assistance. 'No more of this cooing, time for me to butt in and pronounce that you may kiss the bride-to-be and the mother who will now die happy.'

315

Having resolved to put army logistics behind him, Newton, nonetheless, followed any report on what was now fixed in military lore as the 'Malayan Emergency' during his stay in Port Elizabeth. Alive to these tendencies, Esrelle had, not long after he came to lodge at her house, whetted his thirst by obtaining a subscription to *The Times*. Whenever he passed some caustic observation, she delighted in chiding him with, 'My poor, dear Reginald, you're as wedded to Malaya as the rubber that shoots from the ground.'

Even allowing for his armchair perch and the hearsay accounts, he was appalled by the unfolding administrative debacle, recalling his own warnings of its likelihood because the roles of all three arms of the administration were so ill-defined. The various services – police, army and intelligence – waged an internecine warfare, sometimes appearing more vituperative than the actual conflict on the ground, as they jockeyed with each other. Perpetually at loggerheads internally, the players sometimes broke out in unseemly public spats, managing the dubious distinction of increasing newspaper circulation while sapping morale. It was an extension of the powerplay he had experienced, though on a much larger scale since his departure. Esrelle had encouraged him to speak of it, and Henrietta listened in apparent awe at his broad knowledge and insight.

Sir Henry Gurney had remained on as High Commissioner after Newton's departure. Though Malaya was not a unified colony, as the terrorist activity intensified, Gurney introduced rigid emergency regulations, including deportation orders directed at the Chinese squatters who were outside the effective control of the government. Such were enforced by police recruited from the United Kingdom and Palestine. In turn, as designated lieutenants, they trained the special constabulary.

The report, that didn't require reading between the lines, was the one that shocked him and the British government most. Gurney was assassinated in a terrorist ambush in October 1951. The event would send, Newton opined, the most chilling signal to all that not even the highest official was safe.

From 22 January 1952, Newton noted with immense optimism that Gurney's replacement would be none other than the distinguished and redoubtable General Sir Gerald Templer, a man he had briefly encountered in North Africa and who he greatly admired.

*   *   *

Sonning Common, Reading England

Tel. RG4-5981

12 November 1952

Dear Colonel,

Your letter arrived in my mailbox only yesterday so that means a pretty slow postal transit. But from what I can see with the lapse of time, remaining optimistic that you will follow my lead in attending to your correspondence in the future is a given.

Because I must post this hour, I shall keep it somewhat abridged, promising to be more detailed the next time around.

All levity apart, let me begin by thanking you for that jam-packed chronicle of your life, times and perambulations since last we communicated. More than anything within those events, momentous as they are, was the tone and character that I feel and see in your makeup, and even style. Something has indeed happened for the better and it shows!

There you are, having taken up a life so different from the one to which you have been used, and your enjoyment of it need not be otherwise stated. Why, you're as near to fatherhood and domesticity as any man might be but without the ties that holy matrimony imposes. I don't mean to sound blasé, especially given the circumstances which brought on the situation in which you now find yourself.

As to the young boy, speaking from experience, the bonds that you have with him already are of the kind that will sustain anyone with the flintiest of hearts forever, and I know you're not such a species anymore. (Oh, go on with you, that was a joke!)

He sees you as his father, and what a lucky (and plucky he would be, too, under your guidance) little fellow he is to have someone as dutiful as you. Importantly, you regard him as your son. No flesh or blood connection can make it get any stronger than that. If Magnus had lived to see and experience this, he couldn't have imagined a better life in front of him than the one you've a right to expect in the future. He would almost worship what you have done and will sleep well forever hereafter in the bosom of Abraham.

I am also delighted to be told that Henrietta has accepted this situation of you in her son's life, de facto grandfather, if you please, and embraced her birth mother in the process. What a turnaround it's all been and, despite the scars she wears, it seems as if motherhood has been the making of her.

I'll digress for a moment. Not wishing to be seen as flippant, but I just can't see you toadying to and ferrying 'nobility' around in a peaked cap. Ah, now I've got it. You're back in uniform without someone standing over you and issuing orders! Your partner's goodwill is heading south as I write, eh?

Well, as you must be detecting from this rather discursive epistle, I'm rushing this so as to send you and your little 'family' my best wishes.

Me and mine? First, Charlotte is doing good things and, soon after walking on dry land here, I picked up some tutoring. English primarily (there's an irony) and basic mathematics. It opened another door for me and led to being offered a position as a teacher. Naturally, I accepted, and have been doing my bit at a local secondary school for nearly a year. Altogether this earns me a reasonable stipend. Things are quite expensive in England and, without Charlotte's scholarship, it would be tough going. Fortunately, I haven't had to draw on my capital, but touch and go just the same.

Now that you'll be staying put for the foreseeable future, please keep me posted. I haven't mentioned anything about Esrelle's condition because it seems from your account that she's doing well. Let's hope and pray that she becomes restored to full health and strength.

As I said, more to follow soon. Take care and enjoy your deserved new life.

Fondly,

Nancyng Jenkins

✳   ✳   ✳

Except for the officiating officer, theirs was the wedding the bride's mother had wanted. It was private, unobtrusive and tasteful. A request of it taking place in the form and manner she had set out and her final words that she would carry the projected image in perpetuity ensured that Henrietta and Reginald honoured those wishes. Even the doves' release from the steps of the drab government building symbolised the blissful flight of Esrelle's spirit to the heavens.

The registrar himself had acted as celebrant, although even Newton thought his bearing more befitted one of his other duties, the making of entries in a solemn roll supported by medical certificates. In a jet-black suit, white shirt and corporate tie, proclamations bordering on the melancholic set a somewhat disconsolate tone throughout the formalities.

By contrast the bride, her glorious red hair wound in a bun high atop her head and secured by a wreath of pansies, shined as if bathing in the approbation of unseen and innumerable guests and the dust of stars from a heavenly realm. Her well-behaved son, standing beside Henrietta in navy blue shorts held up by braces strung over a blue and red checked shirt with red bow tie, thumb firmly planted in mouth, pressed his head shyly into his mother's pink, ankle-length dress.

The groom, face relatively unlined, head erect and sartorial in charcoal and grey pinstriped suit almost matching his hair and not appearing so differentiated in years from her as to occasion remark, contained a broadening smile, stealing glances with his bride before beaming in admiration as her vows delivered their precision of lifelong commitment. Even the now slightly slimmed-down version of Gerhardus, stolid beside the bridegroom, wore a mustard and brown checked sports jacket strained across massive shoulders over a blue shirt, top button unsecured to accommodate a twenty-inch neck, a motley red tie and brown woollen pants. He was given to shifting his feet and swaying as if to revive the musty room.

The pronouncement of 'man and wife' seemed to have been made just in time. A clerk entered the room, handed paperwork to the registrar and snapped a photograph of the group. Before a chance had been offered for the husband to kiss his bride, the telephone rang. When the receiver was replaced following a number of monosyllabic answers, the registrar told him that the attaché at the British Consulate would be pleased to receive the attendance of a 'Lieutenant-Colonel Reginald Newton'.

'That's you, I take it, sir. A telegram of confirmation will arrive in a few minutes. A little time will be soaked up in some legal procedures as we need to sign the registry book and your certificate of marriage has to be completed, witnessed and sealed in accordance with South African law.'

That accomplished, as they moved into the corridor the telegram was delivered and he put the envelope in his pocket.

'Aren't you going to see what it's about, my dear husband?' his radiant wife asked.

'Not just yet,' Newton sighed.

'I think you should. It's sure to be important.'

'Nothing is more important than finishing what we started.'

Pressed further, Newton read it and, without saying a word, showed Henrietta. The author was General Sir Gerald Templer, the High Commissioner of Malaya.

'Well, there it is, Reginald, Gerhardus, Magnus, we must suspend celebrations and take ourselves off to the consulate,' announced Mrs Newton the second, sounding as confident and sure as the woman who had begotten her. 'Our little celebration can wait.'

*   *   *

Port Elizabeth

10 December 1952

Dear Mrs Jenkins,

I have yours of 12 ultimo for which I thank you. You will soon begin to understand why I won't be responding in other than a fairly matter-of-fact manner. There have been some life-altering events that have taken place since last I put pen to paper.

First, while it was true to say that Esrelle's restoration to vitality bordered on being incredible, not long after my letter was posted she experienced a relapse that hit us all for six. Her health declined in a precipitous fashion as the cancer came back vengefully and she passed away within days of you writing.

While it was a terrible blow to Henrietta, the way her mother comported herself in those final weeks was nothing short of exemplary. As the end approached, they drew the utmost comfort from each other. I couldn't work, of course, and Gerhardus, who has proved to be a Rock of Gibraltar and more, drove the taxi the whole time, that is, if he wasn't going out for medicines, summoning doctors and procuring household supplies whenever they were needed.

Secondly, Esrelle knew that she was leaving behind a fragile young mother with potentially no one to care for her and Magnus in the long term, not that I wouldn't have ensured that they were furnished the necessaries of life.

Thirdly, a further problem recognised by Esrelle was that both of us, as well as the young child, not being South African citizens, couldn't remain in the country open-endedly unless there was ongoing sponsorship by a resident who owned real property. Our visas were renewed every six months on that basis. The exception to that rule was if Esrelle gifted her property to her daughter. This she did, and it meant Henrietta could remain, take citizenship and keep sponsoring myself. Unfortunately, gift taxes had to be paid.

Fourthly, there was Magnus. I couldn't separate myself from this tiny bundle, but how would I be able to stay in the same house with an unmarried woman and a child?

Fifthly, there was but one thing to do. Esrelle knew it, Henrietta wanted it and Magnus believed he had it – a mother and a father. And so we went and got married; no fuss, no grand ceremony and in a shoebox Registry Office. Snookered, if you like. Still haven't woken up from it all!

But there was more. That day I received an offer to go back to the old stomping ground in Malaya under a progressive administration led by the indomitable Sir Gerald Templer. I can't say much about this matter except that it seems more police work, the activities of a nasty criminal first and a communist second. Somehow or other Sir Gerald has been led to believe that my background might assist in being able to track the felon and his gang down.

In the wash-up, we are tidying up loose ends and moving by the end of the month. Gerhardus asked if there could be room for him and I requested that he be permitted to come. He's been approved as one of the family's assistants, as the British authorities so quaintly put it.

Still much to work out. And you may well be wondering about something else. Think no more, as there was no way that I would take the job if it meant leaving Rommel behind!

I told Henrietta some time ago that you and I had been corresponding and she seemed delighted to hear it. In fact, she said to pass on her regards. Who knows, you might even receive a letter from her once we get all settled up in the 'Old Country', pun intended. I think I would like that to happen. She has never forgotten what you did for her on the ship.

Henrietta did happen to ask me rather recently whether you and I were more than mere penfriends, a thing I found a little unsettling. I simply told her that we were odd and rakish sort of friends but nothing else.

Ours, I mean Henrietta's and mine, is an unusual cohabitation for I have not yet fully processed the actual notion of holy matrimony, notwithstanding having been a party to it, strange as that may seem. I have come to care deeply about this young woman who has entered my life as something of a 'misdirected package' – crassly put, I concede – but struggle to comprehend the duties, obligations and expectations of a husband in this exceptional situation. My belief is that the adjustment process will take time, and it is something for which everyone's prepared and about which no more need be said.

Accordingly, and being rather franker than I'd prefer, you may, or perhaps may not, be surprised when I relate that I haven't been able to bring myself to share the same room with her, but neither has there been any sign barring entry. I want to believe that she understands, and I know by the regard she has for me and her manner of observing yours truly when I'm playing with little Magnus, that Henrietta somehow loves me in a way that I am as yet unable to reciprocate.

All of the above must seem confusing to you, perhaps my candour even more so, if not rather startling. I've not shared these intimate thoughts with a single soul, knowing that you would respect confidences and appreciating the relationship we have had.

So saying, may we part with this: until things have stabilised, Mrs Jenkins – and I most certainly don't mean to offend you – given that I'm married, I have begun to wonder if it is perhaps more appropriate for all further correspondence to be curtailed. It goes without saying that this state of affairs has not been prompted by any suggestion of Henrietta's.

In the event and not without some regret, and maybe not for all time, it is the course I've decided to follow.

All the best to you and your family,

Reginald Newton

Chapter 17 – *Concerning London*

As an only son, Thomas Tredwig had been a profound disappointment to his parents. Having attained General rank in the army, his father regarded Thomas as ungrateful and indolent in desiring a police vocation rather than the one mapped out for him from the time he could speak. The boy wanted nothing to do with the army and, once at boarding school, even less to do with his parents. Dropping out at seventeen, he never returned home and supported himself by working in a number of labouring jobs. Having always set his sights on a constabulary career, he studied at night, gaining a Diploma in Criminal Legal Studies and Procedure. At twenty-one, he changed his surname by deed poll and, certificate under his arm, was accepted into the London Metropolitan Police.

It was a calling into which he plunged with all the delirium of a kid in an ice-cream parlour. Beginning duty on the beat, he distinguished himself early as fearless and fearsome, securing a number of notorious arrests. One such scalp happened to be a vicious thug with an unenviable record being sought for murder who had eluded detectives for months. Lining up for a Cornish pastie at a shop near to where he lived, Tredwig recognised the individual from a wanted sheet and called him by name. Instantly, the man broke past him and ran into the street. He was no match for the fleet-of-foot young constable, who tackled him, rugby fashion, after which an all-in fist fight ensued.

The fugitive was given six inches in height and several stone in weight, but Tredwig was a nippy scrapper, ducking and weaving while landing some neat blows before several Bobbies arrived to cuff and subdue him. Though not emerging unscathed himself, PC Tredwig's flurry of punches had left the criminal a bruised and bloodied mess.

Tredwig also had an uncanny knack of intuiting suspicious activity and acting so as to effect an arrest either leading up to or not long after it had been committed. He was recognised through these exploits as someone with a great investigative future. That he was cognisant of the law was one thing, but practical knowledge he also pursued, utilising every spare moment to attend trials in order to become familiar with procedure. Thereby, Tredwig developed an impeccable understanding of the rules of evidence. It prompted his superiors to suggest that his talents were being squandered on the beat and that he should take up the offer of Articles of Clerkship with a prominent London firm who witnessed his expertise in nailing one of their clients embroiled in an elaborate fraud.

He was content to remain with the police, exploiting the powers the office gave him, including the opportunities for advancement not solely confined to rank after he graduated to plainclothes work. Tredwig became friendly with a powerful element of the underworld active in the Soho area. He used some as informers to great effect.

His reputation as an uncompromising pugilist spread fast, as well as his notoriety for having no compunction about the use of firearms when they were needed. He played criminals off against each other and benefited materially for it. By the time he was thirty, he had risen to detective sergeant, sometimes acting as a detective inspector, and was one of Scotland Yard's most formidable investigators.

During this meteoric rise, he saw nothing of his parents until informed by an uncle that his mother was in straitened circumstance after several strokes, his father having died of pneumonia several years previously. A bachelor to that point confining his liaisons to married females, he became remorseful at the way he had treated his mother and effected something of a reconciliation. He had time off from the police and resided with her, arranging for a live-in nurse when he resumed duty.

It became apparent that he couldn't manage the responsibilities at Scotland Yard and look after the ailing woman. He sought a transfer to a lesser position closer to where she lived so as he could spend more time with her, a final illness now evident. It was not long after she passed away that Tredwig heard of an opportunity to serve in Malaya as a police liaison officer. Coincidentally, some old matters in which he had been involved at Soho had taken a sharp turn against him, with his replacement not being as ready to cut corners using seedy contacts as had his cocksure predecessor. Before things closed in upon him, Malaya beckoned and he made an application.

In January 1953, Thomas Tredwig joined an already impressive list of former force members from the United Kingdom to become part of Britain's plan to establish and maintain an effective presence to counter the communist insurgency as it impacted on the Malayan population.

Soon after he arrived in Kuala Lumpur, Tredwig was sworn in as a lieutenant. It was something of a promotion, given that the pay was significantly better than he enjoyed as an officer of the London Metropolitan Borough.

*   *   *

Lynn Lee's fiancé was listed as missing, his plane confirmed as having been shot down over Germany in August 1943. No immediate word emerged as to his fate or that of the bomber's crew. Her prayers for him were boosted when a report suggested that he was a prisoner, but nothing more came with war's end.

Sir Gabriel Litherland was an MP who had earned a reputation for helping the families of missing RAF personnel. A former air force officer, Litherland, having been acquainted with Lynn's plight, became her most unfailing supporter, raising questions in the House of Commons on her behalf and for other women who were searching for their loved ones. After a tip-off from the French, it appeared that her fiancé may have escaped from detention and had been at large in occupied France.

Lynn was desperate to know whether he had survived, given an abundance of gossip and speculation suggesting that some English servicemen opted to start new lives, for multifarious private reasons, rather than return home. Accompanied by Sir Gabriel, she travelled to the continent before confirmation was finally provided that he had been caught and liquidated by the Gestapo. Though no gravesite was ever found to add credence to what was revealed, two independent sources verified his detention in Avenue Foch, and he was never seen again. She was devastated and, after entertaining so much hope, inconsolable.

Litherland had continued to pen letters of support, which she rarely answered, before one came declaring his love for her and containing a proposal. She was surprised and honoured but, having pledged never to marry after her tragic loss, thanked him for his kindness, declined his overtures respectfully and shunned any further attempts at contact. More than six years passing since the airman's disappearance, the Chancery Court on the application of the Department of Defence, declared that he was deceased and made a grant of probate. His small estate had been left to her.

Since they commenced sharing the Sonning Common house, Lynn Lee had more fully unburdened herself to Nancyng Jenkins, her cousin. They had been close, having corresponded over a considerable number of years. Nancyng well remembered the joy she expressed at being engaged to be married to an airman and the devastation at being advised that his aircraft hadn't returned from a mission.

Lynn found solace in Nancyng's gregarious nature, contrasting with that of her own, being shy and retiring. Like her, Lynn was a teacher by vocation, save that she took classes for year two primary children. A petite, late-twenties woman, she preferred to limit her friendships to those with whom she worked, and never of the opposite sex. Nancyng Jenkins respected her cousin's reluctance to socialise in groups. Beyond an occasional visit to the pictures, they rarely ventured out after work, confining themselves to short walks or attending to their shopping.

The imperative to remain indoors was no more evident than on a bitter Sunday evening of 22 December 1952 that had windswept and dusted fields, sealed open cracks with snow and overlaid much else in ice. It wasn't just an unwelcome companion but an officious intruder that no layers of clothing could withstand. Even the local off-licence loomed as one challenge too far despite an occasion that invited a departure from routine. Nancyng baulked at it, but, after tipping her face into the elements as one last test, was encouraged by the cessation of blustery conditions and a starry sky.

'My goodness, it's your birthday, Lynnie. Just this once,

can you try, if only for me? It's not all that bad outside now, crisp but bearable, and we aren't going on a bender,' Nancyng urged Lynn a second time before she relented.

Once inside the *Hoof's Rest*, they spied a quieter nook away from the bar, the choice made easier by the fact that most had trusted to their homes.

'Thank you for braving it,' Nancyng said, holding a sherry and a lager, the beer finding her lips a little earlier than her cousin's when she proposed a toast.

'Mm, that's a treat,' she brightened. 'Warm and cosy near the logs, makes the whole thing worthwhile. 'I'm coming to feel glad we punched through the ice sheet in more ways than one. It's about time I did.'

'And same for me, Lynn, much less daunting once the effort is made, and doubly so for you managing to get me out as well. I've been so cocooned lately. As this really is something of a first, let's hope it won't be the last. You know, we owe it to ourselves not to just sit around,' she offered breezily, receiving a nod by way of acknowledgement. 'Oh, come on, you can do better than that,' she urged.

'Good to be with you, cousin,' her teeth making more of an appearance.

On the blackboard beside a full-length portrait of an airborne chestnut stallion, each hoof depicted as if the farrier had polished it that same day, was the two-line chalked fare announcing shepherd's pie and bread and butter pudding with custard.

'And no need to spend much time ruminating over

the menu either,' she added, warming to the convivial atmosphere, woodsmoke out-scenting that of tobacco.

Nancyng placed their order and received the thumbs-up after lodging an aside into the barmaid's ear. Apart from three loungers on barstools, their faces fixated on nothing but seeming to open their jowls from time to time either talking or, more frequently, tilting a jar of frothy contents, the only other patrons were two young men playing darts and going much harder pint for pint.

'You seem to be chirpier than a little birthday occasion of mine would warrant,' offered Lynn, scrutinising Nancyng in faux suspicion. 'Something has to be tickling your fancy.'

'Well, there you go. Housemates for a couple of years and not even a secret thought is secure. The answer goes not so much to my fancy, rather more like amazement.'

'Is it that letter I saw you reading yesterday?'

'Go to the top of the class, ugh, that awful cliché, again. Alright, I've been dying to open my trap. You've heard tell of Reginald Newton, that colonel chap ex-Malaya I met on the cruise over?'

'Since you received a letter from him, he's all you ever seem to talk about.'

'That's the first decent colour *your* cheeks have made in a while. The sherry's not to blame and I see you're due for a follow-up,' Nancyng Jenkins replied, catching the barmaid's eye from whom came a nod when she held up two fingers. 'Well, get this: remember I told you how he stayed on in Port Elizabeth?'

Her cousin nodded, Nancyng being momentarily distracted by two well-dressed men who occupied the now empty bar as if they had requisitioned it. 'Don't they look important?'

'Uh-hum, that's one way to put it.'

'Almost out of place,' Lynn observed, as one of them nodded towards her.

'Careful, cousin, they might hear you. So, remember that young woman, Henrietta, whose father made her pregnant?'

'Yes, it was revolting, and committed suicide to save face.'

'Well, Lynn, I'm completely flabbergasted. Newton has gone and married her.'

'What? Wasn't she hardly out of her teens and he broaching fifty?'

'Not that close and, anyway, he doesn't look it, even if the colonel acts like he's been fifty all his life.'

'I say, you seem to have done some looking yourself.'

'That's enough from you,' she chided merrily. 'Okay, there's an age difference, but it's not what anyone might think without appreciating, shall I say in his defence, the extenuating circumstances.'

'That's right, for I recall you mentioning that she had recently found her real mother only to discover the poor thing desperately ill.'

'To everyone's amazement she rallied, at least for long enough to see her grandson walk. Meanwhile, the colonel stayed on to help them. Well, the cancer returned of a sudden and she passed away recently.'

'Oh, that must have been terribly distressing for the young woman. The whole saga also says a great deal about the stoicism of this Reginald.'

'Indeed, it does. I mean, he'd become part of the household almost by accident and lived in a semi-detached room. The Colonel appears to have taken a great fancy to the little boy but never was there any concession – well, I wasn't there, but no indication of any romantic connection. Still that's—'

'Hello, ladies.' The more bumptious of the newcomers had swaggered over from the bar. 'Trusting that we aren't interrupting, may we join you? My name's Tommy and this is my mate, Alex.' Not waiting for acquiescence, they occupied the table. 'And you're?' The meals arrived without any answer being given. 'Oh, pardon us, ladies, but you seemed lonely. Excuse me, waitress, could we have ours brought here?'

Nancyng touched Lynn under the table for reassurance and opted for indifferent civility. 'I'm Nancyng and this is Lynn. We're expecting some company soon but fine for the minute.'

'You live around here, I take it?' with the hint not taken. It was the other man, raising his voice to counter a cheer from the dart participants whose level of enthusiasm matched their increasingly determined intake of brown ale.

Nancyng Jenkins sized both men up before replying. 'Yes, not all that far away.'

'Together?' Tommy asked. 'Look, sorry, can't help being inquisitive in our line. We're police officers. Bloody wish we could 'ave normal, simple lives but always we put the public first.'

Nancyng's reply was more interrogative than expected. 'Are you on duty? It's just that I've never heard of the law drinking at work, unless you're undercover or something.'

'Hey, Alex, how about that? Not only gorgeous little oriental wallflowers these, one even with passin' knowledge of policin', eh, Nancyng? So you'd know that the law's always on unpaid dooty. As to our roster, that's another story.' Tommy's patronising familiarity saw the two women make fleeting eye contact before, in unison, each unbound the serviette from her knife and fork.

'It's been a hard day, so don't mind Tommy, me dears,' chirped his companion, as if in the character each employed when on the job. 'It's his last shift before, next week, he takes on policing in a not-so-friendly patch as this one's been.'

'Malaya, actually,' the impending traveller announced as if he had been headhunted for the position, rocking his head from side to side before asking, 'Has either of you lovely damsels ever 'eard of it?'

The women shuffled between glances again. Their unspoken pleas for interruption were answered momentarily by the arrival of the men's plates. 'Thankee, me darlin,' said Tommy, one eye on the portion size, the other exploring the barmaid's cleavage. 'Malaya anyone?' he persisted.

Nancyng responded tartly, 'Not a place for the faint-hearted from what I've heard.'

'You don't speak much, Missy.' Alex directed his eyes to

Lynn. 'I say, Tommy, there's something really fetchin' and allurin' about a woman that's this shy. Good, healthy chaps like us find it real kosha, and we know youse types are always good witnesses in court, Miss. Sorry to embarrass you. I can't help myself when it comes to mystery and our job. And what's your situation, eh, Lynn?'

'Um, just a primary school teacher,' she responded meekly.

'Oh, Miss, come on now, no need to be shy and scared around us fellas.' He touched her hand and she drew back with obvious annoyance. 'You have to get up in front of all those little boys and girls and show 'em who's the boss.'

'Bit like this callin' again, Miss,' chimed in Tommy, 'only that ours deals with big boys and girls, bit less responsive and a ruddy sight more ignorant when it comes to other people unless persuasion is brought to bear, the kind like that brings to mind them pair of ignoramuses playin' darts,' projecting the last words in the subjects' direction when a roar went up.

'Hey, hey, keep it down, alright?' Alex called over to them. 'We can't hear ourselves think, or what these lovely ladies are even sayin'.'

It was as if their insobriety had been notarised and they turned their attention to the interruption.

'You got somethin' to say to us, mate?' the more heavyset of the players responded, advancing a few steps with the other behind him no less intent.

'If you pair o' lags can see anyone else in the bar who's makin' that bloody racket, you might care to fills me in,'

Tommy blurted out, getting to his feet while his partner exuded an air of bravado in the direction of the two women, as if desiring recognition and trying to allay any concern they might have should trouble arise.

'Just making a polite request for youse to settle down,' Alex eventually said, leaning back in his chair. 'There are patrons here beside yourselves, that's all we're sayin', mate.'

'And who might you be to run the bar? Oy, and I don't see the manager askin' us to shut our faces and, until he does, you know what you can do with the fat end of a pool cue,' spoke the other man pugnaciously, stepping forward beside his friend, his face made prominent by a nose, flattened so as to borrow more of his cheeks than it had during childhood.

The manager, recognising those who had made the request, adopted a conciliatory tone and whispered to the players. A last round of pints did little to quell their simmering anger. The darts were deposited in their cabinet and the door shut with a clear absence of decorum. Somewhat less expressively, out of respect for the manager, the empty glasses were returned to the bar. Both found Tommy's eyes and the word 'grubs' was louder than a whisper as they left.

Alex's smile had become a smirk as he was drawn to his dinner, but not Tommy. 'Come on, guv,' he said, tapping the other man on the shoulder. 'Sorry, another time, eh, my dears. We 'ave to love ya and leave ya. Dooty calls. As I said, we're always on it, and that's the trouble. I've got a hunch about them pair. Probably my last little soufflé, but good coppas are born with instinct.'

*　　*　　*

'I say, get some of this?' Lynn addressed Nancyng as she came through the door on a brisk Monday evening. She deposited her handbag, scarf, beanie and coat across the Chesterfield. Having handed her the opened newspaper pointing to the story, Lynn had received an answer before her cousin had sat down, taking in fully the small piece on the second page under the heading, 'Thugs get mugged'.

'Well, look at that.' Nancyng read aloud the final paragraph: 'One of the burglars is seriously ill in a coma while the other remains at large.'

'And what about that business of the two police involved having recently completed their shift had intercepted the men less than a block and a half from the *Hoof's Rest* trying to break into a house.'

'And the poor coppers sustained minor cuts and bruises in the affray,' echoed Nancyng Jenkins. 'I wouldn't buy it if the Prime Minister himself had verified the story, and still more would there be a need for further convincing.'

'I agree,' replied her housemate, 'but there's no mention of the names of the police or the alleged burglars. Yet again, what an extraordinary oddity it would be if different police altogether were involved.'

'And off-duty at that.'

'You know, Nancyng, I guess this sounds a little silly for me in particular but that quieter one had his eye in my direction, sliding around and touchy as he was trying to be.'

'I noticed,' her companion replied. 'Had they not left so abruptly, I almost wondered whether he might ask you out, not that you ever would go with his sort.'

'Or even entertain such a thought. They should be reported.'

Nancyng became thoughtful. 'Reporting? Yes, in principle, but to whom? And the other question is, for what, without knowing it was definitely them, or even how the bashing arose, that is, if it really did occur in the course of preventing an attempt to rob someone's house.'

'What about an anonymous tip-off to someone really high up?'

'Tempting, but what's it to do with us really? They're the wrong sort to tangle with, and, if we phoned, they might trace the call. Come on, Lynn, you're old enough to know what police are like.'

'That Tommy will be off to Malaya any day soon from what he said. If they were the ones, I can't help feeling sorry for those two young chaps in one way. I know they were cheeky and potted, but if they were trying to break into a house – still, somewhat peculiar.'

'They left us rather quickly, I thought, given what was really nothing; almost seemed to be spoiling for something and—' The doorbell interrupted Nancyng's musings. 'Who could that be, I wonder?'

'I'll get it,' came her cousin's reply. She stiffened at the appearance of the visitors and called her cousin.

'Hello again, m'dear ladies, what a special treat. Remember

us? Don't look so alarmed.' It was Alex who led off and broke out into a hearty laugh. 'Hey, Tommy ol' mate, have you got the cuffs ready?'

His partner stepped cheerily into the porch light. 'Sorry, love, just jokin'. I remember you're the quiet one Alex fancied. We're not 'ere to arrest ya or anythin' and, even if we wanted to, I couldn't, since m'badge got handed in and I'm just like anyone else now.'

Her mouth was still agape.

'So are youse going to leave us out in the cold or what?' Alex asked.

Nancyng, in no mood for pleasantries, shielded her cousin, taking hold of the door and narrowing the opening until its progress was stayed by Tommy's knee.

'Whatever it is you two want here, state your business succinctly. Lynn, be ready to ring Scotland Yard.'

Tommy laughed heartily. 'Well, Alex, there's gratitude for ya. We're mindin' our own business, save these women from nuisance drunks, left a plate full o' food, track a couple o' crooks, prevent a serious crime from being committed, earn a shiner or two for our trouble and that's all the thanks we get from 'em.' Tommy turned his head sideways, pointing to his face.

Nancyng didn't shrink from him. 'The other night you told us you were never off duty. Is this evening's call yet another variant?'

The snigger was followed by the application of more pressure with his lower leg and his hand wrapped around her fingers that were holding the door.

'Oh, guv, steady on. I wouldn't blame little Lynn in there for the unwise actions of her surly mate 'ere.'

'Will that be all now?' Nancyng persisted unflinchingly.

The former policeman responded to his colleague's gentle tug at his sleeve but not so far as to permit the door to be closed in his face.

'Weren't you a resident of Malaya at one time, Mrs Jenkins? Strange how ya never mentioned it,' his curious frown deepening. 'Me 'unches never let me down, do they, Alex?'

'Let's be gawn, mate.'

'Been suggested to me that it would be much healthier for you and your daughter to continue to live here rather than ever returning to that place, provided you behave, o' course. Isn't that right, Alex?' his voice fading as they moved towards a car.

Emboldened by Nancyng's stance and wanting to dispel a perception the men might hold that she was any less forthright, Lynn opened the door holding her cousin's hand. Together they stood outside, and she called after them. 'If either of you ever come to this house again, your superiors will hear of it, along with the reasons that brought you here.'

It wasn't merely the truculent stares that saw both women go inside, bolt the door and hover at the window. The two figures remained seated in the idling, unmarked car, interior light burning and from which emitted harsh laughter, cigarette smoke and low conversation before, tooting the horn several times, they sped off.

'Don't know about you, Lynn, but they have confirmed an assumption. I'm glad that the more loutish of the two is going to be out of harm's way. He's cut from shady cloth, and the other, who seems rather in awe of him, might trim his jib from now on.' 344

Chapter 18 – *The Quarry*

Amidst the squalor and privation a remote jungle subsistence promised, one of Nu Li's few remaining liberties was the ravening satisfaction he derived as leader of a gang of communist insurgents that had stalked and executed the British High Commissioner in October 1951. More than a year since the momentous event, pronouncements that every terrorist involved would be hunted down without mercy brought the makings of a curl to his puffy lips. *Not a soul taken, you scum,* he thought. Nu was all about internalising since there, along with the serpent, resided his garden of Eden.

What a potted expedition Nu's had been in the peninsula leading up to the Japanese subjugation of Malaya and Singapore's encirclement in February 1942. Upon that event, lucrative emoluments accruing to him under the cover of his proprietorship of an eatery on the periphery of Kuala Lumpur's business district were peremptorily severed, and financial ruin was the smallest of his fears.

Acquired in 1938 and nurtured under concealed foreign patronage, the nondescript dingy café flowered, becoming a meeting place and clearing house for bribery and clandestine activity while earning a legitimate name as a recommended venue for dining. With Singapore's capitulation and go-betweens – Heenan, the British spy, and his villainous sidekick, Jamal Viranhi – eliminated, an only sister probably dead, and the rest of his family gone, Nu's time of easy endowment had passed.

Like his stature, noticeably shorter than many of those from whom he once accepted favours, so too had shrunk his status. After attempts to put himself at the Japanese administration's further disposal as far as keeping watch on any local elements minded towards insurrection received a mistrustful rebuff, Nu Li was swift to turn bitter and rancorous, traits with which he was more than fully equipped. He became certain that his earthly sojourn had been judged by the occupying power as not worthy of extension. The repulsion felt for traitors, even from once-gratified aiders and abettors, was a universal characteristic.

Nu experienced a nervous tic each time he separated from the confines of his business. Paranoia that he was being watched by the Kempeitai beset him. From experience during the rape of Nanking, he knew that their methods were not guided by such concepts as natural justice. Daily, he lived with the fear that a raid might occur and the Beretta pistol, concealed in his attic, would be his undoing.

Being found in possession of a firearm earned summary execution.

On the street, the Chinese were candidates for unexpected interdiction. Whenever in his vehicle going about commercial activity, each glance in the rear-vision mirror saw sweat gathering on his forehead on the coolest of evenings and sliding down the sides of his face as if imminent arrest was but a 'halt' away. When Nu took to opening and closing his premises at inconsistent hours, the end was in sight as custom dwindled.

This existence had the positive effect of activating schemes as to what should be his next move. Blessed with the originality and acumen of his father and having, since his arrival in Malaya, crafted an exceptional cunning of his own, he wasn't without considerable adaptation skills. Amidst this brooding, the genesis of an idea began to take on the form that might pave a means of escape from the threats he supposed were encompassing him.

Revenge was a powerful inducement to swap sides. The Japanese had no further use for him and, with each passing day, there was a danger that he could be denounced by anyone he had crossed. With torture, beatings and disappearances gone by through his betrayals, there remained any number of enemies or their relatives ready to denounce him and claim a reward. Financially, he was in a strong position to insinuate his way into the underground communist movement and still hold enough back in case the approach was rejected but the cash wasn't. He decided that his future lay in becoming an active supporter and a participant in the movement of which he had been aware well before the Japanese set foot into Malaya.

At the infancy of these ruminations, a break came when a consortium offered to buy the café. Considerable satisfaction was derived from it being one of the few transactions where he had permitted himself to be bested through faking illness and exhaustion as the reason for a swift, under-priced sale. It provided enough working capital capable of gaining the confidence of the communists and he could hide the balance with his one trusted friend in the whole of Malaya, Lemarno Scarfino.

By the time of Nu's conversion to the communist cause, Scarfino's association with him had survived for nearly five years. Both men shared a mutual trait, a preference for their own individual company, though Nu went much further, given a contempt for women bordering on the pathological.

The other commonality was of a kind that dare not be revealed, much less spoken about or admitted to. The Italian, who spent the first decade of his working life as a ship's steward, enjoyed an occupation where one's sexual predilections weren't without exception if kept discreet and separate from daily tasks. On board, the recognised though undeclared proviso was that no other member of the ship's complement was permitted to indulge even covert visits to that person's bunk while at sea. What was done ashore stayed ashore.

Happening to patronise the café, idle, lonely and in search of company, Scarfino met the Chinese refugee. He became the only person Nu Li ever got close to loving. With a pre-existing antipathy to Britain, coming to know of Nu's traitorous activities paving the way for the Japanese invasion proved no barrier to their association. On his vessel's monthly visits to Port Swettenham, Nu engaged with him at various secret locations around Kuala Lumpur. So taken was he with Scarfino that, at his request, the steward jumped ship to be installed in a two-roomed apartment within reasonable proximity of Nu's establishment.

As with the business, Scarfino became the passive partner in the relationship. He would accept any service Nu asked of him. His primary one was to satisfy the not insignificant sexual demands of his keeper and run occasional errands for him. Being reasonably fluent in Malay, at Nu's request he also acquired proficiency in Mandarin and was soon able to negotiate procurement for the café, something in which he was skilful from his time at sea. It also served to relieve the burden on Nu when he was otherwise deployed in stealthy assignments for Japanese agents.

Through his association, Scarfino met Nu's younger sister, Eva, when delivering rice, oil, vegetables and other provisions to the business. She assumed that he was another of her brother's diverse foreign acquaintances, a factor that did not arouse any great interest. Being in complete ignorance as to her sibling's preferences, even the fact that he would sometimes stay overnight at Scarfino's flat aroused no suspicion, although she would never dare to tax Nu over his movements and dealings.

Eva came to like Lemarno Scarfino. She often wondered why it was that he seemed to make a point of never spending any time on the café premises but recognised it without query. In contrast to the domineering and moody Nu, Eva found Scarfino affable, possessive of a ready smile and ever willing to help. Though what had developed into a singular association between her brother and the Italian intrigued her, she credited Lemarno for its longevity. Eva accepted as a noble, dutiful thing that he seemed to worship Nu's every utterance, even of the uncouth variety, and rush to please him at any given summons.

When she asked Nu what his 'story' was, all he would say was that this former ship's steward had lost his position on account of a fabricated allegation concerning the disappearance of food on board. His name was mud on the Malayan coast and any hope of returning to sea a forlorn one. He had come to the eatery, hungry, desperate for a new line of work and offering to do anything to earn his keep. That Nu had presented him a chance she saw as unprecedented, given his bottomless suspicion of immigrants. Even more surprising to her was that they had become close after a relatively short association.

Eva Li's brother confided little when it came to the café's takings and told her even less about his affairs generally. On one occasion, Scarfino had delivered a load of supplies when Nu had been absent. He had a letter addressed to Nu care of the flat and asked her to give it to him. It looked like an account. She was curious and, as it wasn't sealed, read the notice of demand from the water and electricity company directed to Nu as owner of the apartment. She sealed the envelope and left it on Nu's desk, her interest aroused. A few minutes later, a breathless Scarfino returned to say that he would be pleased if she weren't to mention anything about handling the letter herself and to leave it in the cash register sealed. She complied with the request with a certain sense of amusement at being entrusted by Scarfino to be a participant in a tiny subterfuge.

It was the only time in their entire association that Scarfino wrestled with what he saw as a possible misstep. Should he own up to his master or was it really not more than the most trifling of oversights? Nu's sister, because of her ongoing candour, seemed more like blood family than did her brother, and she had always treated him well and with respect. Thus, he never confessed and she esteemed his plea to keep the matter a secret.

With the Japanese victory, Scarfino could look back now on an agreeable association between himself and the sister of his lover, but otherwise it no longer counted. Nu abstained from speaking of her after the British retreat and forbade her name being mentioned. It was as if she had never existed, and so it remained.

There was one last thing needing to be done as a hedge against the future. The flat provided a possible trace to him and Nu decided that, in order to create a different identity, the old life, along with the person who inhabited it, had to become extinct. Identifying a fitting subject to accomplish that object and provide the cover of a downtrodden Chinese coolie from a rubber plantation and processing plant became his next project.

Scarfino found a candidate, resemblance and age sufficiently similar. Hui Tung was single and a labourer with an opium habit, he having fled Nanking himself. Nu attended to the rest, luring the unsuspecting Tung into a drug trap and beheading him. Sufficient identifying documents were left on his person and the civil authorities weren't particular in their enquiries. That Nu was said to have met a grizzly fate with robbery the motive, the subject delighted in reading about.

After that, things moved fast, all the while he lying low. A roomy dwelling was found in a squalid area of Kuala Lumpur's red-light metropolis and Scarfino became the lessee. The title of the abode where Scarfino lived, formerly carrying Nu's name, reverted to the Japanese administrator. It was a loss he dwelt upon at some length in conceiving recompense through manifold vicious ways and means, together with considerable accretions on account of exacting usurious rates of interest.

Becoming part of the Malayan guerrilla resistance established a base from which to wage unrelenting harassment upon the occupiers for every minute of their lives and for him not to surface again until victory had been secured over them. Within a short period, the reborn Hui Tung transformed himself into one of the most feared and committed communists the group contained. For the first time in his life he embraced a cause in which he believed, subsumed as it was to his own.

As he drank in the nightly propaganda lectures, Tung became captive to a much broader creed than merely the elimination of an invader with a red star on his cap. No pangs of conscience about his past as a willing accomplice in the lead-up to December 1941 ever troubled him. There was the perfect cover in that he had been a refugee from Nanking whose entire family were wiped out in 1937. At first, no one questioned his commitment. He played the game early of being a fervent novice where it concerned communist ideology and, over time, became as committed to the movement and more abstemious of habits than any other in the band with which he mixed and operated.

The proof of his conversion came in Tung's actions. During the guerrilla campaign, he had killed and wounded more than one hundred Japanese in the field. This he regarded as incidental to what was to be his chief and most prized occupation, namely, extracting confessions from collaborators. Having devised hideous methods to implement that end, he enjoyed nothing more than deploying the instruments of torture. For him, the resultant executions became the culmination of the often, drawn-out process. Ensuring that the hapless wretches remained conscious of their pending fate remained the ultimate test of his skills, savouring their pleas to be spared much more than the satisfaction he derived from wielding a souvenired Samurai sword to silence them once and for all.

Tung was both feared and highly regarded by those around him. He sought neither rank nor laurels and came to be regarded on account of his courage and ruthlessness as an almost godlike figure, attracting a loyal company of men and some women in his inner circle. Outside of it, he earned the respect of the leadership by insisting on attending to the menial tasks of running a camp deep in inhospitable jungle as much as the next person.

Apart from his manner of dealing with traitors and prisoners, where he had no peer in the brutality stakes, one occasion served as a stark warning that he would never forgive any person who crossed him. It started simply enough with a question being pursued by Yen Ko, one of the older members of the band, about what he had been doing after he had made his escape from China to Malaya and when he joined the communist band. Tung had replied that he was working as a farm labourer at a rubber plantation. This was a story that he promoted to explain why he hated the British almost as much as he did the Japanese. Beatings, cruelty and slave labour conditions on plantations would one day earn not just physical reprisals but political ones he would preach.

'When the war ends, the job will be only half done. Driving out what's left of the Tuan will be the other half,' he passionately declared, adding that it would be achieved in a calculating, determined campaign, steeped in political persuasion to win over the workers and farmers and marked with the threat of unparalleled brutishness should the goals be resisted.

Yen Ko, who was near to Tung in age, had wondered about the new recruit from the moment he stepped into the band but for a time kept any misgivings to himself. A plausible account for possession of the large sum of money was given: he had stolen it by breaking into the manager's office, detecting the combination and emptying the contents of the safe; the timing coincided with the Japanese occupation of the estate; he moved from place to place in Kuala Lumpur before joining the guerrillas.

The explanation was accepted in good grace by the leaders, the foreign currency a preeminent consideration. Over a period of almost a year, Ko and Tung became close to all outward appearances. Ko's wife, Ming, was also a member of the band. A rift occurred on account of a perception that Tung and Ming were more than mere comrades in arms. The suspicion festered when Ming announced that she no longer regarded herself as married to her husband.

A relationship was strictly forbidden in the camp outside of married members and conjugal visits were closely regulated. Trust between the two men had been damaged. Ko began to insinuate that Tung hadn't provided the full account of his background. He sought greater detail on the whereabouts of the plantation where Tung had worked. Claiming to know more than a little about the rubber industry through his trade union affiliations, it was a topic to which he never tired of returning. When Tung finally plucked the name of the estate from a number of which he had been aware, Ko expressed familiarity with it and pressed as to what his labouring tasks had involved. Although not openly disputing anything he said, the insinuation was there, and each point raised in answer led to Ko hinting subtly that its 'functioning must have altered since he knew it' and leaving an impression with Tung that more uncomfortable queries might follow when he racked his recollection further.

One evening after lectures, the two were sitting outside the dormitory with several other disciples when the recurring topic seeped into the conversation. Ko mentioned that he had noticed the relative smoothness of his hands when he had first arrived, along with his uncharacteristically fleshy physique.

'You must have had a good time of it when you took to the life of a robber,' he remarked with what Tung decided was a leer.

'I made up quickly for all they stole from me,' Tung spat out, eyeing the ground rather than his tormentor as if considering whether there was enough loose soil to ram down his throat.

'Yes, but even so, I expected those hands would show some signs at least – a scar or two, a finger or bit of one chopped off – like all of the labourers I've known. They were lean, rough and calloused, but you must have fine health.'

Tung exploded and denounced him on the spot as a Japanese spy who had infiltrated the camp. The two men coming to blows were at once separated. After their commanding officer heard from both, at Tung's suggestion he ordered Ming to be brought before him and spoke to her behind closed doors for nearly an hour. On the same night Ko was arrested, locked up and charged with treason.

The following morning he was tried, though not before a telling piece of incriminating material was located after Tung suggested a search. Secreted under the ground upon which Ko usually slept was a small leather pouch containing a significant store of Japanese paper money. After that find, the evidence of Tung and Ming was almost superfluous in bringing about a verdict of guilty. There followed a lengthy harangue concerning the poisonous slime of Japanese Imperialism and how, even amongst the stolid-at-heart communists, contamination could occur if it wasn't guarded against. The convicted man lashed to a pole, all members of the camp were invited to strike him or spit in his face. Most did both.

'Be vigilant, comrades, lest anyone succumbs to Nippon's wiles and tentacles that can appear at any time and in many guises,' the commander urged all present. 'And never forget the purity of our movement finds its own means of exposing counter-revolutionaries. Likewise,' he railed, 'recidivism will always be uncovered.'

The sentence of death was pronounced, with Tung being delegated to carry out the execution immediately. This was a special honour and he obliged with a performance that sent a chill through even the hardest of temperaments witnessing it. As a grotesque reminder to anyone who might be tempted to flirt with the topic again, Tung pitched the severed head against a jungle tree with such force that it could easily have been mistaken for a watermelon. He took it upon himself to order that the corpse be dragged into a space a few hundred yards from the camp where tigers were known to pass.

Over the next few months, Ming, who had trusted there were now no barriers to sharing his bed as a communist cadre's 'wife', was soon disabused of her assumptions. At Tung's instigation, Ming was told by the commander that she had to prove herself as a loyal soldier first and put all her other instincts to one side until the war was won. Tung could see that she remained the only possible danger to his ascendency. Placed at the forefront for the gang's next raid, if the return fire failed to serve its intended purpose, he would finish the job. As it happened, he had no need to expend a round.

His position was now unassailable and, in the process, had achieved the best of both worlds. As an inveterate despatcher of Japanese Imperialists, he had no peer, both feared and respected by his own side. Even his superiors couldn't help but admire him, not the least because he never sought or attempted to displace them. It was on this account, in combination with the impressive bounty flowing into communist coffers, that permitted him a greater degree of latitude than would be afforded to others.

On the pretext of gaining information about traitors, intended army-inspired sorties or locating potential targets without arousing suspicion, Tung, who had always ventured into Kuala Lumpur and its outskirts alone, was now given more freedom to do so. He took these opportunities to maintain contact and dalliances with Scarfino, who remained as devoted as ever he was.

Since his reappearance back at the camp would coincide with another action plan, not the slightest suspicion of any frolic of his own having taken place ever arose. Scarfino also served many functions as well as being his own most reliable informant. Best of all, the property was the least suspicious of places from which to come and go since every other square inch of the building housing Scarfino's and Tung's crib had been converted into a bordello.

When the Japanese were finally driven out of Malaya, unlike many others who surrendered arms and joined in the celebrations, Tung remained in hiding, more mindful than ever that the past might make an unwelcome return. Only a few hard-core supporters, and some others uncertain of what might ensue, stayed with him. To those of his compatriots who would listen, he was vehement in his opposition to any cooperation with the British. Subjugation was behind the requirement to hand over their weapons became his catchcry.

No one was more satisfied by the breakdown in negotiations, giving him the incentive to rally those who returned into becoming a potent force under his sole command. It was based on the principle of showing no mercy, taking depravity to new heights and making slaughter of European planters and their families a priority. His goal was to terrorise them into submission and retreat.

Fighting what he termed 'the yoke of colonialism', Tung's actual name never came to the attention of the authorities, thus frustrating their efforts to track him down. He was an invaluable financial pipeline to this band of guerrillas because he had a source of regular income that supplanted his illegitimate exploits. By this stage, he was something of an expert who could meticulously plan and execute raids, even taking on daring bank and train robberies. Attacking remote plantation facilities became his specialty, where robbery was the secondary motive.

With his suspected involvement in the assassination of Sir Henry Gurney, Tung earned a high price on his head. Through his preference of operating alone, or only occasionally with one or two fanatical lieutenants who had pledged never to be taken alive, he was able to remain a shadowy and indistinct figure coming to be known only as 'The Huntsman'.

Chapter 19 – *Colonel of Police*

'Though it's getting well past it to say so, Happy New Year, and may I record being absolutely delighted to make your acquaintance again, Newton.'

That it left the patronee of this effusive greeting nonplussed appeared to be its intent. His renowned two-eyed stare came into play: the nearest eye relishing the puzzlement on Newton's face; the right, judging by its inerrancy, undertaking an exhaustive analysis on the state of digestion of the former army officer's recent breakfast.

It was early 1953 and Sir Gerald Templer projected the authority of a man who, having been entrusted by Churchill to the position of High Commissioner for over a year, had impressed himself on the entire peninsula. He had united its disparate elements, moving on the dead wood and set a course that would one day lead to Malayan independence.

Newton's distillation of the occasion surrounding

the general's appearance in Tunisia for a Victoria Cross presentation involved a desperate rummage for some prominent incident that his first recollection might have missed. While he'd hoped to image his having beaten off a would-be assassin, overlooked in the years since through sheer modesty though imprinting an indelible mark on Templer, the best that he could come up with was not much more than the flimsiest exchange of banal greetings.

'The pleasure is mine, sir,' replied Newton, after Templer signalled towards a small table where morning tea awaited. The general was as at home in the King's House study as if he had lived there for his entire life. Behind him, three French doors, arranged bay-window style, opened into a confusion of branches laden with large, dark green leaves abundant with mid-morning light. Family portraits, including one of his distinguished father, were prominently displayed.

He wasn't done with reminiscing and Newton feared a question about the occasion that might defy an answer. 'Ah, but that was a great day, desert sun or no. You'll have some refreshment, I trust, and there's coffee. Take a pew.' He motioned towards a two-seater couch and the two cups.

'Thanks, sir. Coffee will be just the ticket,' Templer's easy style adding spring to his own tone.

'Help yourself to the milk and sugar. You, having lived closer to Kenya than I've ever been, will understand, for once tasted, never forgotten. Before us is the inferior South American bean, though not so bad. Thanks again for coming. I needn't remind you that pulling up stumps after an extended stay in Port Elizabeth and answering my request was not merely a courageous call but a forgiving one.'

'Sir, if I may be blunt, and with the greatest of respect, although duty was a guiding encouragement to return, without my wife Henrietta's acquiescence and support, I wouldn't have entertained it.'

'Women are such wonderfully intuitive creatures, as with my Peggy, for instance. First, they read your mind, then make it up and, afterwards, convince you that the decision has been made for them and you have taken the lead as convention mandates.

'As with yourself, my assuming this job wasn't an army transfer. There was just such a preamble in *our* decision to come. She was all for it, and already has as much work, if not more to do than I, accepting of course the distinction that in your case there is the added consideration of a young family. Your son's how old?'

'A little over three, sir.'

'Yes, quite a challenging handful for these parts.' Templer was already pouring out a second cup for himself and, noticing that Newton hadn't explored far into his first, made the point by topping it to the brim.

'Right you are. Now to business. I told you over the phone that this would be an exacting assignment and couldn't get into much detail for obvious reasons. I also mentioned that what I'm asking you to accomplish may take time. I was unable to be specific about how long, no more than I can be now. You could clean it up in a matter of weeks, if you get lucky, and miracles have been known to happen. On the other hand, six months might be on the conservative side, although, by that stage, the chances of a successful outcome would be remote, and you might be more comfortable plodding the streets here like a London Bobby.'

Newton's wry smile preceded a movement declining the offered packet and didn't earn a sardonic riposte, rather, a throaty cough was the forerunner to Templer's ignition of his own cigarette. 'I must remember to remove tobacco from the list of your necessaries.' The expelled smoke following the observation occasioned a dash of merriment.

'Job's a one-off, and I warrant that there's no agenda to dragoon you back into khaki.'

'Your candour is appreciated, sir. It's a privilege to be here. Ensuring my family's security is foremost.'

'That goes without saying. I'm told you've brought a trusty backup along.'

'Yes. Forgetting his Legionnaire pedigree and size, which are telling reasons why Gerhardus has come with us, there's another. He's like – rather, *is* family, with a close attachment to my son and his mother, having become something of a de facto uncle figure.'

'You made that clear, and I endorse the position you've taken,' drawing on his cigarette with each thoughtful utterance. Apparent from the fingers embracing it confirming tobacco was a constant companion, he exhaled the smoke away from where Newton was sitting before facing him squarely, this time with a compellingly rakish demeanour.

'And I understand your dog's been shipped in. With a name like "Rommel", I trust there'll be no occasion to take me back a decade.' Newton's admiration on hearing this reminded him that Templer had a notorious reputation for demanding a thorough briefing before any meeting. 'Seriously though, a formidable German Shepherd and your Afrikaans colossus will prove invaluable, in a domestic sense, comfort for your wife when the task ahead is sure to keep you on the hoof.'

'God forbid that there may be any occasion, sir, but I want them primarily to be around as protection for Henrietta and little Magnus.'

'Certainly. The question of accommodation has been high on my list of priorities. You will be in a position to deliver a precise answer on that tomorrow after you make a choice. I want you well away from Kuala Lumpur. You're familiar with Fraser's Hill?'

'I am, sir. That's over sixty miles away, as I recall. Your predecessor was ambushed on a road up there.'

'Correct. Had he opted to maintain a decent escort I probably wouldn't be sitting here today. But that's another story. Moreover, as I shall shortly reveal, we suspect a connection between that assassination and the task we are asking you to undertake.'

'As you say, sir.'

'The area was chosen because there are a number of

residences available as well as it being a place of recreation frequented by officials and service personnel.'

Templer produced a photographic assortment and Newton was particularly taken with a site showing two buildings on an apparently elevated piece of land. One, the larger and much lower down, appeared to be a hotel. The bungalow above it garnered interest.

'I'm familiar with the dwelling that's caught your eye. As advised, it's well situated. Ultimately, the final decision is the one you will make. You'll be taken up to the locality tomorrow. As to the job, let me get down to some specifics. My seeking you out was not some pig in a poke or whimsical. I'd thoroughly considered your file. You've impeccable Intelligence credentials and your Force 136 experience led you to understand the communist psyche. You're a talent who languished and was shunted about after the war like a clerk archiving files from deceased estates.'

'The General's redaction of the not-so-eminent sections is kind,' Newton interpolated boldly.

'Look, Reginald,' the duopoly of his gaze at work again sitting atop set teeth and as penetrating as a tiger about to decimate his prey, 'I've had a bellyful of those who, through jealously and incompetence – usually both travel in the same body – hold others back.'

'But, sir, there's more.'

'Newton, I've read your file from cover to cover. If it's that bloody Blunting nonsense, forget it. There's one of her in every little establishment corner, conditional philanthropists parading their beneficence to mask troublemaking propensities when they don't get their way.

'I'll tell you what really piqued my interest. You wrote several reports, but the large one after the war sealed your fate. Thought-provoking and filled with the wisdom of operational experience, as if that hearts and minds stuff was the preserve of one or two. You touched on it as well and it's working just as you forecasted. The late Sir Henry is entitled to some credit in being the author of the policy. If you sowed the seed, well and good.

'Its effects have been that the Chinese farmers now possess capital, for them God's little acre, and we have earned their trust by rigorously policing that investment. Ambivalence, some of it born from fear of the communists and suspicion of colonial motives, has turned to support for what we've done and continue to do. We're overcoming the dread and intimidation the CTs, shorthand you may know for communist terrorists, used to exert to get their food and exact tribute. We aren't at the mopping up stage and, while I'm here, there'll be no occasions for complacency until the CTs are routed, root and branch.'

'I'm wondering whether there's much left for me, sir.'

'There is, and I'm beginning to like you even more, Newton. One individual has eluded us at every turn. You must appreciate that I'm not in the habit of wasting my time, or other people's, so bear with me.

'What's happened in the years since you've been away has been a significant denuding of CT strength which led to a fragmentation of the guerrillas. Instead of a cohesive unit with a central command, we have lots of little subsidiaries. Oh, they're at times no less troublesome and require a diversion of resources. One group in particular is made up of, perhaps, twenty at most and they break down into even smaller hit-and-disappear fragments.

'As much criminal in nature as ideological, the band in question is led by as cunning, vicious and ruthless a species of humanity as God made. Little is known about him other than what he perpetrates. We have a basic description and a grainy photograph. He's elusive, never in one place for long and, by the nature of his signature crimes, has been known to roam over significant distances where procuring bounty is less likely to be difficult.

'On recent indications, given that the CTs have been all but obliterated in Johore, he's rather confining himself to several jungle hideouts adjacent to Kuala Lumpur, notably where Negri Sembilan and Pahang overlap, and possibly as far south of here as Segamat.'

'That's a considerable amount of territory, sir,' Newton observed. 'Apart from the Segamat sector, with which I've had some passing association, it's quite a deal beyond where I was operating with Force 136, not that distances trouble me. And jungle is jungle anywhere in Malaya.'

'I'm not going to suggest that you walk all of it.' Templer remarked grittily. 'But we think the capital could be the key. If feelings count for anything, and rank doesn't elevate mine, he probably doesn't stray far from a fifty-mile arc around this region. Conceded that I'm second-guessing the arc a little.

'We have tagged him "The Huntsman" after the local species of spider that can almost cover the average man's hand. I may not be telling you anything new, but it sizes up its prey, attacks and melts back into the harshest of terrain.' This was accompanied by hand actions as Templer rose to discard the empty and retrieve a fresh packet of cigarettes.

'What I want you to do is become the Huntsman's stalking horse. Find and identify him. Once you get a bead on this individual, his likely associates and, if possible, his movements, our forces will finish the job. My preference would be to take him alive but the reality of that occurring, judging by all we know, is pretty remote.'

'You mentioned a photograph and a possible description, sir?'

'I never thought you'd ask. It and all relevant documents are in this satchel which you must study once you've settled in. Yours is a top-secret assignment, Newton. For its purposes, your rank will become one of an Intelligence Security Colonel – not the army, in case you're experiencing second thoughts, but with all the powers of a police officer, as was already flagged with you.

'Presently, apart from the police commissioner, only one person besides you and I know of the full extent of this project. He is the head of the Special Branch, Cedric Tister. You will be meeting with him when we are finished. I want to keep this operation within tight parameters and Tister has my attitude on secrecy to the forefront of whatever logistical arrangements he makes. With that in mind, choose your words carefully. Not even your wife can know.

'As to the Afrikaans gentleman, while a matter for you, it may be that he can work in some capacity or other, but he mustn't know of the target. Invisibility is going to be the key to success. I'll leave that with Tister, who, I'm sure, will have in mind an experienced policeman to be a go-between and support officer. Are there any questions, Colonel?'

'I can't think of any, sir,' he answered with a humility easily mistaken for hesitation.

'Look, if I wasn't convinced that you weren't the best person for the job, you wouldn't have been asked. I'm more certain now of you being so, but take time to consider the strictures of what promises to be an exacting and potentially quite dangerous task.'

'Sir, I'm humbled by this chance to serve the Malayan people and am willing to proceed without the slightest hesitation.'

'Good. Your record convinced me that you were our man and meeting you hasn't derogated from that conviction. Every indication we get is that the Huntsman is a – I nearly said "dog", for I prefer not to regard him as a human being. Out of deference to canines, most of all your Rommel, "guttersnipe" will better suit. The consistent feedback we have is the universal reluctance by those CTs we've captured to reveal little about him. I think much of this is extreme fear, but also the care he takes to keep to a small and fiercely indoctrinated group. I regret it doesn't offer you much scope.

'Over the last few years there have been a number of atrocities amongst the European planters. We strongly suspect his outfit is behind many of them and he has been at the forefront of their planning and execution. There's a certain hunger for blood that the human mind struggles to comprehend. I can understand vengeful attacks on those who would kill him if they had their chance and summary dispatch of traitors to his cause. And I apprehend that the acquisition of a taste for inventive torture, reading some of the postulations by psychologists, can be a difficult habit to break.

'What I struggle to grapple with is this fellow doesn't just leave it with the belligerents, or the informers, or soldiers or police arrayed against him. He will extinguish the lives of non-combatant innocent women and children as if they were cockroaches or vermin to be crushed underfoot, the more excruciatingly so the better. There's no villainy at which he will baulk. So now you've an inkling at what you're up against.'

'Having worked beside some of the communist cadres, sir, I didn't encounter these propensities in respect of clear innocents and, for me, the South African newspapers contained little more than snippets on what was coming out of Malaya. There were occasional references where gruesome slaughter was involved, sir, but the full account wasn't spelt out. I did however read *The Times* occasionally.'

'You never saw anyone like this fellow in your 136

adventures?' Templer handed him the fuzzy photograph. 'We haven't even got a hint of a proper name to go by, just a number. "Twenty-four" is all we ever prised out of anyone captured.'

'As much as I would like to say I have seen him before, the answer is no, but the tracking him down begins now, sir.'

Chapter 20 – *Closer to the Mark*

When Thomas Tredwig arrived in Malaya, the adaptable personality and bloated confidence accompanied him. He was a man not given to self-effacement and never wasted opportunities for advancing his own star. There exuded an air about him that, unless he rose to at least the upper echelons supervising the Malayan police service within the space of his two-year tour of duty, something of a catastrophe would befall that organisation's future. Fault for failure to do so would lie at the feet of those who were unable to appreciate the many gifts with which he was blessed. Without him, the country would invariably stagger towards communist hegemony.

Possessed of the right credentials to do just about anything in the police line, his most impressive characteristic, as noted in his job application and at interview, was an encyclopaedic knowledge of the Malayan Emergency, its key players, the methods of the CTs and the intimacies of the peninsula's geography. He had acquired so much information about the country and, impressively to his superiors, its politics, that, beyond a few days of on-the-ground familiarity, no resources were required to train him.

Tommy, in further preparation for the swift advancement he coveted, had more than a passing understanding of Malay and Mandarin during an intensive twelve-month course before he stepped onto a Malayan street. On arrival, posing as a tourist, he had gone out of his way to add to his linguistic skills by utilising the spare time available to him in casual conversation with locals. An impromptu offer to undertake elementary language sessions for recent arrivals and not-so-new, jaded officers as a morale-boosting, guest lecturer was quickly taken up and he volunteered his spare time without hesitation. He was lively, personable and impressive.

With the swift acclimatisation, proven record of bravery and resourcefulness and, on its face, impeccable characteristics, the police commissioner had selected Tredwig for a specialist role on the basis that no better aide, mercurial observer with a photographic memory and lethal seconder for Newton existed. A familiarity with firearms and explosives was an additional bonus and his energy was indefatigable.

Not without some reservation, for Newton retained circumspection in all things, he came to accept that if fault existed, it was in his offsider appearing to be an overconfident cop who needed to appreciate that this assignment would be like no other he had undertaken. It didn't take more than a day for Tommy to understand his boss and he was canny enough to make adjustments.

Colonel Newton was impressed by most things about his assistant and valued the inclination to be seen as detached. A caution he registered was an occasional flashiness, more so when demonstrating his language skills. He also had a penchant for seeking endorsement for all that he did. To Newton's disconcerting, though never expressed, unease, this would often be accompanied by him posing a scenario and rhetorically seeking a seal of approval to something he already knew would be accepted. Tredwig would iterate, 'I'm not asking you to endorse … but could anyone really disagree, or am I missing something, sir?' It made other than an acquiescent response difficult, in order to avoid debate were negativity to be evinced.

In weighing up the logistics, Newton, not the easiest of characters himself when in operational mode, determined that his offsider was best kept perennially occupied. Other than when being chauffeured about, assignments of a 'look and listen' nature would be allocated to Tommy, who would report back directly to Newton. He was given a broad discretion to use his own initiative. This sat well with such boundless enthusiasm, but he needed reminding that not all had to be fed back or accounted for, just the relevant information, 'And you're well credentialled to do a good job.' While Newton afterwards wished that the addendum wasn't so much taken to heart, the reaction amused him.

From the beginning, Tommy exempted one sphere

of activity from any comprehensive briefing. Of his own choosing and devices, he had begun to attend the house where Scarfino now lived and managed. The owner was described as a Singaporean Indian called Mulander, an entrepreneur who was hardly ever in the country and had only visited the place on one occasion, that being at the time of purchase. All this was reporting gleaned and accepted at mere face value.

The Italian was willing to afford cooperation with the bright and self-important Englishman who wasn't chary of hinting at being 'in the know'. While a native sense of identifying human weaknesses was one of Scarfino's most abundant traits, such was not needed when it came to Tommy. His undisguised susceptibility to beautiful women, coupled with a conceit that accepted flattery as reward for his very existence, made him a potential informant. Here was an opportunity to ensnare someone who, carefully cultivated, could become a more than useful source, if his intuitions proved to be correct. Scarfino set about ensuring that Tredwig was treated like a sultan.

The encouragement swiftly led to a pattern of visitation for which a discreet, private entrance was availed, with a personal key supplied. Whenever he frequented the bordello, and invariably this was just as the cover of night descended well before the brisk evening trade clicked in, the highest-priced girl was made available. At first, this was at an impressive discount and, within a little over a fortnight, no charge at all was levied. Another justification for the largesse was that, following a fracas with a bullish and drunken Bulgarian who Tommy propelled through the door and into a drain, Scarfino regarded his presence at the premises as an impressive deterrent to any visitor minded to cause trouble. Tommy had no difficulty accepting the characterisation, he having appraised his host that such had always been his stock-in-trade in 'London night club security' circles.

The evening after the most recent of his sorties to Scarfino's, Tredwig was sitting down to a meal with Newton at an inconspicuous teashop in Kuala Lumpur. As insurance against being surprised by his superior's being in possession of collateral knowledge about his movements, Tommy decided to forestall any possible awkward enquiry by telling him where he had been and what he had been doing.

'As part of my intelligence-gathering operations, I've called upon a few joints in some of the less reputable parts of the city, sir,' he told him. 'Unofficially, of course, as in pretendin' to check out the merchandise at each Pelacuran and—'

'English will suffice, Tommy, these words aren't carried around in my head,' Newton said brusquely, 'and while my guess won't surprise you, I want it to be clear from your lips.'

'Pardon me, sir. They were houses of ill-repute. And so I tried my hand at bein' conversational with the madams and, cor blimey, even one "sir".'

'Any specific reason for doing so?'

'Experience, and the hunch of a journeyman to a degree. Sure, this isn't London; pig in a poke, I s'pose. As you instructed, sir, part of havin' a good look around and pick up any information floatin' about.'

'Relevant to your terms of reference, no doubt.'

'Absolutely and indubitably, sir.'

'And did you turn up anything useful?'

'Not yet, except – well, there was a bar at Butik Bintang near to a market, nothin' much there, but another seedier business at Chow Kit worth a further look.'

'What led you to that conclusion?' Newton asked, wishing to expedite the conversation.

'Sixth sense or somethin', based on my gut feelin', maybe. The manager was one of those types who'd do anything to please. Didn't present as a pimp or sleazy; just an effeminate, insipid sort of character puttin' on an earnest, helpful, innocent face, you know the type. Would crack open the pearly whites while bein' held underwater for ten minutes.'

'Did he offer his identity?'

'Naturally, as you'd expect this early, sir, I didn't seek it. He came out and called himself Scarfino, insisted pretty quick that I use his Christian name, Lemarno. Overly friendly to a fault, perhaps even incautious, I thought.'

'You mean apart from touting, or what?'

'Well, I had a drink with him and he rambled over a few topics. There was none of the reserve you expect to get at first meetings. Italian name, and I probed him a touch about that. I used the line from the *Casablanca* film. "Hey, mate, of all the gin joints and palaces in the Far East, this is the last place I'd ever have expected to meet an Italian tourist running a Pelacuran."'

Tommy mistook Newton's facial movement as signifying a supreme compliment.

'Thank you, sir. I thought you'd appreciate that one given that Scarfino did, and started goin' on about how 'e liked that little oozy orbital-eyed Ugarti in the film, the one who stole the letters of transit. "So nice a man and such a shame," he said, with the makin's of a Latin accent. From the way he went on about this cove and never bothered a toss about the smoulderin' Ilsa Lund, it seems the only interest he has in girls is a financial one.'

'What other interest could such a man have?' Newton sighed, measuring his words.

Initially, the response puzzled Tommy. 'Ah, come to think of it, there was the longest manicured fingernails that I've ever seen, and he wanted to show them off. The nail polish I noticed when he handed me a second drink and rubbed my arm, adding, "On the house". Even boasted that he does all the keepin' up appearances stuff.'

'No question then why he was given the task of managing the place, safe pair of hands never inclined to wander over the merchandise. Have you looked into who owns it?'

'No, still feelin' my way with this type. It's delicate and painstaking. He did say some wealthy Indian bought the building and set it up just after the war ended and he's only ever seen him once or twice. I didn't want to push hard early.'

'That's an appropriate strategy if you regard him as a promising lead. And the subjects that spiked your interest?'

'Well, he said that prior to coming to Malaya he crewed as a ship's steward. Of course, the I-ties aren't fussed about our country. I let him think that I sympathised with Mussolini and how he was hard done by and it got me some positive recognition, goin' by his expressions. He mentioned the Emergency and his snide sorta attempts to infer that Malaya might one day shake off the pommy shackles and be independent. I sympathised there, summarisin' o'course, and he was careful the way he put things.'

'Apart from what you've mentioned already, did anything else cause him to be a little broad with his tongue?'

'I painted myself as a bit of a rough-and-tumble drifter with a past, shamblin' through oriental lands but havin' connections. 'e seemed instantly sympathetic, as if I was a sorta kindred spirit. Real touchy-feely from there, regardin' me as somethin' of a friendless soul. I guess that was my intention, to lead 'im on a bit.'

'If you feel that he's worth pursuing, do so. The cupboard has been somewhat sparse so far and almost anything is worth a try. Make some internal enquiries about ownership of the property. That may lead somewhere or nowhere. You're not expected to get into bed with the Italian but, if your enquiries begin to bear any fruit, you are eventually going to have to conjure up a reason for visiting the place, otherwise he will become suspicious.'

'Do you have any suggestions in that line, sir?'

'I'd say this much: we're in an endgame situation. Nothing's off the table. My mail tells me you were selected for this job because you had a capacity to mix and blend with all sorts, your resourcefulness and helpful, ruggedly-handsome features. The third one I can see for myself, the other two I need accept. You mustn't appear or sound like a copper though, and I reason that you don't. If becoming a client is absolutely necessary in order to make progress, so be it. You've a generous allowance. The choice is yours. The utmost care is required, if only for your own health. You know the risks, and the last thing I want to be up for is explaining to the commissioner I've had to bail you out after a vice raid.'

'Perhaps if I *was* arrested my cover would be better sealed,' he offered with half a smirk.

'Absolutely not. You can't risk being identified in any way, shape or form. The local law enforcement generally turns a blind eye to that sort of piffle with much else to occupy them. Nothing further is there?' Newton asked indifferently.

'Ah, well, we've 'ad our little chats in a private sort of parlour. There was a kitchen leadin' into it and I think another room or rooms tucked away somewhere. The girls were on the other side of the buildin' in a reception and, when the bell rang, they'd greet the customer, and take it from there. Occasionally he did. In fact, Scarfino met me at the door on my first visit. And which I should add was made out to be accidental, seekin' a mate who might 'ave dropped in.'

'Well, not much of a linkage there to what we're after, but trust your instincts and you never know. Sometimes what begins as remote, progresses. No more?'

A hundred thoughts flashed by under Newton's penetrating gaze. Tommy's head answered in the negative as if to free it of its principal subject – money. Consideration by way of sexual services was, he suspected, there for the taking and not to be waved away, but fleshly allurements he had encountered many times before. Tangible consideration was harder to come by. Scarfino might be persuaded to release some cream from what appeared to be a rich supply if Tommy played his hand correctly, given his boss's broad imprimatur on the investigative side.

Newton made it clear that their discussions were at an end with the chair's scraping on the wooden floor.

'No, sir. I trust the impression I've given is not one that might lead you to think that we're on the cusp of an endless pipeline of intelligence.'

The only response he perceived was a feeling that Newton wasn't at the stage of thinking all that much about what he was doing, save that it managed to keep him out of his boss's way and he was fully mobile. That was enough.

*　　*　　*

Chow Kit was experiencing its lean and meagre hours where silence reigned in the black, refuse-strewn streets. A furtive visitor crept along its empty lanes in a manner that demonstrated such absolute familiarity with his whereabouts that he may as well have been blindfolded, yet, as always when in near proximity to his haven, ever whipping about, even at the slightest sound, satisfied in this instance of it being a rat gnawing at organic garbage.

A pistol secreted inside his trousers above ankle level was his last resort. The first were the three grenades he always carried in a string bag chockful of his favoured rambutan, langsat and chempedak. Though never having needed to deploy them in these environs, he knew that their effectiveness would be such as to sow mayhem and give him a window of time to escape. The last few yards were always the most dangerous and he slithered along on hands, knees and then chest. Determining it was safe to do so, he slid down the dozen steps and accessed the premises through a low cellar door blocked by an immovable forty-four-gallon drum but just wide enough for access by a slight-figured man.

A considerably earlier attendee had made an impulsive decision to drop in at the uncommon hour of nine o'clock. Possessing a full measure of that natural bent in law officers to turn up unexpectedly, this time he was the one surprised most because Scarfino reacted to his sudden appearance as if it had been pre-ordained.

'Ah, my excellent friend, Tommy, how nice of you to happen by and so opportune a time to arrive.'

'Opportune, how so?' the other asked.

'Tonight, you're going to meet not only the most beautiful courtesan in Malaya, but its most exclusive.'

'And well beyond the means of a poor sod like me.'

'Adelka,' he called out, 'could you step in here?'

Tommy waited for the knock on the louvered door to Scarfino's sitting room separating his half of the ground floor from the other. It never came. Instead, a curtain opened from a passageway plush with Persian carpet, wall paintings and miniature artefacts, the end thereof showing another aspect of the downstairs area with which he was not familiar. An erect, statuesque body of Amazonian proportions accentuated by high heels, moved into the light. Eyes, for such a woman, bore an incongruous, fluttering obeisance.

'You called me, Mr Scarfino.'

'Yes, my precious darling. I want you to meet a special friend from that wonderful English old country. Say hello to Tommy, Adelka.' She made a confident step forward, her figure enhanced by the snug-fitting, sequined, silver gown revelling under the chandelier and held out a hand of never-ending fingers. Tommy received it open-mouthed and could only manage, 'Hello', projecting it from a considerably uplifted jaw.

'You vill call me "Ada",' she mouthed in a husky Eastern European enunciation that sounded more like a command, and confirmed to be when adding, 'Only Mr Scarfino use "Adelka".' Her blonde hair was thatched and plaited about a head that angled back from an elongated neck like Nefertiti's. Bone China cheeks were high, nose long and searching, accentuating full lips opening to reveal a large mouth with an infelicitous placement of teeth that added rather than detracted from a White Russian charisma. In any beauty contest, her eligibility would be challenged on the basis that, at first sight, the judges had become hopelessly compromised by eyes wreathed in bribery.

She never shifted her glance from Scarfino while intertwining Tommy's hand, before drawing him to his feet as if commanding participation in a ballroom virtuoso. He was too engrossed to detect the sign language in which master and servant engaged.

'Adelka has some ideas, and even a few other moves, to discuss with you, Tommy, and time is the least of the many things presently on her otherwise fertile mind. I will be, as always, sir, here at your disposal when you choose to take your leave.' For him, the next few hours became an experience Tommy found unforgettable and was apt to repeat.

All Scarfino sketched to Nu, he sitting up in bed smoking as the morning, signified by the hands of the wall clock, drifted towards the inevitable daylight outside but permanently artificial where they rested.

'You haven't told me all of this for your amusement,' he said abruptly, maintaining his native tongue and showing signs of agitation. 'Me, I have none these days with a price on my head, hiding and weaving, and a hideous description to match, thankful only that it's on the wobbly side. "Prominent jowls in a flabby body." Does this look flaccid, bugger the bastards?' he asked, lifting the sheet and flicking on a torch to show a torso tamed by years of deep jungle adversity and pulling contemptuously at a taut face. 'Even when you feed me here, I can't enjoy much at the risk of bringing it all up. "Huntsman", I don't mind, as they will before long find out to their cost. I get a little enjoyment from eliminating scum who rat on me, but a white man or his fat-gutted wife and bastard children, now, that's another thing.'

Scarfino worked his fingernails across Nu's forehead, kissed it and lavished more attention upon his face. 'You're my "Huntsman", as beautiful as you ever were to me. I know things have been rather dreadful lately on that account. I've been forced to do without you for longer than I can bear. You need to try and relax.' Cradling his head against his lover's bare chest was short lived, as he sprang up and dressed. At a side table, he poured out a large portion of his favourite whisky, added insignificant water and sat on a chair, examining his pistol under the muted light of a battery lamp. Scarfino was unable to take his eyes off him.

'Well,' Nu said roughly, 'what have you been able to find out from your Russian arse, or are we keeping and paying her for nothing?'

'I wouldn't have taken it so far unless I thought what visited here amounted to a rare prize. But Adelka, who has loosened as many tongues as undone trouser belts or braces, tells me that this one has connections with the government, almost like a contractor or supplier of something.'

'Information, attitudes, actions?'

'Ah, Nu, we so think alike, don't we? It might sound a long shot, but I'm certain he's working for them. It's in what capacity and how it can be used that requires further effort to wangle out of him.'

His reception of this news saw a grimmer aspect envelop Nu. 'She hasn't wormed anything of value, and it'll take more than her body to tease out the entirety of his comings, doings and goings amongst that filth Templer and all his minions.'

Scarfino put on his dressing gown and leaned over to light another two cigarettes. Nu took one without a word and his lover dragged a settee over. 'We are doing well in the business. Last week you made fourteen hundred. I've never touched the stash you left other than when you wanted something and have been adding to it all the time.'

'How much do you think it might take?'

'My own dear boy, time, treasure, just leave it to me. The hook is dangling with irresistible flesh; that he's in for her, dead certain. When the money comes into play, it will be line and sinker to follow."

'Something big must be done quickly to smash their colonial arrogance. I want to hit them high and hard again, just as I got Gurney. Why not Templer, or even his wife, someone close to him?' He had taken another whisky and its effect was telling.

'Steady, my precious one. I don't want you to be sick again,' Scarfino said, screwing the lid on the bottle. 'I can feel that this fellow is going to be your salvation. Already he's been here on many occasions over a short period. Once the valve on the pipeline is cracked, he will gush open with it.'

'You had better be right because, even amongst some of my closest comrades, I'm beginning to see signs that they are weakening in their zeal for a new communist Malaya.'

'I will prove to be right, just as Adelka has demonstrated reliability in all things.'

'You need more than the few hours he had with her to get it, otherwise you would have told me something more substantial.'

'I am troubled at seeing you like this, Nu. So—'

'What have you got? Speak fast!'

'It may be trifling but, in their various intimate explorations, she found some tiny words tattooed on the inside of his thigh near the groin, 'Lon-Met Lions'.'

'In the dark?'

'The dear thing always operates with a light burning. When she kept teasing him, he said that it was a secret.'

'You know something that I must be told, Lemarno.'

'Well, my heart, yes. I don't really *know*; more tiny assumptions on my part. If it goes anywhere you will be the first informed. For now, dear Nu, it has done nothing to disabuse me of viewing this Tommy as a real boon to your goals. Meanwhile, having sprung the honey entrapment, and while Adelka maintains the powerful influence over Tommy as she exerts upon any man who has her, when I delve into it further, the immediate aim is springing the money trap. That can start the next time he drops by.'

'You had better be watchful on two fronts. My reaction,

should those enquiries lead back to me, would be less than pleasant for all concerned.'

'I know you don't really mean me, my own one, but Adelka has been a special little project since finding her on the street after she arrived from Hong Kong. She regards me as a kind of father and, as my husband, that makes her your stepdaughter.'

Nu wasn't amused. 'You saved her from the back alleys and slums by hiring her out on in-house employment and outcalls. She's a nothing-but-whore, dispensable, Lemarno, just as all others will be if anything goes wrong,' his voice rising in fury.

Signalling to Nu that he would go and prepare his breakfast, Scarfino closed off the soundproof space, his anguish only departing after he ceased to hear the oaths and dire imprecations.

Chapter 21
– Closing on the Bridal Chamber

Fraser's Hill

3 April 1953

Dear Nancyng,

It's me, Henrietta. I hope you remember. Oh, why should I be so formal and silly? Of course you do, and were expecting me to write after my husband's long-ago invitation. I'll leave the 'proper' stuff to him. It just isn't me, despite my passing flirtation with the Swiss finishing school. My, doesn't that seem an age removed? Motherhood, marriage, etc, but more of that anon.

So where do I start? First, the address. No, it's not some hideout in Scotland (as you can see from the stamp) from which the name derives. I understand it was a Scottish pioneer, Louis Fraser, who set up a tin ore Malayan trading post here in the 1890s and it was named in his honour. Being about four thousand feet above sea level, it's much cooler and not at all humid as in Kuala Lumpur, which is some sixty-odd miles away.

Nearly three months now since we arrived, can hardly believe it! We have a place to ourselves, a smallish stuccoed-brick dwelling with living areas and two bedrooms downstairs and the third, main one, upstairs along with a nursery for Magnus as well. It has been built on the side of a hill that rises quite sharply above and drops as much below us. At the front of the block and about maybe a hundred and fifty yards below us is a guesthouse/hotel that has twenty rooms. It's popular with government and uppity types taking their weekend leave breaks.

Do I like it? Well, yes and no. I love the cooler environment and so does my son, Magnus. I have got to know a couple of families here, and that's a plus as there's children with whom Magnus can play. But I love it much better when Reginald is home, but he tends to be away quite a bit, duty calls and all that guff.

All I know is that he's a doing some secret work and it's not the army but rather police, Special Branch, or something. All hush-hush and winks and nods. He can't tell even me anything much. There is this 'Emergency' going on in Malaya involving the communists who are forever stirring up trouble and agitating to take over the country. There is apparently one really bad gang, an offshoot or something from the main group, creating havoc. The authorities are trying to break them once and for all from what I read. It's sort of a taboo topic with Reginald, although he hinted that his task is tracing these groups and maybe, that's my vivid imagination at work, finding out who the ringleader is and it's up to army or police, or both, to do the rest.

It was something of an honour that the High Commissioner himself designated Reginald for the job and it goes back to what he did during the war when he came to occupied Malaya and went underground. Anyway, cloak-and-daggerish, and I know you'll understand what that means. Please don't admit you have the slightest knowledge of it if you happen to write to my husband.

Let me go back a bit. Once again, though somewhat removed, I must thank you for all you did on my behalf for, without your help, I might never have ended up as happy as now. I found my real mother. We had some glorious time together and, lo and behold, I found motherhood myself – wonderful, excruciating, frustrating but complete joy. I shall never forget Mummy and, through her, experienced happiness and, last but by no means least, I found my husband, the unashamed and unabashed father of my son. And God is good for giving me all of that. Yes, that's a mouthful. You should see how wide my mouth is as I write this down.

It's true that Mummy, hopeless romantic that she was, wanted us to marry but I also know this: despite all that there was with that history stuff and him coming to Port Elizabeth, her view wasn't decisive. Reginald asked for my hand in marriage because he loves me. How do I know?

Well, you're a woman. I always knew he loved me, even as far back as when we met on that ship.

I realise it sounds awfully gushy, but I'm allowed to be, aren't I, even if my husband is older – alright, dammit, much older and, at least in public, staid about such things and much else besides! We have been so happy these last four months since we exchanged our vows in a cupboard called a registry office in Port Elizabeth. He might seem a bit of an old fuddy-duddy, but I can say this much without revealing many secrets: he carried me over the threshold in style and, in the words of the good book, the marriage bed is undefiled. And my lips are sealed!

On the downside, this job he's doing is pretty rotten, not solely on me. Little Magnus also misses him. When his daddy arrives home, he's happiness itself and won't let him out of view, no, not for a minute the whole time. Magnus sleeps in our bedroom and loves nothing more than being between both of us at night as Reginald tells him a story, and he snuggles into us before going to sleep.

When it comes time for his daddy to leave, well, I sometimes wish we didn't have to go through that. Reginald came up with a plan after the little fellow was so upset that he delayed his departure and made his driver cranky. The last couple of weekends (and it's mostly every other weekend that we see him, although occasionally we get two in a row) Reginald has gotten up early, kisses me goodbye and sneaks out of our room before Magnus wakes as it's much easier that way.

I mentioned Reginald's driver. He's actually much more than that, although my husband doesn't say anything about him. Unlike our Reginald, who's as army as a pair of crimped and squeaky black boots, this one's a policeman who arrived from England a bit before we got here. A bright as buttons sort of fellow called Tommy. For reasons best known to him (and he never says much anyway), Gerhardus isn't so fussed regarding him.

I must also say something about that great big South African chap who came with us. Reginald has probably told you about Gerhardus. He's little Magnus' godfather as well. In his sixties and silent at times and getting on, of course, as we all are, but like a grandpop figure to him. If he wasn't around it would be even harder for my little boy when his daddy is called away. At one point he's always there to do anything for you; at other times, with me now married and all that, I sometimes wonder if it will go on after this is all over.

I think Reginald wanted Gerhardus to be able to work with him but it simply wasn't practical and so, close to the family as he has been for the last few years, he has remained with us. He's a giant of a fellow, as I said, and his generosity is of similar proportions. And I suppose I'm never unprotected with him around. I think Reginald feels much better for our sakes that he's here, not that I don't feel safe or anything.

Another 'refugee' from Africa, the one, the only, Rommel, our beautiful German Shepherd, also adores Magnus, and the feeling's mutual. There isn't a day that goes by without them scampering around together.

I really hope this job of his finishes soon. Reginald told me originally that it should be over in a "few" months, perhaps less. When I ask him how it's going, he seems downcast, as if he's not living up to the expectations of those running the damned show. Almost out of guilt, I suspect, he promises to take us to Kuala Lumpur soon as he can for a holiday. If that occurs (I won't hold my breath), it will relieve the monotony of being bottled up here and out of everything. And does my wardrobe need a refurbish! Can't buy a thing in this hillbilly outpost.

Must go now. Magnus is waking from his afternoon snooze and he's always hungry when that occurs. I want to get to him before Gerhardus does. No rest for mums, as you would know. Hope to update you soon and would love to hear all your news.

Bye and best wishes,

Henrietta Newton

✳   ✳   ✳

When Newton stepped inside the Fraser's Hill door, in place of his svelte wife's form, the incongruous silhouette assisting the tiny boy with his dinner bore the unmistakeable proportions of Gerhardus. Rommel, transfixed by the proceedings and bearing the certain conviction that any titbits falling from the board would be his, gave him but a whisk of his tail. Magnus wasn't so subdued, wriggled off his godfather's knee and ran to him calling, 'Daddy, Daddy!' before crashing into his arms, giggling excitedly.

Gerhardus read Newton's enquiry, shook his head glumly and motioned with a forefinger pointing over his shoulder. It was an action that Newton read without needing any elaboration and produced no comment from either man.

'Come on, my beautiful son. Grandpop will take Rommel outside for a run while I see that you finish your dinner. Then it's off to bed, where you know what's next.'

Having accomplished that, the little boy, with Newton's arm around his shoulder, knelt and recited his prayers in which he asked that, 'Mummy be home soon'. Being treated to the story of *Pedro* by his father, he soon succumbed to fatigue and was tucked in for the night.

After dropping the rubber ball at Newton's feet in the kitchen, Rommel licked his master's hand and was rewarded with a sliver of red meat. His intelligent brown eyes asked whether that was all and, with the answering pat, the dog caught the ball and took it to the child's room, where he curled up on a mat beside him.

'Shiz not herzelf deze days,' he said with a maudlin shake of his head. 'Moods, und zeems a diffrant perzon to Soud Africa.'

Newton listened querulously to the apologies rendered on her behalf.

'So it seems. She wasn't expecting me until next weekend.'

'Zspen more time zomeday zoon or maight loz her.'

Newton's sigh was unmistakeable. 'I'm going to take her away for a week soon. Looking after the boy is second nature to you.' Gerhardus nodded. 'Okay, I'll fetch her. Not a word about anything we've discussed.'

'Notdas much as a zound from zis,' finger slow-motioning across his lips like a zipper.

Henrietta, at a table harvesting the attention of a mixed group of revellers and holding a glass of champagne in one hand, began gesticulating with the other when she saw him.

'Oh, what a lovely surprise,' Newton's wife gushed with a poise he greeted as disingenuous. 'Here he is, my distinguished and handsome Colonel – oh, husband of mine, the kernel of my life, you devil,' her finger wagging and lips pursed mockingly.

Her clumsy efforts at recovery didn't improve his mood, as he had always made clear that, for any circles in which they might happen to mix, he was a commercial traveller criss-crossing the peninsula to Singapore and sometimes even in India. Remaining outwardly imperturbable, Newton explained for all to hear that he had returned early from Johore after clinching the sale of farm machinery.

He straightened his shoulders. 'Must make the most of some spare time, ladies and gentlemen,' he added po-faced. 'May I please be permitted to spoil the party and borrow my wife?'

After a boisterous display of public affection from which Newton exerted the ultimate restraint in extricating himself, she accommodated his arm while bidding an elongated farewell.

'Isn't he so, so shy, a real gentleman, and simply wonderful with it? Allows my free spirit to roam while he's abroad making his own merry ways, which is why I delight in the reattachment when he comes home.'

'Henrietta accords me more latitude than is warranted.'

Contemplating whether to linger a fraction longer didn't occupy her mind after she scanned his face. Her glass empty, she waved away the disappointment they expressed at her leave-taking with a carefree, 'See you next time.'

He steadied her when, as they walked outside, she scrambled for balance on the pathway. Instantly, Henrietta became apologetic.

'I'm terribly sorry I blurted that out. Do you think it matters, or anyone would notice, or I managed to cover it? Tell me, darling, please, that you aren't cross. You can't, you mustn't be.'

Newton didn't alter his gaze as he guided her up the steep pathway. 'We should always try to be a little contained, my dear. But I didn't much notice any reaction from those pen-pusher types who wouldn't have a clue what you were saying, other than it being a joke at my expense. And I never mind that, naturally.'

'Oh, thanks be to God. I worry so much, can't help myself. If you were to think me neglectful of Magnus, I'd surely—'

'The only thing I care about is making you happy. It's as your mother asked and as I promised. Being alone so often, you're entitled to become a little jolly sometimes, Henrietta, but it won't be for much longer, if things go to plan.'

She seemed not to hear and began speaking more, as if engaged in persuading herself. 'I do hope it's not obvious, even allowing for three glasses. Great surprise you've sprung. I'm feeling really good and much more settled now you're here. How could I be anything else, or want to be?' Taking short breaths, the climb engaging her, she added, 'And, with Magnus and all that. Phew, can we rest for a second? It's wonderful to have Gerhardus. Magnus is so loved by him and everyone.'

Newton, ever ready to excuse the guilelessness framing one side of her character, managed a pinch of a smile and regarded with benevolence the liberties her other side chose to exert on the facts when they were less than convenient.

'You're an exceptional mother.' He held her to him.

'One day you might think of me as the lover for which you've always craved, the wife of your youth.'

It was Henrietta's most telling riposte. He followed her through the door. Gerhardus served the roast dinner, there being sufficient to go around, apologised for not remaining with an excuse that he needed to take a walk and left them to their table.

Uncomfortable silences persisted between the few things that came up as they ate, he being rather more sparing. Eventually, Newton broke in by announcing his intention to take her to Kuala Lumpur before going on to Penang. 'Just you and I. Gerhardus is willing to look after

Magnus. You deserve a break from this drudgery, as I'm rather painfully aware.'

'Oh, my husband, you've made me so happy,' she exclaimed, taking his hand, stroking her face with it and lavishing the attention of her lips. 'I've never been to Penang and there's some beautiful colonial place to stay I've heard of, the, um—'

'Eastern and Oriental. It's been booked for us, indeed, the bridal suite's reserved.'

She leapt up and flounced around the table, stopping behind him to plant a kiss on his neck. 'You're a dear, darling man. We've never really had any time away, what with our little boy and now your important work. It can be our honeymoon, most certainly it – are you sure you're ready for that, Reginald? I mean, please don't take it as yours truly trying to push things quickly, remembering all that you've said and what Mummy told me. If we have to wait another year, I will, or even—'

'I don't hold any view other than the utmost reverence for you.' She slumped into her seat at the table, feeling more isolated than ever.

'I want us – it, to be right. You're entitled to be treated as a wife in every respect and I intend to fulfil my duties to you as a husband in every respect. The decision to go soon hasn't been a casual whim of mine.'

She moved closer. 'Oh, I know you're anything but casual or whimsical, Reginald. I hope you never think that because we're so different in our natures and us—'

'So separated by hair colour and skin texture?' he offered

in entreaty.

'Don't say that. You're my gorgeous man. I've always liked—' She stopped herself suddenly, perceiving danger in pursuing what an unsteady mind had introduced.

He went to her aid. 'You noticed me on the ship and still happen to fancy me for what I am and what I might soon reveal. No need to be shy,' he quipped with an eclectic gleam in his eye. This time, her kiss searched his mouth in a champagne of desire.

'I can't wait to find out. But mind, you aren't to enter the bride's chamber tonight or tomorrow. We must save ourselves for Penang.'

*   *   *

The following Monday, the chauffeur arrived at Fraser's Hill before the sun had appeared and left the vehicle with the motor idling. Newton was nowhere to be seen when he greeted her saucily.

'I say, Henrietta, your cheeks are glowin' and your slips a-showin'. Should've tooted, eh, and what woulda happened then? Did I think, is there somethin' goin' on? Come out with it, you need to tell your 'umble slave in private before the master arrives to spoil the rum tale?'

Never her best at dawn, she regarded Tommy coolly, asking only that he collect her bags. Rommel barred progress with his great bared fangs before Gerhardus whistled, and the dog stuck close to him as he collected the suitcases, both returning inside without another word.

'Don't think that individual's got a lot o' time for yours truly,' he persisted.

'Nor Rommel,' came the more amenable reply, her changeability an ongoing focus of fascination for him. 'Oh, don't mind them, they're two of a kind.'

'The sort who snap first, eh, Mrs, keep snappy and always come to the party late, like others who must never be mentioned around here.'

'Well, I didn't mean to snap,' she responded, touching him on the arm, 'but I can't speak for Rommel and Gerhardus, who don't befriend easily but, when they do, you're set for life and—' The sound of footsteps on the parquetry stalled her sentence. 'Oh, hello, here's the boss now – yours only. He's my husband and knows his place.' The object of the remark, having purposely made known his approach, made no reply.

Traffic, sparse to begin with, became busier the further they drove. Newton had insisted on Henrietta taking the front seat of the Ford, converted to right-hand drive, while he was occupied with a cumbersome file in the rear.

The conversation between driver Tredwig and the woman gaily adorned beside him was steady. It became much more animated after they slowed to a crawl. He pointed out placid water buffalo being shepherded along the side of the road by a young keeper, whose readiness to give them his devotion made him their loyal favourite. The boy, called to attention as Tommy tossed over a bar of chocolate, grinned wider still when he won a two-shilling piece from her and waved enthusiastically.

Further on, they passed the kongsi communal dwellings, which he explained was a successful development for the Chinese farmers and their families. Following on came the bashas, less prepossessing temporary dwellings housing poorer folk, followed in short order by the stands of almost impenetrable lalang grass growing to the height of one and a half tall men. She listened in awe as he conversed with a group of Malays and caught the eye of a fetching Chinese woman who tried to hawk bags of rambutan as they waited for a lumbering goods train to pass.

'How can you just do that,' she asked, 'as if they're old pals? Did you give the fruit lady a tip as well as your address?'

'Very funny, Mrs Newton. None of that. On m'dooty always in the field and solely about gettin' experience in the job. Goes with the territory of an obedient coppa day in, week in and the rest.'

Newton made frequent, surreptitious checks of the rear-vision mirror. Tommy was too fully occupied with Henrietta to notice, and he continued to listen without the occasion ever arising to offer a comment. It led to a perception that, had he expatiated of any topic, the parties in front might have either missed it or been startled to realise that someone was sitting behind them.

The best he could conjure up was imagining the back seat was now occupied by a newcomer, he having been displaced some considerable time earlier. That assessment held until his wife, apologising for interrupting his paperwork, queried whether he had understood any of the conversations in which Tommy had been engaged.

'Oh, you know, just the odd word here and there,' he responded with customary deft absent-mindedness masking a feeling of resentment. 'Tommy has a great gift all of us in Malaya who've come to know him appreciate.'

'Thankee, sir. Exceedin' kind,' he chipped in idly, not giving occasion for inferences to be drawn against the colonel's remark.

They returned to their own brand of dialogue, a mix of the inquisitive and familiar, while with less ease than ever he resumed the classification of hitchhiker compiling a travel log and losing concentration.

A message awaited Newton at the reception desk as he and Henrietta arrived to check in to their hotel. Its reading and the subsequent call from the house telephone were followed by a rare outward display of frustration. Henrietta waited as he righted himself, realising an announcement not in accord with the plans she was conjuring for dinner was imminent.

'I'm afraid—'

She forestalled the balance of his sentence with, 'You aren't going to be around tonight, are you? Oh well, so be it.'

Unable to deduce whether her countenance was either wholly indifferent or that any residue of disappointment had been suppressed, Newton replied, 'Can't be helped, Henrietta. It's somewhat worse than just tonight. I must go to Singapore immediately and may be there for a day or so. Don't be perturbed. The situation has been explained and—'

'Ah, I've been called many things but never a "situation", though at times whatever I am in this role requires my own daily briefing. What's it to be, no Penang either, I suppose?' she added as a tetchy afterthought.

'First, apologies; indelicate of me, Henrietta. I didn't mean you, as in a person, but the fact that I'd actually brought my wife down here with me, which was known. I had set a few things in order to permit time to take in some of the sights and an evening out before pushing over and away from it all in Penang.'

'Don't mind me. It's, ah, well, I don't know, at the risk of sounding repetitive, a given in this Malayan business. I should be far more ready to accept that my part is to support you rather than make your job more difficult.'

'And you are supporting me. Not sure about HM's government sometimes. Tommy will shunt me off soon to catch the train. I'll ensure that he looks after you for dinner. Perhaps be ready in the lobby at about seven.'

Kuala Lumpur

11 April

Dear Nancyng,

This is a much quicker follow-up than promised, though I trust it won't be as long, you'll be pleased to read.

We're presently bolted down in dreary old Kuala Lumpur. So far it seems about as interesting and appealing as last week's leftovers.

How about this for irony? I was supposed to be here with my husband for 'us' time and, without warning the same day, he's ordered off to a meeting in Singapore for a supposedly short, read two days, briefing or some such. Couldn't be avoided he said. The darling that Reginald is, he's promised to take me over to Penang away from it all. Booked a lovely colonial type hotel over there called the Eastern and Continental or something for a second honeymoon. (Have we finished our first, well might you ask? My lips are sealed.)

Perhaps you've heard of the place. All these unfulfilled promises make a girl a tad cranky, but I'll get over it. He didn't want me to bring Magnus, and of course ever-present Gerhardus was happy to oblige looking after his 'grandson'.

Reginald didn't take anyone with him and asked his lieutenant, that Tommy chap I mentioned, to look after me. He's a gentleman, respectful, but sometimes I think he gets a rather naughty glaze in his eye. Perhaps I need to remind him that I'm an old married woman with a toddler whose husband has the power to hire and fire!

Reginald had promised me dinner tonight at King's House, the high commissioner's place. No, just joking, as only the really important people get to meet Sir Gerald Templer. Reginald's been there, of course, and he wouldn't talk about it or entertain my suggestion that we meet his lovely lady wife over cocktails and canapes. Actually, I'm going to be slumming it tonight with mine 'lecherous' host who's promised to give me a good sampling of the local cuisine, adding that he'd try to find out whether some decent French plonk can be got. Just where anyone would acquire such a thing in this godforsaken dive without paying a month's worth of his salary remains a mystery.

One thing I've had to learn in a hurry is not to become beset by (how's my alliteration going?) disappointments. I could almost call up a string of them since we arrived here, but actually persist/subsist? in a good frame of mind. This is my second stay in KL. As I may have told you, we arrived here first when Reginald received his induction.

I didn't like it then much either. Fraser's Hill is almost heaven by comparison weather-wise, but this time I'm determined to try and enjoy things a bit more, or at least be in a receptive frame of mind. I think having such a gregarious and witty companion in Tommy (something I'm a little unused to because, as you would know, Reginald can be an old stick in the mud) might have something to do with it. Or, on the other hand, an expectation that soon my husband is going to whisk me off to a lovely, romantic isle like Penang, or so I've heard, may also be a factor.

Oh hell! The phone's just rung, and it was hubby. Wouldn't you know, he's got to go on to Johore for another night so looks like I'm here a bit longer. He has already told his underling the news and given strict orders that my every whim must be catered for 'or else'. When I hear him talk like that, so thoughtful in his own dour way, I have to remind myself that life isn't all that bad and what's ahead in England when this is over will be much better.

Now, here's a big secret. Tommy has let it be known that Reginald and he are on the lookout for an evil criminal known in these parts as 'The Huntsman'. There was a blurry photograph of the fellow and a story about him in the newspaper. I'm tearing it out to enclose with this in case you might be interested and just so you know Reginald is not on some junket over here.

But please, all hush-hush, as Tommy wasn't meant to let

on. I asked him after he'd dropped my husband off, having seen the story, and Tommy came out with it. He likes to big-note himself but he's all puff and show. Reginald mustn't know a thing, though, otherwise Tommy will lose his job.

So, there you have it. Apart from being proud of my husband for what he's trying to do, I wasn't all that concerned. The life of an 'army wife' seems to be on a par with that of a policeman's missus but, really, I wouldn't want it any other way. Reginald always makes it up to me and I love him so! .....

I just went out for a long walk. KL isn't so bad, I guess. I looked at some of the shops and was harassed by beggars and hawkers after I incautiously gave in and purchased something. Never go shopping with me unless you've hours to spare! Given all that, I didn't see a thing I liked, except the little toy wooden train which Magnus will love.

There are other things I wanted to add but I'll leave off for now. They'll have to wait for the PS aftermath where the events of the dinner … will be faithfully recorded. Ooh, I'm sort of looking forward to it even though I've nothing to wear. Oh, silly me, who am I trying to impress anyway?

Henrietta

After spending a few minutes twisting and turning in front of the wardrobe's full-length mirror holding the frock she favoured had her husband been the escort, Henrietta decided there was no point and an ordinary substitute would suffice. It was blue with large white buttons, its hem just below the knee and a demure neckline with a pink frill. Her shoes were white and almost flat, consistent with her mood, and she decided not to wear stockings. Had an apology been received on account of Tommy being ordered away himself, she would have accepted it with relief and retired early.

*   *   *

Singapore

11 April

Dear Mrs Jenkins,

Well may you regard me as something of a sneak, if not a hypocrite (perhaps on two counts given my 'sign-off' on the last occasion), for insisting that you retain the sentiments in this letter in conjunction with the understanding that there is a reason for confidence in this somewhat delicate matter. The location from which I write will also have not escaped your casual eye.

I'm here for unexpected briefings, updates, and I need not trouble you with what else, and have time on my hands out-of-hours as well as some privacy. Historically, you have been a patient, considerate listener and thanks are due for that. In an odd sort of fashion, I trifle with the notion that, for someone like me, you have become adept at both knowing the right thing to say equally as well as perceiving what not to enquire upon.

Having already hinted at a few of the difficulties I've been encountering at such an embryonic stage in this marriage I have contracted (and more and more a contract is what it feels like, signed, sealed and unconsummated), you may not be surprised to hear that things haven't really improved, the emphasis being on the real as opposed to the superficial.

I feel older than my middle age and know she is a vibrant and, at times, tempestuous woman, not merely since Henrietta has reminded me that she has wants and needs. I do understand. It's simply that I cannot bring myself, still, to meet my side of the bargain. Her mother may well be reaching from the grave to control another life. It seems I'm feted to accept a similar destination.

Yet, paradoxically, as tediously uxorious it may sound to reiterate, I love her the more as each day passes. She has made clear, mostly by inferences rather than by words, that if I don't change my disposition soon she won't be responsible for any actions on her part. Shuddering when she first canvassed such issues, I am starting to see only too well that she means what she hints at after having observed her unabashed flirtatiousness with my young driver and liaison officer. He's a good-looking 'hail-fellow-well-met' type, though here for just a little longer than me, after, I'm assured, a distinguished career in the London Metropolitan Police and Scotland Yard.

Given that a much-anticipated break has been put on ice, I've encouraged him to chaperone Henrietta while she's at a loose end in Kuala Lumpur until I get back. Having deliberately prolonged my stay – more sneakiness, yes, I own to it – but I believed her when, at its threshold, she assured me that getting used to marriage (your correspondent being senior in years and even more so in ways to her) was something Henrietta wholeheartedly accepted and at which she would succeed, no matter what, 'for better, for worse'. Aren't those words becoming rather hackneyed?

Though I'm loath to recall the *New Zealand Star*, I'm realising rather sooner than I anticipated that a facility for flightiness hasn't quite deserted her. I'm grieved at having to relate this but the other day, on returning early for a weekend to surprise her and expecting a joyous reaction, instead of my wife tending to our son in the evening as any mother does, Gerhardus had been delegated for the task, or so I inferred from what was going on.

He was anxious not to be seen as indelicate, saying only that she seemed rather footloose (my word for his roundabout explanations) and had gone out. She didn't tell him where, but he revealed that the guesthouse below our home might be a suitable starting point. Henrietta was indeed in the bar there, somewhat the merrier/worse for champagne but otherwise better in spirit for the ribald company, becoming rather less so upon my impolitic appearance. Consistent in nature with the person of Esrelle, it's an attribute that's emerged. The sins of the mother, weakness of the father combination, perhaps?

Even the euphoria of motherhood, which had exerted not merely restraint but was, I'd concluded, transformative in her makeup, hasn't long lingered amongst different surroundings. When I'm not around, part of the problem, it must be conceded as Gerhardus now whispers to me following my insistence, is that she seems content to leave even more of the wet-nursing stuff to him and moon about at said bar.

With considerable persistence, I also learned that on one other occasion she didn't return until after Magnus had been put to bed and was deep in sleep. Henrietta offered some justification (again my word) about feeling unwell and retired but the tell-tale signs of inebriation couldn't be disguised from my dependable South African compatriot.

I oughtn't ponder, pending my return to Kuala Lumpur, whether she and my driver have spent a portion of chaperoning time in private in addition to being seen in public, but trying to flee such images from my mind is proving less than easy. Now, you're somewhat psychic, I've noticed. If just uttering some visionary words or something else would be all that was needed to shunt off debasing thoughts so as to be the man she requires, the husband she deserves, show me that magic and I will engage it to the 'on' position.

The really unsettling part of my reveries now is whether I have set the whole thing up to find an excuse to re-embrace bachelorhood and derive perverse pleasure out of personal failure. Worse still is that entrapment has become part of the design. 'Lord, give me some help, some self-abnegation,' I want to pray. How foolish am I?

And still I have this little boy who is the light of my life. Would I suffer any indignity, any humiliation, any ridicule, any torture, being a cuckold, regarded as pathetic and weak if it meant that Magnus could continue to have a mother and father around him every day to love and cherish? You must know the answer.

I don't often drink but, if ever there was a time to break with that convention, it may arrive after this letter is posted. To catch it, I must sign off. As you no doubt would have worked out, like on the ship, the tale has to be all one way. I couldn't talk to anyone else about my marriage, or Henrietta and myself, save that I am of the firm belief that you are a non-judgmental assessor. Even if there was a way for you to write back without the contents being seen, right now I wouldn't opt to avail myself of your valuable insight, so it's best not to even consider it. This expurgation will soon cease.

Without seeming to sound unutterably foolish, I remain sanguine that things will resolve in the end. Also, Henrietta has told me that she wrote to you some time ago, and that's encouraging. In the light of the one-way communication hiatus, resisting the temptation to ask whether she raised any personal issues with you doesn't arise. I'm certain that she would want to keep things bright, breezy and surreal, as if I was her Prince Charming and she the doting little princess waiting at table.

Sorry, that was catty and undeserved. It's a situation we both face and the primary responsibility lies with me since I could have said to Esrelle, 'No, sorry, I'm unable to marry your daughter. She needs someone younger, fresh and dashing.'

Here I am having let the greater part of the last couple of hours slip by without giving any indication of the slightest regard for you and Charlotte. No doubt you would be pleased to emerge intact from another of those horrid English winters. They are the things I miss least about England and, if I ever return there, which Henrietta never stops talking about, by the way, the challenge will be to find a mild, even temperate place to eke out the rest of my life. Who knows, you might even come and visit with me/us with plenty more fat to chew if the memory remains kind.

I also trust you and Cousin Lynn are well and your teaching continues to be rewarding.

Regards,

Reginald Newton

*   *   *

Prior to collecting Henrietta, an assured Thomas Tredwig had managed to allot some time for Chow Kit. It had become a place with whose familiarity he was so enthralled that, if a welcome sign had been nailed up for him above his personal entrance, he would have perceived the gesture as right, duly earned and totemic of his increasing influence and importance.

He was disappointed that Adelka hadn't been in residence,

415

an inference he preferred to draw from the word 'unavailable', and couldn't join him for one-on-one time, though this was soon offset when Lemarno, to whom he now always referred by first name, took from a wooden crate that contained five more of the same, a bottle of 1929 *Pomerol*, in conjunction with an apology that the additional and hoped-for accompaniment, *Pol Roger*, had been unprocurable.

'So, my perfect man, what plans do you have for the disposition of this classic French merlot? Surely not going to waste it on flat-footed and dull Englishmen?' he fluttered, seeking to prise an opening in the other's doings. A dark frown was quickly neutralised. 'Tommy, sweet fellow, I'm jesting.'

'Yeah, I'm 'opin' to enjoy several over the next hours,' he said, as Scarfino passed it over. He confirmed the vintage. 'But it mightn't do to carry more than a few o' these around at any one time. Could get meself coshed or somethin'.'

'I would counsel anyone against trying to take *you* down.'

Tredwig cocked his head. 'Always sayin' the nicest things, Lemarno. Looks pretty good stuff, I guess, but plonk is plonk, I'll vouch, all's the same to me.'

'But surely not just for yourself alone, and you know the old saying about taking drink that way,' Scarfino said, wagging his signet-ringed index finger, its one-inch nail hypnotising Tommy.

'Who said anythin' about either bein' alone or set loose with flatfoots, eh, mate?'

'Now the truth is seeping out,' Scarfino insinuated. 'Someone has caught your roving eye. Do you think *she* might be the sort of creature to fully appreciate such an exclusive vintage?'

'She's a real mixture. Lady, yes, refined, young and beautiful, with some spirit. A challenge that I'm sure to—'

'Enjoy "to the max" as you would say, dear one. Is she somewhat aloof and unreachable? Come on, please tell your little Lemarno. He can only dream of such things and life is about dreams, Tommy.'

'But not of women, eh, Lemarno? That spyhole into Ada's boudoir isn't solely for bosoms and female complementary private parts viewin'.'

'So sharp-eyed and kindly tolerant of my foibles. You understand, I'm sure, and that's why there's so much to like, and you never judge, not even my voyeuristic proclivities. Live and let live, eh? All of us have our weaknesses, don't we, Tommy? Oh, I nearly forgot, something here you better have.'

The white envelope was thicker than usual, its contents readily apparent. Tommy's lips, dampened by a circling tongue, opened avariciously as he fingered the notes muttering, 'Thanks.'

Almost as an afterthought, Scarfino snatched it back and dangled the item just beyond his reach. 'Dear Tommy, Lemarno needs to know who you're about to exert your charms upon. Married, is she? I don't require a name, of course, but the lady is, ah, known about town?' He hesitated long enough for the Londoner to wriggle in his chair, apprehension marking his face. 'Money, sir, it, well, doesn't shoot from sagan trees.'

Tommy swallowed and cuffed a hand around his mouth, leaning towards Scarfino, who turned a scented ear in a gesture of reciprocation. 'Ah, bugger it, she's the wife of a somewhat lowly government official.'

'Oh, my, is that all? For a minute I thought you were going to say Lady Templer's confidential secretary, or maybe even the lady herself. Well, off you go my hot, anxious beau. Here, yours to do with however you wish. She'll love its appearance. Women like to see a man of means and action at their beck and call.' This time Tommy sequestered the item beyond the donor's reach.

A bow of acquiescence played to the dupe's vanity.

'Yeah, Lemarno, I hate soundin' like a tosser, but she likes me, if you must know, mate, a mere skint, coarse and ignorant underlin', like me, eh? How come?'

His benefactor leaned over, mouthing into his ear. 'Your secret is sealed, forever mine. The whole night's ahead. Give time for the oiling up of those cogs so the Tommy charm can attain its rightful climax. She can't resist, and I'll be drooling over your report. Oh, before I forget, may I recommend a romantic venue?'

Scarfino had no difficulty convincing Tredwig to dine at *Lafayettes*. Serving the only authentic French cuisine in Kuala Lumpur, it was the restaurateur, a close acquaintance linked through commission referrals, who had originally supplied the wine.

*   *   *

While Henrietta was waiting for her escort, the concierge mentioned a place and, on the strength of his recommendation, she asked that a booking be made. By the time Tredwig arrived to kiss her hand ostentatiously, she was in humour again and regretted not being more elaborately attired.

'I've reserved two places at a restaurant that would be perfect for the wine and, being French, the only one of its type in the city but,' she raised her eyebrows and lowered her voice, 'might be a little expensive. It was booked by *moi*. Cheeky of me, wasn't it?'

He was relieved when she recounted the name of the establishment. 'What good am I, m'dear, and sorry I'm late, traffic and all. Ah, you're a woman after my own heart, bold, assertive and—'

'And, come on?' tilting her head, canvassing his eyes in anticipation of a saucy follow-up.

It was a signal that left even Tommy struggling. 'Ah, I, I never do go out with timid, petal types. Shall we?'

Following behind as she sashayed towards the doors, he determined that the lobby's waiter hadn't been kept idle. Refusing his hand, Henrietta demonstrated some practical application of Tredwig's characterisation by accessing the driver's side while pointing him to the passenger's door. 'Go on, get in.' He was content to accede by delivering a mock grin.

'Well, that's tellin' me. And I 'aven't even had time to say 'ow real scrumptious you look, Mrs Henrietta.'

'Liar! Complete frump, you meant to say, but *sooo* much better now.'

The evening air was freshened with a film of rain. She followed his directions and asked how he knew of its location. 'An associate, sorta hush-hush, told me, that's all,' he replied. In what seemed to her like no time at all, though to him somewhat longer on account of her indifferent familiarity with road rules, he had opened her door, offered his arm and they passed through the entrance to be royally seated.

The wine flowed inexhaustibly as he exercised listening skills. After the first bottle came another from the house. Eventually, his hand found hers in plain sight. She permitted him for a time without a look being exchanged. Regretting the action, his lips mouthed 'sorry'. Longer silence ensued, she taking to the liquor in abandon before excusing herself with, 'I need to powder my you know what.'

When she returned, her hair, undone and brushed out, glowed like embers in a room otherwise suffused. The soft freckles clustered around her cheeks entranced him.

'You needn't have made the apology, such as it was,' she eventually resumed, her eyes inviting questions.

'Aw, pretty rash and stupid of me.'

'You're a man, aren't you? All men think they're entitled to try these things on,' her voice matter-of-fact.

'Not all jokas would.'

'Are you just a joker, Tommy, or a gigolo?'

His face reddened even with the smirk. 'Hell, no, Henrietta. Look, I mean your husband's my boss away in

Singapore and all that. I know 'e wouldn't be manhandlin' a senior officer's wife at dinner.'

'Can we refrain from any such talk please, Tommy?' the statement's abrupt delivery leaving him uncertain as to the next step.

They continued to eat in silence. All but half a glass of their third bottle remained at the end. She finished it without offering him a portion. 'Can you take me to my hotel now? I'm tired and, well, over things,' she said, standing and dabbing her face with a damp cloth. He went to finalise the bill and was told that Lemarno had attended to it. She drifted backwards at the car's door being opened and he took her arm. Offering no resistance to his kiss beside the vehicle, she was content to let him guide her into the seat, permitting a more intimate follow-up before he crossed over to take the wheel.

'You have another bottle, Tommy,' Henrietta suddenly piped up. 'It could have sliced my ankle open.' She rolled it carelessly in her hands. 'So, you're off to have it alone after you've dispensed with your date, or maybe you'll get lucky elsewhere?'

It was not enough of a question or even a statement to permit a response, but he punted for the one that fancied him most, 'Preferably shootin' up with m' lady luck sittin' beside me. Definitely no other offers, not much else sorta stuff for it.'

'Isn't there? Alright. I'm going to keep it all to meself,' she hiccupped. 'Lord forbid, I'm even startin' to sound like you, Tommy boy.' She cradled the wine to her chest and playfully pushed him away with one hand. A pretend tug-of-war preceded his giving way, correcting the vehicle after it veered dangerously close to a pedal car.

'Okay, Mrs H.' They had come to a halt outside the hotel. 'We're at a stalemate. Wouldn't be fair to let any lady drink alone, especially one as scrumptious as a certain someone a fella might sorta refrain from being bold enough to mention.'

'You'd better not let *the lady in question* do so, as long as you behave,' her words becoming more slurred. He whispered to the bellboy, who pressed a button. A man parked the vehicle and Tommy followed her into the elevator. She handed him the wine so as to prop herself against the handrails and began humming tunelessly.

'Are you alright?' he asked. Henrietta, blank to the questioner, had gone quiet. He helped her into the bathroom and he asked again. She tried to answer, coughed, gurgled and vomited.

Chapter 23 – *A Time Bomb*

Having chosen Newton's young wife as the addressee even though she was anxious to make contact with him, Nancyng sat down with a blank sheet of paper in front of her. Before applying pen and ink to it, she fingered the three letters in her hand, one from Reginald and two from Henrietta. They had found her letterbox in successive deliveries.

She had combed through them carefully and decided that refreshing her memory again as she wrote would ensure that the mixed and, at times, troubling messages emanating from husband and wife didn't lead her to unwittingly betray the confidence with which Henrietta's husband had entrusted her and which Nancyng Jenkins would never take for granted.

Still a tension existed where she wanted to avoid being so stymied, given that duty seemed to exert a pull upon her to proffer something other than platitudes or empty mundanity. Sipping at her second cup of thick, black coffee since the hour was late and Lynn long abed, she began:

26 Vivesta Lane, Sonning Common RG4 Reading, England

20 April 1953

Dear Henrietta,

Many thanks for your two letters, the latest of which arrived yesterday.

By the time you receive this, your little getaway in Penang will be well and truly over. I hope you and Reginald had a relaxing time together. It's a cosmopolitan, frantic sort of place at times. What a treat it must have been to stay at that famous hotel. I'm sure you had lobster and champagne overlooking the sea and, if you didn't, I'm going to brain that husband of yours.

Speaking of husbands, marriage is such a combination (or sometimes combustion) of disparate things. In most cases it's two different people thrust together in close confines who must adjust to each other. It's one thing to live in the same house with others around. Given your experience, I think such a situation can be advantageous as far as transitioning is concerned, and friendship, too, which has obviously become strong for you both in that wonderful period with your mother leading to Magnus' arrival and his toddling about.

Familiarity, along with its potential, not so much as to breed contempt, can be counterproductive. Instead of, as before, having a friend and exchanging sometimes superficial pleasantries and at other times things of substance, you now have a lover (an altogether different beast, no offence intended), a man who will share your intimate life and your body. So with marriage comes a foreign set of norms to consider and to which adjustment must follow on a daily basis. The transition is a long way from a light-hearted stroll through Hyde Park in summer; more like a barefoot weaving amongst briars, thorns and thistles with a few rose petals thrown in between, but hopefully many more of those.

In your case, you seem, by your words, to have made it rather unified, but be on guard. Heaven forbid that I mention this as a negative, but there is an age difference between you and people do change as they get older still. I speak with some experience. What I'm trying to say is grow together, age together and don't let that difference accentuate itself with time. My earnest hope is that the happiness you both deserve will be realised and your love for each other matures with it to an even deeper level.

A binding agent here is a ready-made family, and you've been particularly fortunate in having a man who's a more than devoted father to your son. It's a wondrous thing that Reginald sees the little boy as much as being of his own flesh and blood as would any biological father. I could go on but, for fear that you may think me a busybody, shall leave off sensitive areas. You have only to say the word and the topic will never again be mentioned.

Now to something about which I'm somewhat troubled

and really hope my fears are groundless. You've spoken quite a bit about this fellow Tommy. It may just be a coincidence but there was a police officer by that name who my cousin and I met some months ago when we ventured out, it being Lynn's (my cousin and housemate's) birthday. We went to a local pub or something exempted from that strange six o'clock closing rule.

The particular policeman and his partner had apparently finished duty and invited themselves to our table. Neither Lynn nor I took to them at all. They were intrusive, but that may have been a perception brought about by us not being desirous of male company.

A bit of trouble arose with two young fellows who had been drinking and had become inebriated. They were playing darts and some harsh words were exchanged between them and the police. They then left us, their meals having hardly been touched, not long after the young men had also gone. A few days later, there was a report in the paper of a chap being hospitalised with serious injuries and another on the run or some such thing. The suggestion was that they were found trying to burgle a house and there was a terrific fracas between them and the two officers.

On the evening we read the story, Lynn and I had a visit by those same police. How they found where we lived and the reason for doing so is a mystery made disturbing by their insinuating, intimidating and threatening presentation. Being a hardier specimen when cornered, as it were, than my cousin, it made me wonder whether I should have reported them to someone higher up. We ended being dead against that, fearing that there might be repercussions. We all know how the men in blue stick together.

Anyway, most relevant of all was another word or two about the Tommy character. He said he had resigned from the local constabulary and accepted for appointment to a top position in the Malayan police authority. He indicated that his departure was imminent and added with a leer something to the effect of, 'You can be pleased to know my ex-partner will always be at your disposal if you ever need him.'

If I'm wrong about presuming it might be him, tell me I'm a dill and a busybody. There may well be many such Tommys who were policemen somewhere or other and have ended up in Malaya. I read in the press that there were literally hundreds who took positions there from all over Britain and other parts of the Commonwealth.

However, trying to assist, I'll give you a description. He's fair-haired, handsome in a footballer's kind of way and a nuggetty-built man, perhaps thirty and mid- to upper-five foot in height. Has a tendency to laugh a lot at times and smirks with it, the type they sometimes call a 'smart Alec'. I couldn't tell you much else, other than his lips seem to disappear when he opens his mouth and he's not short of teeth, top and bottom. He's also quite the flirt and I wouldn't trust being alone with him unless one was at a public venue. There's an underlying cunning that he masks by being bouncy of Londoner-type speech and keen for attention, life of the party type.

If that description makes you wonder whether there could be two such men who look alike, my advice would be to have a quiet word to your husband. Whatever you do, please take no steps to ask him about anything I have written here as a means of dispelling any doubts or confirming them. Reginald is in the best position to do some discreet searching. I don't have a surname for him. And, most of all, be careful. I don't want to worry you.

Please give my regards to Reginald. I hope, if and when you come back to England, that we shall continue to be friends. It would be such a thrill to see the three of you together. Also, when Reginald is away, stick close to that South African fellow, like him or not.

And forgive me for asking, but one thing I should love to own is a photograph of Magnus. Even better perhaps, a family snapshot if you have one spare. Oh, and you didn't enclose that newspaper clipping. Next time will do.

Love and best wishes,

Nancyng Jenkins

*　　*　　*

Fraser's Hill

15 June

My dearest Nancyng,

The rain is so heavy as I write that I can hardly hear myself think. I've never seen anything like it since being in this country. It doesn't agree with me much at all.

I trust you have received my letters. I could have misaddressed them as I didn't remember the number of your house. That would add to the delivery delays, and such things are problematic at this end at the best of times.

I don't know quite where to start but perhaps it's best to make a confession upfront. Got you worried? Then stop this instant because I think I might be pregnant! Mostly, I'm as regular as clockwork, but I missed last month and didn't think much of it but now a second has gone by. You're sure to be calculating about our 'honeymoon', exotic location and all that, champagne, candles and Reginald trying his best to be as romantic as a boy of twenty-one. Well, it may have worked and, if Magnus isn't going to have a brother or sister, well I've become an old, worn-out maid in advance of the body clock. Before I get too excited, I had better wait until I see the doctor at the end of the week.

There's not much more I can say. Please write and say it for me!

Hugs and kisses,

Henrietta

P.S. Still raining cats and dogs. Will send photograph soon. Here's that newspaper cutting I forgot to enclose.

Pray for me. Please?

Henrietta went to the window with her letter addressed and sealed and watched the torrents of water charging in rivulets down the macadam driveway to the road. The rain that had gouged away some of the hillside steadied, the last forty minutes having seen the gutters overflow, along with the downpipes. Gerhardus was out in it, raking and shovelling debris and leaves that had blocked the two drains at the front of the house. He was drenched. She opened the window to call him inside. Apart from waving her away with an indifferent arm movement, he paid no heed until the job had been finished. When he re-entered the house, the request to post her letter was obeyed without a further word.

Gerhardus took the only vehicle available, the second-hand Jowett Bradford van he purchased soon after their arrival in Malaya, and parked down at the inn. When it came to enterprise, he had no peer, hiring it out as required and running deliveries. It had also been a useful acquisition in moving furniture.

Over the last weeks, tensions, that had been simmering between he and Mrs Newton, began to magnify. What she regarded as his emerging proprietorial attitude to Magnus had, since her return from holiday, become even more vexing. The little boy having fallen asleep on the floor when the rain commenced, Henrietta covered him with a sheet and put a pillow under his head. As she began to compose her letter, Gerhardus had carried Magnus to his bed. The action wasn't out of the ordinary, but this time it rankled, and Henrietta was in no mood to let it pass. She regarded it as an intrusion, just another of the many examples where she perceived herself as being diminished and relegated.

Fresh in memory was the fanfare generated by his

godfather's announcement that Magnus had graduated from the shortened open cot to a boy's bed, as he put it, while she was holidaying with her husband. The little fellow was winsomely proud to show off his refurbished bedroom, the cot having formed the deposit for the upgrade. Gerhardus had clinched the trade with a local hardware store. She was unusually testy to find the arrangement in place on her return, the more so because of its winning Reginald's immediate and effervescent approval in conjunction with the child's.

Henrietta had arrived at a stage of universal resentment when it came to his ongoing involvement with her son, intuiting it as a sign that she wasn't up to the job. The irony was that Henrietta had willingly endorsed the arrangement that Magnus be cared for by his godfather while she and Reginald were away. Gerhardus knew a showdown was imminent on seeing her demeanour after his return from the post office.

'Juzcort the puzst in time,' he offered as she fixed on him. 'Izder anyding da matta?'

'Plenty, now that you mention it. Sit down, please,' she responded curtly.

Looking sheepish, he did as he was told, the Chesterfield creaking as it sank under the man's considerable frame. She maintained her feet in a show of defiance, eyes at the ready, hand motions activated.

'There are some things you must understand if you're to remain under this roof.' The cadence in her voice rose and fell inconsistently, the presentation of which had never before been delivered. Her skin alternated between being icy pale and wantonly florid.

His first thought was that she had been drinking. The Afrikaner began to apologise but his heavily-accented brogue, an aggravating feature even on a good day, was interpreted as impertinence and she told him so even more stridently. 'You will kindly hold your coarse tongue when I'm speaking and know your place here.'

'Zorry.'

'The first rule you must remember is that I am Magnus' mother. If he's to be put down to bed at any time, I will do the putting. Secondly, he's too young to even be in a bed like that one. He might fall out and injure himself. You had no right to give away the cot, the one I selected for him and paid for, without speaking to me beforehand.

'Furthermore, at night, *I* will read him his story, and you can get out of the habit of lying down with him when he asks for you by making yourself scarce and attending to your duties.

'While on that topic, in future you will confine yourself to looking after the grounds and the garden. I intend to hire someone to undertake domestic service. The mothering will be for me and no other. If you want to fiddle about with deliveries and ferrying people around in that stupid vehicle, that's your business and yours to grow now that you will have more time at your disposal, but Magnus is mine and mine alone. Do you follow me?'

He coughed awkwardly, sighed and nodded. 'Iz wudeva yuzsay.'

'You can still play with him, as I understand how he likes you doing because my husband is so often absent. When it's all over here with your *master's* work, I can say with certainty that our future won't be in Malaya. You need to consider where yours might lie. You cannot put in jeopardy my husband's relationship as father with our son either. Attachments to family are one thing, to a stranger quite another. The more so because when we move back to England after the business here is finished, just think how little Magnus will be confused when you're no longer around?'

As his great grey-dusted head nodded repeatedly, he blinked away more than one tear.

'By the way, when you were out, I received a phone call from Mr Newton and I've discussed the issue with him. He's in full agreement with me, and that includes where we will eventually make our home. So, for now, our business is at an end. Good evening. No doubt with all the rain you've still got plenty to keep you occupied somewhere.'

Gerhardus rose, tipping his fingers to his brow respectfully. From his trouser pocket, he handed her a letter with a local stamp on it. 'Juz remembered diz.' As she was occupied with it at her desk, he checked the phone line in the hallway. It was still out, as it had been before Henrietta sent him on the earlier errand.

*　　*　　*

'How have you been going with that Italian bawdy-house keeper?' Newton's snappy question had drifted at Tommy almost as an unnerving casual aside amidst a wide-ranging discussion about the Huntsman and his cohort. He was exhibiting a continuum of frustration. Since the principal, or even a hint of him, hadn't been sighted once in the last five months, his strategies weren't bearing the slightest hint of a return. How to draw the quarry into the open was the foremost question and Newton was scouring his mind for some kind of ruse that might induce a raid.

An indication of the stalemate was that this had been their first meeting since Newton's short secondment to Singapore and Johore. Newton had scaled back his regular sessions with Tommy after making a request of Cedric Tister that he preferred, wherever possible, to take bus or train travel so as to be less conspicuous. If he required use of a vehicle, he had an absolute discretion to hire one for himself and if, for any reason, he needed the Londoner, whose job it was to assist when required, he could summon him at a moment's notice. In the meantime, for his part, Tommy furnished reports of his own activities directly to the assistant police commissioner where it involved general duties and to Newton if it pertained to information that might be relevant to the Huntsman.

'That source hasn't produced anythin' of substance, I must relate, sir,' stating the position with an underlying air of someone whose mind was otherwise occupied.

'I don't know about that so much,' Newton mused

with a sagacious glance towards him. 'My wife happened to mention that your selection of wine in combination with French dining showed more than a little inside local knowledge.'

The observation sent such an electric shock through him that, under the table, he made a fist of his right hand until the knuckles turned white before parrying at them with the other and twisted his grimace into a smile. He then strove to counter his fear by adjustment, assuming that Newton knew about the night's outing being on the house as well as the alcohol.

'Aw, a bit embarrassing to blow me trumpet, sir. Sheer luck it is. I must be worthy of somethin' that Scarfino wanted of your 'umble offsida for him to take the trouble. I know 'e trusts me and has been led to assume that I deal with the government in a contractual capacity that might mean I can be of benefit to him.'

'That's long-winded. To what end? Cheaper electricity and water? No more raids or inspections? We aren't in the business of running the blinking Vice Squad! Not a soul does,' vexation emerging again, before reverting to the opaque. 'Never mind answering. Go on. And?'

'I don't think Scarfino's lily-white in the sense that no one in his sleazy, manipulative line could be. Corruption has no boundaries, as lurkin' in the old 'aunts in the East End taught me.'

'That must have been a real apprenticeship for you as a young copper, Tommy,' Newton's piercing eyes seeking to draw him out. 'Shaped techniques, hobnobbing with toffs and the riffraff, much of it at the same time. Always on guard in case you mixed them up. Must be of considerable application here from what you say.'

Tredwig remained uneasy but reverted to the blasé accent he preferred to parade.

'Yeah, the good ol' days. Missem sometimes. Course I'm used to grubs and adaptable to their ways. Ya gotta be to get anywhere.'

Newton was at last beginning to enjoy himself. 'And you obviously did, Tommy. It paid off,' pausing deliberately for effect and to gauge his reaction, before adding, 'career-wise, of course.'

'Thanks, sir. Here as there, information, leads that could be useful to us, might, with a bit o' the ol' patience and perseverance, just drip our way. But with respect, fair enough. I've still got little basis for sayin', or even assumin', that Scarfino's directly, or even indirectly, connected to the primary target; more a tiny inklin' or speck o' hope that it may lead somewhere good.' He fidgeted with a house matchbox, avoiding Newton's eyes.

'What about those other areas you were following up?' his colonel eventually asked.

'Ah, now one of mine did net a grub. A CT suspect was caught on the premises after I reported to the chief. Unfortunately, no connection to the H either, but he's bein' cooperative since they found 'im. Funny 'ow weapons can so easily fall into their laps even by accident.' When his guffaw passed without apparent notice, Tommy's tone recovered immediately. 'Possession's a capital offence, so there might be more.'

'If you hadn't reminded me of that incident, I might have forgotten about it,' Newton effected in a tone to which his colleague was unaccustomed and sceptical.

'So are we concentratin' on any particular angle or is it just pressin' on in the usual manner? What I mean is, if ya want me to pursue another line of enquiry?'

Newton pondered momentarily at the mixing of two separate questions. 'Keep at what you're doing. Presently the angles are many, the points almost non-existent. So much so that they just seem to be widening with each day. There is one thing, though.'

'Anything for you, sir; at your service, just name it, tell me how high and I'll jump,' adopting the persona that Newton preferred least to experience even when in humour.

'Nothing operational, trivial really, but Mrs Newton requested me to ask if you had any more of the wine.'

'Really? Aw, well, I'm quite 'umbled, sir. That French joint might. I'll see what I can do for you and your lovely lady, sir.'

'You wouldn't be doing it for me. I have the palate of an Eskimo's when it comes to the fruit of the vine.'

'That's a real beauty, sir, an original,' he replied, craving acknowledgement for the compliment.

'And it's to be paid for up front and regular. Still, she seems keen to educate me. Says that if I tasted something special, I wouldn't look back,' he muttered as if to himself.

'Tell Madam I'm gettin' on it. Might need a bitta time,' he said, sucking at his lips.

'And I trust Mrs Newton enjoyed herself for those couple of days, even if you might have preferred to focus your activities on Chow Kit's all and sundry.'

He evaded Newton's eyes with a petty laugh. 'Gave no indication otherwise, sir. "All spiffing" were her actual words after a big thanks for my "puttin' up" with her. She likes to joke, your lady.'

'Does she now?'

His forehead tensed, revealing more lines than had previously been exhibited. 'Not the slightest bother when any task you delegate comes up, and I trust Madam hasn't raised any problem concernin' me?' Tredwig wanted to wish away the laxity of language that he was certain had prompted the scrutiny upon him, ever more so when Newton's breath touched his face as if anticipatory of some form of rebuke.

'Nothing that I can recall,' Newton drawled, shaping as if the meeting was about to end. 'All gratitude was bestowed as if you were a hand-picked guide. A little tired as she first appeared, Mrs Newton appreciated the company of someone who went out of his way, Tommy. That's it for now. Oh, I almost overlooked it, she passes her best wishes on.'

'That's nice. If you please, sir, tell your charmin' wife the pleasure's all mine.'

'And one other thing. She wanted to go further with a personal note of thanks, so I provided your new address. I'm certain you don't mind?'

'Not for a minute, sir,' he replied with little conviction. 'Ah, been there for a few weeks and prefer to remain a bit incognito otherwise. Upstairs always agrees as makes for better readiness if trouble arises. My cover's basically that I'm moving about a bit but home base is in KL and not far from the seat o' command.'

'Then expect it delivered any day. Good evening.'

Tommy exited the café first. He was edgy and apprehensive, not merely on account of the last question. Instead of returning to his abode, he detoured to the premises doubling as his second home. It occasioned no surprise to him when he found that Adelka was yet again absent. In recent weeks he had come to accept that she was much in demand and, on this occasion, sequestered to an assignment in the Cameron Highlands. Scarfino was quick to excuse the occurrence when they met before moving to his private parlour in the usual manner.

'I have other beautiful company available this evening, if that's your desire, my Tommy, young, virile buck that you are. But first, down to business.'

His companion bit at his scarified nails. 'What's the "business"?'

'Nothing serious, if you can help out bearing in mind what last we discussed; give and take, you Englishmen say. This may sound coarse, but the lady with whom you had dinner and all that lovely expensive wine, the one you squired to her hotel room?'

Tommy began to sweat. His hands found security from

the weight in his coat pocket.

Scarfino assumed a soothing air. 'No, my boy, don't be alarmed. I'm about protecting you and our investment for the future.'

The gesture produced no easing in Tommy's bodily decorum. 'Go on. "Our", you're sayin'? How so?'

Scarfino's casual reply suggested that he wasn't moved by the intimidatory tone. 'It's now assumed that she's the wife of a person here in the, shall I be so bold to mention, "important" people category *you* mightn't give a thought about but who we would like to get to know for, ah, business and economic advantage.'

'So what if she's married to someone or other "important", as you put it? It's of no use to your sort of trade,' permitting himself a sly twist of his mouth, 'not 'ere, surely?'

'My interests' – his interchangeable use of the personal and collective pronoun asked many questions of Tommy, not the smallest being: was there, apart from the Indian landlord perpetually in absentia, much more to Scarfino than he had ever imagined? – 'can be described as somewhat broader. One day, this insurgency will be over, you fellows gone, and Malaya becomes a nice place to have respectable economic standing. Come on, Tommy, just a confirming name or an occupation will do. Get the scene I'm painting? It's one sure to suit your expensive tastes. You don't have to decide immediately. A few days lesser than a week is enough. Until then, my friend.' Standing, he felt an uncertain hand.

'And before you go, dear man, just something more for you

to reflect upon. If the official happens to be who we can only surmise and has a name, next time you manage to call and want to talk to your Lemarno about it, bring a briefcase and a ticket to the Riviera will also be yours in early retirement or, if not, just go on being Mr Tredwig and resume your career.'

The longer than usual time that elapsed between Tommy's exit from Scarfino's and being conveyed by taxi to his own flat did little to allay his prismed mood. Even if the minor accident that caused the delay hadn't occurred, he still would be no further advanced on how to deal with the proposition. *Might the little weasel be onto something or was he flying a kite, and could more be read into 'career'? Fuck it, but the stupid bitch booked Lafayettes in her name. And how would the sneaky poofter know mine? And then there's Newton.*

He adopted extra precautions to see if anyone might have been tailing him. There was now no room for carelessness, as the minutes ticked by and he surveyed the street from a darkened recess, grateful that it was deserted of all but two screeching cats in a circling stand-off, their antics illuminated in the lights of an occasional passing vehicle.

On determining it clear to enter, lacking customary enthusiasm though with trepidation aplenty and a stomach churning around a cocktail of despair and anger, Tredwig took on the sharp stairs leading up to his one-bedroomed apartment as if the treads on which he stomped were the faces of his enemies, only to become even more moribund of spirit when he saw the envelope. The writing was in a hand by no means unfamiliar to him.

For reasons derived from practice and usage of women, he experienced dread of its contents, first fearful that either it would contain an unalloyed expression of eternal love or a declamation that his recent actions towards her had been tried by time and fervent consideration and weighed in the balance. Of one thing he was certain. It wouldn't be a 'kind thank you' without more.

Before tearing it open, his apprehension was of sufficient gravity to steady himself in the refuge of Gilbey's gin. He had swallowed two tumblers in advance of his flat being locked, before he realised the desirability of doing so, given his initial exclamation of, 'Shit.' On his third such pull, Tommy read it slowly and audibly through teeth that so ground against each other as to blanket any vocal sound.

Fraser's Hill

20 June

Mr Tredwig,

There's no point in my exchanging the usual pleasantries with your type of person. An alley cat has more redeeming features. You need no explanation for what that means.

You took advantage of me when I was sloshed and sick. Now, I can't swear on the Bible that it was rape in the normal sense of the word, but you know that it was and will have a difficult time denying it if I decide to take matters further. If I'm comatose with drink, I can hardly consent, can I? <u>And</u> you also know that any hint of a scandal like this finishes your career, kaput! <u>You</u> know that my husband would always believe and stand by <u>me</u>.

I suspected, but didn't want to accept or believe, that you aren't the sort of man who would ever yield to normal moral restraints as far as a woman is concerned. Your silence in the intervening period said one thing and going out of your way to ignore me the other day when you happened to be up here wasn't so smart.

Also, I've been told that your history elsewhere as a police officer has also been less than admirable. The night at that tavern or pub place just before you departed England refers. A couple of single ladies and that young man who ended up in hospital comes to mind. Remember now? You even tried to intimidate, going to their home uninvited to frighten them. So how about that, Mr Smarty Pants, and who would have ever thought it might come back to haunt you? Well, it did.

There is one more thing. Minor, I'm sure, to you, and not that I'm thinking it will make much difference to your situation: I'm pregnant! Did you get that? Yes, with child, or as you cockneys understand, in the family way, up the proverbial duff, bun in oven. And it's your child I'm carrying.

So, what do we do about it? Pretend it's his to let you off the hook or do we just own up to a reckless night of passion and seek clemency? Or do I just say to my husband, 'He got me drunk and I can't remember what happened next?' And don't ever hope that my husband won't support me. Any which way, it wouldn't look good and I shan't think it will turn out well either. Your goose is cooked, boy!

My decision on what I WILL DO will really depend

on what YOU DO about this situation. I needn't add to your woes by reminding great lair Tommy (rotter) that the evidence is on the verge of becoming too obvious to elude further attempts at concealment. Your old 'pal', Gerhardus, already suspects something's up and would be the first to sheet the blame home to you were I to say the word. He doesn't miss much and was right about you.

So, now it's morning and my spewing is about to commence again. Not nice to witness, let alone undergo, as you must recall. I know from experience that there shouldn't be much more of it. The tennis ball has lobbed onto your side. If you have a suggestion that's a gamechanger for both of us, let's have it. But time, as we know, waits for no man or woman. The fuse is ticking away up here.

Need I add anymore? Except I forgot, some of that stuff you were flashing around. MONEY! AND BE QUICK OR ELSE!

Henrietta

After hours in solitary confinement, chain-smoking, drinking, stalking the flat and muffling his random punches with pillows, Tommy made for Chow Kit. At his appearance and subsequent unburdening, no stink of gin or stale tobacco could repress the kisses Lemarno Scarfino planted on his cheeks and neck as he made up a bed for him.

Chapter 24 – *Snuffed*

With the passing of a fortnight since her letter was posted to Henrietta, Nancyng Jenkins made a point of coming home during the luncheon break for any reply. She even called at the post office to alert them that she was expecting important mail from Malaya. Because of her anxiety, she was invited to attend after hours in case it was in the late-delivery bag. Several days of persistence reaped an apology from the manager as he handed her a letter with a place stamp indicating that somehow the item had been mixed with mail destined for Edinburgh. Read on the spot, its short contents did little to allay her fears. The enclosure received but scant attention.

Pregnant, Nancyng's mind was transported into myriad scenarios as she paused on Sonning Bridge. With the Thames rippling in presentiment, she checked the date imprint on the envelope and made an umpteenth perusal. Resuming her homeward walk, even the fairy tale common, an excursion she habitually took after daily exertions were completed, lent no balm. The black, brooding heaven prompted a quickening of step. *Carefree in one breath, delirious in another and then, 'Pray for me.' Why would Henrietta suddenly ask that, bewildering, strange little girl-wife that she is?* By the time she reached her door, Nancyng Jenkins had entreated heaven many times to show mercy.

'There's been a terrible atrocity in Malaya.' The call, coming no sooner had she entered the house, was one she least wanted to hear or take in as Lynn pointed to the headline bannering the top of page three, 'Outrage in Malaya'. But it was the subhead that arrested Nancyng's eye. 'Young mother, workman, killed.' Becoming transfixed, as if her whole body had suspended operations was the prelude to a bout of quavering.

'What is it? Nancyng, please?'

Making no response, Lynn guided her into a steadying position where she sat, head bowed. A tumbler of brandy was placed in a trembling hand that Lynn continued to hold in case she dropped it.

After several long breaths, unintelligible words issued as she attempted to take in the story and an accompanying photograph captioned, 'Scene of Fraser's Hill terrorist horror'.

She inhaled loud and short. 'It must be. I suppose I'd better—'

'No. Nancyng, please let me,' and Lynn read.

Two people were brutally murdered at a bungalow near Fraser's Hill, north of Malaya's capital, Kuala Lumpur.

Early reports indicate that a British woman was one of the victims. Police described the scene they encountered as 'horrific'.

A man of South African extraction believed to be an employee and part of the household was shot to death in the grounds of the property. The bodies of two suspected insurgents were also located.

A band of communist terrorists is believed to have been responsible for the macabre slayings in an area of northern Malaya favoured by day trippers and holidaymakers.

It is thought that the attack might have been deliberately planned. Unconfirmed reports pointed to the perpetrators being a cell of the notorious 'Huntsman' gang of CTs, known for targeting Europeans and who, until this event, had not been active for some time.

The gang and its leader have eluded army and police actions over a number of years despite intensive efforts to eliminate them.

A government spokesman refused to comment on whether the woman killed was related to a senior security officer.

The police commissioner stated that they will track down those responsible.

'No stone will be left unturned to catch these evil terrorists,' he added.

Early reports have yet to confirm the fate of the victim's three-year-old son, but grave fears are held for his safety.

'Is there some way I can help you, Nance?' her cousin asked.

The grandfather clock chimed out seven strokes. Silence persisted with Nancyng tapping her arm in acknowledgement and nodding. She rose and approached the curtained back window as if in a trance. Upon a dilapidated rear garden shed she focused for some minutes with her cousin behind her uncertain what to say. Of a sudden, Nancyng whipped around to take Lynn's hands and spoke, the voice decisive.

'I've all but made up my mind. Before I tell you what I'm intending to do, may I ask a favour?'

'Anything you want; whatever I can do, if it helps.'

'You mustn't presume that I expect compliance. Are you able to look after Charlotte for me? What I mean is, just be here in case she needs support and, of course, when term vacation arrives. Given she's old enough to care for herself, it won't be necessary for you to alter your routine. She's independent for her age, almost too much so, as has become self-evident and wouldn't bat an eyelid if I was gone for some time.'

'Gone? I think she would, Nance.'

'That's kind of you. My thoughts are no more than five months. I should be back before Christmas. Travel time has to be factored in. I realise it's a big ask.'

'Travel time?'

'Yes. My intention is to return to Malaya, not out of choice but necessity. It's vital that I do so, literally as soon as I can conjure a means of getting there. As far as my teaching situation is concerned, I'll see if I can crib some leave, otherwise there's nothing for it but to resign.'

'Are you serious?' glancing at the newspaper for herself before grim eyes answered.

'Never more so.'

'Huge decision on so many fronts. To do with what's in here?'

'No, in one sense, and yet it's true, but much more so as well.' Her mind was not quite directed at the question.

'I still don't quite follow you. Is it going to be, ah, risky?' Lynn spoke as if seeking the answer was superfluous.

'I can't say, but in something like this you must do what instinct dictates, danger or not. More perhaps for those who might be – are, affected by these terrible events.'

'You once told me you'd never go back there. I understand that Malaya holds things from the past which you prefer not to recall, let alone mention.'

'Painful and dark things, yes, Lynn. They're of no moment in the face of the evil behind this wanton slaughter and the motives of the perpetrators. But we're talking about the present.'

'I'm lost for words, Nance.' She steered the conversation elsewhere. 'Dear cousin, the communists will always argue that the ends justify the means. Their noble manifesto trumps every human decency. What's another life or two in *their* struggle? Sorry, I didn't mean—'

'And it seems to work. Look at Mao; supreme butcher, unassailable dictator, master of China's people and destiny,' she spoke with rare vehemence.

'And they'll probably triumph in Malaya. What can *you* do against them, Nance? Why should you even concern yourself, unless there's a reason?'

'You think they are winning? No, that's just it, Lynn. I believe they're losing, and this latest bloodlust, well, it's like that comment ascribed to the man you're so fond of reading, adapted as being "a dying gesture of a revolution three-quarters dead". And there *is* a reason.'

Their hands remained clasped, each following her own thoughts, before Lynn turned her cousin's face to search her eyes. 'Can I just – I mean, oh, dear God, I'll just say it. You've been writing to that army chap you met on the ship and to the English girl you sometimes speak of, Henrietta. Is it about them; I mean, was that where this terrible business occurred?'

Nancyng had been general in her revelations, simply alluding to the fact that letters had been exchanged between she and her former shipmates. On the one hand she felt constrained to say more, yet knew that Newton would be furious if anything personal was revealed. She found some matches and used one to get the kettle boiling, the other to light a cigarette. As she rarely smoked, her cousin knew more was coming besides their tea.

'Yes,' she finally spoke, handing Lynn the cup and saucer and placing her own on the coffee table, 'it's about them, has to be, is. I'm not really disposed to go into it at present.'

'I shouldn't pry, but do you think that she might—' her

hesitation being well-read by Nancyng's questioning gaze, 'I know that one newspaper report is hardly the full account and who knows, the woman, well—'

'There's this terrible finality I feel about the whole thing. I've become, how shall I put it, a sort of confidante to both throughout the time I've known them and, I confess, much more so in recent months. If it's not Henrietta, and my mind's trying to retract first instincts, the coincidences would be extraordinary.'

'Oh, Nancyng.' The two women exchanged a lengthy embrace.

'What's even more troubling is that I can't sweep from my mind a suspicion that the revolting Tommy character might somehow be in the mix of it all. Why, I don't know. Call it stupid, women's intuition or just a readiness to blame anything on that peacock.'

'*Him?* It doesn't bear thinking about. Why?'

'I'll just say that some cur so like his ilk might know Henrietta. Maybe not, but I can't help thinking it, wild as it seems. I don't intend to tell anyone other than Charlotte where I'm going. I know I can rely on you to say nothing of my movements. The only forwarding address I can think of will be care of the High Commissioner's Office in Kuala Lumpur at this present. Once I get there and sort out everything, I will endeavour to phone you rather than send a telegram.'

'Nance, I'm absolutely here for you, but steady on. Have you figured out how long it's going to take to get there?

Flying's out, unless you've a secret benefactor or something. You've got to find a ship that's not going to stop between Southampton, Lisbon and all ports in the Mediterranean, Suez, India and Ceylon, etcetera. That's not sixty days, dear. And then what? You just go out there and hope for the best?'

'Yes, I know all that,' Nancyng replied a little touchily, 'but I'm in this situation where it's impossible to write, or send telegrams or phone.'

'Please dear, I meant no offence. While I've been listening, I've also been thinking. Remember that MP I told you about who liked me and helped out regarding the man I was engaged to marry?'

'I remember you saying that he had rather a soft spot for you.'

She blushed before adding, 'Yes, and I rebuffed him, not that he'd hold that against me, knowing Sir Gabriel Litherland to be a kind and steady gentleman. We can go and see him. I'll introduce you and then make myself scarce. He has contacts galore and I'm sure that they would go as high as the Colonial Secretary.'

'And he's totally discreet and honest, even for a politician?'

'Yes,' she sighed, almost in regret at casting asunder his unrequited fondness for her. 'Sir Gabriel is an irreproachable pair of hands. Once you got there, you'd be fortunate to even get the footman on the phone at Government House or wherever in Kuala Lumpur and, here, you wouldn't get past the street sweeper if you tried approaching the Colonial Office in Whitehall.'

'You're probably right. Who am I but some Chinese import?'

'Don't be so negative, Nancyng. If I happen to call my old friend and tell him about your problem, I reckon he'll facilitate a meeting in a flash.' Lynn clapped her hands. 'He might have re-married by now but it won't change anything. He's a kind of father figure who took this little foreign girl under his wing.'

'Let's see if he'll take another.'

*   *   *

By the time she stepped off the train that had carried her from Singapore to Kuala Lumpur following the interminable flight from London, Nancyng Jenkins was exhausted. Through deliberate decision, no one was there to meet her, nor had she elected to take any rest time on arrival. To her mind, there was nothing more important than that she speak to Reginald Newton as soon as was possible.

The other request, less easily acquiesced in, was that Newton not be informed in advance that she would be present at the memorial service. She promised an unobtrusive entry and early exit, combining it with a compelling submission that she knew both the late Mrs Newton and her husband more intimately than almost any other person on earth.

The letters she had as proof clinched official acceptance, Sir Gabriel endorsing her position when his further enquiries confirmed her worst fears concerning the squalid events at Fraser's Hill and pivotal in facilitating a swift transit.

The timing was exquisite. No sooner had she checked into her hotel than she emerged again, this time in a sea of black rayon that, with hat and dark glasses, almost entirely shrouded her in mystery. It was a ride made shorter through importuning the driver to have her at St Andrews Presbyterian Church by three o'clock if he wanted a decent gratuity. She waited for the bells to ring the hour before creeping into its farthest seat, though to little avail.

That a mere seven people were in the pews only enhanced the echoes of another's arrival. A solitary figure was sitting in the front row. An organist played the only hymn, *The Day Thou Gavest Lord Is Ended*. The apposite words, led by a female soloist with a sonorous voice soaring into every corner of the vast empty space, left Nancyng wiping her eyes knowing that only Newton could have chosen the classic refrain.

The rector explained that the writer, one John Ellerton, had intended the hymn to symbolise the drawing into itself the beginning and end of things. He spoke of the glory in the hereafter as being infinitely preferable to that which preceded it and solemnly thanked God for the life of Henrietta Newton. He motioned for those assembled to rise again, whereupon *The Lord's Prayer* was recited in unison before they resumed their seats.

After a few minutes of quiet meditation, the bereaved husband came to the lectern. Her head was lowered throughout the short address save for the occasional stolen glance his way. The voice was remarkably serene. As he reached the point of thanking those who were present, Newton basked his memories against a commission he was determined to accomplish.

'I will miss your ready smile, your naivety and the vitality that returned youth to a man who thought it had long passed him by. Our son Magnus gives thanks to you for being such a wonderful and loving mother. The world has become a lesser place now. Henrietta, my own girl. I promise you one thing: your life has not been lived in vain and' – he faltered momentarily – 'your death will not go unpunished in one realm or other.'

The last words altered the rector's features but compassion returned when he shook the widower's hand. He did the same with the other mourners and proceeded alone towards the front of the church. Newton stopped directly opposite her, motioning a greeting to Nancyng with his head. She crept along the empty bench and, taking his arm, they walked outside to a waiting car, not pausing to mingle with the assembly behind them.

His only response to her condolences was a transitory twitching of his features while continuing to stare straight ahead. 'How did you know it was me?' she asked as they were driven away.

'Do you think for one moment I might contemplate your not being here if you were in Kuala Lumpur?'

'You knew I was coming from London? That figures, I suppose.'

'Could you conclude for an equal moment that you would have been given a flight only the few can afford if it hadn't been run past me?'

'Please excuse me for saying so at a time like this, but I'm glad that you haven't changed, Colonel Newton. And it's all credit and power to you.'

'Haven't I? Well, what was said in my first and last address from the pulpit might indicate something by way of an alteration.'

'Vengeance is not in your makeup even if, to the priest, it might have seemed so.'

'No more than determination to get justice for Henrietta; perhaps also appeasing my conscience for the abject failures so far to make any mark on those who have destroyed her.'

'And the life of a dear son,' she added. Newton took on an even grimmer aspect. 'So few to hear your beautiful words. I thought perhaps Sir Gerald—'

'I didn't want any officials there. Even six representatives were several too many. Shall I drop you off at the hotel? I haven't been able to inspect your eyes under those shades but—'

Nancyng Jenkins removed them, and he managed the faintest of expressions when she added, 'That's all you need to see of the nearest equivalent to Boris Karloff wearing a skirt. Yes, do deposit me there and we can meet tomorrow, if it suits. There's much to catch up on since last you wrote. But that's not so important as what's pressing upon you at this time in your life. I feel your anguish, Reginald, and wish there was some way I could comfort a man who's lost his entire family in so foul and sudden a manner.'

Newton took an endless, shaky breath before ordering the driver to remain seated. He stepped out to open the door, facing her imperturbably as she stood inches from him. 'Nancyng, Magnus survived. He was saved by his dog, Rommel, whose life was forfeited in the process.'

She began to sob. 'Oh, this is just – Reginald, I'm dumbfounded, what joy, what wonder, what an answer to prayer. My fatigue is secondary compared with what I need to say, if you could graciously permit me some time to do so. Shall we repair to the tearoom for light refreshment and afterwards to business upstairs?'

*   *   *

'Don't perturb yourself about him, dear boy. Tommy has gone and won't be back. Why would he bother us or the British after being so accommodating when seeming to relish his flush of importance?' Scarfino spoke soothingly. He had been housing his paramour on an unusually protracted stay following the Fraser's Hill escapade.

Whether it was the period under Scarfino's purview or on account of reasons peculiar to himself was far from clear, for Nu was as edgy and spiteful as a cobra being poked with a stick, becoming more so by the hour. His mood was such as to permit little more than a snarling, offhand mumble, 'So *you* say.'

'The last I heard he was enjoying furlough in Singapore with the ever-obedient and dutiful Adelka, who promised to keep him both occupied and out of sight.'

'*She* had better be coming back.'

'Have no fear, Nu. Our most illustrious number one will always follow my every instruction. And the latest news from her is that Tommy is leaving these shores any day now.'

'He's fortunate that his permanent resting place wasn't with the other dross after the biggest fish happened to be away when we struck. Now they will be more determined than ever to net *me*.'

'Tommy had no idea what that fish's movements were at any time for that one always worked alone. We got as much as he was capable of revealing.'

'And was, by hell, grossly overpaid at that.'

'Money well spent, dear thing. Two birds, one stone, for my guess is that the tenure of your nemesis in our fair land has all but come to an end. What normal man could go on regardless, and such loss of face amongst his peers?'

'That doesn't mean I'm off their radar any time soon, still skulking like a mangy mongrel. They'll all pay an even heavier price before I'm finished.'

'Why, precious one, I thought you were happy to do so amidst my clean sheets and three lovely meals rather than that jungle hammock, rancid pork and men who you, deep down, really despise.'

'You would do well to remember that yours isn't the only bed open to me around this town, Scarfino.'

The words cut him, coming as they did after a distinct cooling in disposition since the year commenced. Apart from occasional suspicion about fidelity, Lemarno had never been in any real doubt that theirs was a relationship he regarded as impregnable and capable of withstanding the ravages of their many separations. He had excused Nu's moods with the increasing pressure being brought to bear since the new High Commissioner arrived.

In this environment, unquestioning obedience by Nu's remaining lieutenants was solely imposed through fear with the circle of guerrillas around him having dwindled, some through fatal jungle maladies and others defecting to groups where the omnipresent threat of reprisal for treachery, real or constructed, was contained.

Overall support for the communist cause had also diminished, a factor Scarfino realised had plagued Nu. Those who were prepared to go on accepting the abstemious jungle existence without murmur were becoming fewer in number, while others who did were wearying of the propaganda that had promised a socialist nirvana but managed to deliver even less to eat and drink than they had ever experienced.

The allurement of jumping on the free enterprise bus, owning their own land and inviting a better life, had become visual as well as spatial, rather than some illusory dream. Recruiting those prepared to forego a chance to become farmers or earn independent income and raise families in the New Settlements was now much more difficult.

A determined band of hardliners loyal to Peking was all that remained and, although Nu had enjoyed a much more privileged position than his comrades, Scarfino could see that he was developing an obsessive fear that a reckoning loomed much closer than had ever been thought possible.

The intimacy that had been unique to them was being lost and the careless observation made it clear that his own tenure as a permanent fixture in Nu's life was no longer something which he could regard as guaranteed. Rows increased in frequency, with Scarfino invariably accepting liability for their conflict. A mere glancing threat of infidelity was almost beyond any taunting he could endure but he held his tongue.

'I've decided to push off tonight,' Nu flung out without prior indication. 'It's not safe to remain here every stifling minute, even in a soundproof prison like this one, with those sick women upstairs and their depraved men coming and going.'

'But you'd originally said it would take more than two weeks for the dust to settle and getting back to your comrades could be the most dangerous part.'

'Would you have me strung up? I must keep moving to survive. I've made other plans with which you needn't concern yourself. I don't intend to live like this forever. I'll be back in a few days. Now, spend your time managing those harlots and see that I'm not being cheated. We have much to recoup after the avaricious abstractions of that English poser.'

Scarfino left his companion to sleep, not entirely convinced that Nu intended to return to his comrades to boost morale. Were he to reappear, it would be more a calculating, temporary one designed to demonstrate proof of his invincibility and as a means of striking terror in them. Irrespective of Nu's intentions, Scarfino decided, as another night approached, that he might undertake some pursuing of his own, if only to disabuse himself of what he had begun to suspect. Other than a growing physical indifference, the only clue he possessed was a strange comment Nu had made on the visit leading up to the Fraser's Hill attack.

'Lemarno,' he had enquired, 'have you ever heard of Binit's Bathhouse?'

'Who hasn't? Why do you ask?' Situated not more than a mile from where they traded, comprising steam rooms, saunas, a swimming pool, and treatment cubicles, it was a sideline to activities between the young male attendants who waited on an older male clientele.

'I've been there a few times to see whether it's an operation that would be more enriching than the one we have here, and conducive to my mood. From what I saw, it most certainly is.'

'You went as a patron?' Scarfino ventured with trepidation.

'Don't be ridiculous, you bloody old fool,' Nu snarled, thence to derive pleasure from his partner's anguish. 'I enjoyed a sauna, a swim, talked to the owner and drank some whisky.' Further questions led Nu to make him an object of ridicule; he was a 'good-for-nothing jealous queen' who needed to find someone else to 'mother'. So elevated became Nu's agitation when Lemarno started crying and pounding on the wall that only the cold point of a metal barrel thrust into his neck with the word, 'Silence', saw him sink to the floor in supplication.

The Italian's existence in Malaya flashed through his mind. Nu could be rash and hurtful, but never had it come to this. Unquestioning service to the man he had trusted and loved for over a decade was the cornerstone of his life. There was no future for him anywhere were it to end. He wondered whether Nu's reference to Binits was not merely a means of making him jealous but whether other schemes were at play: *Could he be devising a business proposal which doesn't include me? Has he found someone else?*

After thinking it over at length, he resolved to execute a discreet visit to Binits. As it was late at night, the venue would likely be crowded and his presence go unnoticed. Scarfino carefully selected a sequined gown for the occasion and painted his nails a matching fire engine red. Along with the blonde wig, he would merge as just another element of flamboyance in a crowd where that commodity was far from scarce.

On arrival at the front facade, there was a modest queue to enter, something that confirmed his assumptions. After a solitary hour of sipping brandy and dry ginger ale, he passed at the open invitation to join a group in the steam room. A feeling of guilt enveloped him for even imagining that his lover would seriously indulge such decadence.

He emptied the last of his liquor and hammed it up for

the muscly Indian barman, who told him that he was a weightlifter and offered to demonstrate his prowess by bench pressing the slender cross-dresser. Lemarno declined with coquettish flair. On a detour to the lavatory, his confidence returning, he continued in a more carefree and gay fashion, before wheeling about suddenly when he saw Nu coming towards him, his arms around the shoulders of two boys who appeared to be no more than sixteen. With Scarfino pretending to embrace the wall of the narrow passageway as if spaced out on liquor, the trio skipped straight past, Nu smooching the cheeks of each of his companions, who weren't shy of where their hands chose to wander. Seemingly mesmerised by the obvious attachment, Lemarno watched as they dived into one of the lounges. The door was slammed shut and, when he read the sign on the outside, 'Gold Class Members Only', his world collapsed.

He needed one last brandy, this time ordering a double, and made short work of it. As he slunk away, the wiggle of his hips had deserted him. Scarfino felt a pain far more acute than the varicose veins occasioned in his fifty-one-year-old legs that bore him back to Chow Kit. By the time he arrived there, Lemarno Scarfino entertained just one feeling towards the man he had faithfully served and worshipped for so long.

Chapter 25
– Understanding and Deployment

The hotel room allocated to Nancyng Jenkins was a double suite, spacious and comfortable. They sat opposite each other in two matching Queen Anne chairs embroidered with blue and gold upholstery. There was something almost as venerable about these antiques as the continuance of Newton's remarkable self-possession.

He opened. 'You've surely quite a deal more to tell me. I've perused a summary of what you disclosed prior to your leaving London.'

'Where to begin is the question, and I'm reluctant to rehash things that must patently be so raw for you, Reginald.'

'It mustn't be a consideration with the pressure of time. My various duties haven't permitted me to consume all that has taken place and won't be allowed to obtrude given the importance of the information you have,' he said, his countenance persisting in an avoidance of emotion.

'The crux then is this Tommy, on the assumption that he is the same fellow that worked for you, might be somehow involved in the whole dastardly business. My experience of him was detailed in the statement I made for the Colonial Office, some of which I'm sure you've digested. Is he, ah, around? I mean, no updates about him were provided in London, not as if I was expecting that they would be.'

'He's no longer visible at any rate. He departed well before, ah, Fraser's Hill, declaring an intention to move to Australia and take up a position in the private sector. We don't know where he is right now. At the time there was no reason to be suspicious about the motivation behind his sudden resignation. The most he said to me was that neither the job nor the climate suited him and he needed more action. I can confirm with certainty that he is the same fellow.'

'Reginald, I had a low opinion of that individual from the start.'

'That's an understatement that also demonstrates commendable restraint given you and your cousin's experience. He mightn't have fooled you but he certainly conned many.'

She had never experienced such intensity in his eyes before nodding, taking a long breath and attempting to relax. Newton managed to follow her lead. 'But, please, may we just pause here?' He signalled in the affirmative. 'I can't go further without enquiring of your son because the newspaper report said that he was missing. May I—'

'Of course. You've a right to know. About Gerhardus, you were aware of him?'

'Yes, from you, and Henrietta told me a little. Go on at your own pace.'

'From what's been pieced together, the terrorists – there were four of them – struck at about three o'clock in the morning. Was it a random attack? I'll answer my own question by saying that, while it's not entirely clear, it seemed to be initially.'

'Why?'

"Well, at the outset, I've no doubt that if they knew of my actual connection there and the capacity in which I serve they might have staked it out until certain of my being in residence. And therein lies the difficulty about premeditation.

'But let's proceed beyond those sorts of suppositions. Gerhardus was a rugged old ex-Foreign Legionnaire, a bachelor with no family except us. He loved Magnus and was his godfather, as you may have known. The terrorists didn't get it all their way. Rommel alerted the house to the intruders. But it was too late to save Henrietta as they got in through her open window.

'Gerhardus appears to have fought them off within the bungalow. He shot one, sustaining a wound himself, or maybe more, in the initial shootout. He managed to get outside with my son and Rommel close by. Bless the fellow, but he had erected a cubby house adjacent to, and secreted in, the bush for the boy. From there it becomes much more speculative. The dog understood everything and would do whatever Gerhardus told him.

'I think what happened was that he either took or directed Rommel to take Magnus there and remain with him. As a German Shepherd, Rommel was enormously intelligent, had a most powerful set of jaws and could have carried or dragged him out of harm's way. After that, the firefight continued and Gerhardus, though mortally wounded, managed to eliminate another terrorist.

'Before he left this life, and he had been shot multiple times, he managed to converse with an Afrikaans-speaking diplomat from the hotel who had arrived on the scene, telling him that the leader of the group was the man we have been after for some time, the notorious "Huntsman". How he knew this I can't say but the description he provided supported what we know of some of this man's physical characteristics. The manner of the attack itself was another corroborating factor.'

'And Magnus?'

'Even though the light was still dim, I found him not long after I arrived on the scene from Kuala Lumpur. The cubby house, as I said, was well-concealed. This was deliberate as part of the game of hide and seek that Gerhardus, Magnus and Rommel used to play all the time.

'It sounds hard to comprehend amidst all the hue and cry, but Magnus was curled up asleep. There was bedding inside. Near the entrance, I found Rommel. It seems one of the terrorists approached the area where Rommel was standing guard, and no imagination is needed about what happened next. There was a lot of blood in a spot on the verge of the bush. Some of it Rommel's, some human. He managed to crab himself back to where the boy was and there he died. And then—'

'That is just beyond all comprehension. What an extraordinary tale of survival. And amidst all of that, the unspeakable loss with which you've been confronted.' She had approached and was kneeling beside him, her hand on his arm at the point where he had faltered.

'Thank you for using your discretion with what you've revealed to the Colonial Office. It hasn't gone unappreciated.'

'Reginald, I would never have breathed a word of what you had written to me, and I've all but forgotten it now in the light of everything.'

'Back to the chameleon, Tommy, and matters closer to home.'

'Yes, here, you mean,' she responded in a manner tinged with reticence. 'What a pity he's no longer locatable.'

Newton resumed after a thoughtful hiatus. 'Tell me, Nancyng, in the light of my jottings and what Henrietta did, do you hold a view that he would have taken *advantage* of her? You more than faintly hinted at a tendency to be overly familiar in your statement.'

'Restraint he had but little and would stop at nothing if and when it suited, given our own experience. How can I speak of this to you? We do know that Henrietta was *trusting*,' Nancyng managed to say.

'Yes, she was ever so. And my entrapment foolishness managed to facilitate their coming together. Pretty contemptible, wasn't it; what carnage it yielded, fitting or deserved, for me, I mean, damnable—' he faltered.

Nancyng accepted his struggle as an opportunity to alter their focus. 'Sorry, I want to trespass into an area not directly personal – I suppose all is now – but more pertaining to your job of catching the perpetrator. It may well tie in with Tommy or may not.'

'Then the floor is yours, Nancyng. It won't happen again.'

Mrs Jenkins shifted her torso and stood up to stretch, excusing the interval by remarking that the long journey had been a timely reminder of advancing years. 'Did Tommy ever mention a person by the name of Scarfino in the course of his work?' she began.

No matter his fortitude, even Newton couldn't shield the recognition that this question occasioned. In the ordinary course, he would have reverted to type – coughed, cleared his throat, feigned impassivity and disinterest, effected ignorance. He couldn't lie nor immediately bring himself to answer the question either, so he put one of his own.

'And your reason for dropping into our discussion a strange Italian-sounding name in a place like this is?'

'The same reason that I scarpered from you when I was in the middle of my tale on the starboard side of the *New Zealand Star*.'

'Still at somewhat of a loss as to where you're going. Pray, enlighten me.'

'I'm aware that this isn't the time or place to be unkind or worse, deceptive, Reginald,' she said plaintively. 'I mentioned a brother who lived in this country. *That* part was true. I don't believe you accepted a word of what I was telling you at that point. You're so clever, and I don't mean this as uncomplimentary. You had figured me out, admit it; suspected I was not who I said I was and playing me like one of your suspects under interrogation. That's why I broke off.'

'That took some mangling of concepts and language, unlike almost anything I've ever heard fall from your lips. All I can say is, you were quite wrong to draw such a conclusion. I didn't have the faintest idea where you were going or what you were talking about, *then*.'

She felt foolish. 'Hoist me as an impudent crank and now a singing kettle.'

'Not as far as Scarfino is concerned,' he said, permitting a steely smile. 'That's if he's the same person. Go on, I'm listening.'

'If you can find Scarfino, you might be getting closer to the one said to be behind Henrietta's and Gerhardus' deaths.'

'You must have a reason for imagining that. Do you know him, or of him?'

She clasped her hands, twisting the fingers backwards and forwards before speaking. 'I met a man by that name when I was living here before the war broke out. He had always struck me as an obsequious sort but was by no means unfriendly, to me at least. Scarfino had become a sort of accidental resident, having previously worked as a crewman on ships. I was reasonably young at the time and he treated me with deference and decency, something I wasn't used to. He worked for my brother and seemed efficient.'

'What sort of work might that have been?'

'Just odd jobs, running around and the like. Nu, that's my brother's name, had a little distribution business, a sort of middleman buying fresh food directly from farmers and growers and selling it to hotels and restaurants.

'Over time it expanded and Scarfino remained involved. I helped my brother out and, through various errands, came into contact with Scarfino. I can't think of his first name.'

'Lemarno?'

'Yes, that's it,' her eyes noting a calculating sweep entering his. 'He lived alone in a little flat on the northern side of the city. I generally rode over to his place by bicycle because it was a fair walk from where we were staying.'

'So you were living with your brother throughout this time that you had involvement with Scarfino?'

'Yes, on and off, I did,' she said in a manner less convincing.

'Nancyng, let me assure you that this isn't meant to be part of an inquisition concerning your good self. I'm not in the slightest interested. But what happened to your brother, did he get through the Japanese occupation? I'm recalling that there was some mention of your family on the ship. That was during the war, as I remember.'

'Forget the ship. I've had no contact with Nu since those days and don't know what became of him,' she said dismissively. 'I wonder sometimes.' She reached for a handbag and unfolded the newspaper cutting Henrietta had sent her.

'This is the man you've been seeking?'

'We thought so, and Gerhardus' dying declaration has given it some added weight. It's the best likeness we have. As a picture, it's nothing much to go by really. Could be anybody of Asian/Chinese ethnicity. What is it, Nancyng, what's troubling you?'

Perhaps it was his tone of voice, so different from the one she hadn't wanted over the last days of the *New Zealand Star* and in Port Elizabeth, a gentler, kinder concern, an enquiry emanating from his soul, even, she dared envisage, a tentative excursion into hers rather than being in furtherance of his impeccable manners or another agenda.

It might have been his spirit, so depleted by all that had upturned his life. Perhaps Newton had formed the realisation that he might never want to get to the bottom of events were they to reveal the truth about how the gang of communist terrorists and its leader in his sights for so long had found the place where he lodged with his wife and family.

Such a disparate kaleidoscope seemed to make the past appear as if it was incidental, that nothing she could say would shock him or sever the link that she now felt between herself and this figure whose last remnant of stoicism had migrated to a reticent though demonstrative affection for her.

'Thank you,' she said, leaning over to nestle her face against his. With hands cradling her cheeks, his eyes asked her to tell him everything before he even spoke.

'If, Nancyng Jenkins, you think anything could change the regard in which you're held, that would be a profound misjudgment.'

The gesture released the chains in which she had bound herself since those evil days when the Japanese soldiers made sport of her body as a defenceless young girl during the pillage of the ancient Chinese capital. His smile had set her free.

'As blurred as the image appears, the moment I saw it in the newspaper cutting I asked myself whether it might be my brother. Nu was the eldest. He was recruited to spy for the Japanese, having ingratiated himself with them while we were in a camp during the sacking of Nanking. With our other family gone, we ventured to Kuala Lumpur. I became involved with an English spy called Heenan, pimped out to him and anyone who might be useful. So I was a traitor as much as he was. Now you've heard it from my lips, you're released from any obligation you feel might be due and owing to me. I never knew what happened to him nor, apart from getting his just desserts, did I care.'

'The ultimate penalty was extracted before Singapore fell,' Newton interpolated.

'That's not something over which I'll dwell. I cannot recall what occurred between when we were escaping Malacca and me being rescued. I was cared for on Mr Jenkins' private yacht, having been plucked from the waters of the Straits. A ship's officer found with me had saved my life. He and I were on some sort of floating debris but his injuries proved to be fatal. Mr Jenkins was caring for a Eurasian orphan child and on a roving voyage after his wife had died of a stroke. We married and passed the little girl off as ours. That was Charlotte. Pretty much the rest is what I told you before. I was disowned after my husband's death, came back here and all else is immaterial.

'So now you have enough to clap me in irons. But before you do, and not for any reason to escape my just desserts, can I get back to Scarfino and my brother, the one who could possibly be in the photo. If I was to make contact, he wouldn't have the slightest reason to refuse to see me. If Nu is somehow behind this outrage, and you are better qualified to weigh the evidence and draw the necessary inferences than me, I think Scarfino could be the link. It's not just on account of their acquaintanceship all those years ago but because if Scarfino resides in Kuala Lumpur a strong suspicion follows that Nu is alive and the puzzle begins to gather its pieces. Does any of this make sense, Reginald?'

'It does, apart from how remarkable it is that you recognised much of anything in the newspaper plate, but for one matter. Is there any reason why Scarfino and your brother would be still in some sort of partnership? I mean, it's the politics that stump me. That your brother was in league with the Japanese is a given. How could he have gone from there to being a fanatical communist?'

'My take on him may help. We weren't close, even as children. Other than cultural norms as younger sister which demanded that I do his bidding, I never felt anything for Nu and came to detest him as I matured. Having no regard for the ordinary incidents of family, he stole from my father's business, traded favours with the Japanese in Nanking and, in Malaya, manipulated me as if I was rotting meat, not even fit for the sewers but suitable for anyone who might wish to use me. At the end, promises to ensure sanctuary for mother and the rest of the family in Shanghai proved empty. They became expendable.'

'Without diminishing the weight of your biography, may I ask a fatuous question?' A receptive tilt of her head meant he could. 'Have you any theories as to why, were he to be our man, your brother would switch to politics and terror?'

'For what it's worth, Reginald, once the Japs were in charge, his usefulness had passed with business and source of profit gone before the surrender was signed. He may well have been a marked man, not just for the dirty transactions in which he was engaged or the natural disdain a conquering nation has for those to whom avarice is their sole loyalty. But, most of all, he was Chinese, and we know how much they despised us. Along the way, I believe he would have accumulated a large fortune. This is where Scarfino could come in. It had to be kept somewhere, and I spent a lot of time delivering packages from Nu to the Italian, the only man I had ever known him to really trust.

'And here's where, with the benefit of experiencing so much of, well, life, good and indifferent, I am led to speculate, for there's no actual proof. I've never seen Nu associated with a woman, if you take my meaning, nor the Italian, it so happens. Scarfino and he may have more in common than being mere work acquaintances.'

As she was speaking, Newton was nodding his head ever so slowly, the lines in his brow set like trenches, grim, unyielding and deep. 'Then again, these terrorists are dyed in the wool communists. Was there anything else in your brother's makeup that would suggest he had political tendencies of that ilk, even accepting his opportunistic temperament?'

'That's what puzzles me and qualifies all that I've mused upon so far. The answer is a resounding "no". I rather think, if he was anything, it would have been of the nationalist persuasion. The other mystifying factor is courage under fire as well as abject cruelty. None of this I ever saw in Nu. He was a coward who shirked a fight and, I suppose, giving him his due, I never witnessed any example of violence or cruelty.

'But I wouldn't like to cross him concerning monetary matters or possessions. Scarfino always spoke warmly and understandingly of him in every interaction with me. He was careful about any item I brought to him, asking if it was in exactly the same condition as when it had left my brother's hands, almost like he was subject to regular audits from Nu.'

'I realise this is going to be hard for you to answer but—'

'Reginald, I came here to help first and foremost. I will do anything for you, *anything*. And before we continue, may I ask *you* something, please: where is Magnus? I would love to hold your little son, please.'

Now his eyes were vulnerable and he swallowed. 'Ah, he's in a location that I can't even reveal to you just yet, but out of harm's way. There's much pressure on me to pack up and take him home to England in the light of what has happened. That must wait until I finish the job, after what you've just told me.'

'So, if you know about Scarfino's whereabouts, why not just arrest him?'

'On what charge? Bribery, corruption?'

'Now I understand. Mine was an inane query. Here's a suggestion, which you had better believe is serious and not some feminine silliness. Put me in touch with Scarfino. I can spin a story of having been in Australia along the lines you already know and tell him I'm trying to find out if my brother is still alive.'

His stare was of the sceptical kind, but she hardened her frown as if to correct it. 'The idea is, well, almost fantastic – unique, I'll grant. I accept you're serious, but implementing it is impractical since, if Nu is the man we're looking for, he will wonder how you just happened to turn up at this time, story or not.'

'What is Scarfino up to by the way of business?'

Newton emitted a corrective cough. 'That's part of the problem in countenancing your proposal. He operates a business at Chow Kit, the type in polite circles known as a gentleman's retreat.'

Nancyng's mirth was short-lived and her withdrawal from it riven with embarrassment. When he waved the apology away, she spoke in deadly earnest. 'There's another slice of the jigsaw, a promising lead, a piece of fortuity. It's the perfect entrée.'

'You can't be serious, chancy, even dangerous and you're—'

'Ancient, past it? Reginald, look at me for once!' She rose to perform a showy pirouette. 'A figure worth a second glance, equal to many a decade younger.'

'Granted, you won't fail on that account. I'm more concerned for your wellbeing.'

'Forget the safety stuff. I can handle myself. Great heaven, it's zilch in getting to the nub of this riddle and maybe the criminals behind the outrage. You are, after all, speaking with someone of dubious prior expertise in the entertainment industry. Granted that in today's parlance I'm a little decrepit in the skin game but, with the right deportment and makeup, can pass for someone younger. So I roll up at his door as an applicant for a job. I'll be terribly embarrassed when I recognise him and worm my way into his confidence, saying that I always wondered what happened to Nu. At least that part is right.'

'Theoretically, a brilliant suggestion, even if it sounds too easy to be real. One has to ponder where it might progress from there but, if he gives an indication of recent contact, it's a definite lead. Would Scarfino even recognise you? I didn't.'

'You're still to convince me of that. But you'd never met me, anyway, before the *New Zealand Star*.'

'I'd seen your photograph in the past, but bells failed to sound.'

'Incidentally, can you tell me what happened to Richard?' she asked, her eyes contemplative.

'He lives in Australia with his wife and—'

'That's all, please. Now, ah, yes, the context of your non-recognition, Reginald, was different. My darling daughter was with me. I had another persona and a pretty convincing autobiography until I unconvinced myself of its authenticity to avoid telling you the rest of the tale. And there was the scarring.'

'Wasn't obvious, but I did notice something, and even contemplated the lengths you took to hide same, only to file it as eminently understandable and indelicate to visit. Ours *was* rather good banter while it persisted and a basis for lasting friendship laid. The fact that you're here is final testimony to that.'

'And will remain by your side, if you agree, Reginald. Now, let's talk strategy for the thing is settled. I will call upon Lemarno Scarfino about this job and see where it takes me. Should he prevaricate, which is doubtful, if I know him to be as he once was, we may need to consider something else.'

'You must understand that what we are doing is unofficial. As far as the commissioner of police is concerned, I'm on leave, although a policeman is always on duty.'

'Tommy was the person from whose mouth those words last fell on my ears. How ironic. If that scoundrel is part of this, I may have another job to perform.'

'You will never have to mind about Tommy since he didn't

leave any forwarding address. Putting a red alert out for him is unwise, and I wouldn't like to think about him being minded to contact Scarfino with you possibly on the scene.'

480

The Italian hadn't recovered since returning from the bathhouse. The girls had all gone and he forced himself into a careless inspection of the rooms and water closet, cursing at their shambolic state but disinclined to undertake the necessary tasks to effect remediation. He didn't want to imagine what might happen should Nu have reappeared before daybreak, although speculating upon that possibility was short-lived since such an action would be out of keeping with the persona on display at Binits.

Scarfino reclined on the sofa after resuming his day clothes and freeing his face of the makeup. Whether it was several stiff brandies or the advanced sunlight, or both, his next awareness was the sound of the doorbell.

He took time to attend to his toilet thinking, as the hallway clock fell silent on the last of its ten strokes, it might also have exhausted the persistence of his visitor. When that wasn't to be, he went to the door and, through the peephole, saw the slim form of a jauntily-attired woman wearing sunglasses, her hat occupying a sporty angle.

Scarfino, who had more complex an affinity with the female sex than that of the male, softened the more his eyes lit upon her. He was ready and willing to admit the distinguished-looking newcomer, becoming increasingly receptive as she removed her head covering and spectacles in one movement.

'Lemarno? Lemarno Scarfino? Oh no, heavens, no, that can't be, it mustn't be you, can it? Surely I am seeing a mirage, aren't I? Tell me it's not you. Good lord!'

He remained mystified by her utterances but was welcoming. 'Hello there and good morning to you. Why, it's me and only me, your eager servant, madam. Are we acquainted? I somehow hoped we might be and more to understand why.'

'Acquainted? My godfather, this is so embarrassing. Coming to such a place without knowing, or even expecting, a *man* would greet me, let alone this man. And what are *you* doing here?' she pursued with a conviction that demanded greater elaboration.

'Well, my dear, enter and sit down and all may soon be revealed. If I said I'm here every morning to clean up after the follies of the night, I don't think it would pass without comment on your part and I'd have to reach for another excuse.'

'Oh, this is frightful, so awkward, but I will, even if only to say "hello" and maybe reminisce. What must you think, that I was an aspirant for employment or a hawker?'

'I would prefer to believe your being at these premises was either a misunderstanding or a nasty person set you up, or even that you came here seeking directions or something entirely different again,' he said diplomatically. 'Please enlighten me.'

'It might have been all or some of those. You still haven't grasped who I am though, have you?'

Scarfino continued to enjoy and encourage the dialogue, inviting her to go on quizzing and teasing. That she felt the same way was evident to him before she spoke.

'I often asked myself what collision of planets made a man, as nice to me as you were, to be equally as obedient and trusting to someone whom I knew may not have always reciprocated the sentiments.' Features softening further, he remained bemused.

'Oh, come on, guess. Remember "Mr L", a term of affection that he surely couldn't forget. She turned sideways, tilted her head and placed herself as near to him as propriety permitted.

'My, but is it? Yes, it's little Eva, so grown up and mature. I'm mortified. How could I not know? But Eva, you were never your brother's sister—' he broke down momentarily and she helped him to a chair in the empty waiting room. 'Sorry, that was unforgiveable. Everything has kind of overcome me even after, what is it, a dozen years or more?'

'A goodly number,' she said, and, sensing that he had recovered from the shock of seeing her and its association, went on to ask if he would like some water. When he accepted the offer, she filled a glass, brought it to him and touched his face tenderly.

'What am I to say? May I begin by thanking my God.' He crossed himself with considerable ceremony. 'I thought you'd perished during the war. Nu told me that you had disappeared after running off to Malacca with some bad company on a ship. He said a vessel had been sunk and the Japanese were responsible.'

'Well, I'm hale and hearty, as you see. What I'm rather instantly amazed to realise is how he would have come to know about that sinking. It's staggering.'

'Can't help you there. He only mentioned it when I kept enquiring as to how you were going because I hadn't seen you for so long. That's all he said, and contemptuous of his only sister, for he told me never to mention your name again. Things went sour after the Japanese took over. I think he came to hate what they did to you and the family back in China. Becoming a communist, Nu vowed revenge against them for what happened.'

'Really, he actually said that? And did you believe him?'

'Yes, then I did, and the hatred in his face was blood-curdling. He never lost the desire for retribution while they ruled Malaya.'

She let the ambivalence in the answer alone. 'And what became of him? I don't know where he ended up because there hasn't been sight nor sound. They must have flushed him out in the end because, well, Lemarno—'

'I'm here and he's not?'

'Yes, I guess so,' she said hesitantly. 'I don't wish to pry.' Sensing it a subject he preferred she not pursue, Nancyng continued. 'As far as I'm concerned, I thought you must have known about all that stuff I was doing in the past. It hardly matters now.'

'I suspected. You don't blame him surely for your being at this place right now?'

'Blame? Hardly, me being an adult woman and all. Nobody pushed me to this house, and it's far easier to resume a vocation you once practised. I've my daughter who's at school in a famous educational facility. There's no father. She's in Singapore and I couldn't very well peddle my wares around there and possibly shame her.'

'Nu has always been accomplished at using people,' he chimed in abstractedly. 'So much I've had to sweep from my mind, even about you. How callous it sounds, eh? Once way back when I asked him about it, he said you enjoyed the company of men, "the more the merrier" were his words, even when you were barely past being a child yourself in Nanking.'

She swept aside the feeling of repugnance that had begun to blur her features and Scarfino apologised.

'Forgive me, I am deeply sorry,' and he touched her face.

Nancyng retained his hand. 'It's alright, Lemarno, I was blind to so much, to look away, and how he used me as well. Oh, there was food to eat and a roof over my head. He looked after me in those early days and I was the younger sister knowing my place. Later, well, that's another story.'

'I see you now and feel genuine sorrow, a woman, what, thirty and neat of shape, and even the way you dress. I see them all here, some even older than you, but they've known nothing else. You're educated, classy, kind, honourable and you tell me there's a daughter. It makes me feel rather ill at *my* blind pair of eyes towards you, remembering the past and the café and him as well, and—'

This time Eva did the comforting as he sobbed into his hand. She took it and, with Scarfino leaning against her, caught the remnants of cheap, heavy perfume he was still carrying. 'I'm so sorry if I've upset you. All that time you were friends with him I never understood there was more, I couldn't even think it, and—'

'Come with me.' He was hunched over when he stood, making a cadaverous figure, and shaking while still clutching behind at her hand. 'You're not ever going to need to work here, and never again in this rotten business, and I'll show you why.'

Scarfino led her to the end of the hallway. They were met by a seemingly impenetrable stone edifice. He swung to one side the large painting on the wall and tinkered with a handle. A carefully concealed door opened upon a set of stairs that led to the musty, partly-furnished storage cavity where he and Nu slept.

'You see this bed, it's Nu's and mine when he comes and stays, ever since he joined the communists; where he was just a day ago. It was our bed; our little, pathetic love nest, and all the comforts that I provided he used just as he did me. But not anymore.'

He went to the far wall and a low passage materialised as if he'd pronounced some Middle Eastern command. Scarfino disappeared. She dare not follow him into the blackness. From that direction emanated the clunking of bricks being stacked one on top of the other, followed by a series of scraping noises as if a hook was dragging heavy tins across metal shelves. Then there was nothing save that his breathing took on a series of staccato bursts and cries, like a runner straining in a final sprint, as the ferreting intensified.

Coinciding with the cessation of Scarfino's labours arrived an eerie quiet. Nancyng was troubled when there was no response to her enquiry as to whether he was okay. She sat down on the soft bed, favouring the direction of the stairway from which they'd come, before he announced himself again.

'Here!' He began strewing about wads of paper money, predominantly sterling and some American. 'And here!' Gold sovereigns, unleashed from a bag, were pitched around the room, jangling against the stone walls like the ringing of bicycle bells. Some were pelted at the floor and not a few ricocheted in all directions, including his and hers.

Oblivious to Nancyng's retirement to his parlour, Scarfino went into a frenzy of scooping up the lucre and hurling it into the ceiling, screaming out, 'For you, all for you, beautiful sister, and none for Nu!' Laughing hideously, the dance continued, the ripping in half of banknotes, the jamming of coins between his teeth, the spitting them out, the pulling asunder of the sheets, and then he started urinating, beginning with the bed linen, quickly graduating to the paper and coins.

'Stop this, filth. Silence, you hairless hyena, you whore, you ugly, filthy, pox-ridden queen,' screamed a voice Nancyng instantly recognised and sought out.

Scarfino, refusing to heed him and now naked, was yelling gibberish and jigging around as if possessed by a devil. Facing towards the direction she had taken, he spoke loudest of all.

'It's all for you, little Eva; all, everything, every dollar, pound, every speck of gold, every sovereign; all for you, dear innocent Eva, and none for Nu. No, none for that—'

With the deafening explosion came high-pitched moaning. His sister's entry, rushing to the gravely-wounded Scarfino writhing on the bed, saw Nu raise his pistol at her. 'You! You! Now I understand. You and Tommy and that shitbag there, all against me. It's my money you want. Never, you harlot, you slut, no sister of mine. Count yourself lucky, Eva. Your fate will be painless compared with the English bitch at Fraser's Hill—'

'Get down, Nancyng,' Newton yelled, the first shot heeding the beam of torchlight and smashing the wrist of the quarry's hand as his revolver misfired. Legs earning a second and third saw Nu on bended knees before rolling onto his back, screaming and begging to be spared. Nancyng Jenkins retrieved her brother's pistol at Newton's command and they stood, side by side, over him.

'You want mercy? So, is it to be the quality of mercy you

showed towards the woman with child at Fraser's Hill, my own wife?' Amidst the contorted grimacing, there was instant cognition.

'The big man, he, he tried to kill me, what I could I do? Tommy man, he wanted her dead. She carried his baby and blackmailed him, he, he told Scarfino. He boss of it all, he – help, help.' His arms were raised, blood streaming down the right one was negligible compared with that spurting from the leg wounds. His eyes were rolling. 'Eva, Eva, your brother commands your help, his life, pleads to you. I did for you, all—'

As Newton stepped over to assess Scarfino, he asked her to cover Nu's heart, adding, 'If he as much as twitches, pull the trigger.' It was an instruction that brought instant compliance from Nu.

Newton shook his head when their eyes met after he had searched for Scarfino's pulse. Between teeth clenched as if in lockjaw mode, he forced out the words his mind had fashioned on the spot.

'Were he an animal, the kindest thing would be to put the miserable wretch to sleep. As the "Huntsman", *it* doesn't deserve anything less than being crushed underfoot. You had better go upstairs, for I intend to gut-send him into eternity,' Newton said unblinkingly, as he reloaded the pistol, unperturbed by the elevated pleas.

She stood her ground and, betraying an equivalent degree of emotion, replied, 'Since you're on the right, I'll take the left side.' Both pulled the hammers back and fired in unison.

*   *   *

Over the next few hours, the police were picking through the detritus of the Huntsman's concealment. The treasure in gold, foreign and local currency abstracted from the hole in the wall wasn't nearly as valuable as the trove of documents the cellar had also stored.

Camp locations, collaborators, weapon caches and food dumps were identified. In the ensuing months, the terrorists would incur unyielding ambushes, harassment, surrenders and incalculable losses. Such was the relentless nature and extent of the operations that an organisation, already under pressure militarily and politically, suffered irretrievable setbacks. It would later be said that the taking down of the Huntsman was the forerunner of the insurgency having its back broken once and for all.

They returned to the hotel and changed. He told her that they needed to be prepared before he met with the police commissioner to report on what had occurred and formally resign. Not a word passed leading to their reclining in splendid upholstery adjacent to the lobby telephone until he called for drinks.

'Where did you spring from, I mean, getting through the door and?' she finally asked, almost as if they, being old comrades in arms, were in de-brief mode having executed the perfect ambush.

He leaned over and held her hand. 'Mrs Jenkins, you hardly think it likely that you were going to be sent in there and forgotten about? And I've been known to pick the odd lock, also, over the course of active service.' He held up the glass and proffered it. She managed a respectable amount.

'Partners in capital crime, eh?' she said with a tired sigh. 'And, yes, you always seem to cover the whole gamut.'

'Would you mind?' he asked, opening the door to the phone cabinet. 'I've an important call to make. Shouldn't be long. I will handle everything, mind.'

'Do it. Take whatever time you need. It's ours for the making now, Reginald.'

He read Nancyng's eyes. 'Yes, indeed.'

Newton was put through to the High Commissioner's office, where Sir Gerald Templer's aide-de-camp received the codeword that King's House had waited so patiently to hear, 'Spiderdown'. He emerged to retrieve his drink. 'On any other occasion, it would have been champagne.'

'Yes', she replied thoughtfully.

'Sorry, I need to make one final call.'

She nodded, this time more settled, apologising for not enquiring how he was. He told her there was no need to ask anything.

While waiting to be put through, Newton, having decided in an instant that his time in Malaya was over, began thinking ahead. As much as he wanted to be a part of the operation to capture Tommy, Magnus was now his main priority. He realised that, given the momentous events and her like obligations in England, Nancyng Jenkins would be keen to depart and return to the place she called home.

The second conversation was slightly longer than the first. Absent from his oral report was any mention of Nancyng's active involvement or disclosure of her blood relationship. Her information had been vital in netting the target and that was clearly understood. The request that he and Mrs Jenkins fly back to London on the next available flight was agreed to with regret but understanding that Malaya was no place where he would want to remain. He was on the point of pressing one further concession when the commissioner foreshadowed it.

'And we won't be releasing any information about this operation or the Huntsman's fate for the present, having many other fish to fry. Your anonymity will always be preserved, as you wished,' he added. Newton remained imperturbable.

When he re-joined her with the news, she had a request of her own. 'I would like to send telegrams to Charlotte and Lynn that I'll be coming home.'

'Well, you can go a step further, if you choose. It's about six in the morning in the UK. Too early to phone your cousin, or, ah—' he encouraged.

'No, she rises with the birds. I'll let her know now,' she responded excitedly.

'Before you do, timing-wise, I'm advised that there could be space on a military flight to Singapore tomorrow afternoon and with a connection on the Kangaroo route to London not long afterwards. I'd say we will be home in three days, but no more than a week, to be on the safe side.'

'Reginald, I know it's all rather sudden, but may I enquire where you intend to stay when you get back to England? I mean, you mentioned "home".'

'Fair question, but the only answer I have at present is that it won't be some sterile barrack accommodation for me and the little chap. The pound, shillings and pence will play a part. I know where I'd like to end up in my dotage but that's, I hope, some time off yet.'

'So, where might that ending up be, young fellow? And as to that little chappie, I insist on seeing him.' She instantly regretted the request. 'Sorry for my flippancy.'

'Don't concern yourself. You'll meet him soon enough. As to the first query, I've been used to warmer climes now for so long that the English winters are sure to bite harder than ever before. The place everyone talks about as being mild and generous is Cornwall.'

'I've read that it's beautiful.'

'In the interim, Magnus and I will put up somewhere. No idea yet but, longer term, must think ahead to him going to school. Do you have any recommendations?'

'Why, with me and Lynn for now. You know where Reading is. There are two spare bedrooms and the High Street's close. I mean, until you find your feet,' she hastened to add, sensing his apprehension.

'I'll think about it; sounds tempting. There'll be plenty of mulling time on our flight.'

She felt him gravitating towards her offer. 'Look, how about this? I'll tell Lynn to be ready for two guests, you and

Magnus. Hang on, this has to be a three-minute call. My allowance from the Colonial Office won't stretch beyond that.'

'You're an uncontainable organiser. But hasn't it got to be okay with your cousin, it being her house and all. I don't wish to presume—'

'No need to presume anything, Reginald. You might have assumed it was Lynn's house but, actually, it belongs to me. There were problems over her fiancé's will and I bought the property from the trustee. One of the reasons she and I were eventually able to become permanent residents was because we had this place in which to live with me as owner. Now, why I didn't 'fess up' in the first place can be something held over for later discussion. Right now, I'll make that call.'

After several attempts and an animated conversation with a telephonist, Nancyng returned, it being evident that the connection was unsuccessful.

'That's strange. Each time there was no answer. Perhaps she was out early today. And one other little thing. I know you're thinking already about a long-term place where you will stay with your son. Umm, my dear Reginald, so like the real Magnus, eh?'

Nancyng Jenkins accepted his advice about getting some rest before the marathon journey home. Fatigued after the momentous events at Chow Kit and not minded to enlarge upon the cryptic remark in the lobby, she went to her room. For his part, Newton returned to headquarters to compile a report at the Special Branch, though all he was minded to do was embrace his son. The child had remained where he was, with a nanny and armed guard inside the secret dwelling, as well as three burly policemen stationed on an around-the-clock basis in the street.

Having shaken hands for the last time with the police commissioner, Newton hurried to his office and wrote a letter. He arrived at the hotel's reception desk with instructions that it be delivered in person. Two hours later, the doting father was playing with an excited little boy, a German Shepherd puppy and the tangle of string emanating from a ball that the animal bounced around in order to keep it unravelling. Neither he nor his dog once took a breather until Newton decided that it was time for both to be fed and settled for the evening.

It was still dark when Nancyng rose and called for tea. In a short time, it, along with a letter bearing her name in a comforting hand on the envelope's face, arrived.

Dear Nancyng,

There is an awkward confession that must be got off my chest. If the contents cause you to repent of your kind offer of a place for us to stay, that is understandable.

By the way, I didn't mention one other potential guest. He's a puppy we've named 'Rommel'. As the progeny of his illustrious father who, posthumously, was awarded a medal specially created for dogs who showed selfless bravery in action, he has been given permission to travel with us all the way to London.

Now back to what may occasion some pain. I told you about Magnus and Esrelle. You called it, didn't you? Magnus was a figment of my imagination. No such person by that name ever existed, then. There was a friend, my best man and, in many respects, the shoulder who helped me through much of what I related myself doing for Magnus. He died of malaria in Malaya.

Events that were detailed were wholly true, however. There was a marriage and, of course, Esrelle. There was a lengthy army career, the less than savoury entanglements with the two women old enough to be my mother (at least one of them was a widow, if a not so merry one later).

'Magnus' had the feelings depicted of him. Some were as cold and indifferent as headstones in a graveyard, others perhaps manufactured by time and circumstance, less so. He came to love his own mother and cling to her memory as a man may treasure the last droplets of water he might possess several days' march from an oasis.

'Magnus' could never have children. He didn't possess the wherewithal to satisfy the dreams of his wife and understood why she sought other avenues where she could find them. He was, of course, jealous, but too weak to do anything about it. For whatever reason, he took full responsibility for the greatest sacrifice she made, the giving up of her daughter. The heartache that would have occasioned, he accepted, was a direct consequence of his not standing by her.

You are a highly intelligent person, Nancyng, and I always wondered if you ever suspected that the whole thing was an elaborate contrivance, if not entirely a concoction. Your listening to it, the pertinent observations while it was told, were a great source of strength for me and relieved many burdens as well as raising fears. This was my cathartic experience many years in gestation but leading to the best thing that ever happened to me in my life: marriage to a young woman who somehow managed to love me and a son who called me 'Daddy'. There has been tragedy in all of that and...

And I met you, Nancyng.

So, there it is. 'Magnus' is me, Reginald Newton, confidence trickster, coward, in all his wretchedness, but father at least, at last.

Ever Yours,

Reginald

The purification that had streamed from the Copperplate hand had awakened her deepest emotions as she sank back into the bedclothes to press the paper to her lips and re-read the words of the man she would die for. As one who had listened to the story through the prism of her own, now washed away and cleansed by time, hers became secondary to this tale. The face of the narrator and the subject merged as one and she saw Reginald Newton, unedited, complete and unabridged. That he should have granted her the gift of his long-stored frailties was something of inestimable value. As the imagery swept over her, she became infused with an inexplicable longing, and such was its effect that she fell into a dream.

In it Nancyng saw herself in the coastline of an England, dashing, wild and unfamiliar. She had been out walking with an elderly dog, their pace laboured by its aged steps. When even snail movement became painful, the fur child nibbled at her hand. Every pause and pat earned forgiveness courtesy of a sloppy tongue. It was love, unconditional.

There were so many memories, as if the cliffs carved out by the sea retained new pockets and inlets that awoke yet another recollection of all that had preceded it. Nothing lurking in there could be anything but beautiful. This was serenity itself. When she returned to find the empty rocking chair over which was draped the heavy woollen rug that once warmed his legs, she set it into creaking motion and droplets from her eyes pooled on the floor.

Fleeing the dream, she woke to another turmoil, the clock showing it closer to the next hour than the nine which she'd banked upon. The rush to pack began. Nancyng was in a state unprepared to meet Newton downstairs and under hotel dictates to check out. She phoned and they gave her an extra fifteen minutes.

Flushed, but far from appearing bedraggled with the allotment of time open to her, she joined a departing crowd, noting that he had still to arrive. It gave her the opportunity to finalise her bill and try to get through to Lynn again. She figured that the hour, though inapt, should surely have her at home, and her cousin would understand.

When the receiver was picked up, the only sound Nancyng heard for several unnerving seconds was crackling down the line. At the third iteration of her name, coupled with, 'It's me, Nancyng. Please answer,' a fragile voice acknowledged her with a plaintive cry. 'Oh, Nance, dear Nance, thanks be to God.'

'What is it, Lynnie, are you alright? I'm terribly sorry for waking you at this awful hour. I tried to phone a few times yesterday morning your time. Lynn?'

'Yes, I'm here. I, I am here. There've been some unnerving calls on the telephone at all hours of the last few nights.

The first time I just heard breathing, the next laughter, another one was nothing at all and, yet another, someone was whistling followed by a ticking sound like a clock. I'm terribly frightened. No words were said.'

'It might just be some kids, Lynn. Have you rung the police?'

'No. I, I, I'm not sure of them after what happened with those two outlaws after my birthday. So, no, I haven't, no; not said anything. I, you're the first person I've told.'

'Look, don't worry. I'm sorry to ask but have you checked on Charlotte?'

'Yes, she had some holidays. I sent her off to stay with a trusted friend after these calls started. She's fine.'

[Operator: *Three minutes Madam, would you like to extend? We have one minute.*]

'Yes, please,' Nancyng said. 'I only have a minute to tell you that we are coming home by plane. All finished here. Might have a visitor and his young son with me as guests. Should be there in a few days. Why don't you see if one of the teachers can—'

Their connection lost, she returned to the desk to pay for the extension before resuming the same chair in which she'd rested the previous day. A few minutes later a bellboy appeared to advise that a car was waiting. He carried her luggage to a black vehicle.

The driver, a uniformed Malayan policeman, assured her that 'Mr Newton' had sent him to convey her to the airfield where their plane for London was waiting.

'For London, not Singapore?'

'Yes, Madam,' he replied deferentially.

A special crib had been installed in the DC-9, as had a tiny kennel to suit Rommel, though it soon became apparent that the pup preferred to spend more time in the arms of Magnus, wherever he might be, during the protracted haul. The entanglement was mutual.

Newton's response to her fears about Lynn led to calls being made at each stop along the route. At all but one of those, Nancyng was able to verify that there had been no further incidents and this eased her mind.

'Oh, and Lynn seemed happy that you and Magnus might be coming to stay. You are, aren't you?'

'With all that dashed harassment she may not have thought much about it, so we shall see. I would like to reassure her that the police can be trusted. Until my resignation takes full effect, if I do stay, technically, she'll have a police bodyguard in residence.'

She surveyed the drawn, contemplative face beside her and resisted an urge to touch it, instead tapping his hand on the armrest. Finally, it drew him to speak.

'You received the note I trust?'

She acquiesced appreciatively. 'My, but that brain of yours indulges circuitry.'

He wasn't talkative and, for her, it was just right. She was beside the man who meant more to her than life itself and, over the next few days, earned the title of next favourite for Magnus after his father. Having had the presence of mind to acquire a few children's picture books courtesy of the hotel before she left, once they were produced, the boy occupied more waking time on her lap as the journey proceeded than he did on his father's. When he became weary, she would pass him to Newton, and he would remain in his Dad's embrace for hours as they both slept.

*   *   *

The call came while Newton and Nancyng were drinking tea in the lounge at 26 Vivesta Lane, their long trip having thrown sleep patterns awry. It arrived at such an hour of the night when the ringing of a telephone almost displaced them from where they reclined.

Instantly apprehensive, she picked up the phone answering, 'Nancyng here. Hello? Hello?' and held the receiver sufficiently apart from her head so as to admit a second listener. Silence persisted for a number of seconds, before she said, 'Is anyone there? My, it's late for childish pranks. Hello, is it urgent?' There was a growling, grunting noise, followed by a knocking sound as if the receiver had been dropped and left swinging. They next heard a car's engine being started.

Nancyng kept speaking as before. Still there was nothing but the revving of a vehicle and then the sound of it being driven away. More disquieting than the events themselves was the fact that it prevented any further use being made of her telephone.

Newton put on his coat and went to the door, turning to her as he opened it. 'I'm going out to a public box. How far away is the nearest one?'

She gave directions, adding that it was no more than five minutes' brisk walk. 'What are you intending to do?' she asked when he reached the footpath.

'Just a hunch. I won't be long. You need to stay here. Other than the police, don't open the door to anyone until I get back, alright?'

An enveloping fog made it a tricky night and, as the time went by, it became apparent that he was hopelessly lost. Newton backtracked, took a right turn at the first intersection and began to sweat, running the clock down some more. Finally, the faint illumination of the telephone box appeared in front of him. No sooner had he entered than his suspicions were confirmed.

Replacing the handset, he rang the police. Newton's second call wasn't answered because the line was engaged. He phoned the station again and was assured of an instant response before setting off as fast as his legs could carry him. Outside, intuitively, he checked himself on hearing the voice. The reflection from the loungeroom light allowed him to creep around the side, observe and listen.

The two women were cowering in a corner. He was standing over them with a gun. The situation was beyond heroics but demanded action. The floorboards creaked as Newton entered and the gunman turned to him side-on only to realise he was covered.

'Hello, Tommy, nice of you to drop by and spare me the trouble of finding you,' he opened purposefully, as the sounds of screaming sirens, screeching brakes and heavy footsteps merged. 'You're finished Tredwig! Next stop an appointment with the gallows in Kuala Lumpur.'

Epilogue

'That was the oddest dream you had. Are you psychic by any chance?' It was her editor on the phone, Nancyng trusted, for the final time.

'No, Dorothy, I'm not. What have I done now? There must be something I've neglected, a word that doesn't fit, an expression that fails to ring true.'

'Nothing at all to worry about, dear. You're not the sort of biographer or, should I say, auto-slash-biographer who leaves a single fragment out.'

'Rather, after reading the letter Reginald wrote and the dream that followed just before the long haul back to England, I couldn't help staring at a yawning chasm. Surely you must tell me and the hoped-for, tenterhook bookworms out there in reader-land?'

'You want to know why it took so long for us to marry?'

'Now I'm convinced you *are* psychic.'

'Okay, I tell you what, I shall put down a short note, and that's definitely it.'

'Please do it soon, my patient and long-suffering friend, I'm on a real tight deadline for publication.'

*   *   *

Magnus Farm, Cornwall

Dear Dorothy,

Here we go. Within a few months of our return to Vivesta Lane, things became a little awkward. Lynn and her inexhaustible admirer, Sir Gabriel Litherland MP announced that they were going to get spliced and presented us with an imminent date for the nuptials.

Soon after the 'banns were posted', Lynn confessed to yours truly in somewhat embarrassed and apologetic tones to having stayed over at Sir Gabriel's house, with his sister the resident chaperone, after the nuisance calls began. That nice gentleman had never given up on Lynn and renewed his pursuit after she re-energised him into more troubles, and she finally weakened. Perhaps there was something more still and she was reluctant to admit an unabridged account, suspecting a proposal might be afoot.

After all the Tommy business blew up in the public domain, her suitor was regularly at her side, somewhat familiarly, I wondered, at the time. Here was me uncharitably thinking, 'Jolly old impudent politician!' He got his name in the papers when it all came out about his

Foreign Office involvement in getting a 'mysterious, never to be named spy' (me) to assist in the elimination of a certain, most-wanted terrorist. But I was wrong. He resigned his seat before they wed, was a lovely man and good husband to my cousin. Within a year they had produced a daughter. My, some men are devils, and at his age!

Anyway, I digress. This brought matters to a head, although I felt Reginald was never comfortable at Vivesta Lane and, of course, shunned the publicity it initially had occasioned. But rather than any such inevitable discussion about the future (and I would have had no problem if he had stayed on there), his father's house, in which he had the remainder interest, became available on the sudden death of his stepmother, and that sealed it.

I think both of us knew that the time wasn't yet right. Indeed, the decision to put to rest any notion of getting together then was mutual. In his most ingenuous style, Reginald told me that he didn't want there to be any chance of another failure. Naturally, I understood and wasn't insulted (well, almost not). Foremost in his mind was his son, who had been through so much, and no one on this earth was loved as much as that lucky boy.

Strangely, perhaps even perversely, he became a committed Presbyterian in the traditional Scottish style after they moved north. He saw Magnus as the son God protected through Rommel and had gifted to him. Incomprehensible as it may seem, he perceived his own failings as a husband through that child, the grandson of his first wife, the son of his second and there would be no prospect of failure as a father on account of possible disruption by a number three! And there wasn't. He did an outstanding job. I kept my distance, being far from perfect myself.

He and I stayed in fond touch and, you guessed it, pretty much always by a consistent stream of correspondence in the intervening decade or so before Magnus went to boarding school and University. Up to that point, we saw each other twice a year for a long lunch. That was all, and I mean all!

It was around then when we both knew our time had come. He confessed his love for me and begged forgiveness at delaying Cornwall for so long. I told him not to be so pompous and silly and we had a great laugh. We always did laugh together. Even the pages and pages we wrote were full of mutual fun and frivolity. My influence? Perhaps just a little.

I have already mentioned to you how he had found the house there and brought me in as the last (the lucky) Mrs Newton. He said that I was his only 'real' wife. And I can tell you, as the years rolled on, no one appreciated it more than I did. He loved, honoured and cherished me. We always slept together when under the same roof. It was something rare and precious for me.

But before all the beer, skittles and roses, let me relate how I staked out the territory every new bride declares as hers. I refused to have a Registry Office affair and made that clear in no uncertain terms. He was quite apologetic for having the temerity to mention it.

So we did something quite extravagant and 'eloped' to France for our honeymoon after we got 'hitched'. And who solemnised our day? Why it just happened to be the old clergyman from Malaya who Reginald had all but spurned at that terrible occasion so many years ago. Having been repatriated for a hoped-for quiet and uncomplicated retirement, he must have thought delayed retribution was imminent when Reginald turned up at his door. My darling delighted in renewing his Intelligence skills in doing so and, unusually for him, was far from being reticent in explaining the process to me.

Ours was a quiet morning wedding in a chapel with the requisite two witnesses, neither of whom knew us. I think Reginald slipped them a fiver each.

And that's it, Dorothy, that's our story.

Nancyng.